EDDY ROSE

LION OF ZARALL

<TWILIGHT OF BLOOD, BOOK ONE>

www.eddyrose.com

Published by: Phoenix Hollow Publishing

ISBN: 978-1-7637341-1-1

Edited by: GCD Editorial

Cover Design: Miblart

First edition published in 2018.

Second edition published in 2020.

Third edition published in 2024.

This copy is the third edition.

GLOSSARY

THIS BOOK HAS BEEN crafted so that most terms and concepts are either self-explanatory or clarified through the context. However, for further explanation, feel free to consult this glossary. Please note, some entries may contain spoilers. If you choose not to read the glossary and dive straight into the story, I promise you will not feel lost.

Acts of Defiance – Forbidden or taboo behaviours for slaves.

Beast – A type of slave used for combat in the arenas.

Blues/Chinderian Blues – The currency of Chinderia. One Blue is equivalent to ten Greys, and one Grey equals ten Reds.

Chamber of the Twelve – Places of worship dedicated to the Twelve Riders.

Darkhome – One of the three realms created by the Twelve Riders after the Dividing of the Homes. It serves as the prison for Fiends.

Dividing of the Homes – The event following the defeat of the High Fiends, where the Twelve Riders divided the realm into three parts to imprison Fiends and protect *rhoas*.

Earthome – One of the three realms, Earthome is where humans reside, protected by the Twelve Riders.

Farhome – Another of the three realms, where the *rhoas* of the deceased are sent.

Fiends – Mythical beings of fire and darkness, now imprisoned in Darkhome.

First Word – A unique magic word used to temporarily paralyse a purebred slave. Each purebred has their own individual First Word.

Flame – A type of slave trained for sexual services and entertainment, also known as pleasure slaves.

Freeborn – Slaves who were born free but later enslaved.

House slave – Slaves responsible for household tasks and labour.

Kill Word – A unique magic word that triggers the Rage in a purebred beast.

Lor'qas - An angled type of sword with a serrated blade.

Pain Word – A magic word that causes temporary, intense pain in any purebred without leaving a trace or causing damage. Each purebred has a unique Pain Word.

Purebred – Slaves specifically bred and raised for servitude, often trained from childhood in obedience and various skills.

Pyre – A religious figure who serves the Twelve Riders.

Pyrearch – A senior religious figure overseeing Chambers of the Twelve in larger cities.

Rage – A state where a purebred beast loses control, fighting with mindless ferocity until either their target is killed or they are incapacitated.

Rhoa – The essence of a person, believed to contain emotions and everything that makes a person human.

Twelve Riders – The twelve deities who govern the three realms, each riding an ancient dragon. They maintain balance, protect the realms, and oversee the laws of life and death.

Unrage/Bare – When a purebred beast fights without entering the Raged state.

Words – Magical commands used to control and bind purebreds.

CONTENT WARNING

Lion of Zarall is an adult dark fantasy novel and it deals with some heavy subject matter such as ongoing trauma, abuse, torture, graphic violence, gore and non-con. Some parts of the writing is explicit and will draw you into the characters' minds and let you experience their feelings. If any of these things are triggers for you, Lion of Zarall may not be the best book for you. I can't guarantee the below list is exhaustive, but I've done my best to be thorough.

- Amputation

- Bodily harm

- Captivity

- Childhood abuse and trauma

- Coercion

- Death of a wild animal (self-defense)

- Death threats

- Descriptive gore

- Depression

- Dissociation

- Emotional abuse

- Gore

- Injury

- Imprisonment

- Mature language

- Mature sexual themes

- Murder

- Mutilation

- Non-consent

- Physical abuse

- Profanity

- PTSD

- Self-harm

- Sexual assault

- Slavery

- Strangling

- Suffocating

- Swearing

- Torture

- Violence

If you or someone you know is in crisis, help is available. Get in touch with your GP and/or mental health professionals in your area, or call a helpline.

Australia: Call 13 11 14 or text 0477 13 11 14 or go to lifeline.org.au

New Zealand: Call 0800 543 354 or text 4357 or go to lifeline.org.nz

US: Call 800-273-TALK or text 988 or chat 988lifeline.org

UK: 0800-689-5652 – the National Suicide Prevention

Canada: Call 988 for the Suicide Crisis Helpline

1

LION

He knew it was over when he blinked and stared at the severed hand at his feet.

He had learned to take his time waking up from the Rage. His senses rushed back to him all at once, but he only focused on one at a time. The harsh sunlight glaring off the bloodstained sands. The smell of sweat, leather and death filling his nostrils. The taste of blood and bile, coppery and bitter, lingering on his tongue. His muscles aching with a fatigue that hinted at the ferocity of the battle he could not remember.

He closed his eyes and took a deep breath. Not even fragmented images of the battle survived the Rage that had consumed his mind. He didn't even remember how he fought, only that he won. Otherwise, he wouldn't be standing here, waking up from it.

Opening his eyes again, he surveyed the mutilated remains of his opponent. He wondered what it would be like to die while Raged. His heart pounded in his ears. The roar of the crowd was distant at first, then it crashed over him like a wave. They cheered and chanted the name he was given.

Lion of Zarall. Lion of Zarall. Lion of Zarall.

Finally feeling steady enough, he shifted his weight to wipe the blood and sweat off his face. Although it was only mid spring, the battle had left him overheated and breathless. When he lifted his arm, a sharp pain flared in his left shoulder. He didn't look, didn't even falter. He pushed through the pain and wiped his face.

The eyes of the thousands in attendance were on him. He didn't dare show them that he was injured. *Minor*, he thought to himself. It was only a minor injury. It was nothing. As he lowered his arm, he almost gasped at the pain. He kept his face a perfect mask of indifference. *Minor*, he thought stubbornly. *It's nothing.*

He walked up to the grandstand overlooking the arena where his Owner was seated. It was separated by walls and soldiers clad in black and gold uniforms. Lion was used to hiding his discomfort. His shoulder ached with each step, as if an invisible hammer was pounding at it. But he kept his back straight, and his arms relaxed at his sides.

His lor'qas, an angled type of sword with a serrated blade, still rested in his right hand. He had a shield too, but he must have lost it at some point. He stopped directly in front of the grandstand. He dropped to one knee, his head bowed, and he raised his sword in salute. He suppressed the soft, warm flutter that he felt in his chest. This part of the battle, saluting his Owner like a free man, always made him feel that flutter. But he was quick to extinguish that emotion.

King Leonis Zarall accepted his salute with a slow nod. He was clad in layers of golden-black fabric, rich and opulent, designed to draw attention. His frail and aging figure was concealed beneath the loose garments and elaborate accessories, a deliberate attempt to distract from his physical weakness. His weak limbs and aching joints were a secret well-known within the castle walls but carefully masked from the public eye.

Lion stood slowly, his head still bowed. He turned from the grandstands and from the carnage he had painted at the arena, and he headed for the looming gates that led underneath the arena structure. The gates, named the Gates of Life, were elegant and imposing. They swung open slowly as he approached.

He kept his head high, his posture unwavering, despite the throbbing pain that threatened to undermine his strength. He blinked at the shadowed passage beyond sight from the prying eyes of the spectators. As he crossed the threshold, the roar of the crowd faded and was replaced by the cool, dark sight of the corridor.

Here, his team waited. A small group of trainers, physicians, weapons masters and guards. He could fool the spectators, but he couldn't fool them, especially Master Badimar. As soon as the gates swung shut behind him, Master Badimar's eyes landed on Lion's shoulder. "How bad?" he asked.

"I am well, Master." Lion's reply was prompt.

"Like fuck you are." Badimar took Lion's blood-stained sword and handed it to one of his assistants. He then glanced at Sir Dramesh, one of the king's personal guards who was assigned to ensure Lion's and the team's safety. "Sir Dramesh?"

Sir Dramesh answered from the door that led further into the arena structure. "We're clear."

"Let's go."

A group of guards, all armed to the teeth, fell in step around Lion. Badimar took his place next to him. The trainers and the rest followed behind.

Lion used to find it odd that all these free men, the king's personal guards selected for their talent as well as their nobility, were ready to fight and give their lives to keep him safe. Not that he needed it. If anyone dared to ambush him in the corridors underneath the Switchblade Arena, which had its own security too, Lion was more than capable of defending himself. He didn't see the point of being escorted by guards. But he wouldn't question the wisdom of free men.

The corridors were empty. Sir Dramesh and his men must have cleared it ahead of time. They didn't have to walk too far to reach the preparation room. Each beast and their teams were given rooms like this by the arena management as they waited for their turn to fight. Being the king's champion beast, the room allocated for Lion was the most spacious and closest to the arena. Sir Dramesh and his men waited outside as Lion and the others walked in.

Located right underneath the stands, the steady hum of the crowd was a constant, oppressive presence in the room. Badimar had brought their own armoury and other equipment from the castle. Two racks displayed an assortment of weapons. Sharpening stones, whetstones, and various tools for weapons and armour maintenance cluttered a long table. Nearby, a barrel of water and a stack of clean clothes waited. Two stands held Lion's spare armours, their metal plates polished and ready. The third stand was bare.

Master Badimar pointed at the corner of the room, where Lion usually stood as they prepared him for battles. He walked to the corner and faced the room, his hands relaxed at his sides and his eyes fixed on the ground.

Vanalten, the physician responsible for the king's beasts, approached him like a man with a mission. "Where?"

"His left shoulder," Badimar said. He hovered nearby, his arms crossed over his stocky chest, a grim expression on his face.

Vanalten scowled at Lion's shoulder, which was hidden under a shoulder plate. He waved his hand at the two slaves who waited nearby. "Remove his armour."

The two men, both humble house slaves dressed in plain, earth-toned uniforms with worn leather belts and frayed cuffs, started undoing the straps that held Lion's armour together. Both slaves were familiar. They were the ones who often helped with maintaining Lion's armour and weapons before and after fights. The older slave with the weathered face and bony fingers had been around for as long as Lion came into King Leonis's possession. Yet, Lion never knew the name their Owner had given the man. They had never talked, never even acknowledged each other. But the man's presence eased Lion's nerves.

As he stood still, letting them undo the straps, Lion distracted himself by staring at the tattoo on the left side of the old man's neck. The faded ink displayed a plain, circular frame around a hand, marking him as a freeborn house slave. Despite being a freeborn, the faded colour of the ink suggested the man had been enslaved for longer than Lion's age. His perfectly obedient manner was proof of that.

Lion had a tattoo on the left side of his neck too, though his was a more intricate circle of jagged lines, flowing curves, and sharp angles. The unique pattern of shapes and symbols framed a dog-like creature. The tattoo identified him as a purebred beast. A perfect warrior, bred and raised for the arenas.

Once the straps loosened and the armour came free, Lion braced himself for the pain he knew would come when they lifted the armour over his head. Although he didn't grimace, he couldn't help but clench his jaw. Luckily, the old house slave had stepped in front of him and concealed his expression from

Badimar. Before the slave stepped out of Badimar's view, Lion relaxed his jaw again.

Next, they removed the padded jacket he wore under the armour, then they pulled the thick shirt over his head. Lion's bare chest was damp with sweat and sand that clung to his skin. Arena sand always found its way under the layers of armour and clothes he wore. It was an irritation he had grown accustomed to as the old battle scars that adorned his skin. Among these marks, three brands on his chest stood apart, each made by hot iron that seared his skin.

The tournament brands were Caesh's idea. During a drunken celebration following Lion's first tournament victory, he had suggested that the Lion of Zarall should display on his skin every tournament he won, as a way of distinguishing him for the rest of his life. It would increase his value in the future too, if the king ever decided to sell him. The king liked the idea, and so, they had started the tradition of branding Lion for each major victory. He had three round brands in a neat row just beneath his collarbones, representing the three major tournaments he won: a stallion, a rose, and a maiden.

He would receive a fourth one, a sparrow for the Golden Sparrow Tournament, if he could win the next fight.

As soon as Lion's chest was stripped, Master Vanalten pushed the slaves aside and ordered Lion to sit on the bench. He started with a visual examination first. Lion's entire shoulder and upper arm was a canvas of with dark, angry bruises. It wasn't bleeding, but it was swollen. Lion interpreted the lack of blood as a good sign, though Vanalten's lips pressed into a thin line.

Next, Vanalten started poking various sections of Lion's shoulder. He didn't bother asking Lion questions. He knew the slave would do anything to downplay the severity of the injury. Instead, Vanalten put one hand on Lion's neck, monitoring his heartbeat, and he kept a very close watch on his expression.

Badimar crossed his arms, standing as close as he could dare without annoying Vanalten. The other three trainers – Joharin, Caesh, and Doha – gathered behind him. They each held their breaths. Doha, their youngest, kept shifting his weight.

The two house slaves hung his armour on the empty stand. Moral, the armorer, was examining the integrity of the armour. He started replacing the left shoulder plate, which had a massive dent on it. As he worked, he kept glancing at

Vanalten, as if expecting the physician to say Lion won't need his armour today. Or ever.

A knot twisted in Lion's gut. *Minor*, he thought as he tried so hard to breathe normally. *Just a minor bruise.*

"So, how bad is it?" Doha asked.

Vanalten grunted, but he didn't speak. Still carefully watching Lion's expression, he started moving his arm up and down and from side to side. The pain intensified, but Lion stared at the floor and kept his expression still. Vanalten lifted Lion's arm over his head, bent his elbow and pressed his palm against his. "Push," he ordered.

Lion pushed against Vanalten's hand and pain exploded in his shoulder. It was so intense and unexpected, a small gasp escaped him.

"Shit," Caesh cursed. He started pacing.

Doha leaned against the wall, his shoulders sagged. "It's bad, isn't it?"

Lion's eyes widened, surprised at his lapse in control. He was ready to push through the pain, but Vanalten pulled his hand back. His bushy eyebrows knitted closer together. He resumed his examination, moving Lion's arm in different positions and instructing him to push.

Above the room, the crowd's low hum intensified into a passionate cheer. The second semi-final battle had started. The winner of that battle was going to be Lion's next rival for the tournament final. Thousands had gathered in Brinescar for this event. To watch King Leonis's champion beast win the Golden Sparrow. If Lion couldn't fight, the king would have to concede and Lion would be in so much trouble, depending on the severity of the injury.

Badimar's face darkened as he continued hovering behind Vanalten. Moral tossed the shoulder plate at the table and stopped to watch the examination, no longer in a hurry to fix the armour. Even Sir Dramesh kept peering from the door he guarded. For long minutes, all they could hear was the spectators' muffled roar.

But all Lion could hear was his own panicked thoughts. *Minor. It's just a minor injury. It's nothing.*

Finally, Vanalten stepped back and sighed. "Well, good news and bad news."

Lion's heart skipped a beat.

Vanalten waved his hand towards Lion's shoulder. "I can fix that. It's not permanent."

Lion didn't let his relief show. He continued staring at his feet, his face perfectly flat and still.

"But only if he doesn't aggravate it," Vanalten added.

Nothing changed on Lion's face, but his mind went cold and blank.

Doha scoffed. He waved his arm towards the arena. "How is he not going to aggravate it? He's got another fight in what? Less than an hour?"

The room went silent. Lion knew. He glimpsed the answer in Badimar's face, too. He understood what Vanalten suggested.

Doha took his time, but he caught on. "Oh shit."

The soft sound of metal scraping against metal filled the room. Moral resumed his task of fixing the armour. He replaced the shoulder plate with a spare.

"You guys can't be considering this," Caesh said.

Joharin, senior amongst the three assistant trainers, crossed his arms as he shook his head at Badimar. "It's risky. He might lose."

"Might?" Caesh spat. "It would be like pitting a freeborn beast against a purebred beast."

"A Raged purebred beast," Doha added. He motioned his arm towards the arena centre again. "Whoever wins that fight, they'll Rage him. No one is stupid enough to send their purebred Unraged. Especially against the Lion of Zarall."

Caesh pointed at Lion as he spoke to Badimar. "And we'll send Lion Unraged?

"He will be at a disadvantage," Joharin said. His objection wasn't as passionate as Caesh's. He was merely stating the facts.

"A big one," Doha added. He pointed towards the arena again, as if they'd looked hard enough, they could see past the walls and watch the battle as it unfolded. "These are Blackmaw and Skullsworn. They are... They..." He scoffed. "Well, you know how brutal they both are. One of them will be Lion's next rival, and we'll send him out there Unraged? He won't win."

"Well, if you Rage him, he might win." Vanalten lifted a finger. "But it will undoubtedly be his very last fight."

Lion's heart sank, though he suppressed the emotion. If he couldn't fight again, he would have no use for his Owner. He would be as good as dead.

He took a slow, measured breath and reminded himself that he only lived to serve and breathed to please. He would do whatever he was ordered to. He would accept whatever happened.

"So that's it, then," Doha said. "These are the options? Let him lose and die, or help him win and become useless?"

They all looked at Badimar. He was the king's Master of the Beasts. The head trainer. He would make the decision. Lion tried not to hold his breath. He inhaled and exhaled steadily.

Badimar stared at him long and hard. Despite being a head shorter than Lion, he was an imposing figure who made everyone feel small in his presence. Badimar was the best trainer Lion had ever served. He pushed the king's beasts to their limits while also prioritizing their health. He made sure they all received good meals, kept physical punishments to a minimum, and he generally followed Vanalten's advice.

That's why his decision struck Lion like a blow.

"We can't let him lose," Badimar said. Pity flashed across his face, but it was gone when he looked away at Moral. "Get him ready."

Moral nodded and did his last check of the armour. Vanalten pointed a finger at Badimar, then at the rest of them. "You all heard my advice."

"Yes, it will go on the record."

"The king will be disappointed to lose the best purebred beast he's owned in over a decade."

"He will be more disappointed to lose the tournament held to celebrate the Zarall family's hundred years of reign."

"I will decide what would make me most disappointed."

King Leonis Zarall's entrance caught everyone except Sir Dramesh by surprise. Lion was the first to snap out of it and react. He dropped to his knees and pressed his forehead to the cold floor. The two freeborn house slaves did the same, while the free men in the room greeted the king on one knee, and with their heads bowed slightly.

King Leonis waved his hand impatiently. "Up."

Lion stood tall, his hands clasped in front of him, his eyes firmly on the floor. The king looked him up and down, his eyes lingering on his shoulder, before he turned his attention to Badimar. "Shame on you, Badimar."

"Your Majesty?"

"If it wasn't for Sir Dramesh sending me the word, you were just going to throw away my investment without consulting me?"

Badimar shot a glare at Sir Dramesh, who simply shrugged and returned to watching the door. "Your Majesty," Badimar said. "I was merely..."

"Shame on you for lacking faith in yourself. Have you not spent the last three years training this beast?"

"Yes, Your Majesty."

"If, after all this time, he is still unfit to face a Raged purebred beast..." The king walked across the room slowly, his steps measured and careful. He shook his head and clicked his tongue. "Then perhaps it is not the beast's worth in question, but your own competence as a Beast Master."

"It's not about my competency, Your Majesty. I promised you a victory. I'll make sure..."

"What have I named this purebred beast?" King Leonis raised his voice with a sudden anger. He paused for a response and also to catch his breath. Doha glanced at the stool across the room, but kept his mouth shut. King Leonis steadied himself, though his anger crept up his cheeks. "Has Kyrus stolen your tongues? What is the name of this slave?"

"Lion of Zarall," Caesh muttered.

"Lion of *who*?"

"Lion of Zarall, Your Majesty."

"Now imagine my people uttering these words:" He paused after each sentence to gasp his next breath. "Lion of Zarall got injured and retired. *Retired*. Do you grasp the weight of that word?" He didn't expect an answer, but he paused anyway, before hissing, "Weak. It implies he became weak."

The room was dead quiet. No one dared to make eye contact with the king. "Master Vanalten," King Leonis said, controlling his voice.

"Yes, Your Majesty?"

"And what becomes of those injured beasts whom you cannot heal?"

"As extensive as my competencies as a physician, we all know it is not always possible to recover from some injuries."

"What happens to those who cannot do what they are bred to do?"

Lion knew the answer. Every slave did, whether they were freeborn or purebred. He suppressed a shiver that crept up his spine.

"The fortunate ones are sold to the tribesmen of the North."

"To keep a beast that cannot fight is sheer wastefulness." King Leonis nodded. "And I refuse to send my champion beast to those cannibals."

Badimar bowed his head. "I understand your wish, Your Majesty."

"Do you?" King Leonis examined the armour, which hung on the stand. He swiped his finger across the breastplate, still dusty and stained from the last battle. When Moral elbowed the old freeborn house slave, the man rushed to wipe the breastplate clean until the golden lion engravings shone bright.

"I do not wish him to lose," King Leonis said. He picked up the metal half mask from the table, which was custom made to complement Lion of Zarall's arena gear. It wasn't much of a helmet; it only provided protection for his upper face, leaving his bearded chin unprotected. It was shaped like a lion's face. With his bushy blond beard and rich blond hair framing the metal mask, Lion's head resembled a lion while he wore it.

Turning and twisting the mask between his bony fingers, King Leonis made his way to Lion. "Can he win, Master Badimar?"

"Yes, Your Majesty," Badimar said quickly. Lion knew the Master of the Beasts enough to hear the lack of faith in his tone. The king didn't seem to notice, and nodded like he was given what he wanted.

"What do you think, purebred?" the king asked quieter. "Can you win?"

"I live to serve, I breathe to please, Owner." Lion's reply came within a heartbeat.

"Purebreds don't have opinions," Doha started, but King Leonis snapped. "I am not talking to you, child. I am well aware of what purebreds are."

Above the room, the crowd's cheer exploded into a series of roars and exclamations, followed by thunderous claps, marking the end of the fight. Next was the final battle between the winner and Lion.

King Leonis pressed his palm against Lion's chest over the brands that marked his past victories. He lowered his voice, so only Lion could hear. "You want to fight him, don't you? You want to fight him bare. As yourself."

Lion's fingers twitched. The word *yes* crept to his lips, but he didn't say it. There was only one way he could answer this question. "I do as my Owner wills," he said.

The king stared at his face, then smiled. Lion's heart pounded loud in his chest. His blood rushed.

"Then I am willing you to win." Leonis placed the mask on Lion's face. "The Lion of Zarall shall not fall."

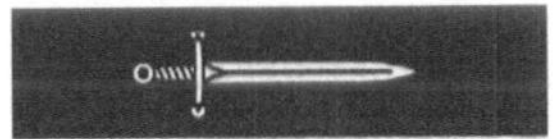

LION STARED AT THE vertical line in front of him. Bright daylight outside squeezed into a line between the two gates that remained shut in front of him. He slowed his breathing, using each inhale to steady his nerves and each exhale to focus his mind.

"Do you understand what you need to do?" Badimar asked for the fifth time.

"Yes, Master," Lion replied respectfully. He understood, and he barely kept himself from bouncing from one foot to the other. His heart thrummed, and his muscles tensed, ready for action. Yet, he remained still and focused. He needed to control his mind more than ever in this fight.

Badimar, on the other hand, made no attempt to conceal his nerves, pacing back and forth and checking Lion's armour over and over again. It was just the two of them in the launch room. Sir Dramesh and the guards secured the door, giving them privacy. The rest of the team had gone up onto the stands allocated for them to watch the fight. Outside, the announcer was making a long speech about celebrating House Zarall's hundredth year of reign. His voice was muffled by the thick stone walls and the sound of Lion's heart beating too loud in his ears.

He clenched and unclenched his fists. He was itching to charge out there and fight.

"You got to keep level," Badimar reminded him, as if he could sense Lion's eagerness. "Don't overthink but use your brain. Control the fight."

"Yes, Master."

Badimar tapped Lion's left elbow. "Keep that arm tucked against your side. Vanalten said no pulling or pushing, and no lateral movement."

Outside, the announcer said something, and the crowd cheered ecstatically.

"Yes, Master," Lion said. He flexed his neck muscles and bent his knees slightly. His grip on his weapons tightened.

Badimar stood beside him and put a hand on his right shoulder. "Steady."

Lion exhaled a slow breath. *Focus.*

The announcer spoke louder. Lion could almost hear the spectators holding their collective breath. The entire Switchblade Arena was filled with anticipation. His muscles twitched.

He inhaled. *Steady.*

He heard the announcer say his name. The doors broke apart, inviting the bright daylight into the room.

"Go!" Badimar yelled.

Lion was already out, sprinting across the pale sand reflecting the brutal sunlight. He carried a trident in his right hand, and a weighted net was draped loosely over his left shoulder. The crowd's ecstatic shout greeted him. The noise was so overwhelming, it shrouded his thoughts for a moment. That was fine. He didn't need a lot of thoughts. His body knew how to fight.

The opposite gate across the arena opened at the same time. His opponent charged into the arena. The name he carried was Skullsworn. He was a purebred beast too, but unlike Lion, he was Raged.

Lion didn't need to see Skullsworn's face to know he was Raged. He moved like a Raged beast. Fast, focused, feral. His mind was quiet and dark. Kill Word quietened all the thoughts, took control, and left no memories. Lion knew that. He had experienced that blissful state many times. Stripped from any thoughts, feelings and distracting sensations like injuries and pain. Raged state gave the purebred beasts an indisputable advantage.

One Lion didn't have in this fight.

Lion lifted his trident over his shoulder and switched to a throwing grip. He didn't have the advantage of being Raged in this fight, but he still had a strategy.

"One third of the battleground," Badimar had instructed before the fight. "Adjust your speed, so Skullsworn reaches the centre first. You need to control the space."

Skullsworn, who wielded a one-handed mace and a round shield, charged at a dead speed. Lion timed his approach, then slowed down. He planted his feet, aimed, and threw the trident. As soon as the shaft left his palm, he resumed running.

Skullsworn sidestepped without breaking his stride. The trident flew past him. Lion had perfectly calculated its downward tilt and the weapon plunged into the sand just behind Skullsworn. Lion's eyes remained locked on his rival. He ignored the spectators' disappointed exclamation at the failed throw. In one fluid motion, Lion pulled the weighted net from his left shoulder and threw it with practiced precision.

The net sailed through the air, aimed directly at Skullsworn. The Raged beast, still moving at full speed, twisted his body and narrowly avoided the net.

Another disappointed howl filled the arena. Using the momentary distraction, Lion veered sharply, darting past Skullsworn. The Raged beast lunged for him, swinging his mace with the agility of a predator. Lion dodged with grace, his feet barely touching the ground as he sped toward his trident. Skullsworn pursued, but Lion was already out of reach. With a swift dive, Lion's fingers wrapped around the shaft of the trident, pulling it free from the sand. He rolled to his feet, the weapon now back in his hand, and faced his opponent.

Skullsworn didn't hesitate. From this close up, Lion caught a glimpse of the beast's eyes through the slits of his helmet. A wild fury burned through Skullsworn's shrunken pupils. The Raged beast swung his mace. Lion parried. The sound of their clashing weapons rang through the arena.

Skullsworn's mace swung again, relentless and brutal. Lion used the trident's long range to keep him away.

Wielding the trident with one hand, Lion was limited with the range of moves he could use. He only used his left hand to support but avoided putting pressure on it. Most defensive moves required a two-handed grip, so he would have to drive the exchanges and keep moving. He jabbed, aiming at Skullsworn's neck. The Raged beast brushed it aside with his shield and followed with a relentless counterattack. Lion kept moving. He spun and skipped from one side to the other, jabbing rapidly and barely keeping Skullsworn at bay. He cleared all thoughts from his mind as he kept his eyes on Skullsworn's shield. He watched how the Raged beast lifted it and brought it back down after each parry.

"When he does an overhead strike," Badimar had instructed him, "he tilts his shield to the left." The Master of the Beasts had spent weeks gathering information about Skullsworn and other likely opponents, watching them, building strategies. He was the best trainer in all of Chinderia. And there was a reason why he sent Lion out here with a weapon clearly designed for a two-handed grip, despite its limitations.

Skullsworn raised the mace for an overhead strike. The shield tilted slightly to the left.

Lion's trident sprung forward like a snake lunging at its prey and caught the shield between the prongs. He gripped the shaft with both hands, twisted, and pushed it upwards.

Skullsworn's shield was strapped to his left forearm. When Lion pushed the shield up, Skullsworn's arm was dragged with it. The Raged beast tried kicking and swinging his mace, but his shield was locked with Lion's trident. He could neither close in nor step back.

The crowd roared with anticipation of blood. The fight hadn't lasted long. Only several intense minutes had passed since the gates had opened, and it was already about to finish.

Lion pushed the trident, forcing Skullsworn to move with it. He had to put more pressure than he wanted on his left arm, because Skullsworn was big and heavy and very reluctant to cooperate. Lion's shoulder throbbed sharply, warning him not to push harder. He changed his grip and pushed with his chest. Skullsworn stumbled towards the direction Lion wanted him to go. He stepped over the edge of the net.

The crowd gasped, only now noticing how the weighted net was perfectly spread wide, exactly like how Lion threw it. A few more steps and Lion could...

With an enraged grunt, Skullsworn yanked his arm free of the straps. The sudden loss of resistance made Lion fumble. Before he could fling the shield away and regain his stance, Skullsworn was within range. The beast brought his mace down in a vicious arc, catching Lion on the left shoulder.

Pain exploded through Lion's body, nearly causing him to drop his weapon. He stumbled back, gritting his teeth. Raged or not, he was an experienced fighter who knew how to ignore the pain and stay focused. He spun, twirling the trident in one hand, and he brought the end of the shaft on Skullsworn's unprotected side. He followed through with two quick jabs, one at Skullsworn's helmet, and the other at the centre of his chest, with enough force to push him back out of close range.

He breathed through the pain. The agony, he could ignore. The thoughts, he couldn't. His shoulder was throbbing like a nightmare. If he wasn't wearing shoulder plates, the mace would have crushed every bone in his upper arm. It might already have. He couldn't help but test the damage by moving his fingers. The pain became worse.

How bad was it? Was it still treatable? Had he just aggravated it?

He narrowly dodged Skullsworn's next blow. As the mace flew past his face, one of the spikes caught Lion's face mask and yanked it off. Lion withdrew further, barely keeping Skullsworn from rushing him. He kept his left arm close to his torso, yet it still throbbed.

Was the injury going to be permanent? Was this his last fight? If he couldn't fight anymore, he was going to die regardless of if he won here or not.

Skullsworn swung his mace wildly. Lion parried and dodged, then followed up with one handed swipes and jabs. The Raged beast didn't even care that he didn't have the protection of a shield anymore. He didn't see Lion as a threat. He had every advantage in this fight: uninjured, Raged, unburdened by thoughts and fears that flooded his head.

Lion growled as he dodged another strike. He hated that he had thoughts. He hated that he had to think about the possibility of this being his last fight. Thoughts didn't belong in a fight.

Anger did.

With a roar, he landed a strike at Skullsworn's helmet, causing it to twist just enough to partially obscure his sight. The Raged beast yanked the helmet off and threw it away. He barely parried Lion's next strike. The trident became a blur. Fury drove Lion's strikes, the pain and fear fuelling his anger. He launched at Skullsworn with renewed ferocity, each strike carrying the weight of his rage.

He drove the prongs of his trident deep into Skullsworn's unprotected side. They tore his light armour and found flesh.

Skullsworn wouldn't register the pain, so Lion didn't wait for a reaction. He didn't just want to hurt the purebred beast; he wanted to kill him.

The arena seemed to blur as Lion's focus narrowed on Skullsworn. Their weapons clashed in a brutal dance. Skullsworn, despite bleeding from his side, fought back with wild, relentless energy. Lion stabbed his arm next, but Skullsworn fought on.

Lion's strikes, fast and precise, were driven by a desperation to end this fight before it took a bigger toll on him. He drove Skullsworn back with every attack, forcing him to withdraw, step, dodge to the side, withdraw again, and step to the same side. He herded Skullsworn like a shepherd's dog. When Skullsworn stumbled, his chest opened for another attack.

Lion didn't take the shot.

Instead, he tossed his trident aside, rolled to the ground and pulled the net.

He flung it over Skullsworn, and the Raged beast swung his mace without thinking. The weapon got tangled in the net. Skullsworn struggled, his movements hindered by the weighted mesh.

Lion wasted no time. He pulled the net tight, catching Skullsworn's limbs and further restricting his movements. Skullsworn thrashed wildly, but it only tightened the net around him.

Lion picked his trident back up. Moving without hurry, he drove it into Skullsworn's chest.

The arena erupted in deafening cheers. Lion stood over his fallen opponent. He watched Skullsworn's face as the purebred beast blinked rapidly. He was waking from his Raged state. Lion had wondered many times what it would be like to die in Rage. If he would wake up from it in time to understand that he was dying? He saw the answer in Skullsworn's face.

The purebred beast, now conscious and himself, coughed and spat blood. His eyes found Lion.

He spoke.

Despite the crowd's overwhelming noise, Lion heard the words.

"I will see you in Farhome," the purebred beast said.

Lion stared at him in shock until Skullsworn's eyes glazed and his expression stilled. This shouldn't have happened. Purebreds didn't speak to each other. It wasn't permitted. It was an Act of Defiance.

Purebreds didn't go to Farhome either. They couldn't. They didn't have *rhoas*.

Lost in his confusion, Lion stood over Skullsworn's dead body longer than he should have. He looked up. The spectators filled every available space in the rows. No one was sitting. They were all jumping up and down, chanting the name he carried.

Lion of Zarall! Lion of Zarall!

His chest heaving, and the pain in his shoulder throbbing with each breath, Lion spared one last glance at Skullsworn's lifeless body.

I will see you in Farhome.

A shiver ran down his spine.

He moved away. He took two steps towards the Gate of Life, before he remembered he hadn't saluted his Owner yet. He turned sharply, hoping his slip-up would go unnoticed. He approached the royal grandstand, dropped to one knee, and raised his trident.

Like a free man.

He suppressed that annoying flutter in his chest. He stood back up, keeping his head down respectfully.

The Gate of Life swung open, welcoming him into the cool shadows behind.

2

GLADWIEL

THE SMALL WAREHOUSE WAS cluttered with rusty cages, crates full of chains, and old furniture. The wind beat against the walls outside and howled through the boarded-up windows, urging Gladwiel to hurry and finalize this business. Autumn had rolled in early, with its miserable weather and destructive storms. If Gladwiel and his men couldn't return to Kiore before the storm picked up, they would be forced to stay overnight in this filthy place. And that was the last thing Gladwiel wanted.

Dravik, the leader of the four collectors, had made himself comfortable on one of the dusty crates. His posture was relaxed. In one hand, he casually flipped a knife, the blade catching the dim light of the lanterns. His three men spread around the warehouse: one watching outside through the cracks between the boards, while the other two leaned against the canvas-covered wagon that brought them here. The vehicle was weathered and worn, its wheels caked with mud. Their tired horses were underfed, their ribs visible under their damp coats. The canvas over the wagon was thick but old, torn in places.

For the time being, Gladwiel avoided looking at the wagon.

He knew what Dravik was trying to accomplish, leaving the back flap open just enough so Gladwiel could partially see the man lying inside. Dravik wanted him to get curious and ask what else he had in there. The sleazy collector would then claim that this particular slave was special and act as if he didn't want to sell him. But Gladwiel was in the business for long enough to know every strategy. So, for now, he ignored the wagon and the mysterious man inside.

He kept his attention on the seven slaves who lined up on their knees in front of him. The slaves reeked of sweat and blood, the smell forcing Gladwiel to stay at least two meters away. His robe, adorned with intricate embroidery and shimmering jewels, stood in stark contrast to the slaves' dirty, tattered rags. He scrunched his nose with dissatisfaction as he watched his assistant, Hasrey, examine the slaves.

After checking the last slave's teeth and limbs for any obvious injuries, Hasrey walked up to Gladwiel. He pulled a handkerchief out of his pocket and wiped his hands. "Well," he said. "They're all freeborn."

"Of course they are," Gladwiel said with obvious disdain. This wasn't where he acquired his high-end products. He didn't expect to find anything other than questionably enslaved freeborn slaves here. He let his face show what he thought of Dravik's merchandise.

Dravik smirked, showing a mouthful of crooked teeth.

Gladwiel glanced at the wagon. He suddenly understood what Dravik's play was. He tilted his head slightly as he listened to Hasrey's report with boredom.

"Tattoos seem genuine enough," Hasrey said. "Fresh ink…"

"This is a mistake!" one of the slaves, a man with dark hair and a missing ear, shouted. Bruises and bloody gashes covered his face, and he blinked rapidly whenever someone moved, yet he was still reckless enough to challenge them. "These tattoos are fake! We're not criminals."

"That one is freeborn house slave." Hasrey pointed at the raving slave. He moved his finger to the next two. "Those two are freeborn beasts, but their tongues cut out."

Gladwiel rolled his eyes at Dravik. "Mute slaves lose a lot of value." That was true. Buyers were cautious about freeborn slaves who had their tongues cut out. That usually meant someone didn't want these slaves talking. It indicated a suspicious background that could lead to potential trouble.

Dravik shrugged. "They're good fighters. They don't need tongues."

"This is illegal enslavement!" the reckless slave kept shouting. "Do you know who we are?" He yelped and shrunk when one of Dravik's men walked up to him with a club. Dravik's brute beat the man into silence.

Hasrey had to raise his voice over the slave's whimpers. "One more house slave, not the healthiest. The other three are flames. They're young enough to be receptive to proper training."

Gladwiel glanced at the last three slaves wearing a flame tattoo on their necks; a young man and two women. They trembled and kept their eyes on the floor. They seemed docile enough already. Gladwiel's slave trainers could turn them into obedient pleasure slaves within a few weeks. Those three promised good returns on investment. He could make a decent profit out of the freeborn beasts too. Underground arena enthusiasts didn't mind buying wild freeborns, as long as they could fight. Overall, this seemed like a good trade. He was glad his hour-long trip outside the city of Kiore in this terrible weather would be worth his time.

He glanced at the wagon again, wondering.

"Of course, the flames would need to be checked for any diseases," Hasrey said.

Gladwiel nodded. "Nobody wants diseased pleasure slaves."

Dravik shrugged. "Suit yourself. My men didn't touch them."

"Do you want me to arrange Master Tekdar to come and check them?" Hasrey asked, already knowing the answer.

The rain pounded on the walls and ceilings outside. Water leaked from a corner. Gladwiel longed to be back in his office inside the city, sit by the fire, and start sorting out paperwork for these sorry batch of slaves. "No need," he said with a sigh. "I'll take them."

Dravik smiled his toothy grin again. He flipped his knife between his fingers. Gladwiel's two bodyguards, who stood behind him, openly scowled at the blade.

"This is wrong," the slave with the missing ear cried softly. "You'll pay for this."

"I'll pay a Blue each for the flames and the beasts," Gladwiel said. "And eight Greys for the other two."

Dravik scoffed. "Three Blues each. For all."

Gladwiel dug his hand into the brown sash around his waist and pulled his leather purse out. He started counting large blue coins, making sure each one caught the glint of the flickering lanterns. Dravik didn't let his greed show, but his men glanced at each other with grins they couldn't hide.

"Dravik, you and I have done enough business to know, there are costs involved in training slaves," Gladwiel said. "I can't sell these wild things without properly training them. And training costs money. And time."

"They'll learn quickly."

"I doubt that." He lifted his eyebrows at the pathetic slave, who still sobbed and muttered his objections at the legitimacy of this trade. Gladwiel looked back at Dravik, with clear exasperation on his face. "I'll give you six Blues for all."

Dravik scratched his stubby chin. He stood up and stretched his neck muscles. Gladwiel's bodyguards loomed menacingly at him, their eyes fixed on Dravik's knife, which he kept twirling between his fingers. Dravik's jaw clenched as he casually walked to the sobbing slave.

Dravik grabbed the slave's hair and slit his throat.

A scream escaped from one of the female slaves. The three flames and the house slave huddled closer together, as they watched the blood spurting out of the troublesome slave's neck. The two freeborn beasts stirred in shock. The slave with the missing ear collapsed facedown, gurgling and choking in his own blood under the horrified gazes of the others.

"What was the point of that?" Gladwiel asked as he gestured his bodyguards to stand down.

Dravik smiled his crooked grin. "Just lowering your costs. Now they'll be easier to train. More eager to learn." He glared at the remaining slaves while he wiped his knife on his dirty pants.

Sadly, he was right. The flames and the house slave bent down eagerly, touching their foreheads to the dirt floor. They sobbed and shivered. Even the beasts hunched their shoulders and avoided their gaze. Gladwiel tilted his head as he studied them more carefully. He could tell these two were not lowlife thugs before they were collected and enslaved by Dravik. They came from a life of comfort, if not luxury. Perhaps personal guards of a wealthy merchant. Until this moment, they must have been in a state of daze, not quite accepting what was really happening.

As they watched the noisy slave bleed to death, realisation struck. Gladwiel could see it in their eyes. Only now, they were realizing what kind of life awaited them.

"You're welcome," Dravik said, spreading his arms with a mocking bow. "I've done half the job."

"But now I'm purchasing six instead of seven slaves."

"Six very trainable slaves."

"I'm still not paying three Blues each for these."

Dravik lifted his knife. "Should I off another one?"

"Put your knife away, Dravik," Gladwiel sighed. "I'll pay you ten Blues for all six, and I'll let you show me what else you've got in that wagon."

Dravik pursed his lips, pretending to consider the offer. Gladwiel let him play the reluctant seller. They both knew ten Blues was a generous offer for this bunch. Dravik sighed and nodded unwillingly. "Fine." He raised a single finger. "But this one is very special."

Gladwiel made an impatient gesture, urging him to hurry up and bring the slave out. Outside, the wind blasted against the walls. If they didn't leave within the next few minutes, they would get caught in the torrent. Gladwiel didn't look forward to getting drenched.

While Dravik and his men pulled the slave out of the wagon, Hasrey gestured to the bodyguards to move the other slaves into Gladwiel's wagon, which stood at the edge of the room. His horses stamped their hooves impatiently.

"Here it is," Dravik said as he rolled the slave at Gladwiel's feet.

"Is this a joke?" Gladwiel covered his nose with the sleeve of his robe and stepped back. "This is a carcass. Do you expect me to pay for a corpse?"

The slave was unconscious. His chest rose and dropped with each laboured breath, but he was on the verge of death. Anger rose to Gladwiel's cheeks. This wasn't worth his time.

"He's a purebred beast," Dravik said, as if that was all Gladwiel needed to hear. Gladwiel's intense glare pierced through the collector. Dravik didn't look away. His smirk returned to his face. "See for yourself."

"And how could you possibly get your hands on a purebred beast?" Gladwiel asked with open disbelief. Purebreds were expensive. They were not like random travellers who had the misfortune of crossing paths with Dravik and his thugs. Purebreds were born and raised to be slaves, trained from birth. They were valuable possessions.

"Come on, Master Gladwiel. All these years we've been doing business, you know better not to ask me that question." Dravik patted the road dust off his clothes and pretended to fix his shirt. "As far as you know, I'm a legitimate merchant running a perfectly legal business."

Gladwiel clenched his jaw. His bodyguards had loaded the purchased slaves into his wagon. He glanced at the doors. He could leave. A dying purebred beast wasn't worth his time.

Dravik licked his lips. "When did I bring you trouble, Gladwiel? No heat coming after him. Especially not with what's been happening at Brinescar. Everyone's too busy with the riots and the fallout."

Dravik had a point. Slave trade definitely blossomed in the last six months, since the Serpent's Grip Tournament and the events that followed it. Nobles and the city lords were too busy with the riots and securing themselves, they rarely patrolled the roads other than the main trade routes. More and more travellers disappeared off the roads, and hardly anyone asked about the origins of so many fresh tattooed freeborns.

Still, Gladwiel looked grim as he continued negotiating. "His recovery is going to cost me more than his worth!"

"He's a *purebred*!"

Gladwiel hesitated. His instincts were telling him to turn and leave. He'd already bought the others. He would make a good profit off them. He didn't have to take a chance on a dying slave with suspicious origins.

He glanced at the shivering, filthy man who lay on the verge of death. A purebred beast. He had paid Dravik ten Blues for the six freeborn slaves. He could sell the flames for fifty Blues each. Freeborn beasts went for anywhere between ninety to one-hundred Blues, depending on how well they fought. Even the house slave could sell for at least twenty Blues, with appropriate training in manners. More if he had literacy.

A purebred beast was worth at least two hundred Blues, if sold at a legitimate auction, with appropriate paperwork in place. And Gladwiel knew people who could handle the paperwork.

His greed got the better of him.

Dravik flashed his crooked grin and waved a hand at the purebred. "Examine him, at least. See for yourself whether he's worth it."

With a resigned sigh, Gladwiel stepped closer. His polished leather shoes crunched on the dirt and grime that covered the floor.

The slave's eyes were closed, though his eyelids trembled as if he was dreaming. His breathing was laboured. His face was bruised, like the rest of his naked body. Blood trailed down from a minor cut on his forehead. His skin was tanned from spending most of his life training under the sun. It looked even darker because of the thick layer of mud and filth that coated him like a hardened cloth.

"Did you drag him through mud or something? Why is he so filthy?"

Dravik shrugged. "Would you pay more if he was clean?"

"No."

Dravik smiled and nodded, like they had agreed on something. Gladwiel rolled his eyes and returned to his examination. The slave was tall and large, though maybe a little underfed, his ribs flaring too visible with each shallow breath. That was okay. Gladwiel could fatten him up. He smelled like a mixture of urine, blood, and infection. After covering his nose with the loose sleeves of his robe, Gladwiel leaned forward to examine the purebred's face better. His long, dirty blond hair was curly, tangled, and grungy. His beard was bushy and messy. Under all that bruising and dirt, his face was good looking. Gladwiel held back an approving grin. Slaves who were nice to look at always found buyers quicker and easier.

Gladwiel pushed the slave's chin, tilting his head to the right. He leaned closer to get a better look at the tattoo on the left side of his neck.

"Hasrey," Gladwiel called out to his assistant. "Bring me a rag."

"Yes, Master."

Hasrey borrowed a waterskin from one of the bodyguards and poured some water on his handkerchief. He kneeled beside the slave and scrubbed the layer of dirt from the man's neck, uncovering the details of a slave tattoo.

The first thing Gladwiel noticed was the colour of the ink. It was faded grey. Old. Unlike the others who had fresh ink, this one was tattooed as a child. Intricate swirls of lines and symbols framed a dog-like animal in a circle. The pattern of shapes was unique for each individual purebred, and almost impossible to imitate. Gladwiel smiled. The slave was a genuine purebred beast.

"Told you he was purebred," Dravik said with triumph. "Would have left him in a ditch if he wasn't."

"Don't start counting your Blues yet, Dravik." Gladwiel shifted to examine the purebred's injuries. A thick layer of mud and dried blood clung to the slave's torso, obscuring the contours of his muscles and hiding old scars. There were no open wounds or excessive bleeding. Gladwiel didn't see any missing limbs or broken bones either. The only concerning injury seemed to be the one on his right leg, which was bandaged poorly.

"Hasrey." Gladwiel gestured to the injury.

Hasrey used his knife to cut the bandage around the slave's right thigh. As soon as the wound was revealed, the putrid stench of decaying flesh and infection assaulted Gladwiel's senses, making his stomach churn with disgust.

He was right to call the slave a corpse. It was going to take Twelve's miracle to save this man.

Gladwiel glared at Dravik with distaste. "Why would you let this happen?"

Dravik, who still played with his knife, now cleaning under his fingernails with the tip of it, blinked innocently. "He was like that when we found him."

Gladwiel growled with frustration. The purebred's thigh was bright red and swollen. Yellow puss leaked out of the deep cut. The wound wasn't new. This could have been prevented with timely care and treatment.

Hasrey proceeded to wipe the wound with the wet cloth. The slave's eyes snapped open. He howled in pain, his breathing frantic. He growled at Hasrey and swatted his hand off. "Don't touch..."

"*Padlociatius*," Dravik said quickly. He had taken a piece of paper out of his pocket, though he spoke the word from his memory, with barely a glance at the paper.

The purebred's hands dropped to his sides. His whole body relaxed as if he'd just lost consciousness, though Gladwiel knew he didn't. His eyes were still wide open, fully aware of his surroundings. He'd simply lost control of his body.

Gladwiel shared a look with Hasrey. The shocked expression on his assistant's face confirmed Gladwiel's belief. "Did I just hear this slave speak without permission?"

"It's an Act of Defiance," Hasrey said in a hushed tone. "I've never heard purebreds commit Acts of Defiance."

"It's the fever," Dravik explained. "He's not himself. Don't worry, he's like a normal purebred when he's properly awake." He shook the paper in his head. "Besides, at least you got to see how he responds to his Words. In case you still doubt whether he's a genuine purebred or not."

He was right. Freeborns didn't respond to Words. The Words were what made purebreds even more special. Although still disturbed by the slave's behaviour, Gladwiel was pleased to see the demonstration.

Hasrey finished cleaning up the wound and examined the infected cut. Gladwiel narrowed his eyes at Dravik, looking for a sign of deception. But the collector was probably right. Despite their excellent discipline in obedience, even purebreds weren't immune to fever induced craziness.

When the purebred started showing signs of regaining control of his body, Hasrey stood and stepped back. He hadn't been gentle with his examination of the slave's injury, so as soon as the effects of the First Word faded, the slave gasped in pain, then passed out.

"It's bad," Hasrey said. "I'm not even sure if we can save him."

Dravik didn't bat an eye. "Of course you can; he's strong, and you've got those expensive herbs and stuff."

"Those *expensive* herbs are very expensive," Gladwiel said. "I only use them on injuries I know I can fix."

"I'm telling you, give this purebred what he needs, and he'll fight to live."

Gladwiel lifted an eyebrow at Hasrey, a subtle question. Hasrey wiped his hands with the clean edge of his handkerchief, his eyes on the purebred, contemplating. "Maybe," he said slowly with a sigh. But the discrete look and the subtle nod he gave Gladwiel was confident. Yes, the man could be saved.

Gladwiel sighed. "I'll give you five Blues for him."

Dravik scoffed. "Five? How about thirty?"

The slave moaned, his head rolling from side to side as he blinked rapidly. His breathing went erratic once again. He grabbed his thigh, howling in pain. He made an effort to raise his head and take in his surroundings, which Gladwiel took as a good sign. Terminally injured slaves did not usually have the strength to move or yell in pain.

"Ten Blues," Gladwiel said, raising his voice to be heard over the purebred's moan. Dravik laughed, shaking his head. "He's Tribesman food if I end up having to chop that leg off," Gladwiel insisted. "Ten Blues is a fair price for a corpse."

Dravik snorted. Spinning his knife between his fingers, he walked up to the slave.

"Oh, please, no need for that," Gladwiel sighed.

Dravik kneeled beside the purebred, grabbed his grungy blond hair, and pressed his knife against his neck. "I'd rather slit his throat right now than give him away for free."

The purebred's hands grasped Dravik's wrist. Gladwiel couldn't help but take another step back. The purebred's hands shook with a desperate strength and inched the knife away from his throat, before Dravik spoke his First Word and paralysed him again. The slave's limbs went slack, though his eyes remained wide open. Despite feeling disturbed by another show of defiance, Gladwiel was pleased to see the purebred still had strength.

Dravik pressed the knife against the helpless man's throat, drawing a few drops of blood.

"Enough," Gladwiel gave in. "I hate wastefulness. I'll give you twenty Blues for him, and that's my final offer."

Dravik pulled back. "Deal," he snorted, standing up. After putting his knife away, he rubbed his wrist discreetly. How strong was the purebred's brief grip? "He's all yours." He flashed another crooked grin.

Rain pounded on the roof and the wind howled through the cracks in the walls, causing the lantern flames to dance and cast eerie shadows on the purebred's face. With the effects of his First Word fading once again, the purebred snarled and moaned. When Gladwiel's bodyguards grabbed his arms and dragged him, the purebred struggled against them.

"His Words?" Gladwiel held out his hand. He narrowed his eyes at the purebred, who was growling and resisting maybe a little too fiercely.

Dravik placed the piece of paper in Gladwiel's palm. After looking at the three words written on it, Gladwiel read the first one out loud: "*Padlociatius.*"

The purebred's body went limp. When his snarls and howls suddenly died, the only sound that echoed through the warehouse was the storm outside. Thunder struck, and a flash of lightning sneaked through the boarded windows. Gladwiel gritted his teeth as he watched Dravik's men climb back into their wagons. This transaction had taken longer than he wished, and it was going to be a wet and uncomfortable trip back to Kiore.

Gladwiel's bodyguards tossed the slave into the wagon, with the other purchased slaves. Gladwiel pulled his purse out and counted thirty Blues, for the purebred and the others. Once he handed the money to Dravik, his purse felt disturbingly light. As he climbed into the driver's seat, preparing himself for the miserable trip back to his office, he tried to cheer himself up by thinking about the auction value of a purebred beast.

The slave had the will to live. All he needed was a good physician, some rest, food, and a bath. He was going to pull through and one way or another, Gladwiel was going to make his profit.

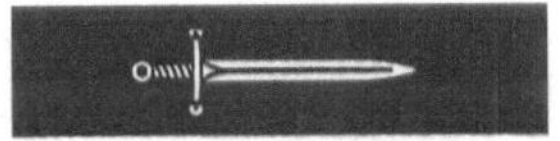

GLADWIEL'S WAREHOUSE, NESTLED WITHIN the city, was smaller than the one he'd met his suppliers outside. It consisted of two sections. The front office was a picture of wealth, with heavy tapestries hanging between the tall windows, and a thick, spotless carpet muffling the sounds of footsteps. This was where he handled the private sales. The operations section at the back was where he stored, prepared, and trained the slaves.

Ample sunlight streamed through the tall windows of the operations section. It was open space with uneven dirt floors and not much furniture. Three rows of large cages, which held a total of fifteen slaves including his latest purchases, occupied one side of the section. The opposite side was meticulously divided into separate work zones, each designated for various types of training and preparation. One of those distinct work zones, intentionally located nearest to the cages, drew attention to an imposing chair and tables full of torture devices.

Gladwiel walked the three rows with his head trainer, Master Kamal, at his side. Kamal, a lanky man who wore a leather whip at his belt, crossed his arms over his chest as he studied the new slaves Gladwiel had brought last night.

"The flames should be easy to train," Gladwiel said, suppressing a yawn. He had arrived at the city well after the storm hit and was drenched like a street rat. After securing the slaves in the warehouse, he had gone home to get changed, then came back into the office to organise the slaves' paperwork, so everything looked by the books. He had napped on the couch in his office for a few hours, but still felt tired and grumpy. "Do a three-week training plan, and I'll evaluate them." He raised his voice so the three slaves with flame tattoos could hear him. "If they're not profitable by then, I might consider selling them at a red ribbon auction."

The females didn't react, but the male flame's eyes widened. He clearly understood the extend of Gladwiel's threat and hopefully would explain the stakes to the others, ensuring their obedience and commitment to training.

Kamal nodded with a grunt and followed Gladwiel to the next cage. Gladwiel hardly stopped at the next cage storing the house slaves. He pointed at the newest one. "See what talents or skills he has and if you can add any value to him."

Gladwiel stopped at the next cage, where the two new freeborn beasts were locked. "Test their talents, see how good they are. But be careful. They're at that stage where they might consider taking their chances with the Hunters."

"I hate that stage," Kamal grunted as he glowered at the two men who stared back at him. "I might just start with some intense discipline."

"Sure," Gladwiel said, distracted. In the training zone nearly, his second trainer, Dalle, was training one of the other slaves Gladwiel had purchased several weeks ago. The slave was young, with a fresh-faced beauty and shapely hips. Although she was mellow, she seemed to pick things up very slowly. Gladwiel had a private sale coming up next week and was hoping the girl would be ready.

"Tell me all the Acts of Defiance," Dalle said, tapping his rod against his palm.

The girl stood naked in front of him, her head down and her hands clasped in front of her. "I will not make eye contact," the girl said timidly.

"How much time do you want me to spend on these beasts?" Kamal asked. "Can they even be trained properly?"

Gladwiel, still watching the training, replied thoughtfully. "You know every slave can be trained properly, with enough time and dedication." He rubbed his chin. Watching the girl recite the Acts of Defiance made him think of the purebred beast he had just purchased. He remembered the purebred beast looking at Dravik, making eye contact with him. It struck him as odd.

"I know," Kamal said. "But not all are worth the time and the effort."

"I will not speak without permission," the girl said next.

Gladwiel scowled. The purebred had spoken without permission last night. But like Dravik had said, he had a fever. Purebred or not, people sometimes raved when they were feverish. It was fine.

"I'll test how good they are and do a training proposal, with costs and timeline. You can decide whether they're worth it."

"Yes, yes," Gladwiel said with a dismissive wave. He was still focused on the girl and the training.

"What's the next one?" Dalle yelled.

Unable to remember the answer, the girl sobbed and teared up.

"What is it? We've done this a dozen times!" Dalle slapped the rod against this palm. The sound made the girl flinch. She opened and closed her mouth.

"What is the next Act of Defiance?" Dalle asked harshly.

Kamal followed Gladwiel's gaze and let out a disapproving sound. "She'll figure it out. Even the most stupid ones learn, eventually."

Gladwiel's stomach dropped. He couldn't explain why watching this scene gave him goosebumps. He couldn't explain why it made him think of the purebred either. That purebred... There was something about that purebred. The more he watched the training, the more on edge he felt.

The girl blabbered, crying and sobbing. "I... I don't know... I'm sorry..."

Dalle struck her hard with the rod. She raised her arms to defend herself. "That right there!" Dalle barked. "If your Owner decides to strike you, you will not raise your hands. Now keep them down."

Gladwiel felt hot and sick. The purebred had pushed the knife away when Dravik threatened to slit his throat. Raving with fever or not, Gladwiel clearly remembered the wild look in the purebred's eyes when he grabbed Dravik's wrist. And he remembered the bruise his grasp left behind.

"She still has that reflex," Kamal said, watching Dalle beat the girl. "It takes a while to teach them to suppress that reflex."

"Not purebreds, though," Gladwiel muttered. "They don't have that reflex."

"Of course," Kamal said with a chuckle. "Breeders beat that out of them when they're kids."

Gladwiel glanced at the doors leading to the office section of the warehouse. That's where the infirmary was, where they kept the sick slaves until they were healthy enough to be trained or sold. The door opened, letting Hasrey's nephew in. The snotty little brat had no use other than carrying messages, and Gladwiel would have gotten rid of him if it wasn't for Hasrey.

"What is it?" Gladwiel snapped, pulling the boy out of his fascination with the naked flame Dalle was still beating.

The boy blinked at Gladwiel before remembering what he was here for. "My uncle says you should come and see something."

"What?"

"I don't know. He wouldn't tell me. Says it's urgent." His eyes moved to Dalle and the woman, distracted again. The flame was finally keeping her arms down and taking the beating.

"Where?" Gladwiel sneered.

"Huh?"

"Where is Hasrey?" He held his breath, already guessing the answer.

"Oh, he's at the infirmary."

Gladwiel barged through the boy, almost taking him out. Behind him, Kamal muttered something about taking care of the rest here. Gladwiel hardly heard anything. His heart was pounding in his chest; a sense of impending trouble almost suffocating him.

This was about the purebred. He just knew it.

Gladwiel hurried through the doors, entering the warmly decorated and much brighter front lobby. He took the hallway to his left and followed it to the infirmary, which was the very last door.

He's dead, he thought. The purebred is dead.

And he had paid twenty Blues for him. That was a big write-off.

When he walked into the sick bay, Gladwiel found the room evacuated, save for Hasrey and the purebred. His anxiety soared. To his knowledge, there was at least one other sick slave who needed some rest, and if Hasrey had kicked him out of the infirmary, he must have had a solid reason. The physician was nowhere to be seen, either.

Gladwiel's eyes scanned the room and settled on the purebred. His chest heaved up and down under the blanket. Gladwiel released his breath, though he didn't quite relax. Okay, at least the purebred was still alive.

He scowled on his assistant's pale face. Hasrey looked as if he needed to lie down on one of the beds himself.

"What's happening?" Gladwiel snapped, his eyes flicking between Hasrey and the slave. The purebred lay sprawled on the bed, unconscious yet restless. Damp strands of dirty blond hair clung to his face. His eyes darted beneath closed lids, and a soft moan escaped his cracked lips.

"Why are you looking at me as if you've seen a fiend crawl out of Darkhome?"

"You have to see this," Hasrey muttered, as he gestured Gladwiel to come closer. He pulled the blanket down and stepped back.

The slave's muscles twitched. Sweat trickled down his skin, which was scrubbed clean now. The mud and blood were washed off to reveal bruised ribs and old, white battle scars, which was not a foreign sight on a beast's body.

"What's wrong..." Gladwiel started, then paused after noticing the marks.

Gladwiel's jaw went slack. Blood withdrew from his face, and his expression matched Hasrey's. He couldn't pry his eyes off the four circular marks on the purebred's chest.

"Do you think that's Him?" Hasrey whispered.

Gladwiel didn't answer. He couldn't. His eyes were fixed on the marks burned into the slave's skin, each one seared by a hot branding iron. The brands displayed four figures in a neat row just beneath his collarbones, meticulously positioned at equal distance from each other. A stallion, a rose, and a maiden were the first three, old enough to appear faded and pale, their edges smooth and sunken into his skin. The fourth brand was the newest, mostly healed but still slightly raised with uneven edges. A sparrow, for the Golden Sparrow Tournament.

Four brands for four tournaments won.

There should have been a fifth, Gladwiel thought grimly. *A serpent…*

"I thought they were maybe imitations," Hasrey said, babbled, "but the first few ones are older, and the sparrow is the newest…"

"That's him," Gladwiel cut him off. He studied the slave's face. The blond locks of hair splayed wildly on the pillow. Together with the golden, bushy beard, they looked like a lion's mane.

Gladwiel pulled the blanket over the slave's chest to hide the brands. He looked around the empty room. "Has anyone seen these?"

Hasrey shook his head. "As soon as I noticed what they were, I kicked everyone out." He chewed on his thumbnail, as he did when he was stressed. "Bastards coated him in mud to hide those."

Blood rushed to Gladwiel's ears at the thought of Dravik and the collectors. "I'll make sure they'll conduct no business north of Riverdam ever again."

"What do we do? Do we… Do we take him to Brinescar? Do you think we can get a reward?"

"A reward?" Gladwiel sneered. "We'd be lucky to keep our heads to ourselves, let alone a reward."

Hasrey ran his hand down his face. "What… What then?"

Gladwiel considered his options. There weren't many. He picked the safest — though least profitable — option.

Reaching out with a shaking hand, he pulled the pillow from under the purebred's head and handed it to Hasrey.

"Are you sure?" Hasrey muttered as he took the pillow. "You just paid twenty Blues for him."

"Flay those brands off his skin when you're done. Make sure no one finds the body."

Hasrey held the pillow between his hands and approached the purebred cautiously. He brought it over the slave's face, swallowed, then pressed it down.

The slave woke up as soon as the pillow touched his face. He made a muffled noise. His back arched as he tried to breathe, but Hasrey pressed the pillow firmly.

Gladwiel found himself chewing his thumbnail; a nasty habit he'd copied from Hasrey. Fear brewed in his stomach. The slave started flailing his arms, trying to push the pillow off his face. His hands hit Hasrey's face. Then, his fingers found Hasrey's neck.

"M-Master Gladwiel," Hasrey whimpered as he craned his neck, trying to shake the purebred's clutch off.

Gladwiel watched in horror. The slave's fingernails scratched Hasrey's neck, drawing blood. He was defending himself. He was resisting. He was drawing blood from a free man.

He was what they said he was. He had gone broken. Disobedient. Mad. Rabid.

"Master Gladwiel, a little help!" Hasrey begged.

The blanket fell off as the slave started kicking wildly with his good leg. He had managed to push Hasrey back just enough to steal a shallow breath.

Gladwiel snapped out of his shock. His hands dipped into his pocket and found the paper with the purebred's Words written on it. He dropped the paper, picked it back up with trembling hands, and read the First Word out loud: "*Padlociatius.*"

The slave's arms and legs went limp on the bed, paralysed.

Hasrey was out of breath. He put all his weight on the pillow, as if the harder he pressed, the quicker the slave would suffocate. Blood trickled down his neck as he stared at Gladwiel in shock. "Have you seen what he just did?" Hasrey whispered.

"It'll be over soon." Gladwiel swallowed.

"Master Gladwiel!" Hasrey's useless nephew opened the door without knocking.

"Not now!" Gladwiel roared. Remembering the blanket had fallen off and the purebred's brands were visible, he positioned himself to block the boy's view.

The boy blinked at him, then at Hasrey and the pillow. He shook his head, as if seeing them strangle a slave with a pillow was nothing new. "That farmer woman from West Kilrer is here, Master Gladwiel," he announced.

The purebred's arms started twitching as he regained control of his body. He made an angry noise under the pillow. His hands jerked up, searching for Hasrey's neck again.

"I said not now!" Gladwiel sneered at the boy. He turned his attention back on the purebred and repeated: "*Padlociatius.*"

The slave's body went limp. For the last time, Gladwiel hoped.

"But she says she'll come back with the constables if she doesn't see you now," the boy insisted. He kept staring at the slave, his eyes not too far from discovering the famed brands.

Gladwiel stormed at the boy, grabbed his arm, and shoved him towards the door. "Tell her..." he started, then paused.

Tell her what?

Gladwiel didn't want constables in his warehouse, especially not when he had Him in here. They would recognise the purebred, and then Gladwiel would have to part with his head. He needed more time to get rid of the purebred's corpse, making sure it never led back to Gladwiel.

That annoying woman... She was relentless. Couldn't she have found another time?

"Tell her what?" the boy prompted. His head turned back to the slave. Hasrey continued pressing the pillow down, trying to finish him off before the First Word wore off again.

A brilliant idea started shaping in Gladwiel's head.

"Take her to my office. Tell her I'll be with her shortly." Gladwiel pushed the boy out and slammed the door shut behind him. He rushed to the bedside and pulled Hasrey back. He flung the pillow aside.

"What are you doing?" Hasrey yelled. He went to pick up the pillow.

"Just wait." Gladwiel held out a hand. He stared at the purebred, whose face had turned purple. The slave's eyes were flat, glassy, and were fixed on the ceiling. Red blotches had appeared on the whites of his eyes.

For a moment, Gladwiel thought he was too late. The purebred had passed. Maybe it was for the best.

Then, the slave's arms started twitching as he slowly came out of his paralysis. He sucked in a shaky breath, coughed, blinked. He propped himself up on his elbows in jerky movements. His grey eyes found Gladwiel's and fury twisted his face.

Hasrey took a step back.

With his tangled, mane-like hair and beard, the slave looked like an angry lion, ready to leap out of the bed. Gladwiel swallowed as he kept the First Word at the tip of his tongue.

"What are you doing?" Hasrey whispered.

"Hasrey, go get him some *pemitoin*," Gladwiel said, making an effort to keep his voice steady. He didn't break eye contact. Outside, his other slaves were learning how making eye contact was one of the Acts of Defiance. This slave had committed at least three Acts within the last five minutes and looked ready to commit a dozen more.

"*Pemitoin?*" Hasrey repeated. "Why?"

"Hasrey," Gladwiel growled impatiently. "Do as I say and hurry."

Hasrey hesitated only a split second before leaving the room. They'd kept the ingredients for *pemitoin* in Hasrey's office, not trusting the expensive mixture with their physician.

The purebred narrowed his eyes, no doubt recognizing the name of the mixture and what it did. Sweat trickled down his face.

Gladwiel forced himself to take a step forward. He was within arm's reach of the slave now. His mind screamed at him, telling him to get away from the dangerous creature, but he stayed put.

"I know who you are," Gladwiel spoke, barely keeping the fear off his voice.

One of the slave's hands shot up to his bare chest, over the exposed brands, and he scowled.

"You will do as I say," Gladwiel demanded. "You will play along. And maybe you can walk out of here alive. If you try anything, I will make sure Hasrey finishes what he'd started."

The slave glared at him for nearly a minute. When he finally parted his lips and spoke, Gladwiel almost flinched.

"Yes, *Owner.*"

3

OLIRA

Olira scrunched the skirt of her dress in her fist.

She hated being here. She hated doing business with the likes of Master Gladwiel. The slave merchant studied everyone with a calculating look, as if they all had slave tattoos on their necks and he was appraising what he could get for them at an auction.

Olira's father always argued the Domestic Assets Trade Union and men like Master Gladwiel were the source of everything that was wrong with Chinderia. Being here — sitting on this comfortable chair, breathing in the heavily incensed air — made Olira imagine the disappointment she would find on her father's face if he was still alive.

She unclenched her fist and straightened the crease on the thick brown fabric. Her jaw ached from grinding her teeth. Guilt gnawed at Olira's *rhoa*. She crossed her arms over her chest to stop her hands from fidgeting. She didn't want Master Gladwiel to mistake her discomfort for weakness. She came here unannounced, not allowing Master Gladwiel to elude her again. She wasn't bluffing when she'd told the boy she would bring the constables with her.

She would not leave this office empty-handed.

She pushed a strand of light brown hair behind her ear as she studied the lavish office with disgust. She'd been here many times in the past, and Master Gladwiel didn't spare any expenses furnishing this room. His oak desk was carved elegantly.

He fashioned a long-backed, ornate chair for himself behind it. A purple velvet cushion, moulded into the shape of Master Gladwiel's backside, rested on the seat. Two comfortable armchairs were placed in front of the desk. Olira was sitting on one.

On the other side of the room, a couple of sofas were positioned to face the wall. More velvet cushions littered them, and a side table between them housed a bowl of fresh fruits and empty glasses.

Olira scowled at the furniture. She guessed this must have been where Master Gladwiel's business transpired; the slaves would line up against the wall, while the customer sat on the soft pillows, munching on their refreshments, and browsing their next slaves to take home.

It disgusted Olira. She despised slave owners, and she regretted ever getting into business with a slave merchant.

She was rehearsing the argument she was about to have with Master Gladwiel inside her head when the office door opened behind her.

"I am so sorry for making you wait this long, Mistress Olira," Gladwiel said as he hurried inside. "I just had to oversee something myself."

Olira blinked at the second man who trailed after Gladwiel. She mumbled a response to accept the apology.

Gladwiel closed the door behind him and gestured to the man to stand in front of the sofas. Then he hurried behind his desk and sat down on his cushioned chair.

"You're here for your payment, I presume?" Gladwiel smiled warmly.

"Yes…"

Olira was distracted by the other man's presence. At first, she thought the man was one of Gladwiel's workers. He was clothed in a plain, faded yellow shirt, a pair of dark pants, and leather shoes. He stood in front of the sofas, with his back against the wall, his eyes cast down and his hands clasped in front of him. When she spotted the slave tattoo on the man's neck, she looked away. Gladwiel must have been expecting a customer to display this slave after meeting Olira. She shook her distaste and focused on her argument.

"Master Gladwiel, I've been waiting patiently for my payment…"

"Yes, of course, I sincerely apologise for the delay," Gladwiel interrupted with a calming gesture. "I have your payment ready."

"You do?" Olira blinked, momentarily thrown off balance. Her argument evaporated from her mind.

"Yes, of course. Again, I'm so sorry for taking this long. You know how business is. Things still haven't stabilised after what happened at Brinescar last summer."

"Oh, right. That's okay, I understand." She bit her lips, suddenly feeling guilty for threatening the man about bringing constables. The anger and frustration that had been bubbling inside her since the early morning of her two days' journey to Kiore suddenly dissipated.

"Can I offer you some refreshments?"

"Oh, umm, I'm good, thank you." She eyed the slave merchant's face suspiciously. Over the few months they did business together, he'd never offered her any refreshments. "So... My payment?"

"Right." Gladwiel stood and gestured at the door. "My assistant, Hasrey, is in the next room, finalizing the paperwork. It shouldn't take too long."

"That's great to hear, thank you." Olira gathered her satchel and stood. A mixture of relief and bewilderment almost made her laugh. Then, her smile froze on her lips. "Wait. Paperwork?"

"Yes, the sales papers." Gladwiel rolled his eyes. "Need to keep them on you when entering or leaving a city. Guards will always ask to see them."

"Sales papers?" Olira scratched her head. "The city guards never asked for any papers from me before."

Gladwiel chuckled. "Well, you've probably never travelled with one before."

"Travelled with what?"

"A slave, of course."

A knot of unease twisted in Olira's stomach. Her eyes darted between Gladwiel and the slave, who stood against the wall like a statue. She recoiled when she understood. "Oh, no," she said, shaking her head and pointing a finger at Gladwiel. "No. No, no, no, no..."

Gladwiel blinked with a surprise that matched Olira's. "What? What's the problem?"

"I'm not buying a slave!"

"You're not... I don't understand, Mistress Olira. I'm making you a payment."

Olira's face flushed red. She forced herself to sit back down and regain her composure. "You're making me a payment?"

"Yes."

"With a slave?"

"Yes."

She inhaled a deep breath and held onto it for a while until the urge to slap the audacious man diminished a little. "I'm not buying a slave, Master Gladwiel."

"I know. I'm making you a payment." He sat back down, too. Propping his elbows on the table, he leaned forward. "I don't understand what the problem is?"

Olira gritted her teeth. The problem was, she despised the slave trade, and even the idea of owning a slave made her want to gag. The sentiment was deeply ingrained by her parents. Growing up, her father had been a vocal advocate against using slaves for labour. The more slaves business owners used, the less work became available for free men and women. It led to poverty, which forced more people to commit crimes. And the process of enslaving people due to these crimes was so dodgy and poorly regulated. The Domestic Assets Trade Union gave slave merchants and breeders such unchecked power. It was terrifying.

And the purebreds... Freeborn slaves, she could understand. She still disapproved, but she could understand. But the existence of purebred slaves was like a spit on the Twelve Riders' faces.

She didn't see any point in making this argument to Gladwiel. The man had a rock for a *rhoa*. Instead, "I don't need a slave, Master Gladwiel," she simply said through gritted teeth.

Gladwiel narrowed his eyes at her. He was eerily quiet for a long moment. Olira didn't break eye contact. Her jaw ached from clenching.

"Mistress Olira," Gladwiel finally said with a deep sigh. "How much do I owe you?"

"You owe me eighty Chinderian Blues for a bag of *Palleogano*, forty Blues for *Oxeron* and *Stripefang Blossom* roots, and another thirty for a whole rack of other rare herbs. That's hundred and fifty Blues, Master Gladwiel. Cash."

Gladwiel shook his finger. "We never said cash." He pointed the same finger at the slave. "This is how I'll be paying you."

"I don't accept this payment. I want my money."

Anger flashed on Gladwiel's face, but he reined it promptly. He took a deep breath, ran his fingers through his hair, and settled on a different approach.

"Mistress Olira," Gladwiel said patiently as he walked around his desk. "I just paid one-hundred and eighty Blues for this slave. He's worth more than what I owe you. Come, have a look." He walked over to the slave and gestured Olira to join him.

"I'm good, thanks." The last thing Olira ever imagined herself doing was sitting on those sofas and browsing a slave.

"Please, come have a look at him."

"Master Gladwiel, I don't want a slave."

Gladwiel mumbled to himself. Rather than giving up, he grabbed the slave's arm and brought him over to Olira.

"Merciful Alunwea..." Olira muttered to herself. Anger and embarrassment painted her face red. Gladwiel positioned the man to stand in front of Olira. She remained in her chair while turning her face away. "What part of–"

Gladwiel put a hand on the slave's shoulder and shoved him down, hard. The slave dropped to his knees with a thud. He blinked once and clenched his jaw but recovered his blank expression in an instant. He let out a slow, quiet breath, fixed his eyes on Olira's knees, and remained still.

"Master Gladwiel–"

"Look at his tattoo." Gladwiel grabbed the man's face, turned it right, and tilted it back to reveal the slave tattoo on the left side of his neck. The slave didn't even cringe at the rough handling.

"Do you see this?" Gladwiel continued, poking a finger at the slave's neck, pointing at the dog-like beast displayed on the tattoo. "This means he's a beast."

When Olira took a deep breath, she noticed the man smelled like soap. Part of her wanted to cover her eyes or look away, but she was afraid Gladwiel would make the man sit on her lap until she looked.

She eyed the slave, taking in the short-cropped blond hair and the hard lines of his face. He seemed older than Olira, though no more than his mid-twenties.

His skin looked pink, as if he'd just been scrubbed clean, confirming the smell of soap. A layer of light powder concealed yellow bruises all over his face. His cheeks looked red and irritated, and Olira spotted minor cuts left by a hasty razor. Freshly shaved.

"I know what a beast tattoo stands for, Master Gladwiel," Olira grumbled. Beasts were the type of slaves who killed for entertainment. They were even worse than the flame tattooed pleasure slaves.

"Do you know what these lines stand for?" Gladwiel continued, pointing at the intricate lines around the dog-like creature. "These lines mean he's a purebred. His parents were meticulously matched, and he's been raised as a slave since the day he was born. Trained to fight in the arenas since he was old enough to stand. His kind are the best slaves anyone could afford."

Disgust washed over Olira. She'd never seen a purebred up close. The slave's grey eyes were blank, communicating no thoughts or emotions. Not a trace of anything that made a person human. Even animals had feelings. This man was completely empty.

He had no *rhoa*.

She glowered at Gladwiel. "Master Gladwiel..."

Gladwiel cut her off as he continued. "Purebreds never disobey. Ever," he emphasised with a passionate shake of his finger. He pushed the slave closer to Olira's chair, as if his proximity would help change her mind. "They don't think, they don't feel. They never disrespect or upset their Owners and Masters. They have no human urges, nor desires. They never want anything. Not even their freedom."

The slave's expressionless face confirmed everything Gladwiel had said.

"And look at his size! Look at these shoulders, these muscles. He's big and strong and healthy. He's only got twenty winters behind him. Good looking too..."

Olira stood up. In her hurry to get away, she almost kneed the slave in the face. She walked around him and invaded Gladwiel's personal space until her nose almost touched his chin. "I. Don't. Need. A slave," she said, drawing out each word. "I need my hundred and fifty Blues."

Gladwiel's jaw hardened. For a brief moment, he appeared as if he was a heartbeat away from striking her. When Olira didn't step back, Gladwiel took his frustration out of the slave. He yanked the man onto his feet and shoved him towards the wall. The slave stumbled, recovered, and resumed his position in front of the sofas. Hands clasped in front, eyes down, shoulders straight.

Gladwiel walked behind his desk and started pacing. "What kind of person refuses a purebred beast?" he shouted, waving his hands aggressively. "I'm practically giving him away for free."

Oddly, Gladwiel's lapse in controlling his anger made Olira feel calmer, nearing triumphant. She tipped her chin up. She'd discovered that often times indifference infuriated people more than a heated argument. She sat in her chair, leaned back, and crossed her legs.

"I refuse," she said. "And you're not giving him away for free. You're trying to sell me a slave I don't need and I can't afford."

"Mistress Olira, be reasonable!" Gladwiel almost yelled. "Just take him off my hands."

Olira sighed. "For the last time, I don't need a slave."

"Well, think of him as an investment!" Gladwiel argued. "Take him now, keep him until the fight season approaches, and put him on auction. You'll double, heck, triple your investment! Even if you sell him right away, any private buyer will happily pay at least two hundred or two fifty for him."

Olira blinked lazily. "If he's so valuable, why don't you sell him and pay me in cash?"

A muscle on Gladwiel's cheek twitched. "Because you're here and demanding payment now. Just take him and we'll call it even."

"The answer is no," Olira said stubbornly.

Gladwiel blinked once. Twice. He narrowed his eyes as if an idea occurred to him. He sat down, leaned back. A smug smile stained his face. "Okay," he said docilely.

"Okay?"

"Okay."

Gladwiel pulled a paper in front of him and started reading it, indicating he was done talking to Olira.

Olira chewed her lower lip, squinting at the slave merchant. She glanced at the slave, but didn't see any explanation from him either. She would describe his face as made of stone, but even rocks expressed more emotion. She returned her gaze to Gladwiel and allowed the silence to stretch for as long as she could tolerate.

"So then, do I collect my payment from your assistant?" she finally burst out.

Gladwiel raised his eyebrows, pretending like he'd forgotten Olira was there. "Oh, no, Mistress Olira. I won't be able to make you any payment today. Come back in a month. I'll see what I can do then."

"Are you saying you're not paying me?"

"No," Gladwiel said without looking. "I'm saying if you want to be paid in cash, you'll have to wait."

"You've been delaying for two months already."

"And I'm deeply sorry for that," Gladwiel said, with no hint of sincerity.

"I will go to the city court."

Gladwiel flashed her a poisonous smile. "Go ahead. Go make an official complaint. Do you know what will happen?" He leaned back and started examining his nails carelessly. "The constables will write down your complaint. They might arrange a visit to my office, maybe in two weeks, if they're not too busy. I will tell them that I made you a very generous offer — and anyone would agree to that — and that you refused. I'll tell them I have every intention of paying you back. They'll give me a deadline which wouldn't be earlier than a month after they visited me. And then, if I'm having any financial trouble, I have a right to ask for an extension. Twice."

Olira noticed a pang in her palms. She had clenched her fists so tight, she drew blood. Flexing her fingers, she grabbed the arms of her chair. "This is extortion," she whispered. Her rage consumed all her energy to speak any louder.

"No," Gladwiel said, pleased with himself. "This is business."

Olira snatched her purse and stormed to the door. A headache was blooming at the crown of her head. Jygan had warned her against doing business with city merchants, but she hadn't listened. She knew she could get better value for her goods in the city. She was right, but what that value was going to cost her?

She paused with her hand on the doorknob and glanced at the slave. There was something different in the man's posture now, though she couldn't put her finger on it. He seemed... alert.

No, not alert. Alarmed.

His grey eyes remained fixed on the floor. He didn't look up, but when Olira curled a finger and beckoned him, he saw it and he hurried after his new Owner.

4

OLIRA

"Olira Aryanna," Olira replied flatly.

"That's a beautiful name," Hasrey said. He wrote Olira's name on the sales papers. "And what would you like to name him?"

"Umm..." The question caught Olira off-guard and dimmed her rage with a dose of discomfort.

Hasrey's office was smaller, stuffy, and dimly lit. Leather-covered ledgers and scrolls, chests, and cabinets took up most of the space. There was barely enough room to fit Hasrey's small desk and a wooden chair for Olira to sit.

She turned to glance at the slave who stood next to her with the same blank expression on his face. "I don't know," she scoffed. "What was his real name?"

Hasrey leaned forward with a polite smile, his head tilted slightly to the side. "Slaves don't possess names, Mistress Olira," he explained softly, his tone kind and measured. "They can't possess anything. Their Owners choose their names."

"What did his previous Owner call him?"

"You know what, don't rush," Hasrey said, waving his hands dismissively. Olira caught a glimpse of uneasiness on his face but couldn't be sure. "You don't have to name him now. Take your time and when you decide, get your village Agha or Bailiff to write the name on here." He pointed at a blank space on the paper.

"I know how to read and write," Olira glared.

"Excellent!" Hasrey flashed his teeth. He continued to scribble on the paper, his smile looking more forced every second. He prepared two copies and turned both papers towards her. Pointing at the bottom of the pages, "Just sign here and here, then he's all yours."

Olira pulled the papers from under Hasrey's clutches and started reading. Hasrey placed a quill pen at the edge of the table in front of her. He drummed his fingers on his desk and sighed. His efforts to rush her didn't escape from Olira's attention. She leaned back in the uncomfortable chair, ignoring his impatience. Her eyes went back and forth between the two pages.

"So, do you have any other business in Kiore, Mistress Olira?" Hasrey asked casually.

"Yes," she said distractedly. She didn't look up from the pages, making sure they were identical, word for word.

"An excellent day for shopping, isn't it?"

"Uh-huh." She bit her lips when she came to the section describing the slave's physical appearance. The sentence below read: *I was given a chance to inspect the property before purchase and I accept the property in his current physical condition.*

Blood rushed to her face. Most buyers stripped the slaves and examined them naked before purchasing. She didn't think she could stomach it. She studied the slave's face with quick glances, making sure at least the facial description matched: blond hair, grey eyes, tanned skin, thin-lipped, jutting jaw... He did look strong and healthy, as Gladwiel had claimed.

"So, what are you going to shop for?" Hasrey asked.

"I need to get some supplies for winter and a few bolts of fabric," she said, returning to the paper.

"Ah, wonderful," the assistant said, leaning forward. "I recommend Rumur Seamore for the best grains in the city. His shop is right at the crossing of Orchid Street and Middle Lane. As for fabric, I wouldn't go anywhere other than Tidor Softfeather's shop. Stay far away from Erick Fjalar's fabrics. He had a pest invasion last month. Every one of three bolts he sells has holes and—"

"Who is Master Valder Babrozi?" Olira interrupted. She was frowning at the bottom of the pages.

"Oh, that's Master Gladwiel's business partner," Hasrey said, waving a hand dismissively.

Olira narrowed her eyes. "I didn't know he had a business partner."

"Oh?" Hasrey blinked in surprise. His eyebrows shot up as if saying, 'How can you not know this? Even a five-year-old child knows Valder Babrozi is Master Gladwiel's partner!' With a bemused shake of his head, he leaned back slightly, crossing his arms. "Well, he'll make an appearance today, probably in the afternoon, if you wish to stay and meet him. Master Gladwiel is originally from Calae, but Master Valder is a Kiore resident. That's why we put his name as the seller. For tax reasons, you know?" He winked.

Olira stared at him a while longer. She couldn't decide if she believed him or not. It didn't matter. She was not going to walk out of here with her money, so she might as well take whatever she could. Finally, she reached for the quill pen and signed the bottom of both pages.

"Congratulations!" Hasrey said with a big grin. He took one of the copies while Olira kept the other. "You are an Owner now."

Olira didn't respond. She rolled her copy and stuffed it in her bag. She stood, eager to leave.

"Before you go," Hasrey said, reaching for his pocket and bringing out a small piece of paper. "Here are his Words."

"His Words?"

"Yes, every purebred slave is bound by specific Words," he explained. "That's what makes purebreds special."

"Right." Olira knew this. "They're born without a *rhoa*, so their bodies have to be bound by Words to spare them from the ill influences of Darkhome." She'd heard this from the sermons held at her local Chamber of the Twelve. The Pyre at her town preached how Twelve Riders guided people's *rhoas* to Farhome after their death, but purebreds were long lost, and only a few Words kept them from being possessed by fiends. She touched four fingers on her forehead and drew the Twelve's sign in the air.

"That's right." Hasrey smiled and nodded. He pointed at each of the three words written on the page. "That's his First Word. It is used to temporarily paralyse him. If he's doing anything he shouldn't do... Not that you'd ever need it. The second one is his Pain Word. It's used to punish him. Again, not that you'd ever have a reason to use it."

Olira brought the paper closer to her face. "Prij... pri- prihjti..."

The slave flinched. It was very subtle, but Olira caught it. He stopped breathing, though his expression didn't change. Hasrey interrupted her before she could finish the word. "Perhaps it is best not to pronounce those Words unless you mean to use them."

"Oh." A small crease appeared on Olira's forehead. She searched for a trace of that subtle sign of life on the slave's face again, but couldn't find it. "And what is the last Word for?"

"That's his Kill Word," Hasrey said. "Speak it and he will go into a Raged state. He will not be stopped until he kills whoever you want him to kill. Again..."

"Not that I would ever have a reason to use it," Olira finished.

"Exactly." Hasrey flashed another smile, full of teeth. "Also, I'm obliged to warn you: If you ever use the Kill Word, legally, you are still accountable for the murder. In the end, he is only a tool."

"Right." Olira took a few more seconds to quietly memorize the Words, then put the paper in her bag. "Is that all?"

"Almost."

Hasrey walked around his desk and rummaged through one of the large chests in the corner. He pulled out a metal collar with a chain attached. "City regulations," he explained. "Slaves have to wear chains on the trade roads and within the cities. You can take them off at your farm."

Hasrey put the collar around the slave's neck and snapped it shut. Olira held her breath, expecting a cringe or any sign or discomfort from the slave, but there was none. The metal collar was only loose enough to allow two fingers between it and the slave's neck. It looked uncomfortable. The slave didn't seem to care.

"You are now the property of Olira Aryanna," Hasrey recited. "You are given no name for now. Acknowledge."

"I am now the property of Olira Aryanna," the slave spoke. His voice was raspy and rough. He sounded older and more tired than he looked. It sent a cold shiver down Olira's spine. "I am given no name. I acknowledge," he finished.

Hasrey nodded his satisfaction. He handed the key of the collar to Olira, which she dropped into her bag.

"He's all yours." Hasrey grinned, holding the free end of the chain to Olira.

She fixed the folds of her skirt and her travel cloak, hung her bag across her shoulders, and fixed her dress again, before picking up the chain.

Hasrey walked her out of the office. "I wish you a pleasant day, Mistress Olira. It's been a pleasure doing business with you."

She didn't respond. The chain clinked annoyingly behind her at the slave's each step as they walked into the streets.

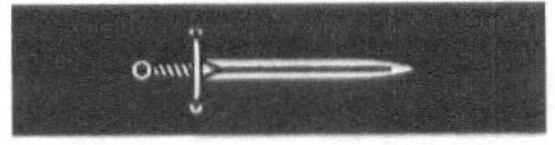

THE CITY OF KIORE was built on the sunny side of a green mountain, which loomed protectively above it. Its paved streets had a gentle slope. Buildings stood either adjacent to each other or in proximity, forming narrow, winding alleyways. Despite the early morning chill, the sun's warmth promised a pleasant afternoon.

Warrior's hooves clacked on the stone roads as Olira led him through the streets. She patted the mule's grey mane when the animal brayed and tilted its ears again.

She'd hitched the slave's chain at the back of the packsaddle and Warrior was oddly uncomfortable by the slave's presence, flicking his tail and shaking his head frequently. Olira didn't judge him. She was too.

Now that she was paying more attention, she was seeing several people with slaves trailing after them, all wearing collars and chains. Only one out of every ten slaves were a purebred. The rest were freeborns; mostly house slaves and flame tattooed pleasure slaves. They all kept their heads down and attempted to look indifferent, but at least they still looked like people trying to bury their emotions. Purebreds were different. They had no feelings to bury.

Olira had given up glancing at the purebred's face, searching for a sign of life. He walked on the left side of Warrior, his gaze down. He matched pace with the mule, keeping the chain loose between them. Now and then, he raised a hand to scratch his cheeks, confirming Olira's suspicions that he was shaved recently.

Olira had enough self-awareness to notice that her dislike for the slave trade and her frustration at Master Gladwiel for forcing her into this made her want to lash out at the slave. She reminded herself that this wasn't the purebred's fault. He probably never even asked to exist. She forced her scowl away from the slave and tried not to be annoyed at the clink of the chain. Sooner she could finish her business in the city, sooner she could leave and remove that annoying collar off him.

Her first stop was the perfume shop. She tied Warrior to a post at the side of the building. Sweet, intense smells of fruits and flowers wafted out on the street. After a moment's hesitation, she began unloading the goods from her packsaddle into the slave's arms. She took the chain off the saddle and led him inside the shop.

The shopkeeper kept her waiting for an infuriating amount of time while he chatted with a customer. The customer had a freeborn house slave behind her, who carried a basket on her back. The freeborn kept fidgeting, rubbing her shoulders, looking around, and eyeing the expensive bottles of perfume with curiosity.

Olira's slave stood like a statue; the bags of herbs on his arms, no sign of getting tired or getting bored waiting.

When the customer finally left, Olira started stacking the sacks on the counter. The shopkeeper opened his ledger. Olira opened each sack and showed the contents while the shopkeeper crossed each item off his ledger. He added up what he owed and counted three Blues and eight Greys on the counter. Olira sighed as she dropped them into her purse.

This was why she'd made business with Master Gladwiel. She grew rare, exotic herbs that most small shop owners couldn't afford. *Palleogano* plant only bloomed once a year and its petals were used to cure burns and a skin disease called Wither Pox. It was an immensely rare plant, difficult to care for in this region, and had a high value on the market. *Stripefang Blossom* could cure fever and *Oxeron* was a strong sedative and painkiller, used to make boosters like *pemitoin*.

Master Gladwiel made a fortune buying sick slaves, healing them with Olira's herbs, and selling them back. Olira couldn't find any other buyers near her town, or at Kiore, who could afford her prices.

Olira and the shopkeeper agreed on a date for the next order. With their business concluded, Olira left the shop and set off to make her remaining deliveries. Her next stops included a pharmacist, a scribe, and an alchemist. By the time the sun reached its highest, she had emptied her packsaddle and filled her purse with ten more Blues and twenty-two Greys. It was not nearly enough to pay off her debt to Master Tholthus, and she still had to buy supplies for the winter, but the leftovers should at least be enough to pay one instalment.

She paid two Reds to buy a loaf of rye bread for the slave from a street vendor. Since she hadn't expected to end up with another throat to feed, she had only packed enough food for herself. She sat by a statue at a town square and took out her lunch from the saddle bags. She contemplated how much this man would eat over the winter and how much extra resources she would have to buy now and how long until she could get rid of him.

She grimaced. A weight burdened her shoulders. Getting rid of him meant selling him. Like a slave merchant. Like an Owner.

Her inner strife was shattered when she noticed how the slave was devouring the loaf of bread she gave him. Sitting on the floor, he had hunched over the bread, as if afraid someone was going to take it from him. He tore into the crust, his hands trembling, and he took another bite before swallowing the first. A soft growl rose from his throat as he tore yet another piece with his fingers and stuffed it into his mouth too.

She felt a flush of shame rise to her cheeks as she noticed the man's hollowed eyes and sunken cheeks that spoke volumes about his hunger.

"Merciful Alunwea," Olira gasped. "Slow down, you'll choke yourself."

The slave coughed a chunk of half-chewed bread on the paved ground. He swallowed what was left in his mouth after barely chewing. His movements slowed, though he was still desperate to shove that bread down his throat as quickly as possible.

"When was the last time you ate?" Olira asked harshly.

"I don't know, Owner," the slave said with a full mouth. He shoved another piece into his mouth and gulped it down.

"How do you not know the last time you ate?"

"I don't remember, Owner."

Olira felt horrified as she watched. It had only been a few seconds, and the bread was gone. She offered him her waterskin, but had to take it back after the slave attempted to drink the whole thing without even stopping to breathe. Next, the purebred picked up the chunks and the crumbs he'd dropped off the ground and ate them too, licking his fingers clean.

Olira nibbled at her sandwich, feeling guilty and embarrassed. She'd made him walk all over the city and carry her bags, without even considering if he was hungry or not. She took another bite to suppress her hunger and gave the rest of her food to the slave. He made the sandwich disappear within seconds. Then he sat, doubled over, with a hand over his stomach and his eyes closed.

"Are you okay?" Olira asked.

The slave opened his eyes and stared at the ground. A subtle shift occurred within him. The look of desperate hunger vanished from his face, replaced by a vacant expression. Slowly, he stood, clasping his hands in front of him with a sense of resigned composure. "I live to serve; I breathe to please, Owner."

Olira scowled. That sounded like a well-rehearsed statement rather than an actual answer to her question. She stared at the purebred's face, waiting for another spark of life, but captured nothing. The man had gone from a mindless slave to a starving animal, then back to a mindless slave within seconds.

"Didn't Gladwiel feed you today?" she asked.

"No, Owner."

"Why not?"

"I am not privy to my superiors' thoughts, Owner."

She scoffed. She propped her hands on her waist and glared at him. "Why didn't you tell me you were hungry?"

The slave stared at the paved ground. His focus shifted from one cobblestone to the next one. "You haven't asked, Owner."

Olira rubbed her jaw and took a deep breath. She waited for more, knowing she wouldn't get anything else from that blank face. "Well?"

The slave focused on the cobblestones. His eyebrows twitched. When he didn't speak, Olira sighed. "Are you still hungry?"

"No, Owner." He swallowed.

"Are you thirsty?"

"No, Owner." The slave's throat moved visibly. Olira offered him her water-skin anyway. The man took three big gulps, and then another one, before handing it back to Olira.

"Do you have another need?" She grimaced. "Do you need to pee or something? Are you tired? Do you need a rest?"

"I am well, Owner," the slave said quickly.

Something about his attitude unsettled her. All his responses sounded rehearsed, almost memorised. She wondered if he might be a simpleton. She noticed people were glancing in their direction, making little effort to hide their smirks. Someone even made a snide comment about having a conversation with a purebred, their voice dripping with disdain. She decided not to pursue her answers now. The sun was moving fast, and she still had stops to make.

Leading Warrior and the slave back through the paved streets, Olira started shopping. She bought cloth, wool, and food supplies for the winter. She could have bought all of these from Master Tholthus, who ran a General Store at Oxreach, but it was cheaper in Kiore. Besides, she didn't want to add more to her debt to Master Tholthus. She tracked the cheapest stores, avoiding the ones Hasrey had recommended. It all cost her sixty Greys — six Blues — leaving her with ten Blues in her purse. It felt annoyingly light, but the packsaddle looked full enough to ease her mind about the winter.

For the first time all day, her worries lifted and she could breathe easier. She smiled, telling herself everything was going to work out fine.

5

OLIRA

SEVERAL HOURS PAST MIDDAY, Olira and the slave had joined the crowd of people leaving the city.

City guards were taking their time, stopping and questioning some travellers and merchants, checking the contents in their carts randomly, but letting most people go without so much as a second glance.

One of the guards gestured Olira to step aside and asked for the slave's sales papers. Olira handed them over and waited patiently as the guard inspected the slave's physical description. He tilted the slave's head to the side to study his tattoo. His quizzical gaze flickered between Olira and the slave. He even sized Olira up and down, taking in her plain dress and old travel cloak.

Olira scowled at the man, daring him to make a comment, but the guard kept his judgement to himself. Yet, he didn't fail to investigate the genuineness of the seal at the bottom of the page.

"That'll be seven Blues and five Greys, ma'am," he said, holding out his hand.

"Excuse me?"

The city guard looked at Olira as if the Twelve Riders haven't been generous with her. "That will be seven Chinderian Blues and five Greys, ma'am," he repeated, slowly and clearly.

"Seven Blues and a half for what?" Olira asked after taking a deep breath.

The guard rolled his eyes. "Domestic assets tax, ma'am. You bought a slave and you're exiting the city with it. You pay five percent of the slave's value." He shook the sales paper. "He's worth a hundred and fifty Blues. So, that's seven and a half—"

"*Domestic assets tax?*"

"Yes, ma'am." The guard flexed his jaw, fidgeted impatiently. "Are you paying or not?"

Olira was having difficulty breathing. Rage coloured her face. She mouthed a silent prayer to Alunwea, demanding to know what she did to offend the Goddess of Mercy. This day was a nightmare.

"What happens if I don't pay?"

The slave, who was scratching his neck lazily, stopped and brought his hand down. He didn't raise his head, nor did he glance at Olira, but the muscles on his jaw twitched.

"If you don't pay, we'll confiscate your slave. You'll have thirty days to pay off, or the city will repossess him."

Olira rubbed her temples and took a slow, deep breath. She glared at the slave's indifferent face, like this was his fault. She forced herself to look away. The slave was a mindless thing. He didn't ask to be sold to Olira. He wasn't to blame.

"Are you paying or not, ma'am?" The guard raised his voice. "I ain't got all day."

"Yes, I'm paying," Olira hissed. She counted eight Blues. Two. She only had two Chinderian Blues left in her purse now. It almost hurt physically. The guard had to pry the coins out of Olira's fingers.

"Wait here," the city guard mumbled as he walked into the guardhouse with the slave's paper. Twenty minutes later he returned with her change — five lousy Greys — and handed the paper back to Olira. She eyed the scribble at the bottom of the paper, confirming she'd paid the slave's tax. After rolling it carefully, she placed the paper back in her bag.

By the time they left Kiore, the sun was stretching their shadows long. A fair number of travellers littered the road, some heading in the same direction while others going towards the city.

Olira followed the signposts pointing to West Kilrer. After every intersection, the well-maintained dirt road became less and less busy. When they took the narrow pathway leading south, they were the only ones left.

Olira's head throbbed with an ache. Her face muscles were hurting from scowling and gritting her teeth. She wanted to scream her anger out. She wanted to yell at someone.

The slave walked on the other side of Warrior. He snuck his hand under his collar, scratching the irritated skin. He didn't even look guilty for all the troubles he'd caused to Olira.

She exhaled through her nose and somehow collected herself. Taking her anger out on the slave would be wrong. Gladwiel was the one she should've been mad at. The slave merchant forced her to take the slave and didn't even mention the tax. The slave didn't deserve to be the target of Olira's resentment.

Plus, it wasn't like Olira wouldn't profit from this either. The idea of trading a slave made her feel dirty, but the money... She couldn't stop herself from imagining how much that money could help her and her brothers. The thought gnawed at her, a constant internal struggle between her morals and her desperation. She pictured her brothers' faces, their weary expressions, and what they had to endure last winter. She had to cave in and beg for supplies from Master Tholthus. She was supposed to pay what she owed to the man before the end of summer, and she had already delayed.

As she weighed her options, the sun continued its slow descent in the sky, casting long shadows on the road. It was only an hour before sunset when she noticed the slave was falling behind.

He dragged his feet behind Warrior, still remaining within the range of his chain. Warrior twitched his ears and let out a bray. Olira patted his neck. The animal was getting tired and hungry, but Olira didn't want to stop yet. There was a roadside inn not too far from here. They could make it before sunset.

When she noticed the slave had been breathing laboriously for the last few minutes, she glanced over her shoulder. The man was stumbling after the mule, the chain stretched tight between them. He was walking crouched and his face remained hidden.

Olira tugged Warrior's bridle to stop the animal. She walked around him; her eyebrows drawn together.

"We're not stopping yet," she scolded. "You need to—"

She covered her mouth with her hands to stifle a scream at the sight of the slave. She flinched a step back, trying to comprehend what she was seeing.

The slave dropped to his knees. He let out a gasp that sounded more like a cough.

"Merciful Alunwea!" whispered Olira. She drew the Twelve's sign in the air and touched her fingers to her forehead.

The slave wheezed. His fingers clawed at his collar, pulling it futilely. His neck was red and swollen to the size of a watermelon. The collar was cutting deep into his flesh until his chin had disappeared. His neck looked like a second head, only redder and uglier.

"What... What's happening...?" Olira babbled.

The slave's fingers left bloody trails all over that bulbous globe which used to be his neck. He coughed. He was staring at Olira's bag as he tugged his collar desperately.

Olira snapped out of her shock. She dipped her hands in her bag and started searching for the key to the collar.

The slave sucked a rough breath in and coughed again. His face was turning dark. The collar was choking him. Olira turned her bag upside down and spilt the contents to the ground. She fumbled through her belongings with trembling hands until she found the small iron key.

The slave opened his mouth, gasping for air. His face was an ugly tone of blue now. Olira kneeled beside him. The collar, slick with blood, had almost disappeared under the swollen flesh. She searched for the keyhole. The slave's eyes shut as he swayed on his knees. Olira grabbed his shoulder to steady him. She found the keyhole and pushed the key in. The collar snapped open.

The slave opened his eyes and took a raspy breath. When he swayed forward, his forehead touched Olira's shoulder. The collar had cut his skin deep and left a bloody mark around his bulging neck. He was breathing easier, but his neck was still swollen, and it seemed to get bigger by the second.

Olira grabbed the man's shoulders and pushed him back. "Look at me," she said, still fearful. "What's happening to your neck? What... What happened to you?"

"Pem..." the slave gasped, but was interrupted by another cough.

"Pem what?"

"Ton..." He collapsed on his back, wheezing and coughing uncontrollably.

"Pem... ton?" she mouthed desperately. "Pem... *Pemitoin*?" She paled, shifting away from him. "*He gave you* pemitoin?"

The slave didn't respond, couldn't respond. Olira took her head between her hands. She felt dizzy, and she struggled to breathe. "He gave you *pemitoin*!" she repeated, more an accusation than a question now. A cold shiver ran down her spine as the weight of the revelation sank in.

The slave was going to die.

The man's skin was already stretched tight over his neck. It was going to continue swelling, and the worst was yet to come.

She was familiar with *pemitoin*. It was made from *Oxeron* roots – the same ones Olira sold to Gladwiel – it dulled pain and boosted strength. But its effects were short-lived, lasting no longer than half a day, and it required an antidote from Crastic root. Without the antidote, the aftereffects could be devastating. And Olira was looking at the start of it.

Olira went through the spilt contents of her bag and picked up her purse. She took the two blue coins out of it and stuffed it into one of the saddle bags. Folding the leather purse in half, she kneeled beside the slave and slid it between his teeth.

"Bite this," she instructed. "Don't spit it out."

The slave stared at the sky, his eyes displaying no sign of comprehension. He gaped his mouth, trying to breathe around the purse. He coughed it out. Olira pushed the leather back in, pulled its strings, and tied them around the slave's head.

"You have to bite this, or you'll lose your tongue in a few minutes."

She wasn't sure if the slave understood her and she didn't have the time to make sure he did. She jumped up to her feet, pulled her skirt up, and started running back the way they came from.

She found the stream a couple minutes off the road. She'd remembered hearing the gentle sound of the water as they walked past it before. The stream flowed carelessly through rock and mud, dragging dead leaves and small pebbles with its current. She looked around frantically until she spotted the bright green squiggly leaves of the plant on the other side of the stream.

Not caring about getting her feet soaked in the icy water, she walked across to the other side of the bank.

Etegon Thorn.

The plant commonly grew near water. All she needed was a handful. She used the hem of her travel cloak to rip the thorny leaves off, making sure not to touch them directly. The thorn was poisonous, and although it was not deadly, it could severely numb the skin, and that was the last thing Olira needed right now. After sparing a moment to secure the precious leaves inside her travel cloak, she ran back to the road.

Just as she'd feared, the aftereffects of the *pemitoin* had progressed rapidly. The convulsions had started. The slave's arms and legs jerked in every direction, his muscles twitching as he spasmed violently. His back arched, his heels dug into the ground. His eyes had rolled back in his skull as his teeth were clamped tight around Olira's purse.

Olira didn't waste any time checking on him. She had to hurry. Grabbing a bowl from one of her saddle bags, she crushed the thorn with a rock. The thorns released a sharp, peppery smell, and she added a dash of water to turn it into a soggy paste.

The slave's arms jerked uncontrollably and hit Olira when she sat beside him with the paste. The skin around his throat looked so tight, Olira was afraid it might pop under her touch. The purebred's tattoo had stretched and the dog-like shape was distorted. Dodging the jolting arms, she dabbed the hem of her cloak into the paste and rubbed it all over the slave's neck.

The slave's thrashing grew so violent, he could hurt himself. Olira had to keep him safe until the paste started working. She caught one of his arms and pinned it under her knees. She reached over his chest and grabbed the other arm.

She smelled urine and wasn't surprised to see the crotch of his pants glistened wet. The spasms had caused him to lose control of his bladder. She turned her head up, breathing through the mixed odour of urine, sweat, *Etegon* paste, and something else...

Rotten flesh?

She placed all her weight on the slave's torso, yet barely restricted his convulsions. His legs kicked the ground with such force that she feared they might break. She pushed down on his thighs as hard as she could. The slave's skin was too hot to her touch. His body radiated heat. Sweat trickled down from Olira's face and mixed with his.

There was nothing else she could do, other than pray for Alunwea's mercy, and hold him down.

The slave's neck deflated and returned to its normal proportions, but the convulsions continued violently until the last light of the day. When they finally weakened, Olira sat back and rubbed her aching muscles, breathing heavily.

The slave's eyes fluttered. He took shallow, raspy breaths as he blinked at his surroundings, looking confused. His muscles still twitched, though not as hard as before.

His grey eyes met Olira's.

"Aftereffects of *pemitoin* are swelling in the neck, difficulty breathing, and violent muscle contractions," Olira listed. "Fever is not among them."

The slave swallowed.

Olira untied the strings of her purse and pulled it out of his mouth, but the man remained silent. The whites of his eyes were bloodshot. He averted them from Olira's gaze.

"Don't touch your neck," Olira muttered when the man took a trembling hand towards his neck. She went to fetch her waterskin. After wetting the hem of her ruined travel cloak, she wiped the leftover paste and the dried blood off his neck.

She helped him sit up and held the waterskin to his mouth while he guzzled. He was both burning with fever and trembling visibly. His eyes were half-closed, his head sagging forward, exhausted.

Olira stepped back. "Get up," she ordered.

The purebred blinked his eyes open. To his credit, he attempted to comply without delay. Yet, it took four tries to climb up on his feet. Olira watched each failed attempt with increasing frustration. He held back a moan and slanted awkwardly to his left. He swayed on his left foot, favouring his right.

"Pull your pants down."

The slave untied the strings with trembling hands and dropped his pants down to his knees. Olira stared at the bloody bandage around his right thigh. The sight of the hastily tied, dirty cloth left Olira teetering between the urge to cry and the need to scream.

She took a deep breath before ordering: "Untie it."

The slave picked on the knots with clumsy fingers until the bandage came loose. The putrid odour of the infection struck Olira hard. She gagged, pressing her palm over her mouth and nose. One glance at the red, inflamed wound and the yellow puss spilling out of it, and she knew what she was dealing with.

"Why haven't you said anything before?" she said. "Why haven't you said anything about the *pemitoin* while we were in the city?"

The slave swayed on his feet. "You haven't asked, Owner."

His tone was neither arrogant, nor audacious, but it still flushed Olira's cheeks with hot rage. She curled her hands into fists, her nails digging into her palms.

"Are you kidding me?"

She hadn't intended it as a question, but the slave answered anyway: "No, Owner."

Olira ran her hands through her hair. She turned her back to him, because the slave's mere presence was filling her with fury. She started packing the contents of her bags, hoping she hadn't missed anything in the dim light of late afternoon. She unrolled the slave's sales paper and held it up, forcing her eyes to read the neat lines in the faint light. She found the statement she was looking for:

I was given a chance to inspect the property before purchase and I accept the property in his current physical condition.

She felt a burning sensation in her stomach, fury churning inside her. She scrunched the paper in one hand and almost threw it away, before collecting herself and stuffing it back into her bag.

The slave stood where she'd left him; his eyes on the ground, his pants still down, trembling and swaying wearily.

"Pull your pants up!" Olira snapped.

The man complied with resignation.

"Walk!"

Olira tugged Warrior's lead behind her. The mule twitched his ears nervously as he followed Olira. The slave stumbled after them. He stifled his groans and kept up for the first twenty minutes, until his legs started trembling too violently. More than once, he had to clutch at Warrior's saddle to regain his balance. The mule brayed crankily each time.

"There's an inn just behind that hill," Olira said. "We can get help."

Of course, the slave wasn't done ruining Olira's day. He tripped and fell unconscious only a couple of minutes later.

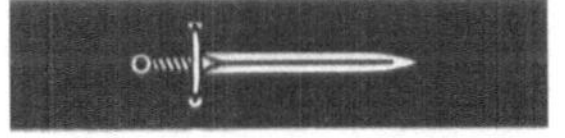

"Get up, you piece of meat!" Astaldo's whip lashed at his face and neck, sending waves of pain through his body.

"Get up!"

"Get up!"

A haze of brown hair hovered over his face. A cold glimmer lit up her brown eyes. His new Owner was relentless.

Furious.

Cruel.

Astaldo struck again.

She struck harder.

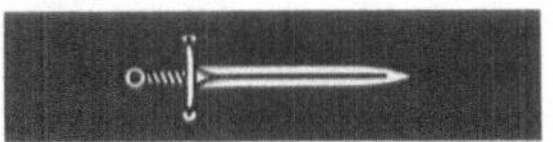

The slave flailed his arms. His eyes bulged in their sockets, frantic.

"Calm down," Olira frowned. "Stop. Calm down."

He rolled to his side, thrashing, trying to climb up on his feet. He was disoriented. He accidentally smacked his injured leg and doubled over, crying in pain. Nevertheless, the pain snapped him out of his confused state. He shook violently, blinking at the dark road.

Olira gave him some water. "We can't stop yet," she said, hating the apology in her voice. "You have to keep walking."

She helped him up and told him to hold on to Warrior's saddle. It was past sunset, and the road seemed different in the dark, but she was sure the inn was just behind the next hill.

She was wrong.

It wasn't behind the next one either.

The slave collapsed again.

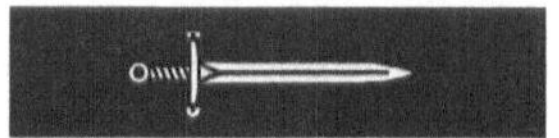

"WERE YOU LOOKING WITH your eyes, or with your mind?" Badimar asked.

"With my eyes, Master."

"Then what was your mind looking at?"

When he told him, Badimar ordered him to kneel and take his shirt off. The whip cracked at his back. Blood and sweat mixed. Pain was hot. His muscles burned.

His new Owner with cruel brown eyes snatched the whip off Badimar.

She flogged him until his flesh fell off his bones.

She struck harder and harder...

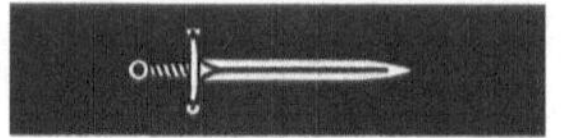

THE SLAVE CRIED OUT hoarsely. Panic flooded his eyes.

"It's okay! It's okay!" Olira repeated.

His fever must have been getting worse; he was talking to himself. He'd said something about his eyes. Olira gave him some space until he calmed down.

"Your fever is getting worse," Olira said. "But I have nothing on me that could help you."

She knew a few herbs that could be useful to break his fever, and although they were common enough to find, it was too dark to search. She frowned ahead. The next hill was barely visible in the darkness. She wasn't even confident if the inn was behind that one, or the one after.

Desperation sucked up all her strength.

She helped the slave up again, but this time, she didn't let go. Her feet ached. She'd been up since early morning, walking with little rest. Her battle to keep the slave safe during his convulsions had left her muscles sore. Her stomach growled. Yet, she supported the slave as best she could, while pulling Warrior's lead with her other hand.

She led them out of the dirt road, searching for a sheltered place to set up camp for the night.

When the slave collapsed one more time, Olira knew he wasn't getting up again tonight.

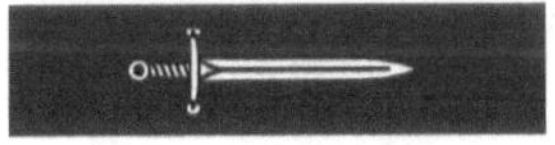

THE BEAR REARED ON his hind legs. His muscles rippled under his thick brown coat. He was full grown, the largest he'd ever seen.

Fierce.

Enraged.

Bloodthirsty.

Marzul's furious roars mixed with their laughter.

Curious.

Excited.

The bear threw himself against the bars of his cage. He gnawed at them, clawed through them, relentless.

Dark shadows sneaked inside the cage. They filled it until the bear disappeared behind them. Marzul's roars faded. The laughter quietened.

The bars of the cage turned silver. They shone bright. Blinding. Shadows twirled inside; like a thick, black smoke trapped in the cage.

Imprisoned.

"Slave," whispered the darkness behind the bars.

"Who are you?" he asked.

"I am what's left after death."

"What do you want?"

"The same thing you do."

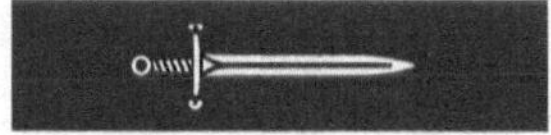

OLIRA LOCKED HER ARMS under the slave's arms and pulled.

Her back hurt. Her feet hurt. Her whole body hurt.

The slave reeked of death. Olira breathed through her mouth and pulled again. The slave's heels left a trail on the soil as Olira dragged his unconscious — and considerably heavy — body under a scrawny tree.

She lowered his head gently, then stood and rubbed her back. This place wouldn't be her first preference to set up camp, but she'd tried — and failed — to wake the man up again and she couldn't have dragged him any further.

She unsaddled Warrior and fed him, before fishing a handful of bread for herself and sitting down. She ate enough to quieten her growling stomach. Exhaustion still surged through her body, though she felt a pinch of her strength returning.

She reached out and felt the slave's forehead. Her hand recoiled immediately. He was burning hot. His eyes fluttered beneath closed lids, and his lips moved silently. Dreaming, or having a nightmare. Sweat drenched his shirt. He trembled.

He was dying.

He had been dying since Olira bought him, maybe even before that. She was in the middle of nowhere, with no resources and no clue how to save him.

He wouldn't make it through the night.

6

LION

THE SUN WAS SETTING behind them as Lion and the others made their way back to the castle ahead of King Leonis and his retinue. Badimar and his team's spirits were high, and their laughter echoed through the streets as they passed in heavily guarded carriages, surrounded by Sir Dramesh and his men. As they approached the castle gates, a small crowd gathered outside, cheering and waving. Sir Dramesh and his men had to push the crowd back to navigate the carriages into the castle courtyard. Once the elegant, high gates closed behind them, Badimar instructed Lion to step out of the carriage. People peered through the iron gates to catch a glimpse of the Lion of Zarall, and they shouted with excitement when they did.

Caesh spun Lion towards the crowd, grabbed his right wrist, and lifted his fist in the air. The crowd's cheer erupted into a thunderous roar, echoing through the castle courtyard. Caesh grinned and blew kisses to a few women amongst them.

"That's enough," Badimar grunted. He was protective of the beasts, particularly of Lion, when it came to dealing with public attention.

Entering the castle, they were greeted by the familiar scent of stone and wood, mingled with the faint aroma of the evening meal being prepared. The corridors were alive with the sounds of activity, servants bustling about, moving furniture and decorations, cleaning the hallways, and lighting the torches along the walls. The king was holding a feast tonight, to celebrate his latest victory.

The group made their way to the barracks hall, a large room with long wooden tables and benches, a central hearth casting a warm, welcoming glow. Castle residents crowded the barracks hall, mostly guards who were off duty, and servants who were idling for a few minutes, to witness the tradition. They applauded when Badimar, Lion, and the others walked in.

Knowing what was expected from him, Lion walked straight to the high-backed chair placed in the middle of the room. He avoided glancing at the hearth and the table near it. Careful not to move his left arm too much, he shrugged his shirt off and sat down.

When Badimar took his place near the chair, the crowd cheered passionately. His hands on his waist, Badimar waited patiently until the room fell silent.

"Is it true he fought Unraged?" one of the castle guards asked. The crowd buzzed with surprise.

Badimar took his time before answering. He let their curiosity build until they were almost holding their breaths, waiting for Badimar's answer. The Master of the Beasts pointed a thick finger at Lion. "This mother fucker *destroyed* Skullsworn Unraged!" he announced.

The room erupted into a mixture of cheer and exclamations of surprise. Badimar continued passionately, his voice raised to be heard. "He faced a Raged purebred and buried him in Switchblade! He's ruthless. He's feral. He's a fucking beast!"

Cheers echoed off the walls. Somebody gave Badimar a mug of ale. He gulped it down and tossed the mug, continuing his speech with a sly smile on his lips. "What do you think I do with these beasts?" he raised his question, without expecting an answer. "I fucking train them to be the best! I push them beyond their limits. You think he won by chance? I had no doubt Lion could kick his ass, Raged or Unraged!"

The crowd murmured in agreement. Joharin raised a toast to Badimar. Someone fetched Badimar another mug. Lion reclined slowly, resting his hands on the armrests. He stared at the ceiling as he prepared himself for the next part.

As the noise subsided, one of the off-duty guards pointed at Lion's left shoulder, which was bruised and swollen, and he asked, "Is he injured?"

Badimar nodded at Vanalten, who had approached the hearth and started his preparations. He folded his sleeves up to his elbows and hardly even looked up at the crowd. "Just a bruise," he said with a dismissive wave. "A few weeks' rest and he'll be fine."

The crowd celebrated the good news. It was a bit more than a bruise. Vanalten had thoroughly examined Lion's shoulder straight after the fight and declared it was something called Shieldbearer's Shoulder, also known as Shieldsmashed. He explained it was a type of injury that involved the muscles and tendons which stabilised the shoulder joint. All Lion needed to hear was that if he avoided heavy lifting and combat training for a while, he would recover. Despite the fatigue and other minor injuries of the battle, he had felt rejuvenated and so relieved after Vanalten's assessment.

Even now, as he listened to Vanalten telling everyone that he would be training again in no time and would be ready for the next tournament, the Serpent's Grip, Lion was filled with that immense relief. If he had a *rhoa*, like the free men and women did, he would be praying gratitude to the Twelve Riders.

But purebreds didn't have *rhoas*. He dismissed the confusing comment Skullsworn had made about going to Farhome — the purebred was probably rambling out of blood loss — and focused on the ceiling.

"All right, here it is," Caesh said as he handed Vanalten a long and slender package, neatly wrapped in cloth. Vanalten put the package on the table and started unwrapping it under the curious watch of the crowd. He raised it above his head to let everyone see the custom-made branding iron.

Whoops and cheers erupted in the room. After examining it and nodding his admiration at the craftsmanship, Vanalten placed the bird shaped tip of the branding iron into the hearth. Then he approached Lion. While the iron heated, Vanalten prepared Lion's chest. He measured and marked the spot for the fourth brand, then measured it again, to be precise. He cleaned and shaved the area, then lathered it in a generous amount of oil-like substance that smelled sour. The familiar smell made Lion vaguely nauseous.

He focused on the shadows in the far corners of the ceiling where the flickering lights couldn't reach. He felt his mind nearing the edge of *that place*. He breathed and watched the shadows. *It's not my body, it's their property*, he thought the words clearly in his head. He kept repeating it silently. The words helped him slowly distance himself from his body. After the fourth repetition, his mind had slipped into *that place*, where he didn't have a body. His body was a thing that belonged to King Leonis Zarall, and what happened to it didn't concern Lion. He wasn't burdened by the fear and the anticipation of pain. The tightness in his stomach eased.

The branding iron was glowing an angry red now. Vanalten gave Lion a folded leather band to bite on. Then, he slipped heat proof gloves on his hands and carefully lifted the iron.

The people in the room made a cacophony of excited sounds. Some people whistled sharply until Joharin gestured for them to be quiet. Vanalten needed to focus. The physician positioned the iron over Lion's chest, his hands perfectly steady.

Not my body, Lion thought. He clutched the armrest, bit the leather, and stilled himself.

Vanalten waited for Lion's next inhale, then pushed the iron against his skin.

Cheers erupted, echoing off the walls as people clapped each other on the back. Drinks were raised in the air, a toast for Badimar and his team. Someone struck up a lively tune on a lute, and soon the room was filled with the sound of music and laughter. People began to sing along, their voices blending into a raucous chorus.

Drowning under the sounds of their joy, Lion sunk into his chair. A searing pain radiated from the burn and sent waves of agony through his body. The smell of burnt flesh filled his nose. The effort to hold back his scream left him weak and lightheaded. The pain didn't ease even after Vanalten pulled the iron back. He slumped in the chair, breathing laboriously, his jaw clenched tight as he bit down hard.

Sending his mind to *that place* didn't stop the pain. It only helped him distance himself from the fear and the hopelessness associated with it.

His fingernails had left long marks on the armrests, but he had kept them there, as if they were tied by invisible ropes. Music, songs, and laughter suppressed any noises that escaped his throat. Vanalten came back with a jar of paste and he spread it over the burn. The paste wasn't for pain; it was to make sure the burn never healed properly and left a mark for the rest of his life. The physician made his final checks, nodding his satisfaction, and pulled the folded leather out of Lion's mouth before leaving to join the celebrations.

Lion kept himself quiet on the chair, his head sagged, his trembling hands still clutching the armrests. People approached to see the latest brand, but they mostly left him alone. Tables were cleared to make room for dancing. Every corner of the room buzzed with animated conversations and hearty toasts. Feeling himself slipping from *that place*, Lion repeated in his head: *It's not my body, it's their property... Not my body...* Breathing steadily, he distanced himself from his body again, forcing himself to see what the people in the room saw: just a thing sitting on a chair.

Other than a reminder from Joharin to sit up straight, no one interacted with him. Lion surrendered himself to the pain and the music and the laughter, drifting along as if carried by a current. He lost sense of time as he waited for the next part. Some time later, after most of the servants had returned to their tasks and half the castle guards were drunk enough to look for a fight, Lion heard Raydon's voice nearby.

"Looks good," the Master of the Slaves said as he leaned forward to examine the new brand.

"I'm just gonna have to bandage the left shoulder and arm," Vanalten said. His speech was slightly slurred.

"Very well. I can make do with that. I have an attire that will conceal the bandages. Is he fit to take a bath?"

"Yes, just avoid touching the shoulder."

"Will he be required to keep the bandages at night?"

"Yes. Why?"

Raydon scrunched his face and sighed.

"Why?" Vanalten asked again, scowling. "What's going on?"

"Lord Hosten finally earned an audience with the king."

Vanalten stared at him for a second, then shook his head. "Unbelievable."

"Indeed."

"How did he convince him?"

"It eludes me."

Vanalten's face darkened. "I'll have to examine the girl."

"Yes, certainly. I shall bring her to you later this afternoon." He nodded at Lion. "Has he eaten yet?"

As if the question gave Lion permission to acknowledge his hunger, his stomach growled.

"No," Vanalten said. "He can eat as usual, if he has the appetite."

Lion always had an appetite for food. Pain never stopped him from eating when they put food in front of him.

"Very well. Let us go and prepare him."

Raydon gestured Lion to follow him. The king's Master of the Slaves was a young man with neatly combed dark hair and sharp eyes that missed nothing, constantly scanning the slaves for any sign of imperfection. He hardly found anything to criticise in Lion's demeanour and hardly ever paid attention to him. If he did, he would have noticed the flash of dread on Lion's face when he heard Badimar catch up after them.

"I just need a minute with him," Badimar said as they stepped into the corridor. Badimar closed the barracks door after them, muffling the sounds of the celebration and leaving them in a tense silence.

Vanalten sighed. "Do you have to? Can it not wait?"

"No." Badimar sounded drunk and reeked of alcohol. He waved a hand at the two of them. "You go on ahead. I'll send him after you. It'll only take a minute."

"Do not aggravate anything," Vanalten mumbled as he and Raydon walked away.

Badimar looked around at the empty corridor, then pulled Lion to a secluded corner. A knot tightened in Lion's stomach and made him forget his hunger. He was expecting this. He was already so tired and in so much pain, yet he still knew this was coming. He had seen it in Badimar's face back at the Switchblade Arena, straight after the battle. Given his condition, he had thought maybe Badimar would leave it until the next morning, but he hadn't fostered any hope.

"What was that?" Badimar growled. "What did I see at the arena?"

Lion dropped to his knees, his head bowed. "I forgot to salute my Owner after the fight, Master," Lion said flatly. He had remembered it with only a few seconds' delay, but Badimar's sharp eyes had seen the slip-up.

"You forgot?" he repeated.

"Yes, Master."

The Master of the Beasts towered over him in silence. Sweat beaded on Lion's forehead. A freeborn would have begged for mercy and forgiveness, but begging was an Act of Defiance, and purebreds never committed those acts. Begging was too close to wanting, requesting, and demanding. Not to mention it required speaking without permission, which was another Act of Defiance. So Lion kept his mouth shut. He had made a mistake. If Badimar chose to punish him, Lion would suffer it.

Badimar's penetrating gaze sliced into Lion's flesh. As the silence dragged, Lion's stomach twisted with anticipation. Vanalten and Raydon had stopped at the other end of the corridor, waiting patiently. He clenched his jaw and desperately tried to seek comfort in those words again: *Not my body. Not my body. It's their property. Not...*

Badimar finally uttered the Word: "*Prihjtivaviula.*"

Lion collapsed on the floor with a pain that he had no words to describe.

Nothing could match the agony inflicted by the Pain Word; not the soreness from the battles he had survived, not the throbbing shoulder injury, not even the searing pain of the hot iron pressed against his skin. Pain Word was worse than everything combined.

The pain didn't focus on a single part of his body; it was everywhere, and it was everything. He felt it in his blood and at the tip of every single hair on his body. Invisible flames consumed all his flesh, veins, muscles, and bones. He couldn't even scream to let the pain out, because the air in his lungs was on fire, and all his muscles — including the ones on his neck — were cramping. No sound could crawl out of his throat. He simply lay there in a silent cradle of pain as his body convulsed, and his back arched, and his rigid limbs shuddered violently...

Then, it was over.

The effects of the Pain Word only lasted for half a minute, but it felt like a lifetime. He didn't remember where he was, and why he was lying on the cold stone floors, and why Badimar was angry at him. He took strained, broken gasps that sounded more like sobs. As his mind started to catch up, he rolled face down, bringing his knees to his chest, and he wrapped his arms around his head, with his forehead pressed on the floor. He shook and whimpered like a kicked stray dog.

Badimar watched him without moving a muscle. He continued to torture him with his silence, maybe waiting to see if Lion would beg. Lion bit his tongue to stop himself from speaking. He tasted blood. Tears wetted the stone beneath him, and he shuddered as he waited, drowning in helplessness. He didn't beg.

When Badimar finally opened his mouth and took a breath to talk, Lion flinched. "I don't want to see you making stupid mistakes like those again. You're a purebred, not a half-trained freeborn. Do you understand?"

"Yes, Master," Lion said. His voice shook.

Badimar waved his hand. "Now go and get ready for the feast. Play your role as the king's favourite toy."

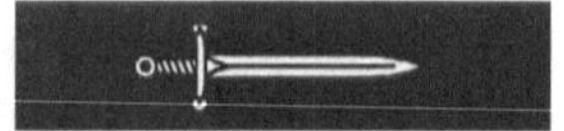

THE BANQUET HALL WAS the second largest room in Castle Brinescar, surpassed only by the throne room. It had the highest ceiling in the entire castle, creating a sense of grandeur and openness. Suspended above the guests was a chandelier holding five hundred candles. It was crafted from a unique metal that shifted colours depending on the viewing angle. Even the flames flickered with exquisite hues. Some guests swore they could see the face of Kahil of the Twelve Riders, the God of Craftsmen, reflected in the intricate design.

King Leonis Zarall sat at the main table. Only his queen and the most important of his guests were seated with him. The rest of the guests — all noble families and successful merchants — sat on the two long tables that stretched along the length of the room. In the space between the tables, a band of musicians were playing cheerful songs.

The food had already been served, though only a few guests were actually eating, which was a shame, considering how delicate the dishes looked. They were more occupied with walking around in the hall with their cups in their hands, talking to each other, making connections, spreading rumours, or doing whatever free men did at dinners: anything other than eating.

Lion was given a hasty and modest supper. He was on a strict diet — rich in meat and poor in taste — which was carefully planned by Doha and Vanalten. Doha had strong beliefs about how beasts should eat three meals and two snacks each day, and that eating certain types of food would help them build muscles and have more strength. Lion had heard some servants saying it was crazy talk, but Badimar agreed with Doha, and that was good enough for everybody. If Lion hadn't been in so much pain, the sight of the feast spread across the tables — fried goose hash, lamb roast and mushroom, smoked boar kebabs, baked duck and lentils, cherry crumble, roasted liver pasties, apricot pie, blueberry cake and many other foods that he didn't even recognise — would have made his stomach rumble.

He took a slow, deep breath, and let it out steadily. The smell of the food distracted him, but he did his best to focus on his breathing.

He was positioned at the other end of the hall, opposite from King Leonis's table. The platform he stood on was three feet high off the ground, so all the guests could get a good view of him from where they sat. Although slaves typically stood with their gaze down, Lion was instructed to keep his head high and his eyes straight across.

Like a proud lion, so many of the guests had already commented with admiration.

Raydon had spent quite a long time working on Lion's appearance, which was surprising considering how little clothing he was wearing.

After a scalding hot bath where they'd washed his hair and scrubbed all the sand and blood off his body, Vanalten had wrapped his shoulder in a snug bandage. Then, the physician had abandoned Lion under Raydon and his assistants' care, to be groomed and pampered for the feast. After drying his blond, wavy hair, Raydon's assistants had spent an hour shaping it, giving it more volume to make it look like a lion's mane. They had trimmed and cleaned the dirt out of his nails, shaved the rest of the hair off his chest, and lathered him in a perfume that faintly smelled like wood and spice.

Raydon had chosen Lion's outfit himself. A pair of black leather pants and black boots were the main items of the outfit. His accessories were a pair of golden greaves on his shins, a large, golden belt around his waist, and a black half-cape which hung over his left shoulder to conceal the bandages. He held the trident in his right hand. It was the same one he used at the battle, with Skullsworn's dried blood still on its prongs. After a debate, Raydon had decided not to give him the weighted net, because it would take the attention away from the outfit. But he had agreed to fold it neatly and leave it next to Lion's feet on the platform, just to complete the appearance.

Lion's chest was left bare, displaying the four brands, including the latest one. It was glaringly red and raw, the skin swollen and blistered, with angry edges. Vanalten would keep applying that sour smelling paste every day to reduce the swelling and to ensure the area would develop a thick and even scar tissue.

Lion took another deep breath, held, and released it quietly. His chest hurt like a nightmare. He could still feel the searing touch of the hot iron on his skin, as if it had never left, and the acrid smell of burnt flesh lingered in his nose. He kept thinking about his bed and wondered when he would be excused.

"What's gotten into Vanalten?" Sir Gennald asked quietly, pulling Lion out of his thoughts.

Two of the king's personal knights stood on either side of the platform, keeping the Lion of Zarall safe from any potential threats, including the drunk and handsy guests. King Leonis loved displaying Lion at every event. But he was also paranoid about his safety. He always tasked one or two of his royal knights with protecting him. One was almost always Sir Dramesh. Tonight, the other was Sir Gennald.

"Seating arrangements," Sir Dramesh smirked subtly.

Deep breath in, hold, exhale slowly. Lion couldn't help but glancing at the table where the king's revered staff were seated. Badimar and Vanalten were sitting somewhere around the middle of the table. Badimar seemed to be enjoying the food, his plate stacked with meat and pastries, and he was engaging in conversations with the guests around him. But a sour look covered Vanalten's face, glaring daggers at the three old men sitting near the head of the table.

Lion recognised one of them as the king's head physician. The second man — wearing a white robe with red flames embroidered on its cuffs — was also from the king's court. Some sort of advisor. The third man was wearing a plain black robe. Lion had never seen him before.

"Who's the black robe?" Sir Gennald asked suspiciously. "Looks like he's from Eternal Pillar."

Sir Dramesh scoffed. "Hope not."

Lion didn't know what that meant, and they didn't elaborate, so he went back to his breathing.

Free men and women were complex. He didn't understand why they'd get touchy about frugal issues such as who sat where, but it wasn't his place to judge the actions of his superiors. He only lived to serve and please.

The feast went on for another two hours. Then, the celebrations moved on to the throne room. Lion followed Sir Dramesh and Sir Gennald and climbed up onto another platform placed nearby the throne.

Guests were served drinks by well-dressed house slaves carrying the Zarall coat of arms — a black and gold lion — on their uniforms. A group of male and female pleasure slaves with flame tattoos on their necks performed a steamy dance on the stage set in the middle. Free troubadours, fire-eaters, acrobats, poets and bards took the stage as well, though none could get the attention the pleasure slaves received.

Despite his tiredness, soreness, and the lingering pain on his chest, Lion felt energized from being in the throne room. Here, he had the opportunity to see the intricate map of Chinderia drawn on the floor.

His orders were to look straight ahead, but his eyes itched to examine the map. Rivers and mountain ranges were drawn meticulously. Cities and larger towns were marked by squiggles that he identified as writing. The thick golden lines that linked some of the cities were trade roads. Forests were depicted with a delicate pattern of leaves and trees, and the sea that framed the western end of the country was rendered with swirling lines that seemed to shift and move.

The entire map was a living, breathing work of art. Looking at it made the hairs on Lion's arms stand up. He had memorised almost every detail of the map. Moreover, he had a secret about this map; a secret that could send him straight back to Faychill Ranch for some brutal retraining with Breeder Astaldo.

The thought of doing something wrong and being punished stirred Lion's stomach. He imagined what Badimar would do if he ever discovered what Lion was doing in his room — the memory of the Pain Word was still too fresh in his mind — but he couldn't stop himself. He had to finish what he had started. He would get rid of it once it was complete. They would never know. He just had to finish it.

He risked stealing a few glances at the floor, etching the elegant lines into his mind. The beauty of the map even made him forget about the burning pain on his chest and the ache on his shoulder. He fixed his gaze ahead when he noticed a group of guests were approaching to gawk at him.

One of the men was dressed elegantly. A nobleman. The second man was a slave Breeder; identified by the whip hanging low on his hips. The last member of their group was a female slave.

Lion had learned to examine people out of the corner of his eyes keeping his gaze ahead while still taking in the girl's striking appearance. She seemed only a few years younger than Lion. Her long, flame-red hair spilled over her shoulders, catching the light, and her pale skin looked impossibly smooth. Her full, red lips stood out, but it was her bright blue eyes that caught his attention the most. He wouldn't have noticed her eye colour if she hadn't been staring right at him, head held high, like a free woman. The collar around her slender neck kept most of her tattoo concealed, but the brightness of the ink and the flaky skin around it proved she had just been enslaved. A fresh freeborn. She hadn't even mastered the basics yet.

Lion tightened his jaw, holding back a scoff. A freeborn. She clearly hadn't had settled into her new life yet. Even her face was still very expressive. She studied Lion with wide eyes. Then, she turned and looked at the map on the floor and looked back at Lion.

Lion's stomach dropped. Had she seen him glancing at the floor? Had others seen him? He thought he was being careful.

"I don't like any slave being treated this way," the Breeder grunted quietly, as he sized Lion up and down. "It's not good for their training."

"He's a purebred," the noble lord said.

"Even purebreds need scheduled maintenance training," the Breeder snorted. "Especially ones who are being revered and spoiled like this." When he noticed the female slave was entranced by Lion, he yanked her chain sharply; not hard enough to make her scream, but firm enough to remind her to keep her eyes down.

"I would have preferred more time with her," the Breeder growled, without taking his gaze off the girl. "She's a slow learner."

The noble waved his hand dismissively. "The king finally agreed. I have no intention of giving him any time to reconsider." He glanced at her. "She'll do."

"Lord Hosten?"

Raydon, followed by Vanalten, approached the noble and his two companions.

"I am Raydon, the king's Master of the Slaves." Raydon bowed slightly. He raised his eyebrows at the female slave. "Is this her?"

"Yes."

Raydon gave her a thorough once-over. The corners of his mouth twitched downwards. "Well... Come this way please, My Lord. We can discuss the arrangements while Master Vanalten examines her."

Lord Hosten and the others followed Raydon. Raydon's involvement and Vanalten's 'examination' only meant one thing; the king was buying a new slave.

Yet, it was odd. Despite her beauty, the girl was untrained. Most of Leonis's slaves were either purebreds, or highly disciplined freeborn.

Once again, Lion reminded himself not to assume he knew anything about his superiors. *I live to serve, I breathe to please,* he recited in his head. He knew his place.

He continued breathing slowly, pretending his chest didn't hurt. He discretely looked around for Badimar, but the Master of the Beasts must have left. When he thought it was safe enough, he glanced at the map again.

The party progressed into the late hours of the night. The guests got louder as they got drunker. King Leonis and Queen Arasanara excused themselves after a speech. The guests raised their cups for another hundred years of Zarall's reign.

After the king and the queen withdrew, the guests started departing one by one. Finally, one of the other knights released Sir Dramesh and Sir Gennald of their duty. Lion was escorted back to the dressing room by Raydon's apprentice. He shrugged off his outfit, put on a simple tunic and pants, then he was released to return to his room on his own.

Being the king's favourite beast, Lion had a small room at the staff quarters, right next to Badimar's larger bedroom. Master of the Beasts liked keeping a close eye on Lion. As he dragged his feet through the corridors, thoughts of sleep and fatigue occupied his head. The female slave with the flame-coloured hair was the last thing on his mind.

That was until he opened the door and found her in his room, naked.

7

OLIRA

Olira was up before the first light of dawn touched the sky.

She procrastinated sitting up for as long as she could, feeling the weight of exhaustion settling in her bones. She allowed herself to keep her eyes closed and pretend she didn't have a gruesome task to do today. But she couldn't escape it for long. With a sigh, she finally mustered the willpower to sit up, which she immediately regretted. Her muscles were stiff and aching from yesterday's physical labour of dragging the slave off the road and nurturing him. Sleeping on the cold, hard ground had locked her muscles stiff. She'd only shut her eyes for no longer than two hours. It was the shortest, most uncomfortable sleep she'd ever had.

This was not how she'd planned this trip to go.

She was supposed to spend the last night at the inn further down the road and wake up as a well-rested and happy, rich woman with hundred and fifty Blues in her pocket.

And where was she now? In the middle of nowhere, with a poor, dead slave in her hands.

Her stomach churned when she glanced at the slave's outline under the dim light of the fading night. She sighed again. She would have to bury him before she continued her way home. It felt wrong to leave a dead body out in the open like that, even if it belonged to a slave. She considered holding a sending ritual, but the purebred didn't have a *rhoa*, so there was nothing to send to Farhome.

Last night, she'd bundled the slave's trembling body up in her spare blanket and the rolls of cloth she'd bought. She'd tried to give him water frequently, but he was unconscious most of the time, and trembling so violently that was a wasted effort. All she could do was keep his head cool with a wet cloth and make him as comfortable as possible until he passed. Feeling hopeless and defeated, and not wanting to watch a man die in front of her, she had gone to sleep.

Olira stood up and stretched. The sun was rapidly painting the sky in red hues of light. Reluctantly, she approached the slave's body and paused sharply when she noticed the movement. His chest was moving. Olira gasped. The slave was still alive!

"Merciful Alunwea!" She drew the Twelve's sign in the air as she hurried to snatch her waterskin. She kneeled beside the slave. He was trembling and his lips were moving without noise.

"Hey." She shook him gently. "Can you hear me? Can you sit up?"

The slave's eyebrows twitched, but his eyes remained closed. The cloth on his forehead was hot and dry. Olira damped it with water and wiped the sweat off his face. She slid a hand behind his back and supported him to sit up.

The smell of sweat, urine, and infection made her gag, but she managed it. His body was too hot to her touch, and hard and heavy with solid muscles. His dried lips parted when she brought the waterskin. He drank some and sputtered the rest.

Still alive, partially conscious, and willing to drink. His heart was thumping fast but strong under Olira's touch. He was fighting teeth and nails to stay alive. This was as good as Olira could dare to hope.

Olira carefully lowered his trembling body back down. His lips moved again, but the sound he made was more a whimper than words. She soaked the cloth in water and placed it on his forehead. Then she stood up.

She chewed her lip as she considered her options. She was fully expecting to bury the slave this morning and move on, but this changed things. Warrior, who was tied nearby, raised his head and brayed at her, his intelligent eyes gleaming with curiosity and hunger. He tilted his ears back and brayed again.

"I know, you're hungry. I just need a second."

The supplies she bought lay in a heap near Warrior's packsaddle. She narrowed her eyes, trying to estimate how much they weighed. Rolls of cloth and a few bags of grains, dry goods, and cured meat surely didn't weigh more than the purebred beast. The man was tall and wide, with layers of bulging muscles. She sighed.

"I'm sorry, Warrior. You're not gonna like this."

Warrior twitched his ears and huffed.

"You're gonna have to drag him." She grimaced. "And I'll carry the supplies."

Warrior brayed loudly and shook his head.

"Yeah, I know, I know. I'm tired too. But we'll only have to get to the inn. It can't be too far and once we get there, we'll figure something else out."

Her farm was only half a day from the inn. She didn't know what help she could ask for once she got there, but at least that would be one step closer to home. She had a stash of *Asennamon* root at home, which was used to fight the infection. She could send word for Varelya, Oxreach's healer. Olira knew basic wound care — raising four reckless and energetic brothers, she had to learn quick — and of course she had extensive knowledge of medicinal herbs. But Varelya's skills would certainly save the slave.

Hope replenished her strength better than the two hours of broken sleep did. She got to work. First, she released Warrior to graze on the cold, barren patch of grass nearby. The animal's intelligent eyes continued to follow her as he nibbled at the grass. She then turned her attention to her next task, her breath visible in the frigid air. She gathered branches and sturdy sticks to fashion a makeshift stretcher. She pulled out the hunting knife Gilann had insisted she took with her and started slicing through the wood. From her bags, she reluctantly took out rolls of cloth, carefully tearing them into strips. She winced at the thought of ruining them, but hoped she could at least salvage the scraps once she returned home.

Using the strips of cloth, she tied the branches together, creating a sturdy frame. She worked quickly but meticulously, ensuring the stretcher would hold the slave's weight securely. Once satisfied with her work, she left her knife on a nearby rock and sat back for a moment to rest.

The sun was climbing fast, casting a cool light over the landscape. It didn't do much to take the chill of the early morning air. Her eyes fell on the slave, still shivering unconscious. His face was pale and covered in a sheen of sweat. He was still burning, and the cloth on his forehead had dried already. She grabbed her waterskin to offer the man more water and noticed it was nearly empty.

"I'll get some water and be right back," she told Warrior, who paused and stared at her with his ears pricked up and a mouthful of grass sticking out of his velvety mouth. "I'll be back," she repeated. "Just don't go anywhere." Warrior lowered his head and resumed eating, swatting his tail lazily.

She headed towards a small stream she had noticed the day before. She filled her waterskin quickly, then headed back to the camp. When the campsite was in sight, she stopped abruptly, then resumed walking faster.

The slave had moved.

He had rolled facedown, and seemed to have dragged himself a few feet, before passing out again. The blanket had tangled around his legs. His right hand rested near his face, while his left hand reached forward. Olira's heart skipped a beat, a sense of unease washing over her as she traced the distance between the man's left hand and the small rock she had left her knife on. It almost looked like the purebred was dragging himself towards the rock.

She brushed the thought, though her eyebrows knitted deeply. He must have been searching for water or something. He was feverish.

She hurried over to the slave, her pulse quickening. Carefully, she lifted his head and brought the waterskin to his cracked lips, letting a small stream trickle into his mouth. He sputtered slightly, but then drank eagerly.

Satisfied that he had taken some water, Olira turned her attention to breakfast. She pulled out a strip of cured meat for herself, chewing it quickly while her eyes never left the purebred. Then she tore a piece of rye bread, mashing it with water to make it easier for the slave to swallow. She brought one of the grain bags over to use as a support. She helped him sit up with his back against the bag. As she prepared to feed him, his eyes snapped open, and he grabbed her wrist with surprising strength.

"Easy now," Olira said, trying to remain calm despite the tension rising in her chest. "You need to eat."

His grip tightened as he blinked rapidly, his eyes dry and bloodshot. He looked without seeing, as if he wasn't really here, his mind elsewhere. Olira wondered where he was. Then, she marvelled at how strong the man was still, despite the fever, the infection, and surviving the brutal aftereffects of *pemitoin*. He shouldn't have had the strength to lift his arm, let alone grip Olira's hand this tightly.

Then, the marvel turned to horror as she realised again *how strong he really was*. This was a purebred beast, raised for the arenas. A mindless, emotionless weapon who had no *rhoa* to call him human. If not for the ingrained obedience the slave breeders diligently instilled in them, purebred beasts would be the most dangerous things in all of Chinderia.

And she was taking him home to her brothers.

"It's okay, you're safe," Olira said, trying to stay calm, despite the stinging pain on her wrist. She firmed her voice and ordered. "Let go!"

Just as she pried his fingers from her wrist, the slave's grip loosened. He slipped back into unconsciousness, his brief moment of strength fading.

Olira exhaled slowly, the adrenaline still coursing through her veins. She resumed her task of feeding him the mashed bread and water. He swallowed reflexively, his breathing shallow and uneven.

Her heartbeat picked up when the purebred's eyes fluttered open again. This time, he didn't grab her and he looked more alert, his feverish haze lifting for a moment. He scanned the campsite, his eyes lingering on the makeshift stretcher. Then he stared ahead, his gaze fixed on nothing.

"Hey," Olira said carefully. "Can you hear me? How are you feeling?"

"I am well, Owner," the slave said. His voice was dry and scratchy, so Olira offered him more water.

"You're anything but well," Olira huffed. "But it's good that you're awake and eating and talking." She looked up towards the road. "If I can get you home, I can treat that injury. You'll most likely be okay."

The purebred didn't reply. He blinked and resumed staring at the campsite.

"How long have you been like this? When did it get infected?"

"I don't remember, Owner."

"And why didn't Gladwiel do anything about it? I know he has the resources to treat this."

"I live to serve, I breathe to please."

Olira scowled and gritted her teeth. "Why do you keep saying that? That's not an answer."

The slave remained quiet. His head sagged, and he seemed to focus on his lap.

"Why didn't you say anything back at Kiore? You helped Gladwiel deceive me."

She stared at the man's clean-shaved face. His grey eyes were still bloodshot as he blinked slowly.

"How did you get this cut, anyway?" Olira asked. "From a fight or something?"

The purebred reached slowly and touched the bandaged leg. Olira saw a flicker of dread and determination on his face. Before she could react, he clenched his jaw and punched his injured leg with all the strength he could muster.

Her eyes widened as the purebred cried out in agony, his body convulsing briefly before he slumped back. He was unconscious once again. She stared at him, her heart pounding. Had he just chosen to knock himself unconscious to avoid Olira's questions? For a long moment, she couldn't do anything but stare at the man's closed eyelids. That feeling of unease crept back to her.

She was taking this man home.

She checked his pulse and made sure the idiot was still breathing. Doubt gnawed at her mind as she went to prepare Warrior. She saddled him and then fastened the straps of the makeshift stretcher to the saddle. Using the leftover cloth, she fashioned a large pouch to hold the rest of her supplies. She tied it snugly and created two sturdy loops to serve as shoulder straps, allowing her to carry the weight behind her like an oversized backpack.

As she worked, she kept glancing at the purebred. Who was this man? What had driven him to hurt himself so severely just to escape a conversation? Questions swirled in her mind, each more troubling than the last. The man's avoidance made Olira more curious and determined to get her answers.

Before she went to secure him onto the stretcher, she fetched her bag and found the small note Hasrey had given her. The purebred's three Words were written neatly. Hasrey had assured her she would never need those, but she took a moment and etched them in her memory before going near him again. Knowing she could control him with these Words somewhat eased her concerns.

The morning sun had fully risen, casting long shadows and warming the chilly air, though her breath still fogged. She checked all the straps again, then took a deep breath and put her backpack on, her knees almost giving under the weight. Once she regained her balance, she took Warrior's reins and started walking.

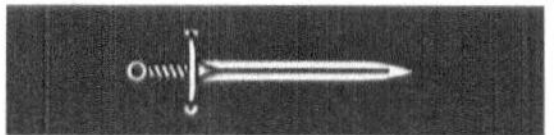

OLIRA HAD BEEN WALKING for about an hour, her steps growing heavier with each passing minute. The makeshift backpack strapped to her shoulders was unbearably heavy. The straps dug into her skin, leaving scars. Every muscle in her body screamed in protest. She was already exhausted from the previous day's efforts, and now her legs felt like lead, each step a battle.

She couldn't burden Warrior with this weight. The mule was already struggling with the man's weight, who had remained unconscious.

The inn couldn't have been too far ahead. The hill they had been climbing seemed familiar. She was certain the inn was behind this hill. She could even see the faint smoke rising behind the inn.

Finally, as the sun climbed higher, she reached the top of the hill and looked down at the clearing where the inn should have stood.

Her heart sank at the sight. "Merciful Alunwea," she gasped as she covered her mouth.

The inn was nothing more than a smouldering ruin made of charred beams and ash. A faint smoke still lingered in the air.

She staggered down the hill, her mind struggling to comprehend the scene. Warrior snorted and tilted his ears back, the smell of smoke making him uneasy. Olira tugged his rein assuringly.

As she moved closer, she spotted the remnants of the inn's sign scattered on the ground. It was scorched beyond recognition. Among the wreckage, she noticed a charred pile, burned with such heat that it had melted together. She turned away and threw up.

Bodies.

Her heart pounded, and she felt sick. She looked around, finally acting with a delayed caution. Until now, she hadn't even considered the possibility of this not being an unfortunate accident — an unattended brazier, a spilt oil lantern, a curtain catching a spark from a hearth when everyone was in deep sleep. But those bodies... They all seemed to be in the same room when they burned all together.

Like they were trapped.

There were no signs of anyone else around, though she still didn't let her guard down. She dropped her backpack and surveyed the wreckage quickly for any survivors. The charred ruins were cool to the touch. This was done a while ago, maybe last night. She shuddered. If she had made it to the inn last night like she wanted to... She glanced at the pile and almost threw up again.

The back wall of the inn remained half standing. There, she found the message; large, messy letters scribbled across the wall with a dark red, dried paint.

Not paint. Blood.

"Lion of Zarall shall not fall," she read the words out loud.

Pushing her hair back, she took a deep breath. So, it had spread all the way up here to Northern Chinderia. Jygan had been wrong. He had assured her that West Kilrer and the rest of the Northern Chinderia would stay out of it. But people here were the most loyal. How could they stay out of it?

Bandits wouldn't have done this. Bandits robbed unprotected travellers that they could easily outnumber. They didn't burn down inns.

She returned to where she left Warrior and her backpack. The slave was still unconscious. Her heart sank as she stared at the heavy backpack. The last hour was like a century of torment in Darkhome. There was no way she could carry all that weight home. And she couldn't risk overburdening Warrior either. The man was heavy enough.

She stared at the slave's anguished face, his eyelids fluttering as he breathed irregularly. The purebred had brought her nothing but pain and trouble. Not to mention, there was something off about him. Bringing him home was only going to cause her more problems. She glanced at the precious supplies. They couldn't survive the winter without them. She would have to beg Master Tholthus for his generosity. The thought was enough to choke the air out of her.

She stood there, the decision weighing heavily on her shoulders, her heart aching with the gravity of the choice before her. She knew what she had to do, and she hated it.

8

LION

LION'S MUSCLES FROZE IN shock. He stood by the door, dumbfounded. He briefly wondered if he had opened the wrong door, but he recognised the room. This was the room assigned to him.

He remembered a famed storyteller visiting the king's court last year. The storyteller had told the tale of Elrimandel and Galeahil in this very hall. It was a love tale. It described how time stopped for Elrimandel when he first saw Galeahil, and how he had felt like struck by lightning, which Lion didn't understand its association with love, as it sounded extremely painful. Although he didn't quite understand why the story had left half the guests in tears, the way he froze now at the sight of the girl reminded him of that story.

The girl retreated to the furthest corner, trying to cover her privates with her hands. Her red hair cascaded down her firm breasts. Soft curves of her body trapped Lion's eyes. Her skin was milky-white; smooth and clean. She must have bathed recently, as her hair was still damp, and the room smelled of soap. The only imperfection on her body were the perfect freckles sprinkled over her nose and shoulders.

Lion snapped out of his shock. He swallowed, his throat suddenly dry. When he closed the door behind him, the girl flinched. Her sky-blue eyes widened with panic. Lion moved towards the washbasin and she took a step back, as if trying to merge with the wall or pass through it. She was still trying to cover her breasts with one hand and the ginger patch of hair between her legs with the other.

Careful not to strain his injured shoulder, Lion took his tunic off. He filled the basin with cold water from the pitcher, splashed some on his face, and quenched his thirst. The room was small, but luxurious when compared to the cramped rooms in the slave barracks where all the slaves slept together. The pitcher was always refilled with cold water. There was a soap and a towel to clean himself. The bed was a real bed, although small, and there was a pillow too!

He soaked the towel in the water and touched it gently against the searing brand on his chest. He let out a soft sigh, the coolness of the damp cloth offering a brief respite from the pain. He wondered how many more of these brands he would get before he had his Grand Blood.

The room was nearly dark. He wasn't given any candle or a lantern, as he didn't have any use for those. The room had a small window facing the courtyard, which was lit with torches. The flickering torchlight that seeped through the window was the only source of light, casting long shadows that danced across the stone walls. His eyes flicked to the corner of the room where the girl stood and watched him like watching a wild animal. She looked like a wild animal herself; one that was trapped. Her plump lips formed a firm line, her eyes gleaming with courage. She was holding her head high, like a free woman.

Her demeanour annoyed Lion. He rarely spent time with freeborn slaves and never enjoyed their company. They cried a lot, they always tried to talk, and they were obsessed with freedom. Lion shivered at the thought of freedom. Why would they even want that? He didn't understand their fixation with it.

Freeborns were trouble. He eyed the healing skin on the girl's neck, where her freeborn flame tattoo was inked. Too fresh, a couple of weeks at most. What was she even doing at Castle Brinescar? She was practically an untamed savage. Why would King Leonis purchase someone like her?

And why would they store her here?

Uncertainty gnawed at him. He thought maybe Raydon ran out of beds in the slave barracks and decided the girl could sleep here until they found her a bed. But it didn't make sense. Did they run out of clothes too? Why hadn't Raydon dressed the girl?

He shifted slightly when he thought of Caesh and how the trainer always boasted about celebrating Lion's victories by sleeping with as many women as he could. Was this some sort of celebration reward? Putting the towel aside, Lion splashed the cold water directly at his chest. Purebreds didn't need rewards, and King Leonis never offered Lion one. Besides, he was too tired and too sore for this. Despite Vanalten's recommendations for rest, he still had to show up at training with the others, and he needed his sleep.

He kicked his shoes off, then dropped his pants down, as he was used to sleeping naked. When he moved to the bed, the girl jumped back and screamed, "Don't touch me!"

Without thinking, Lion launched, clamping a hand over her mouth and pressing her against the wall. Cold sweat ran down his spine. *Stupid freeborn brat!* She hadn't even bothered keeping her voice down! Her eyes widened as she struggled against him, but he held her firmly, his heart pounding.

He glanced nervously toward the thin wall separating the room from Badimar's room. If Lion could hear whenever Badimar sneezed in his room, then Badimar could hear the girl's voice.

The girl's struggles intensified, but he kept her pinned. He held his breath, watching the door, expecting to see it burst open any time, and Badimar barge in. The memory of his Pain Word scorching him from inside out was still too fresh in his mind. If Badimar thought Lion was speaking to this freeborn, committing an Act of Defiance... He swallowed, his stomach twisting in fear. Long seconds passed as he expected to hear Badimar's angry footsteps, but he heard nothing.

Maybe he was out for the night, as he would occasionally do with other trainers.

The girl's fists pounded against his chest and shoulders. One of her blows landed squarely on his sore, branded skin, sending a jolt of pain through his body. He winced, but didn't release his grip. When she tried to punch his bandaged shoulder, Lion grabbed her wrist with his other hand. She was trying to talk and yell, but her voice was muffled under Lion's palm.

He glanced at the door again, convinced that Badimar was out, but still not relaxed. What was he going to do with the girl? As she thrashed to free herself, her naked limbs kept brushing against his bare skin. Lion bit the inside of his cheek.

He couldn't stay pressed against her like this all night. He had to find a way to keep her quiet.

He considered squeezing her slender neck until she passed out, but that wouldn't keep her quiet all night. She could wake up when he was sleeping and start screaming. He looked around the room for something he could cover her mouth with, but then he would have to tie her hands too.

There was one more thing he could try before he resorted to tying her up, though he wasn't confident if it would work. He released her wrist. She immediately resumed punching him with those harmless fists. Still muffling her defiant screams with one hand, Lion pressed his finger to his lips. He fixed his eyes on a spot on the wall above her head. He was careful not to look her directly in the eyes, as eye contact was another Act of Defiance, though she didn't seem to care about that one either. Freeborns were so relaxed with eye contact. It was different for purebreds.

The girl narrowed her eyes and stared at Lion's face. She took quick and shallow breaths through her nose, exhaling warm air on Lion's hand, her breasts heaving. Slowly, her resistance weakened. She stopped hitting him and stood still, though she shivered. Her body was warm against his. She put both her hands on Lion's wrist and pushed, not forcefully, but persistently.

Hoping she wouldn't scream, Lion eased his grip but kept her pinned against the wall. His hand hovered near her face, ready to silence her again if she so much as whispered. She took a deep breath and pressed her lips shut, her eyes wide with fear. They stood still for a few heartbeats, Lion's body, nearly double her size, trapping her shivering form against the cold stone.

Her chest heaved with each shaky breath, but she made no sound. Lion watched out of the corner of his eyes, careful not to look directly. His own breathing was ragged from the effort of maintaining control. He could feel the tension in her small frame, the fear radiating from her in waves.

Moving slowly and carefully, as if he would become aggressive at any sudden movement, the girl put her hands on his chest and pushed. Lion slowly backed away, his eyes still fixed on the wall, ready to react if she showed any sign of breaking the silence. She remained still, her eyes following his every move. Seconds passed by in tense silence. Finally, Lion lowered his hand and relaxed his shoulders.

Without a second glance, Lion turned and dropped himself on the bed. He pulled the blanket up to his waist, slid his hand under the pillow, and turned his back to the girl.

Falling asleep had never been a problem for him before; he could shut his eyes and drift within fifteen minutes. However, sleep didn't come as easily tonight as it usually did. His ears were too alert to her presence in the room. His body was too alert too; the memory of her soft skin brushing against him was still too fresh. He stifled a frustrated groan and tried to relax.

He could hear her ragged breathing, interrupted by sniffs and sobs. His ears pricked when she moved, her bare feet padding on the stone floor. Before he could stop himself, he was imagining how her hips would look like when she walked. He resisted the urge to lift his head and look. She settled on the furthest corner of the room, which was still within arm's reach from the bed. If he wanted to take her, she had nowhere to run or hide.

She was lucky he was a purebred, and he didn't want things.

Lion swallowed. His throat was parched again, but he didn't dare get up for a drink. If the girl was startled, she would squeal again. He noticed that his shoulder and burnt chest hadn't been bothering him for the last few minutes. The girl had been a distraction from his pain, but now he needed a distraction to take his mind off the girl. So he rolled facedown, letting the coarse sheets irritate the raw wound on his chest. He clenched his teeth, soaking in the sharp sting. The pain surged through him. It was a crude way to refocus, but it worked, drawing his attention away from the unsettling presence of the girl.

Not my body, it's their property, he repeated the soothing statement in his head. Within seconds, he had dissociated from his battered body. His mind drifted into *that place*, and he experienced a sense of floating free, as if he was looking at his body from above.

He crawled deeper into *that place*, and everything numbed. He felt nothing. Just an empty void. Even the details of the room seemed to blur into indistinct shades of grey as the colours drained away.

He ignored the tiny haze of red in the far corner of that dull, grey void.

9

OLIRA

THE SUN WAS SETTING down in the sky, casting long shadows over the farmhouse, when Olira finally arrived home. Her body ached with exhaustion, her muscles screaming from the weight of the small backpack she carried. She had left most of her supplies behind, taking only the essentials, and yet even this amount was enough to leave her shoulders sore.

The man had been in and out of consciousness, his feverish mutterings a constant, unsettling background noise. At first she had tried to soothe the man — he was begging, saying 'please, no' over and over again — but he didn't seem to hear her. After a while, she started to ignore him. Whatever nightmare he was having, Olira couldn't help him with. She hardly had the strength to talk.

Her small farm came into view; a modest, single-story building with a dense forest behind it. The farmhouse, constructed from rough-hewn timber and stone, looked weathered but sturdy. Smoke curled lazily from the chimney, making her think of the warmth and comfort that awaited her inside.

To the left of the house stood a small barn. The roof was patched with straw and old shingles. Beyond the barn lay a field of odd-looking, twisted plants. Some had gnarled stalks that reached up like skeletal fingers, some looked furry like animals crawling out of the soil. Some were protected by tarps, while some others stood alone in isolated patches, with no other plants nearby. Olira's herb garden required careful planning and tending to keep the fragile and rare plants alive.

A small shed sat to the right of the house, used for storing tools and firewood. The door hung slightly ajar, swaying gently in the breeze. Beyond the farmhouse and the field was a small structure burrowed into the ground. A root cellar, to keep their winter supplies and produce to sell. The area around the farmhouse was cluttered with broken wagon wheels, discarded barrels, and an old plough that had seen better days. It appeared her brothers didn't care to keep the farm neat in the few days of her absence.

Olira's eyes, heavy with fatigue, scanned the familiar scene. She longed for the comfort of her bed, the thought of sinking into the rough but welcoming sheets barely keeping her moving. She dismissed the thought. Sadly, she still had things to sort out before she could surrender herself to sleep and rest.

She trudged towards the house, leading the mule with the unconscious man still strapped to the makeshift stretcher. As she drew closer, a flash of movement caught her eye. She spotted a horse tied to the fence outside her house. Her heart sank with a mix of feelings. She recognised the horse. Not many people in Oxreach or neighbouring farms kept riding horses like that. Mules and donkeys were more affordable and perfectly suited for hard work. A few of the larger farms down the south of Oxreach had slow but sturdy plough horses. Thoroughbred riding horses like Jygan's was a luxury. Jygan hardly ever travelled outside Oxreach and he rarely left his tannery where he lived alone. Yet, he adored this old chestnut mare.

Olira flushed with warmth and embarrassment, and a sprinkle of irritation. Jygan was here. His presence likely meant he was worried because she had been delayed. The thought was comforting, yet she also felt a twinge of annoyance at the idea of needing to be looked after.

When she was near enough, she put two fingers in her mouth and whistled sharply. The sound cut through the air. She waited, her breath visible in the afternoon chill. Less than ten seconds later, Gilann bolted out of the front door, closely followed by Jygan and Torren.

Gilann was the first one to reach her. At sixteen years of age, he was the oldest of Olira's four younger brothers. His mousy hair was the same brown colour as Olira's and his dark eyes were too serious for anyone his age. Worry was etched on his face and his brows were drawn together when he noticed the man on the stretcher.

"Olira," he gasped, before skidding to a stop in front of her. "You're late! Townsfolk said there were sightings of bandits near Attlecana Grove. I thought you were—"

"Not bandits," Olira said. "Loyalists." She shared a look with Jygan.

The tanner's eyebrows twitched, but he didn't comment. Not in front of the kids. "We were about to go search for you," he said. "Are you okay?"

From this close, Jygan's smell would have watered Olira's eyes. Tanning leather was a stinky business, and the smell had sunk deep into Jygan's skin and beard. However, the slave had already ruined Olira's sense of smell. As soon as she took care of the more urgent business, she was going to pray to Alunwea for a new nose.

"I'm okay," she sighed. "Just help me get him inside."

"Who's this?" Gilann narrowed his eyes on the slave. "Is that a slave tattoo?" His scowl deepened and his face twisted in disgust.

"Wow!" ten-year-old Torren exclaimed after inspecting the slave. "Not just any slave! He's a beast!"

"Olira?"

"I'll explain later," Olira snapped. She softened her voice as she turned to the tanner. "Jygan, can you do me a favour?"

"Anything," he said without hesitation. He was ruggedly handsome, and he had a muscular build. Despite the permanent smell that lingered after him, Olira found him somewhat attractive, and extremely irritating, because their every encounter left her feeling confused and full of self-doubt.

Olira shrugged off her backpack and pushed it in Torren's arms. She turned to Jygan. "I left the rest of my supplies behind, at that inn near Attlecana Grove."

"The Wicked Mirror?"

"Yes, that's the one."

"I'll go fetch them," he said without waiting for her to ask. He scowled at the stretcher. "I'll give you a hand with him first."

Gilann was still staring at the purebred, his eyes wide with fury. "Olira, why do you have a slave..."

"I'll explain later. Torren, take that bag inside and boil some water."

"Is he a purebred?" Torren's eyes gaped at the tattoo with awe. "What happened to him?"

"Clean bandages, *Asennamon* roots, and *Stripefang Blossom* leaves. Go!" Olira said firmly. Torren flinched and hurried inside. "Where are Andar and Kowas?" Olira asked as she scanned the farmyard.

"I sent them to Kantors' house to stay overnight," Gilann said. Olira sighed in relief. At least she didn't have to deal with them tonight. "Olira, seriously, did you *buy* that slave?"

"I said later," Olira snapped. "Can you please give Jygan a hand and get him inside? Then I'll need you to go get Varelya."

"Now?" Gilann glanced at the orange sky. "It'll be night in a few hours."

"Tell her it's an emergency. He's dying."

Gilann opened his mouth to protest, but Jygan tapped his shoulder. "Come on, do as your sister says. Give me a hand." He nodded towards the stretcher.

Together, Jygan and Gilann carefully lifted the man, grunting under the weight but managing to carry him through the farmhouse door. Olira led them to the boys' room where Torren, Andar and Kowas slept. Torren could sleep with Gilann tonight. She would find another place for the slave later.

The slave's breathing was speeding up, becoming shallow and loud. The fever was consuming him. Olira shook her travel cloak off. Before she got to work, she turned to Gilann. "Go get Varelya," she repeated. "Hurry."

Gilann shot one last look at the slave, then grabbed his coat and bolted out of the house. Olira pulled Jygan aside and described where she had stashed the bags, behind the inn.

"Why haven't you left them with the innkeeper?" Jygan asked, confused.

Olira shook her head. "Be careful on the way there, okay."

"Why?"

The slave started shaking and muttering those pleads again — "Please, no, please, don't" — so Olira shook her head. "Just tell me you'll be careful."

"Okay." Jygan nodded, though he seemed disturbed.

When they both left, Olira stripped the slave of his clothes and unwrapped the dirty bandage on his leg. She briefly glanced at the old scars and the round burn marks across his chest. As long as they were not life threatening, they didn't warrant a second glance.

An ugly, yellow puss leaked out of the wound and the surrounding flesh looked purple and rotten, with red blemishes spreading from it. Olira chewed inside her cheek as she wondered if it was too late. How far had the infection gone? Were herbs and poultices going to be enough to give the slave a fighting chance?

Just as she opened her mouth to call for Torren, the boy dashed into the room, clean bandages in one hand, and a bucket of cold water in the other. "I'm boiling some water in the kitchen," he muttered, before dashing out again to bring Olira's herbs.

Olira sent him to put Warrior in the barn before coming back to help her. They spent the next hour cleaning the slave's wound with water mixed with *Gissuri* powder and other herbs. Torren followed Olira's instructions to make a paste with the *Asennamon* root and spread it on the infected wound. The roots were good at soaking up the infection of the flesh. Olira made a mixture out of *Stripefang Blossom* leaves and helped the slave drink it.

The slave's eyes fluttered, but never stayed open for long. He was still shaking, but not as violently. Olira wasn't sure if that was a good sign or a bad one. She wiped his forehead with a damp cloth and gave him more water. His whimpers made her uneasy and, as selfish as it felt, she wished he would stop. At least he was quieter now.

"Please, please, no," the slave whispered, breathless and with a quiver in his voice. His fingers twitched.

"That one looks like a bird." Torren pointed at one of the circular brands on the man's chest. He had been studying the purebred's battle scars with fascination.

"They're just old scars. We're done here." Olira pulled the blanket over the slave's chest. "Nothing else we can do until Varelya gets here. We'll let him rest."

"Is he really a purebred?" Torren whispered, as if he was afraid the slave would hear. "They say purebreds don't have *rhoas*. Is it true?"

"Don't you worry about him," Olira said tiredly as she hurried him out of the room.

Torren kept talking excitedly as they headed into the small but cosy living area with an open kitchen and dining table.

"Are we keeping him? How did we afford him? He's a beast, isn't he? I've heard they were monstrous! He doesn't look monstrous..."

Olira rubbed her face, suddenly feeling all the exhaustion of the last two days collapsing on her shoulders. Her eyes drifted to the wall-mounted stove in the kitchen area. Her stomach was rumbling. She played with the idea of cooking herself something to eat.

Maybe after sitting and catching her breath for a couple of minutes.

She dragged her feet to the space in front of the old stone hearth where Olira and all four of her brothers had a comfy chair or cushions to sit on at night. They'd either read on their own, or talk about the Twelve Riders, townspeople, or herbs.

She dropped herself on her large armchair. "Did you make sure Warrior is comfortable?"

The armchair had been a mistake. As soon as the soft cushions of the chair hugged Olira's back, her eyes closed. Somewhere far away, Torren was talking, but Olira had already drifted into sleep.

THE SMELL OF PORRIDGE woke her.

She moaned softly and rubbed her eyes with her fists, trying to straighten up. She had been dreaming about searching for a wild plant in the woods, one with invisible leaves and a face with sharp teeth and blank, grey eyes. Just as she'd spotted it, it had reached out and snapped Olira's hand off with its teeth.

She scoffed, shaking off the weird dream. Those grey eyes belonged to the slave. Her mind was too preoccupied with him, that was all.

A bowl of porridge sat at the table. Despite the mess in the kitchen, she smiled. Torren, Alunwea bless his heart, must have thought she was hungry and tried to cook for her. Almost burnt it too, as the smell suggested.

Just as she moved to get off the couch, she paused, scowling at the bowl. There was no steam rising off it. She glanced out the window, trying to figure out how long she'd been sleeping. It couldn't have been much. The sun was only just setting. Where was Torren? Why hadn't he woken her up?

Then she heard it again.

It wasn't the smell of burnt porridge that woke her. It was the sound. A soft thump, barely audible. A kick. Coming from one of the bedrooms.

She lunged out of her chair, dashing into the boys' room.

Her stomach churned with dread even before she pushed the door open. The sight that greeted her inside was the embodiment of her greatest fear ever since she'd laid eyes on that purebred monster.

The room was in disarray, the few belongings of the boys scattered across the floor. The blanket and the pillows were tossed aside. In the middle of the room, the purebred loomed like a raging animal. He had pinned Torren under his weight, his massive frame dwarfing the small, helpless figure of Torren. His hands were wrapped tightly around Torren's neck, his fingers pressing into the soft flesh with terrifying strength. Torren's mouth was slack, and his arms twitched weakly. His face was an ugly shade of purple.

The slave jerked his head up. His face was contorted into a mask of rage, and his eyes were glazed with fever and pain. With his lips pulled back, revealing a snarl, he looked less like a human and more like a beast. In a single heartbeat, Olira was convinced that everything they've said about purebreds was true: They didn't have any *rhoas*. They weren't human. That twisted face, those eyes, couldn't have belonged to a human being.

The slave blinked, a glimmer of confusion dawning in his face. His hands relaxed on Torren's neck a split second before Olira opened her mouth.

"Prihjtivaviula! Prihjtivaviula! Prihjtivaviula!"

The slave's limbs convulsed with such violence, he was thrown off Torren like struck by an invisible force. He didn't make any noise as he collapsed and went rigid, shaking and spasming on the floor.

Olira rushed to Torren, grabbed him under his arms, and dragged him to the door, away from the slave. The boy's face was still purple and his eyes were rolled back in his skull.

"Torren!" Olira screamed, rocking him. Was she too late? "Torren! Torren, wake up." Her voice quivered as she slapped the boy's face with enough force to leave a handprint.

Torren coughed. His eyes fluttered and he took a wheezing breath in, then coughed more.

"Merciful Alunwea," Olira gasped.

She cradled Torren's head in her lap, supporting him to sit up. Dark marks bloomed on his tender skin. Tears streamed down his face, and red veins streaked the whites of his eyes. He kept coughing and gasping shallow breaths, but he was alive.

"It's okay, you're okay," Olira said, doing her best to coat her voice with calm. She hugged Torren to her chest as her eyes trailed back to the slave.

The beast's back was arching, his heels digging into the floor. His mouth was open, but his voice was stuck in his throat. A silent agony twisted his face. There was no visible source of pain, but he sure seemed like his bones were on fire, eating his flesh from the inside out.

Pain Word is used to punish him, Master Hasrey had told.

So, this must have been his Pain Word. In her panic upon entering the room, Olira didn't have time to recall his First Word. She'd memorised them all, but had blurted out the first one that came to her mind.

If he wasn't hurting enough already, Olira would have grabbed something and started hitting him. Rage boiled inside her. He'd attacked her little brother! After everything she'd done for him. All the trouble she'd been through to save his life! And this was what he'd done?

A few seconds. If Olira had been a few seconds later, Torren would have been dead.

She had brought a monster into her house. A mindless, deadly weapon. Her hands curled into fists as she shuddered in fury.

The slave's convulsions weakened, though his muscles continued twitching. Olira tensed, holding Torren close protectively. She half expected the slave to attack them and readied to speak his Word again. Her voice froze on her lips when the slave rolled face down, his forehead on the floor, and locked his fingers behind his head. Shudders ran down his body as he tried to bite down a whimper. His posture was a surrender. Although he wasn't begging out loud, the way he stilled his body and tried to appear as unthreatening as possible was a silent plea for mercy.

"Why did you attack him?" Olira yelled, her voice sounding more shaken than she would have liked. Torren coughed again, still gasping laboriously.

The slave shook his head. His face was hidden under his thick arms. "I... I don't know, Owner," he said. His voice was strained, like it was hard to talk.

Olira frowned. That wasn't a good enough answer. When Torren wheezed painfully, she prioritised. She had to make sure Torren was okay. She was going to deal with the slave later.

"Stay where you are. Do not move a muscle, do you understand me?" Olira snarled.

The slave nodded vaguely. "Yes, Owner."

One moment, he was a monster trying to strangle a little boy. In the next one, he was a docile slave, eager to obey. Olira didn't trust him. Not at all.

"*Prihj...*" she started, then snapped her lips together before finishing the word. Part of her took pleasure in the way the slave had tensed and flinched in fear. She narrowed her eyes, trying to remember the correct word. "*Padlociatius,*" she said hesitantly.

The slave's muscles went slack. Olira scowled suspiciously. According to Master Hasrey, the slave would stay paralysed for a minute. It would be enough.

Scooping Torren up in her arms, she backed out of the room, leaving the door open. Keeping an eye on the slave over her shoulder, she opened the door across from Torren's room. She put Torren on Gilann's bed, still glancing back at the slave through the open doors and listening for any sign of movement.

"It's okay, you're gonna be okay," she muttered as she tilted Torren's head back to check on the bruising on his neck.

Torren's body tensed and he pushed Olira away as he bent over to the side and vomited.

He wheezed and coughed, and when he had enough breath, he started crying. Olira soothed him in her arms, coaching him to take slow and calm breaths.

It took a lot more than one minute, which meant the slave's temporary paralysis had passed. When she looked over her shoulder, she could still see him. He was lying on the floor with his hands behind his head, just as she'd asked him. Had he passed out from his injury? Or was he just behaving now?

"Torren, what happened? What were you doing there?" she asked when Torren had calmed down enough to talk.

"His pillow," Torren said hoarsely. "I was checking up on him. His pillow fell, and I was tucking it back under his head. He attacked me."

"Don't ever go near him again, okay?"

Torren nodded, lowering his gaze.

Olira stood, pushing her shoulders back. "Stay in Gilann's room until I come back."

"Where are you going?"

She glared at the slave across from the hall. Her face turned to stone. "I'm going to take care of him."

10

LION

Lion woke before sunrise, feeling like he hadn't rested at all. His body was heavy with fatigue, and the dull ache in his shoulder and chest had bothered him all night. He sat up slowly, careful not to make any noise.

In the dim light, he eyed the girl warily. She was curled up in the corner, fast asleep, with her back against the wall. At some point during the night, she had gotten cold and put on Lion's tunic; the fabric draping over her slender frame. The tunic was baggy enough to let her tuck her knees in under. Her arms hugged her legs, and her face was buried on her knees. A turmoil of red hair hid her features.

He quietly slipped out of bed, his muscles protesting with every movement. He moved towards the small basin in the corner and splashed cold water on his face, the shock of it helping to chase away the remnants of sleep. The chill of the water stung his branded chest, but he welcomed the sensation, needing something to ground him in the present.

He dressed quickly, pulling on his pants and shoes. Then he stood and watched the girl. She was still asleep, her breathing steady and soft. He needed his tunic, and he had to find a way to pull it off her without making her scream. He could hear the Master of the Beasts' snoring through the thin wall between his room and Badimar's. At one point last night, Badimar had returned to his room, so Lion had to keep the girl quiet.

He approached softly and clamped his hand over her mouth. Her eyes snapped open, and just as he had expected, she tried to scream. But he kept her head pinned against the wall, his palm covering half her face and muffling her protests. He made that gesture again, with his finger against his lips. Her eyebrows dipped when she saw it. She made an angry noise and tried pushing his hand away. Lion, his eyes fixed on the wall, waited until she was reliably quiet before removing his hand.

She glared at him, her lips pressed tight. Lion abruptly pulled the tunic off her, grabbed his blanket, and tossed it at her before bolting out of the room.

He only relaxed when he closed the door behind him. Bloody freeborn savage almost got him into trouble! He pulled the tunic over his head as he walked down the hallway. The fabric was still warm, and it smelled like the girl. He could still feel the softness of her mouth on his palm. An abrupt groan rose from his throat, but he swallowed it back down. He pressed his finger against the burn on his chest. Once again, the pain brought him back to himself.

He went straight to the main training yard in the outer court. He took his tunic off and started stretching his muscles while waiting for Doha.

Slaves and servants were the first ones to rise in Castle Brinescar. House slaves were pulling water from the well for the kitchens and for the baths. Kitchen hands were bringing food from the pantry. The lower kitchen of the castle was getting ready to feed the king's more than a hundred slaves. Lion could see the smoke rising from the eastern kitchen and the keep kitchen as well, where they served the castle guards, servants and the nobility. Guards with tousled hair and sleepy eyes were heading to replace the night watch on the walls, watch towers and the gates. Nobody shot another glance at Lion.

His shoulder was stiff, but it relaxed when Lion flexed it gently. The cool morning breeze soothed his burnt skin. Soon, when the sun rose high enough to warm the air and when salty sweat started running down his body, the brand would start scorching again.

Doha arrived at the training yard a few minutes late, his appearance dishevelled and his eyes bloodshot. He was holding his head as he grimaced. "Start running," he grunted, waving his hand dismissively. He leaned against the fence surrounding the training yard and closed his eyes against the harsh morning light.

Lion began to run laps around the yard. The rhythmic pounding of his feet against the dirt was soothing. He never understood the appeal of alcohol. He had tasted it once — Caesh, too drunk one night celebrating the Black Stallion tournament, had offered him a sip — and found that it tasted too acrid and bitter. The experience was like swallowing liquid fire, the sting lingering on his throat. He didn't understand why free men and women drunk that foul tasting beverage, knowing they would be rewarded with a hangover the next day.

Halfway through his laps, he heard the unmistakable sound of retching. Doha was heaving on the ground. The young trainer straightened up, wiped his mouth with the back of his hand, and stumbled towards the water trough to wash himself. Lion pretended not to notice. He had discovered a while ago that free men and women did not appreciate slaves observing their misery.

When Doha returned a few minutes later, he seemed slightly more composed. He called Lion over and directed him to switch to core exercises, with careful instructions to avoid anything that would strain his injured shoulder. When the sun was up and the mouth-watering smells of breakfast wafted from the lower kitchen, Doha instructed him to cool down. Holding a hand over his head to cover his eyes from the sun, he headed back inside without waiting for him.

Lion went to the lower kitchen on his own. Caesh was already there, supervising one of the cooks who prepared Lion's meal. Badimar was ever cautious about what went in Lion's body. One of the trainers always supervised his meals, not just to make sure Lion got all the nutrition his muscles needed, but also to guarantee nothing else was added in the food. Beasts getting poisoned before tournaments was not unheard of, considering the amount of money bet on those fights.

Lion ate his breakfast — half a chicken, bread and roasted potatoes — while Caesh kept himself busy groping one of the kitchen servants. When he grabbed the woman's butt, she shrieked then giggled. Caesh pulled the woman to his lap, ignoring her half-hearted protests. Lion kept his head down and oddly found himself thinking about the girl he had left in his room. He hoped she would be gone by the time he returned tonight.

When he was nearly finished, Caesh told him that Badimar wanted to see him at the Feline Yard after breakfast. Lion stuffed the last piece of the bread in his mouth and hurried to the Feline Yard near the western walls of the castle.

A group of beasts were doing speed and agility drills under Joharin's instructions. Badimar was standing at the side, watching them. He was shading his eyes from the sun and he had the same sour expression on his face as Doha.

Lion stood beside Badimar, his hands clasped in front of him. Badimar didn't look, nor did he acknowledge his presence for several minutes. He rubbed his head and studied the drill with an impatient grimace on his face. He was not in a good mood this morning, though he was not in a good mood most mornings, anyway.

"You'll go to Vanalten after lunch and get your shoulder checked," he grunted finally.

"Yes, Master."

"I assume you've met Lord Hosten's female?"

The memory of the girl's naked body pressing against his skin made Lion's blood rush. "Yes, Master," he said flatly.

Badimar gritted his teeth, looking furious, though not at Lion. "I don't know what Lord Hosten offered King Leonis that the king didn't already have, but he bought himself your seed."

Lion's heart fell into the pit of his stomach. Luckily, Badimar's words were neither a question nor an order, so he wasn't expected to speak. He wasn't sure if he could find his voice. He dreaded where this conversation was going.

"Vanalten checked to make sure the girl is virgin and fertile..." His lips curled into a sneer. "And doesn't carry any diseases. Kiejain forbid! I still believe this is some clever plot to sabotage you out of the Serpent's Grip."

Still not a question, and not an order, so Lion kept quiet. His heart pounded against his chest.

"Bed her. Work on her every night until she kindles with your seed."

Work on her, he repeated in his mind, as he replied, "Yes, Master."

Badimar spat. "Wait until the other nobles get a whiff of this. They'll keep sending their whores... Go sit down and wait."

"Yes, Master."

Lion sat down with his back against the fence. He tried to distract himself by watching the drill, but his mind was like a bee's nest.

Work on her...

She was an untrained freeborn, clearly hadn't adjusted to her new life. The way she reacted to Lion last night was a strong indication that she wasn't willing to comply with her Owner's wishes for her to breed with him. She was going to resist.

Lion swallowed hard as he realised the implications. His Owner wanted him to breed with the girl, and if she wouldn't comply... he would have to force himself onto her. The thought made him sick to his stomach, though he couldn't understand why. He rarely felt anything about any of his orders. He was exempt from the moral values that bounded and restricted the actions of free men. He was merely a tool.

Still, he felt like throwing up.

He forced himself to sit straight and take steady breaths. *I live to serve, I breathe to please*, he repeated his discipline in his head. It didn't help much.

He watched the other beasts exercise with glassy eyes. Caesh and Doha had joined Joharin. They divided the nine beasts into three groups and trained them separately.

Seven of the beasts were purebreds like Lion. The other two had been free warriors once. Lion often caught them staring at him, their eyes narrowed. He understood those sidelong glances were a display of jealousy, though he couldn't fathom why. Jealousy was a pointless emotion, a distraction from discipline and focus. Freeborns wasted a lot of energy on useless emotions and ideas when they could just be following their training and obeying their orders.

And now, Lion was filled with a useless feeling too. He didn't have a word for the emotion, but thinking about what he would have to do to the girl tonight made him sick to his stomach.

I live to serve; I breathe to please. I live to serve; I breathe to please. I live to serve...

Badimar supervised the three groups, dished out criticisms, and gave instructions to the trainers, then started setting up Lion's exercise drill. He placed three upturned cups on the ground in a row, spaced a short distance apart, and positioned a fourth one a bit farther back. Instead of using the usual harness, Badimar opted for a weighted belt around Lion's waist with a sturdy rope attached to the back to focus on leg strength and agility without straining the shoulder.

Lion took position behind the fourth cup while Badimar held the other end of the rope. At his command, Lion dashed to one of the first three cups, then retreated as quickly as possible. Badimar called out the cups in a random order, and Lion lunged at each one with lightning speed, leaving no room for hesitation. Every time Lion ran, Badimar pulled back on the rope, offering enough force to challenge Lion but being careful not to worsen his shoulder injury. Lion had to listen intently, make split-second decisions, run fast, and drag Badimar's weight behind him.

After fifteen gruelling minutes, they were both out of breath. Badimar wore thick, leather gloves to protect his hands from rope burns, but his knees and elbows were grazed from tripping and falling repeatedly. Despite being dragged across the ground, he never got mad at Lion; he only yelled when Lion couldn't pull hard or quick enough.

Lion couldn't help but respect him. Badimar was a great trainer; he was dedicated, and he pushed Lion hard. Even with an ugly hangover, he gave his best to the drill. Lion feared and admired him at the same time.

Lion took the weighted belt off and got a drink while Badimar set up the next exercise. It was a balance drill. Lion climbed onto a meter-high pole, the narrow top barely providing enough space for him to balance on one foot. Once he was steady, Badimar handed him a small, round shield. Without warning, the Master of the Beasts began hurling rocks at Lion, who had to either dodge or parry them with the shield while maintaining his balance.

They ran two more drills — agility and footwork — then finished up for lunch.

All of Badimar's drills required Lion's full concentration. He had no room to think about the girl. However, as soon as he was heading to the kitchen for his lunch, Lion's mind went back to what was waiting for him in his room.

Work on her...

That disturbing feeling he couldn't name had returned, along with the nausea. He struggled to swallow his food and to keep it down.

After lunch, Lion went to Vanalten as he was told to. The old physician examined his shoulder, grunted at the unkempt state of the bandage. He replaced it with a sturdy, stretchy fabric that allowed him to move his arm more freely, though still kept it snug. He put an ointment on the burn mark on his chest, which intensified the pain. Lion let the pain distract him from the girl as he went back to the main training yard, setting his jaw and flinching every time his tunic touched the burn.

Afternoons were reserved for weapons training and sparring between beasts, but Lion was excused from these today because of his shoulder. Badimar instructed him to sit and observe the fights instead. He asked him questions about them; what they did wrong, what could have been done differently, what techniques could counter that move or disarm the opponent from that position.

He never praised when Lion gave the correct answer, but he punished him with his Pain Word when Lion's answer didn't satisfy him. It inspired Lion to pay more attention; to be a better beast. He was a damn good trainer, Badimar was. By the end, Lion had only heard his Pain Word twice, and he had developed so much insight from the other beasts' errors.

Once the beasts switched to weight training, Lion was sent to the servants' bathhouse to clean up. He was the only slave who had permission to use this bathhouse. Other beasts washed with cold water in the slave barracks near the stables. He slipped into the steaming pool, keeping his chest above water, and scrubbed the day's filth off his skin. After dressing up, he went to the kitchen for supper.

He had to wait for Doha to come and supervise his meal preparation. He didn't complain; he would do anything to delay going back to his room. He ate his dinner — roasted beef, potatoes, and green vegetables — slow enough to make Doha question his appetite. He had to speed up to convince the trainer that he wasn't unwell, though he felt like he could throw up at any moment.

On his way to his room, Lion's feet felt like stones. He had to drag them across the floor, each step heavier than the previous one. When he reached his door, he paused with his hand on the doorknob. Closing his eyes, he worked himself up for what he had to do. He desperately resorted to his training.

I live to serve; I breathe to please.

His only purpose was to obey. He had no choice.

It's not my body, it's their property.

He didn't have any control over this. He had no choice.

The girl had no choice either. Her Owner wanted her to carry the Lion of Zarall's offspring. It didn't matter how she felt about this. It didn't matter how any of them felt about this.

Lion pushed the door open. His face was as hard as Badimar's fists.

The girl jumped off the bed where she had been sitting. She wasn't naked anymore. Raydon must have brought her meals and clothes. She wore a plain, dirt coloured dress and her hair cascaded down her shoulders. Something she saw in Lion's demeanour alarmed her. She took a small step back, her face paling as her eyes widened.

Lion closed the door behind him. He was tired, in pain, and he wanted to get this over with, so he could close his eyes and numb himself to sleep. He pulled his tunic off, then kicked off his shoes.

"No!" the girl said firmly. Out loud. Commanding. "I don't want this."

Lion's hands halted on the straps of his pants. She had done it again; she had talked out loud, like a free woman. Anger sparked inside Lion's chest as his lips curled into a menacing snarl. Despite knowing Badimar probably hadn't returned to his room yet, Lion couldn't help but glance at the wall. The last thing he needed today was Badimar walking in and yelling his Pain Word at him.

He stood frozen, his head down, his body taut with a silent fury. Stupid freeborn thought she could *want* or *not want* things? Like she had a choice? She had no choice. He had no choice either. What they had was their orders.

The girl shifted, as if sensing the dark storm brewing inside Lion's chest, radiating out of his coiled muscles. His jaw clenched, his fists tightening at his sides. The girl shook her head and took another step back. "No! Stay away from—"

Her words ended in a shriek when Lion snatched her wrist and swung her to the bed. He climbed on her, pinning her between his thighs, and muffled her mouth with his palm. As if expecting this, the girl bit his hand and stole a surprised groan from him.

"Get off me!" she screamed, slapping and kicking.

Lion growled softly. Blood trickled down his hand. He stared at the mark the girl's teeth left at the base of his palm. She drew his blood! He rarely let this happen in a fight against a beast, and this little wild thing managed to bleed him?

He tossed his head back in time to dodge a wayward punch. Grabbing her wrists with one hand, he pinned them against the bed.

She was still screaming, "No! Let me go! Get off me!" Her legs were kicking wildly, some landing at the wall between Lion's room and Badimar's.

Worry twisted Lion's stomach, which fuelled his rage. He desperately reminded himself that Badimar probably wasn't in his room. It was too early. He often preferred eating at the castle and then heading down into the city for drinks with his trainers and some of the guards. He wouldn't hear this. Yet, Lion flinched every time the girl yelled at the top of her lungs and smacked her feet against the wall. He needed to restrain her and keep her quiet.

He shifted his weight to pin her legs. She somehow managed to twist one of her arms free and raked her nails across Lion's face. He hissed in surprise as the sharp nails left deep scratches across his cheek. Blood trickled and filled his sight.

Twice. She drew his blood twice!

With a snarl, he caught her arms again and pressed them down on the bed. He wrestled her legs between his thighs. She was still screaming like a wild cat. Lion ran his free hand over his face, trying to locate the source of the blood. She had scratched along the side of his face and had barely missed his left eye. Horror filled his chest when he noticed just how close she had come to blinding him. If he sustained an injury that compromised his ability to fight... A chill ran down his spine.

The door was kicked open, the sound of it rebounding against the stone wall left Lion frozen in dread.

"What the fuck is this ruckus?"

Lion was wrong; Badimar hadn't gone to the city tonight.

The Master of the Beasts barged into the room, half-dressed in a nightshirt, his hair tousled like he had just jumped out of the bed.

Lion sprung off the bed and stood ready, his head down and his hands clasped together. His chest heaved. The woman scrambled to her feet too and stood ready with her head down. The savage at least had enough training to remember how to behave in the presence of free men.

Badimar's granite eyes scanned the room and stopped on Lion's face. Blood from the scratch dripped onto the floor. Badimar's eyes widened.

"What the…"

He grabbed Lion's beard and tilted his head up, examining the scratch. He wiped the blood off Lion's face, trying to understand how bad it was. "Are you fucking injured?"

"I am well, Master."

"Are you *injured*?"

"I am well, Master."

Lost in panic, Badimar didn't seem to hear him clearly, as he kept asking and ignoring Lion's calm and prompt replies. He kept wiping the blood, smearing it all over Lion's face, as he tried to assess the damage.

"Did she blind you?"

"No, Master."

"Did she fucking blind you?"

"No, Master."

"Can you still see?"

"Yes, Master."

"Lion!" Badimar pulled him by the beard, bringing his face close. He covered Lion's right eye with his palm. Clenching his jaw and visibly trying to compose himself, he asked: "Can you still see?"

"I can see, Master," Lion replied, clearly and calmly.

Badimar finally let his beard go and straightened. He nodded, inhaling deeply. He turned to face the girl, who stared at him like an idiot. Her eyes widened, and she shrunk.

"You stupid bitch!"

Badimar knocked the girl down to the floor with a backhanded slap. She yelled out in pain. When she raised her arms up to defend herself, Badimar kicked her in the guts. Grabbing her by the hair, he slammed her face against the wall. He kicked and punched her repeatedly, while swearing and yelling.

"Are you trying to blind him, you fucking whore? I fucking knew this was a plot! You're trying to sabotage him! Why else would they send an untamed savage?!"

Lion fixed his eyes on the floor while Badimar beat some discipline into the girl. He told himself she deserved this. She had it coming. She was untrained, unruly, disobedient... She needed to know her place. A good beating always inspired freeborn slaves to learn quicker. This wasn't the first time he witnessed another slave receiving a beating. Yet, he hardly stopped himself from flinching every time he heard Badimar's fists land on the girl's flesh and he almost felt the pain of the blows in his gut. His jaw ached from clenching.

He subtly wiped the blood that seeped from his right hand against his pants. He curled his fingers into a fist to hide the bite marks in his palm. Seeing more blood on Lion's sword hand would just anger Badimar even more.

When the girl started begging him to stop, Lion barely kept himself from grimacing. She had to stop speaking without permission if she wanted this to end quicker.

The girl's pleas intensified Badimar's rage. Last time Lion had seen him this angry was when one of the cooks had used bad meat in slaves' food and all his beasts had been sick in bed, vomiting and writhing with violent stomach cramps, just before a lesser tournament. Badimar had beaten the cook bloody, almost killing him.

He eventually stopped, maybe realising she belonged to someone else. He grabbed her hair and yanked her bloody face up. "Are you going to behave, slut?"

"Yes, Owner," she sobbed, tears flowing down her face.

Badimar slapped her again. "I'm not your *Owner*, stupid freeborn. It's *Master* to you."

"Yes, Master."

When he released her, she curled up next to the bed, hugging herself, trembling and whimpering quietly.

"And you..." Badimar turned to Lion.

Lion didn't flinch, neither did he change his expression. He kept his eyes on the ground, face perfectly neutral, just like he was trained to do.

Badimar yanked his beard again and took another look at the scratch, making sure it wasn't serious enough to warrant an emergency visit to Vanalten. His face darkened when he saw how close her nails had been to the corner of Lion's eye. He glared at the girl, his body tensing, as if hardly restraining himself from hitting her again. Lion's heart beat faster. The girl wouldn't survive another round of beating. Fortunately for her, Badimar shook his head like she wasn't worth the effort.

Badimar pressed a bloody finger against Lion's chest. "I am giving you permission to beat her unconscious if she so much as lifts a finger," he said loudly, making sure the girl had heard him too. "If she resists again, break her arms and legs."

It was a clear order.

"Yes, Master," Lion said compliantly.

"Can I trust the king's champion beast to fuck a girl without getting his ass kicked?"

"Yes, Master."

"Get it done, Lion," he growled. "I don't care how you do it. And keep her quiet."

"Yes, Master."

Badimar stormed off, slamming the door behind him. Moments later, the door to the adjacent room banged open and shut, followed by the sound of him stomping around, yanking drawers open, and cursing under his breath. Shortly after, the door opened and closed once more.

Lion held his breath, half-expecting him to come back and beat the girl again. However, Badimar's fast-paced steps faded away .

Lion let out a breath. His heart was still pounding. His stomach churned when he eyed the girl's bloody frame. She was facing the wall, cradling herself, sobbing and crying uncontrollably. There was blood on her hair and dress, which was torn at the back, revealing her bruised skin.

He had his orders.

Get it done.

Break her arms and legs if she resists.

He couldn't disobey.

Get it done.

The girl's hunched shoulders trembled with broken sobs. She tried and failed to suppress them as they kept coming.

Lion couldn't take his eyes off her. His muscles were frozen, refusing to move. He had to get it done. He had his orders...

What if she resists?

He imagined his fists pounding against her petite body. He had never felt any reluctance about hurting another slave. He was raised to hurt, to kill. He was bred for it. Yet, this felt different. The idea of breaking the girl's bones left him paralysed. Sick. He closed his eyes, tensed and flexed his fingers.

He couldn't hurt her.

He couldn't disobey his orders, either.

His stomach cramped painfully. He didn't have a name for this emotion. It was like drowning, sinking under a thick liquid, his muscles too heavy to move.

What if she resists?

He couldn't move. If he took a step toward the girl, she would start screaming and fighting him again. And he would have to break her legs and arms. His head spun.

Can't disobey.

I can't disobey.

Her sobs were tearing a chunk out of his heart. He didn't *want* to…

His eyes snapped open. He didn't have the luxury of *wanting* or *not wanting*. He wasn't some untamed freeborn. He was a purebred. He lived to serve and breathed to please. He inhaled a deep breath and released it slowly, fixing his eyes on the floor.

It's not my body, it's their property.

He summoned that numbness, sending his mind to that dark place, so he could be the thing Badimar ordered him to be. He blocked out the girl's sobs. His heartbeat slowed down. He was nearly there, on the edge of *that place*, where he could tuck his mind away safely and detach from his body, when he heard the girl stand with a groan.

He held his breath, still lingering between here and *that place*. Without taking his eyes off the floor, he watched the girl with all his senses. She was still sobbing quietly, though she seemed more controlled now. Lion held his breath as he waited for what she was going to do next. Would she attack him? Would she try to run?

She walked past him, holding her head down, and went to the sink. She filled the basin with water and started washing the blood off her face with trembling hands. She had a busted lip and a bleeding nose. Bruises were forming at the side of her face. She gasped softly and shuddered when the cold water touched her skin. The water in the basin turned pink with her blood.

Lion still stood frozen. He hadn't moved since Badimar left. His muscles were taut, ready to snap into violence. He turned his head ever so slightly to keep the girl in his peripheral.

She straightened, dried her face with Lion's towel, leaving red stains on the fabric. Then she unbuttoned her dress and slipped out of it. Her milky white skin was tarnished by ugly bruises and several weeks old lashes. Still keeping her head down, she went to the bed and crawled under the blanket.

Lion exhaled a shaky breath, feeling the tension drain from his body. She wasn't going to resist! The sudden relief left him almost lightheaded, though he still felt like he was about to throw up. He took deep breaths, trying to ease those knots in his stomach. When he noticed the girl staring at the ceiling with vacant eyes, he had to look away.

What was happening to him? He needed to snap out of this. He recognised the expression on the girl's face. She was trying to send herself to *that place*. Why did that bother him? *That place* was safe; that numbness, that void was better than the alternative.

He took another deep breath and willed himself to move. He tugged his pants down and climbed into the bed. She twitched when Lion touched her. He was wrong. She hadn't fully escaped into *that place* just yet. She hadn't dissociated. When he moved to spread her legs apart, she tensed and clenched them together.

A suffocating feeling sat on Lion's chest. She was resisting. She covered her face with her hands, sobbing and trembling violently.

Can't disobey.

Lion closed his eyes, preparing for what he had to do. He opened them back, a new idea blossoming in his mind. Badimar had also told him he didn't care how he would do it, as long as he 'got it done'.

He didn't have to hurt her. He just had to make sure she wouldn't resist.

So, he waited.

He didn't touch her, he didn't move a muscle. He fixed his gaze on the wall and waited patiently. He would wait as long as he had to. He couldn't disobey his orders, but if the girl didn't resist, at least he wouldn't have to hurt her. He could make this easier for her. So, he waited. And it worked. The girl took deep breaths, and she recollected herself. Her muscles relaxed.

When Lion put his hand on her thigh again, she cupped her hand over his. Lion paused. She didn't try to push it away. She simply kept her hand on Lion's, staring at him intently. Why was she looking at him like that? He couldn't interpret her expression. Was that fear? He supposed it was. He probably looked big and menacing. There wasn't much he could do to appear less intimidating, especially considering he still had blood on his face.

Her pale skin gleamed in the dim light, with dark blotches forming on her ribs, just beneath those perfectly round breasts. He could almost hear how loud and fast her heart was beating. Slowly and gently, Lion pushed her legs apart. She didn't resist, her delicate hand still resting lightly on Lion's. When he positioned himself between her legs, she tensed and Lion froze again.

He waited. He studied the wild patterns her red hair formed on the pillow. They reminded him of untamed flames. Every part of his body that touched her soft skin was on fire, while he still felt cold and sick inside. The contrast left him dizzy.

She was still staring at him, shivering under him, her chest heaving rapidly. She wiped her cheeks with a palm, her other hand still on Lion's. Slowly, she slid her hand up Lion's forearm, then his bicep, and rested on his right shoulder. She relaxed and gave him the most subtle nod. It was so obscure; it could have been nothing more than a suppressed shiver. Whatever it was, it eased some of the knots in Lion's stomach. He continued, carefully avoiding the sore bruises all over her body, and monitoring her reactions.

He stopped every time she squeezed his shoulder and moved again when she gave him that little nod. They were communicating, without speaking. Without breaking any rules.

When he was done, he lay next to her. The bed was so small, their bodies were moulded together. Spent from the tension and the release, and that odd sickness in his guts, Lion closed his eyes, eager to drift into sleep and leave this day behind.

The girl spoke softly. "Saradra," she whispered, her voice barely audible. "My real name is Saradra."

No, it's not, Lion refuted silently in his mind. She was 'the girl'. 'The female slave', or whichever name her Owner chose for her. She didn't possess her previous name anymore.

Without opening his eyes, he pressed a finger against her soft lips. She didn't speak again. She turned to face the wall, her back nestled against his chest. Her hair tickled and irritated his brands, but he wasn't bothered. He fell asleep, breathing the smell of her hair.

11

OLIRA

Olira walked out of the shed, a large hammer gripped tightly in one hand, and a lantern in the other. The farm was shrouded in darkness just after sunset, the light of the lantern barely keeping the night away. Long shadows stretched across the yard as she made her way towards the barn. Her face was a mask of cold determination and the crunch of gravel under her boots echoed in the still night.

Torren burst out of the house, his small frame silhouetted against the dim light from inside. "Olira, please!" he cried, his voice still hoarse. "Don't hurt him! He only attacked me because I startled him. He's just scared and confused."

Olira's jaw tightened, but she didn't break her stride. "Get back inside, Torren."

"But Olira," Torren pleaded, running to keep up with her. "He's sick and feverish. He's probably—"

"I said go back inside," Olira interrupted, her grip on the hammer tightening. Her eyes were fixed on the barn ahead. Part of her knew she wasn't thinking clearly. Anger had wiped common sense clear from her thoughts. The image of Torren's bruised neck and frightened eyes haunted her mind, fueling her rage.

Torren's pleas grew more desperate as they neared the barn. "Please, Olira! You're not like this. You can't hurt him!"

Olira stopped abruptly, turning to face her brother. The look in her eyes was enough to make Torren flinch. "I will handle this," she said, her voice low and dangerous. "Go. Inside. Now."

Torren hesitated, tears welling in his eyes, but Olira's fierce expression left no room for argument. He backed away slowly, watching his sister with a mixture of fear and sadness.

Olira turned back towards the barn, her steps echoing in the night. The weight of the hammer felt reassuring in her hands. She didn't try to be quiet. *Let him know I'm coming,* she thought recklessly. The barn door creaked as she pushed it open, the shadows inside running from her.

The startled sounds of the animals greeted her. Warrior brayed tiredly. The cows shifted in their stalls, and the goat bleated curiously.

Olira made her way to the stall where she had dragged the man into. After making sure Torren was okay, she had returned to the boys' room and spoke the purebred's First Word again. The slave had passed out, so it was hard to tell whether the First Word had worked or not, but she didn't trust him one bit. She had run and fetched the stretcher, and spoken the First Word again before pulling him onto the stretcher. She had dragged him to the barn, her back and shoulders screaming from the strain, and had kept repeating the First Word every minute despite the slave never showing any sign of waking up. Then she had rushed to the shed to retrieve a hammer.

She expected the effects of the First Word to have faded, but hoped the man would still be unconscious. Still, she clutched the hammer tightly as she walked to the stall, the word ready on her lips. She pushed the stall door open to find the slave stirring awake. He lifted his head, breathing laboriously. His eyes widened with pain and confusion. He took a sharp breath, as if to speak or to spring into action. Olira didn't give him a chance. "*Padlociatius.*"

The purebred's limbs went slack, and he lay perfectly still on the stretcher, his face vacant, and his eyes intense as he stared at the ceiling without blinking. *So helpless,* Olira thought as she scowled at the purebred beast, fully awake but unable to lift a finger. The image of his monstrous figure strangling Torren flashed in front of her eyes again, and she remembered the suffocating feeling of helplessness. The slave's eyes reflected that same emotion now as Olira looked down at him with a hammer in her hand.

Olira set the hammer down briefly and placed the lantern in the corner, out of the way. She reached into her pocket and pulled out a sturdy iron hoop and a handful of nails she brought from the shed. She picked up the hammer again and began to nail the hoop onto the wooden wall of the stall.

As she worked, she watched the slave in her peripheral. The slave gasped when the effects of the First Word ended. His muscles twitched as he stirred, like it was hard to move. *So he can't start moving immediately then,* she thought. That was good. He wouldn't be able to catch her unaware. He grimaced as he tried to look up, his face reflecting dread and worry.

"*Padlociatius,*" Olira said as she resumed pounding the nails on the wood. The slave crumpled onto the stretcher, his eyes bulging with fear.

She repeated the First Word three more times as she worked. Then, a disturbing suspicion started bugging her. The man had stopped stirring and trying to move when the First Word faded the last time. His face was an utter mask of agony. He wasn't trying to be deceitful. The changes to his breathing and the miserable noise he made gave away when the effects were fading. But the expression she saw on his face bothered her.

She stopped and moved to the other end of the stall, as far away from him as possible. With the hammer still casually resting in her hand, she leaned against the wall and waited. The slave blinked rapidly, gasped, and groaned softly. He lay still, an anguished expression on his face, and his muscles twitching slightly. She gave him another minute to recover from the paralysis before she spoke.

"When I say your First Word," she said sharply, "does it cause you pain?"

The slave kept his eyes on the ceiling, a subtle grimace deepening the lines on his face. He swallowed several times and grunted as if he couldn't yet fully control his throat muscles. "No, Owner," he said finally. He clenched his jaw and pressed his lips tight before he spoke again. "I won't move," he said softly, quieter than a whisper.

Olira narrowed her eyes at the purebred's battered, muscular frame, still as a statue. She wasn't comfortable turning her back to him. Not when he was allowed to move. He must have sensed her decision, as he closed his eyes tiredly.

"*Padlociatius*," Olira said, returning to her task.

The look of anguish was wiped clean from the slave's face. With his eyes closed, he almost appeared to be in a peaceful slumber, though she knew he probably wasn't.

He's not in pain, she reminded herself as she worked faster. He had said it himself. It was probably just unpleasant, lying there helpless. She didn't mind letting him feel what she felt when she walked into the room and found him nearly killing her little brother. Breathing out her fury, she wiped the single tear that trickled down her cheek. She couldn't shake the bloodthirsty expression she saw on the purebred's face and couldn't let herself forget this man was bred and raised for violence. She had to keep her brothers safe.

With the final strike of the hammer, the hoop was firmly in place. She walked into the next stall, where Warrior's packsaddle was stored, and she found the chain and the collar. Returning to the slave's stall — remembering to repeat the First Word at intervals — she attached the end of the chain to the hoop. Then, she clasped the collar around the slave's neck and stood.

Olira's eyes flickered between the purebred beast, who was built like an ox, and the puny little hook she nailed to the old wooden wall. If the man wanted to, he could easily rip the hook free from the wall and let himself out. She took a deep breath. She had to convince him not to try anything. As she waited for the paralysis to fade, she thought about what she could threaten him with.

"You will not get out of this stall unless I tell you to. Do you understand?"

"Yes, Owner," the slave whispered, his eyes still closed.

Olira swallowed. She tried to muster every bit of resolve and filled her voice with conviction before she continued: "If I see you outside of this stall, I will say the other word."

She didn't ask if he understood. She had seen his shiver. He clearly understood what she meant, and how determined she was to follow through with this threat.

She picked up her lantern and hammer, then turned to leave the stall, casting one last glance at the chained man who shuddered with fever and fear. The hammer felt heavier in her hand than it did before.

12

LION

Lion woke up beside the girl, not feeling rested at all.

The bed was small, and he was not used to sharing it with another. No matter how petite the girl was, it was cramped and uncomfortable. However, it wasn't the lack of space that kept him up all night — it was the girl's silent sobs.

She'd been crying again.

She was facing the wall as usual, with the blanket pulled over her hips. The room was dark except for a dash of moonlight seeping through the narrow window. The moonlight bathed her body, making her skin appear pale and delicate, almost like the porcelain statues one of the Northern lords had gifted to Queen Arasanara. Lion's eyes traced the soft curve of her hip, the scars on her back, and the outline of her shoulder blades. Her body shook with silent sobs and soft cries.

He glanced at the square window. The moonlight was still bright. He wasn't allowed to leave his room this early.

This had been their third night together, and he had woken up to her silent sobs on every one of them. Hearing freeborn slaves cry at night was nothing new to him. He could sleep through any noise, but this one kept him awake.

He was being gentle with her; following her lead, making sure not to touch her bruises, being slow and careful. He wasn't hurting her. She wasn't in any physical pain, as much as he could tell.

Then why was she crying?

And more importantly, how could he make her stop?

The sound of her sobs made his chest tight. He had tried to ignore them; he had tried numbing himself to sleep, sending his mind to *that place*. Nothing had worked. Every quiet sob she let out felt like a spear going through his chest and left him feeling like... like he was bleeding out on the arena sands. He had to make her stop.

Hesitantly, he reached over her and pressed a finger against her lips.

She tensed, but stopped sobbing. He could feel her heart beating faster. He shifted closer, his large body spooning hers. He nuzzled his face in her wildfire hair; his blond mixed with her red. His fingers caressed her face, wiping the warm tears away. For a brief moment, it seemed to be working. He was almost proud of himself.

Then she pushed his hand away, firmly.

The rejection felt like a punch to his guts, and he had no clue why. She inched away from his warmth, though there was not much room to move. She chose to snuggle against the cold wall rather than accept the comfort of Lion's body.

He blinked at the back of her head. Although he wasn't hurting physically, he still felt like hot branding irons were pressing deep inside his chest. He could hardly wait until the moon started fading. As soon as it was light enough to justify leaving his room, he rolled out of the bed, got dressed, and left.

The rest of his day went by as usual: he trained, he ate, he trained more. Badimar was still cautious about straining his shoulder too much. Lion didn't share his caution today. His mind went blank as he immersed himself in the training drills, pushing his body harder than he ever did before. The more intensely he worked, the less he had to think about the confusing tightness in his chest. That girl was a distraction. What she did to him was a distraction. He couldn't afford that. He was the king's champion Beast. He was the Lion of Zarall. He was a purebred, not some emotional freeborn.

He made no mistakes in any of the training drills. He even elicited two appraising grunts from Badimar. Not only were they rare, they were also unexpected, given Badimar's current mood.

The Master of the Beasts was snappy, intolerant, and on edge ever since the incident with the girl. After Lion's first night with her, Badimar had dragged him to Vanalten first thing in the morning to check his eye. Although at first the old physician was shaken by the sight of dried blood that still clung to Lion's face and beard, he was quick to dismiss the scratch after examining it.

Throughout the examination, Lion had clasped his right hand in his left casually, hiding the bite mark in his palm. After witnessing their concern over a minor scratch like this, he wasn't sure how Badimar would react to another injury, no matter how insignificant the injury was. He imagined Badimar storming back to his room and beating the lights out of the girl. He had kept his hand dirty for the rest of the day to hide the scars.

He had found out that Badimar had tried to kick the girl out. He had requested an audience with King Leonis, but was fended off by Fauwyn, the royal secretary, saying the king would not annul his agreement with Lord Hosten over a scratch. Badimar had breathed fire for the rest of the day, being exceedingly generous with his whip and his use of Pain Words against all the beasts.

Even today, every time Badimar glanced at Lion's face and saw how close the girl had gotten to blinding him, he barked at the nearest beast for anything they had done wrong, and cracked his whip.

Lion found himself looking forward to the sparring session this afternoon, and was disappointed when Badimar grunted at him to sit this one out too. He hadn't held a weapon for more than three days; he had never gone this long for as long as he could remember. The frustration was more potent than he had anticipated, and he barely kept his hands from forming fists at his sides. He watched the other beasts pair off, clashing swords and exchanging grunts.

After dinner and a bath, he headed to his room early, scratching his chest absentmindedly. The fourth brand had stopped hurting and had started itching instead. It was starting to scar, and Vanalten's poultices only made the itch worse. When he arrived at his room, he walked straight to the basin to soothe the brand with cold water. He didn't even glance at the girl until he was out of his tunic and pressing the wet towel against the mark on his chest.

His eyebrows were drawn together when he finally looked at the girl sitting cross-legged on the bed. There was nothing unusual about that, since there was no other furniture to sit on. Her red hair reached down to her elbows in unruly waves. Her freckles stood out against her pale skin, almost translucent in the dim light.

But there was something different about her today that made Lion's skin crawl. Although her eyes were still puffy from crying over the past few days, they were dry now. Moreover, they had a gleam in them as they perused Lion's face attentively. Her lips were pursed, and a curious scowl graced her features. She sat still, looking both excited and guarded at the same time. Her expression unnerved him.

Just when he'd decided to ignore her and put the towel away, he froze. Her hands were resting on her lap and one of them was tightly closed around a small object. The sight of her clenched fist sent a shiver down his spine. When he saw what she held, the towel slipped from between Lion's trembling fingers.

A grin played across the girl's lips, while Lion's stomach plummeted into a dark pit.

He lunged at the girl, at the same time, she jumped out of the bed and held out a hand. "Stop, or I'll scream," she hissed without hesitation.

Lion halted, frozen only by an arm's reach from the girl. She was holding her free hand in front of his chest and had tucked the other one behind. Lion could easily grab her, restrain her, and snatch the object out of her fingers.

As if reading his thoughts, she forced a confident smile on her lips. "Go ahead and beat me unconscious for all I care. The first thing that'll come out of my mouth will be 'look under his bed'."

Lion let out a weak groan that sounded like a whimper. She licked her lips. "That's right. You hurt me, and I'll tell your Masters all about my discoveries. Now, back off!" She pressed a hand against his chest and pushed him away.

Lion walked backwards until his back hugged the far wall. The girl wasn't yelling, but she wasn't whispering either. Anyone who walked past the corridor outside could hear her. His eyes darted to the door, then to the wall which neighboured Badimar's room. She followed his gaze.

"He hasn't returned to his room yet," she said with a sneer. "I've been listening all day. I recognise how that prick walks."

It didn't matter. If any free man or woman heard what Lion had done, he would be sent straight to White Tower.

The thought of White Tower sent his mind into a spiral of unfinished thoughts and fractured images that blended together in a chaotic jumble: *White Tower... White Tower! I'm going to White Tower. The black hooded figure... Not human... A whole lot of them... Pale, wrinkly, parchment-like skin... The cold, wet tongue on his palms... Mouth and teeth sucking the blood off his fingers... Sucking everything out of him... I'm going to White Tower! The slave named Ratsack... Like an empty shell... Slicing his own ear, biting his fingers off.*

"Hey!" the girl hissed cautiously. Lion barely heard her. The sound of his heart pounding in his ears blocked everything else. "What's wrong with you?"

Black spots started flying across Lion's sight. He couldn't think, he couldn't breathe. His life was over. The fate he dreaded the most, the one he believed he could avoid by adhering to his training and being a good slave, had now become his reality. All his efforts had been in vain, and his worst nightmare was now irrevocably sealed. Like a tight collar around his neck, slowly shrinking, strangling him.

"Merciful Alunwea, you're shaking like a leaf," the girl frowned. Despite looking angry, she lowered her voice. "Relax. I won't tell them anything..."

Lion was leaning against the wall, his legs shaking under his weight. His throat was so dry, he half expected it to bleed when he swallowed.

She won't tell. She won't tell them anything.

He clung to that promise as if his life depended on it. It did. He managed to reign in his growing panic.

Until she added, "... as long as you do what I say."

Lion groaned.

She grinned smugly. Coldly. Her eyes glimmered with a ferocity that reminded him of every freeborn beast he fought against. That girl who had sobbed and cried underneath him was gone. She had the power to ruin his life, and she had no reservations about using it. She stood straighter, like a free woman. Her busted lip and bruised cheekbones no longer marked her as a victim. They made her look like a fierce fighter.

Can't disobey.

If she asked him to do things that conflicted with his orders, with his training... If she asked him to commit an Act of Defiance...

Can't go to White Tower either.

He was trapped. His life was finished either way.

She brought her other hand in front of her, turning and twisting the object between her fingers. It was a piece of hard rock, small enough to fit into her palm. One end was sharp and pointy. Her grin spread wide as she studied the longing etched across Lion's face. She relished the helplessness that suffocated him.

"I saw this under the bed the first night I was brought to this room," she explained quietly. "I thought it was just a piece of rubble. A useless rubbish. Then I realised; there is no rubbish in this room. You're not allowed to possess anything, not even rubbish."

Lion's shoulders sagged. His stomach clenched as he listened to her continue.

"Then I realised how this is sharpened. You must have spent *days* grinding this thing against the floor to make it sharp like this. At first, I thought maybe you wanted a weapon or something, but you are a weapon yourself, aren't you? You don't need a primitive thing like this."

She shook her head, then continued, her voice low and laced with something that almost sounded like pity. "Then I thought maybe you were just planning to... you know... end your misery. Slit your wrists or something."

Lion was leaning against the wall with his full weight now. His knees wouldn't carry him. He kept his eyes fixed on the girl's hands. She shrugged. "But I know purebreds don't do things like that."

She was right, and she knew she was right. She grinned with pride as she whispered, "Then I had another look under the bed."

Lion glanced at the bed and shuddered. The girl stared at him like she was trying to split his skull open with her gaze and see what he hid inside. "Care to explain, why do you have a map of Chinderia carved under your bed?"

Lion's head sagged. He closed his eyes. No, he couldn't explain this. Not to her, not to Master Badimar, nor to anyone. Not even to himself.

The girl's face lightened, her breath caught. She lowered her voice until it was barely audible. "Are you planning to escape?"

Lion flinched and snapped his eyes open. He shook his head frantically. Escape? Never! He would never, ever even think about escaping.

Hunters always find you.

Hunters were not human. They could track escaped slaves all the way to the Darkhome. And the punishment for escape was a straight trip to White Tower.

No. No, no, no, no. He would never escape.

Besides, he didn't even want his freedom. What was he going to do with it? Not having someone to tell him what to do was terrifying.

The girl's face hardened. She levelled him with a glare. "Then why did you draw the map?" When Lion didn't answer, she snorted. "You'll have to speak to me."

Lion shook his head again. He wasn't going to speak without permission from a free man or woman. She flashed him a cruel grin. Tilting her chin up, "Speak," she ordered. "Tell me to stop now, or I'll scream."

Lion glanced at her face, trying to assess if she would really do that. Surely she knew how much trouble she would be in as well. He imagined the events that would occur if she screamed; Badimar or someone else walking in, the girl telling them about the map before they started beating her. He imagined the look on Badimar's face as the Master of the Beasts flipped his bed upside down and saw the map. He would probably arrive at the same conclusion as the girl; that he was planning an escape or something! Every scenario he could think of ended in Lion heading to White Tower with the Hunters.

"Tell me to stop, or I'll scream," the girl hissed again.

Lion shook his head. He wouldn't commit an Act of Defiance.

"Fine," the girl said with a shrug. She took a deep breath and opened her mouth.

"Stop!" The word burst out of Lion's mouth in a harsh breath. He resisted the urge to cover his lips with both his hands.

The girl closed her mouth and flashed him a loathing smile. "See?" she said arrogantly. "It's not that hard."

Lion swallowed hard. She was wrong. Sweat trickled down from his face and his body felt too hot. He had committed an Act of Defiance! He half-expected to hear Breeder Astaldo's voice bark his Pain Word. He wiped his forehead with the back of his hand and took deep breaths to suppress the nausea.

"Why did you draw the map?" she asked. "Speak."

Lion pressed his lips together. He shook his head, his mouth too dry to speak.

"Why did you draw the map?" she asked again. When Lion still didn't reply, she took another sharp breath in, filling her lungs and straightening her shoulders to yell.

"I don't know!" Lion hissed through clenched teeth. He tapped the back of his head against the cold wall behind him, closing his eyes and grinding his teeth. "I live to serve; I breathe to please."

"What do you mean, you don't know?"

"I live to serve; I breathe to please."

She scoffed and rolled her eyes. "You live to serve, you breathe to please..." She held up the little rock. "And you sharpen rocks to carve maps under your bed. A very detailed map, too. Did you draw it from memory?"

Lion tapped his head on the wall again. His jaw ached from grinding his teeth, and he still felt like he was about to pass out.

"Are you saying you just woke up one day and decided to carve a map under your bed? For no reason?"

"Yes, Mast..." Lion slammed his mouth shut just in time before he finished forming the word. He clenched his fists, his nails digging into his palms. She was a freeborn brat. How could he almost call her Master? The girl's lips pressed tight. She didn't find the slipup funny.

He couldn't explain why he drew the map, because there was no reason for it. Lion had been studying and admiring the map on the floor of the throne room ever since the day he was bought by King Leonis. Unconsciously, he had begun memorizing its intricate details until the map floated before his eyes whenever he'd closed them. It had haunted him. For over three years, he'd denied its call. But several months ago, he could no longer resist the urge to bring those vivid images to life.

Like a relentless itch begging to be scratched, he had crawled under his bed and started carving under the wooden bedframe with his fingernails. No one would have noticed it unless they had crawled under the bed and looked up. Even then, the darkness made it difficult to discern any shapes.

He was making very slow progress with his fingernails, not to mention risking splinters and drawing unwanted attention to his bleeding fingers. A couple of days later, he managed to smuggle a rock from the training yard into his room. By grinding one end against the stone floor, he sharpened it until it was sufficiently pointed. After that, his progress was much quicker.

He was close to completing the entire map when the girl was dumped into his room. He hadn't had the time or the opportunity to crawl under the bed and hide the rock more effectively. Any attempt to do so would have aroused her curiosity. He hoped she would be gone before she'd made the discovery.

He was wrong.

He was doomed.

She squinted her eyes at him, studying his face carefully. Lion felt like he was being displayed at an auction, naked, being prodded and examined by potential buyers. He hated to think of the girl as a Master or an Owner. She was a slave.

Yet, she had power over him now.

"I'll keep your secret," she decided, still twisting the rock between her fingers. "But you'll do exactly what I say." When Lion shifted uncomfortably, anger flashed across her face. "Relax. I won't ask anything nearly as difficult as lying still under a slobbering repulsive animal, praying to Alunwea he won't break your arms and legs."

Lion flinched. *A slobbering repulsive animal?* He had gone out of his way to be careful and gentle with her. The quiet fury and the welling tears in her eyes indicated she didn't see it that way. Lion's shoulders sagged and blood rose to his neck as he drowned in disgust.

The girl tilted her chin. "I want you to look at me," she ordered. She said it so casually, not realizing her request was impossible for him. He shook his head, his eyes bulging in panic.

She took a step forward. "You'll do as I say."

He shot a quick glance at her face, focusing his eyes on a freckle on her cheek. She shook her head. "No. You'll look into my eyes."

A whimper slipped past Lion's lips. He shook his head again as his breathing quickened. She didn't understand. He couldn't do it.

She took another step forward. "It's not that hard," she said. "Just do it. Look at me."

Lion's head was spinning. He had no choice. Helplessness struck him like a physical pain. He closed his eyes, and he was back at Faychill Ranch, standing in front of Astaldo. The slave breeder was yelling...

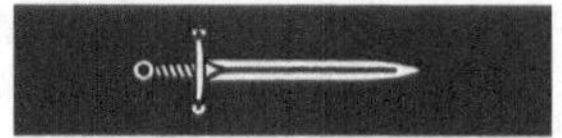

"Look at me!"

The slave who wasn't given the name Lion of Zarall yet, had no more than nine winters behind him. He had lined up in front of Breeder Astaldo, along with four other boys. They all had their heads down, hands clasped in front, eyes on the floor; their stances had already been mastered.

Astaldo paced back and forth along the line, looking down at the young slaves. Each had a Beast tattoo, the ink still dark and fresh. They were all naked, trembling slightly under his hard gaze. Unless it was part of an armour, they never wore any clothing. They were used to nudity. Feelings such as embarrassment or shame have long been scraped off of them. The only thing left was fear.

Not fear of physical pain.

Fear of disobedience.

Astaldo stood in front of a boy. "Look at me," he ordered.

The boy's chest heaved. He forced his head up, his neck visibly clenched with the effort. As soon as his eyes met Astaldo's, the slave breeder spoke: "Caniarepetois."

The boy fell down, consumed by excruciating pain. Astaldo watched his thrashing, convulsing body until the effects of the Pain Word receded.

He ordered him to get up. The boy had to bite his lips until they bled, just to stop himself from begging. They'd learned that begging was another form of defiance; it was no different from rejecting the punishment, or requesting for mercy. All punishable behaviours.

The boy kept his mouth shut. When he took his stance, still shaking, Astaldo spoke again: "Look at me."

The boy forced himself to obey, lifting his head until he met Astaldo's eyes again.

"Caniarepetois," said Astaldo, the second they made eye contact. The boy fell one more time.

They practiced this a few more times — Astaldo ordering the boy to get up, to look at him, and speaking his Pain Word as soon as their eyes met — then Astaldo moved on to the next boy.

"Look at me."

They'd been practicing this for weeks already. His body started shaking as soon as he heard the command. His knees felt weak. He raised his head, slowly, to look at the Breeder's eyes. They were dark as pain.

"Prihjtivaviula."

He fell, writhing in agony. It was hard to believe the Pain Word only lasted for thirty seconds. One eternity was trapped in every heartbeat. His blood, bones, and flesh burnt from the inside, consumed by pain.

"Get up," Astaldo ordered, and when the boy did, "Look at me."

They continued the training at different times of the day, with different trainers. Even an accidental eye contact was punished immediately. Sometimes the trainers even went as far as tricking them into looking up, just to catch their gaze and punish them for it. By the time he was auctioned at fourteen, the slave had become an expert at avoiding any eye contact. Even the thought of looking at another person in the eye was enough to make him tremble.

"LOOK AT ME," THE girl repeated impatiently. "Now!"

Lion held his breath, closed his eyes, tilted his head up slowly. He tensed, his stomach clenching. Forcing his eyes open, he looked at the girl's sky-blue eyes. It only took the length of a heartbeat for his body to react.

He dropped to his knees, doubled over, and threw up. His body shook with the expectation of the Pain Word. The pain was not there, but the fear was strong enough to trick his body into believing it was. His muscles twitched and convulsed. He hugged himself, clenching his teeth and gasping for breath.

It's not real. It's not real.

It was surprisingly difficult to convince himself that there was no pain; just the memory of it.

For freeborn slaves, eye contact was just a taboo. For purebreds, it meant pain.

The girl mumbled something that sounded like, 'What have they done to you?' under her breath. She paled. By the time Lion had finally recovered and stood, shaking slightly, she had an irritated glimmer in her eyes.

"Again," she ordered.

Lion stomped down the urge to beg her. He retched again, but had emptied everything in his stomach. He desperately reached for the words in his head: *It's not my body, it's their property. It's not my body. Not my body.*

"Look at me."

His attempts to escape from his body weren't as effective this time, but he managed to calm himself. He sucked in a deep breath, tensed his stomach as if bracing for a gut punch, and raised his gaze. He almost expected to see Astaldo's cruel eyes. But his eyes met hers once again, and he held for two heartbeats before he averted them and crumpled against the wall, hugging himself and shaking. It was just as bad as the first time.

"You'll get better," the girl said triumphantly. "We'll practice every night. You'll look at me and you'll talk to me. I want you to tell me something nobody knows about you. Not even your Owners and Masters."

A sickening chill ran down Lion's spine. He rested his head against the wall, his eyes closed. *Every night?* He pressed his palms over his eyes. Why? Why was she doing this? Revenge was another abstract concept free men and women were obsessed with. Was she torturing him because he fucked her? Didn't she understand he didn't have a choice?

When she came near him, carefully stepping over the puddle of vomit, he flinched. She picked up the towel he dropped earlier. The little rock was nowhere to be seen, hidden from him. There weren't many places to hide it here. He could ransack the room and find it.

"I know you have to keep... *following your orders*," she said the words with a sneer. She walked over to the basin, soaked the towel, then wrung the excess water. "I won't even try to stop you. And you know I won't resist."

Even if Lion found the rock, she could still tell them about the map. How was he going to keep her quiet?

She kneeled beside him and tilted his chin up. He recoiled from her touch. "But I will make you talk to me," she said. "Tell me something about yourself. Now." She reached to wipe his mouth with the towel. Her hand rested on his cheek, steadying him.

He could kill her.

The thought turned his stomach upside down. Just this morning, he was trying to comfort her, and now, he was contemplating killing her. But this was her fault. She left him with no other option.

"It could be anything," she said, moving down to wipe his hands. "Like your favourite colour or song."

Lion could see himself killing the girl. It wouldn't be hard. He calculated how much trouble that would bring him. Free men and women did not appreciate slaves killing each other outside of an arena. Those acts warranted punishments. The girl belonged to someone else — Lord Hosten — which meant if she died while under King Leonis's possession, it would put the king in a difficult position.

"Tell me something about yourself," the girl repeated, putting the towel aside. She watched his face expectantly.

Lion could make it look like an accident, as if he lost control and broke her. Or he could stage it in a way that would seem like she had killed herself. He would still get into trouble, but he doubted he would be sent to White Tower over this. His Masters would perceive the act of drawing a map under his bed more incriminating than accidentally killing a freeborn. He was the Lion of Zarall. And he had a feeling Badimar would be pleased to get rid of the girl.

"Speak," she commanded.

Lion's eyes glazed over. His heartbeat picked up, though this time it wasn't the fear that drove him. It was the anticipation of violence. He stood, and the girl followed suit. Her eyebrows twitched as if she had sensed the quiet change in him, but she kept her head high, not showing any sign of concern. Like he wouldn't dare harm her.

"Speak," she whispered. "Tell me something about yourself."

Muscles on Lion's neck tightened, and the girl swallowed. She lost her composure for a moment and took a small step back. Lion snatched her arm and held her in place. Her breath caught, but she still didn't make any noise. Lion stepped in and brought his mouth to her ear. "I'm a slobbering, repulsive animal," he whispered through clenched teeth.

He found those words echoing in his mind. She had threatened him with his greatest fear, of being sent to White Tower. She had filled him with horror and left him feeling hollow and carved out. Yet, of everything she had said, those words stung sharper than any weapon.

He seethed with a mix of anger and violence that brewed beneath his muscles. He tightened his fists around the collar of her dress and yanked, ripping the fabric from neck to waist. Her bare shoulders popped out.

He expected her to cower in fear or struggle against him. He was prepared to muffle her screams and restrain her. Her fight would help the violence spill easier out of him. Instead, her jaw twitched with defiance and she hissed, "Fine."

She shrugged out of her dress, kicked it away, and stood naked, her shoulders pushed back and her blue eyes burning with spite.

"Is this how you wanna pla—"

Lion grabbed her by the throat, not rough enough to elicit a scream. Not yet. She was dumber than he thought, for still not realizing what Lion was about to do. For not seeing that he was wound tight, on the verge of unleashing his aggression. She rested her hand on his arm, so casually, and she relaxed her neck, as if coaxing him to go ahead and crush her throat. Her eyebrows twitched and the corner of her plump lips curled.

Without taking her fiery eyes off him, she reached and fiddled with the strings of his pants.

Stupid, *stupid* girl.

Lion pushed her onto the bed. Air whooshed out of her, but she didn't scream. Within a few heartbeats, Lion had freed himself from his pants and was prowling on her with the grace of an animal getting ready to devour its prey. He pinned her legs apart and sheathed himself in her, much rougher than any of their previous nights. He was prepared to smother her screams, but she only gasped and let out a soft moan, which didn't sound at all like an expression of fear.

He found his rhythm, still working himself up for the bloodshed. Kill her, make it look like an accident, like he'd lost his control. It wasn't hard.

He tensed with wariness when he felt the girl wrapping her legs around his waist. A paranoid voice in him wondered if this was a wrestling move, an attempt to throw him off? Then the girl started thrusting her hips in sync with his rhythm.

Lion froze, so taken aback he stopped moving. What was she doing? His mind raced. Was this a trick?

The girl continued grinding against him. She slid herself up and down along the length of his shaft, moving slowly, like she was savouring the pace. The sight of her writhing underneath him left Lion breathless.

What was she doing?

She moved her hands over the hard muscles on his chest, shoulders, and arms. Her hands were soft and gentle, leaving a trail of fire on Lion's skin wherever they touched. She avoided his brands and her delicate fingers were careful as they trailed past his bandaged shoulder. She still rocked her hips against him, her perky breasts bouncing with each movement, drawing Lion's attention. Then, he finally noticed the smug grin on her face.

The bitch was playing. She was having fun.

Lion was about to kill her, and she thought...

He shook her hands off him, ignoring how his skin mourned the loss of her touch. He wanted her to fear him. To hurt. He grabbed one of those round breasts, savouring how it filled his palm, and he squeezed hard enough to make her yelp.

She bit her lower lip to keep that yelp from turning into a scream. Lion's eyes were drawn to those lips. Were they always this red and full?

She snaked her hand along her navel, over her ribs, and cupped her other breast. Lion forgot how to breathe as he watched her play with herself. He hadn't realised when he started to thrust again, matching the rhythm she desired.

"I know what you're trying to do," she whispered with a self-satisfied grin.

No, she really didn't.

Lion covered her mouth with his palm, so he wasn't distracted by those lips and that triumphant smile. Her eyes twinkled like she was winning a game he didn't know they were playing. With his other hand, he cupped her hip, digging his fingers into her soft flesh. He had to erase that arrogant spark from her eyes. He ploughed her with the ferocity of a barely leashed animal. Her thighs clenched around his waist, her entire body tensing, like she was getting close to snapping. She grabbed his biceps, her fingernails raking his skin. She was whimpering, her muffled moans reverberating against his palm. Her warm and wet breath burned his skin.

Then, violent shudders took over her body.

Lion couldn't hold back a groan as he watched her shake with wave after wave of release. How could she... She was not supposed to take pleasure from him. She was supposed to fear what he was doing to her, not enjoy it.

He watched breathlessly as she pushed his hand away, then guided his first two fingers into her mouth. She started sucking them, her tongue twirling around his digits. He made another animalistic sound. She still squirmed under him, panting, like she wanted more of him. Sweat plastered her hair to her face, blood rushed to her cheeks. She pushed his fingers back out. One of her eyebrows curled up as she smirked. "What's wrong? Why did you stop?"

Lion growled, deep and low. "Fuck you."

She giggled. She actually *giggled*!

He flipped her facedown, yanked her hips up, while pressing her head down. She gasped when he plunged himself in. She was drenched! He pounded her, his skin slapping against hers with a wet sound. She flailed her arms, and she bit her lips to keep herself quiet. He gathered her wrists at the small of her back and kept them pinned with one hand. He made a primitive sound when she thrashed to break free.

He found his speed, his fingers grabbing her thigh so firm, they left red marks. She turned her head and watched him over her shoulder, her face flushed, her eyes half closed, and her mouth open. Somehow, she freed one hand and reached back, holding onto his thigh. She urged him to move faster, plunging her nails into his skin. His body obeyed begrudgingly. Her pleasure built up to a climax, and she buried her face into the pillow to smother her scream as she came undone again.

Lion spilt himself into her, his grunt louder than he expected. He came down from a high he had never been to, and he was spent as he collapsed next to her.

She turned her head, watching him with those cunning eyes. Her red hair partially covered her face, her cheeks bright with colour, sweat glistening on her forehead. She smiled.

Lion grunted. He spun her, so she faced the wall and didn't allow her to roll back. He couldn't bear watching that glowing, victorious, arrogant expression.

"Animal," she muttered.

Lion expected her to snuggle against the wall, as far away from him, like she had done the previous three nights. Instead, she shifted and spread, forcing Lion to retreat to the edge of the bed. She kept fidgeting, like she was trying to find a comfortable position, and she thrusted her hips against his crotch way too many times to count as accidental.

Lion faced away from her, shut his eyes, and willed himself to sleep. He was too tired to kill tonight. Too spent. The violence was drained out of him. *Tomorrow,* he thought. He would kill her tomorrow.

13

OLIRA

Olira led Varelya through the farmyard, the lantern in her hand flickering as they approached the barn. The cool night air was filled with distant sounds of rustling leaves, and the moonlight painted the weathered wooden structure with an eerie paleness.

The healer didn't hide her confusion as she scowled at the barn and followed Olira with hesitant steps. Her dark hair was pulled back into a tight bun and she walked with a rigid gait. "Why is the patient in the barn?" she asked, her voice tinged with curiosity and disapproval.

"Yeah, Olira, why is the *patient* in the barn?" Gilann repeated,. He followed them behind, carrying Varelya's large bag of medical equipment and supplies. His emphasis didn't escape Varelya's attention, as the healer shot Olira a penetrating gaze.

Olira pressed her lips together. "It's complicated," she said. "You'll see in a minute."

When they reached the barn, Olira pulled the heavy door open for Varelya. Before Gilann could follow the healer inside, she pushed him back, and snatched the bag off his hands. "You wait outside."

"Why?"

"Gilann!" She didn't say more. Gilann gritted his teeth as he stubbornly continued the staring contest. It was getting harder to win arguments against Gilann, but tonight she could not lose. "Go check on Torren."

"Why does Torren need to be checked on?"

"Go find out."

"Can I get some light in here, please?" Varelya asked impatiently.

Olira followed Varelya inside and shut the door behind her, leaving Gilann to fume quietly outside. She raised her lantern, the warm light casting long shadows across the barn's interior. The animals raised their complaints at the sudden light disturbing their sleep and retreated further back into their stalls. Warrior brayed sleepily.

"Why am I here?" Varelya asked with a sigh. "Gilann didn't say much, only that it wasn't one of your brothers who needed urgent help."

"It's this way." Olira guided Varelya to the farthest stall, chewing her lower lip with the anticipation of her reprimand. She had made sure the slave was still in his stall before Varelya showed up; she had spent the last two hours watching the barn doors, and she had walked in to check on him just before. He had been feverish and unconscious, but still alive.

She pushed the stall door open and stood aside. The air smelled like sweat and rot. She could tell the slave hadn't moved since her last visit. He blinked his eyes at the light filling the stall, then stared blankly at the ceiling. His skin was pale and clammy, and his chest heaved rapidly. He made no effort to move, maybe because the fever had left him too weak to move, or maybe out of fear of being paralysed again.

Varelya took one look at the man, her eyes widening with confusion. "Olira, why is this man chained?" she demanded, her voice sharp.

Before Olira could answer, Varelya's gaze fell on the slave's tattoo. Her confusion turned to shock and disdain. "A slave?" she spat, her tone dripping with contempt. "Olira!"

"It's not what you think."

"You *bought* a slave?"

"I didn't buy him."

"But you own him, right? And keeping him chained. In your barn?"

"Varelya, please don't say anything."

Varelya gave her a long stare that left Olira feeling like a child caught being naughty. Her cheeks flushed with a mix of embarrassment and anger. She met Varelya's gaze but didn't offer much explanation. "It's complicated."

Varelya shook her head. "Your father would have been appalled," she said softly.

The truth in those words stabbed Olira's chest. She didn't need to hear them from Varelya, she already knew. "Can you just help him?"

Varelya's expression hardened. "What are you planning to do with this poor thing, Olira?"

Olira wanted to object and say he wasn't such a poor thing. He was a purebred. A natural killer. "What do you think I'm planning?"

"You know your father—"

"I know my father was against the slave trade. And yes, I own him. And I plan to sell him, because the idea of keeping him is just as disgusting. So now, can you please help him?"

In all the years they had known each other, Olira had never spoken to Varelya like this. The healer, though only ten years older than Olira, was one of the most revered people in Oxreach. She was also a close friend of her mother's. Olira felt the weight of Varelya's disapproving gaze, the silent judgment pressing heavily upon her. She refused to crumble under that gaze.

Finally, with a resigned sigh, Varelya took her coat off. She moved closer to the man as she began to examine the wounds. Olira put the healer's bag near her and brought the lantern close so there was plenty of light. "His right leg," she said. "Infected cut. Nothing else seems that urgent."

Varelya ignored her explanation and examined the man from head to toe before focusing on the leg. Olira remained silent, her attention divided between watching Varelya work and monitoring the slave, ready to speak his First Word again at the first sign of violence. The slave's laboured breathing picked up when Varelya pulled the bandages free and started examining the leg, but he closed his eyes and kept his hands flat on the stretcher.

"I put *Asennamon* and *Stripefang Blossom* on it," Olira explained.

Varelya nodded but didn't reply. She resumed examining the slave's leg, her experienced fingers gently probing the inflamed, discoloured flesh. Olira already knew the infection was severe. Varelya concluded her examination and sat back for a moment, considering her options. She reached for her bag and started pulling her tools out. Not the poultices and powders she typically used, but the sharp instruments wrapped in dark leather.

Olira's stomach clenched with dread as she watched Varelya lay out the tools: a bone saw, a thin knife, and heavy bandages.

"No," Olira said. "There has to be another way."

The dread in Olira's voice drew the slave's attention. He turned his head, causing the chain to rattle slightly, and glanced at the sharp tools. His eyes widened, and he went very still.

"The infection is severe, and it's spreading," Varelya said.

"I put *Asennamon*—"

"You were too late. This wound is clearly at least a few weeks old, received inconsistent care, and is now turning gangrenous."

The purebred was so still, it sent a cold shiver down Olira's back. His fingers twitched, his eyes fixed on the bone saw, as he listened to the two women discuss his fate.

"I can't let you sever his leg," Olira said.

"That's the best way to save his life."

"But if you cut his leg..."

Varelya gave Olira a disgusted look. "He will be worthless, right?" Olira clenched her jaw. Shame was like a bucket of cold water poured down her head. She bit her tongue to hold back an angry retort.

"You can't make a profit out of a one-legged slave," Varelya continued with spite. "So you'd rather let him die than lose the leg."

Olira's blood rushed to her cheeks, but she was relieved when Varelya shook her head and pushed the tools aside. With a resigned sigh, she started pulling other tools out of her bag: a flat needle and a bowl. "I can try draining it, but it's already spread so much. If I can't get it all out, he may die."

Olira cast a quick look at the slave's frozen expression. "It's worth the risk."

"This will be excruciatingly painful for him. You better get Gilann in here to help hold him down."

"I can restrain him," Olira said through clenched teeth.

The slave stared back at the ceiling and looked somewhat deflated. His throat bobbed when he swallowed, his chest heaving rapidly.

"Olira, I'm going to drain the pus out. I have to be very *very* thorough and this will be *extremely* painful for him. I need him to be perfectly still. How are you planning to restrain a man triple your size..." She trailed off, her eyes drawn to the purebred's tattoo. She only now noticed the intricate details that marked the slave as purebred. She hardly contained her surprise.

"How did you—"

"It doesn't matter," Olira dismissed.

"Olira! Purebreds are abominations."

"I'll restrain him," Olira said. "Tell me when."

She refused to squirm under Varelya's judgmental gaze. The healer's expression hardened and Olira knew she would never be able to earn the woman's favour again. With another shake of her head, Varelya began to prepare for the procedure. "I need clean water," she demanded, her voice cold and demanding. "A fresh cloth, warm towels, and the darkest *Exiram Leaves* you have. Heat it into a warm poultice and add *Gissuri* and *Bitter Rue* if you have any. I'll need a separate batch of *Gissuri* with *Abyss Ice*, watered down."

"I don't have any *Abyss Ice*. I sold it all..."

"*Etegorn Thorn?*"

Olira nodded.

"It'll do. Go."

Olira hurried to gather the items the healer requested. She had already prepared boiled and cooled water, clean towels, and some of the herbs she had anticipated Varelya might ask for. She had another pot of boiling water on the stove as well. It didn't take her long to gather everything else and return to the barn.

Varelya immediately set to work. She soaked the cloth in the water and began to clean the wound with gentle, deliberate strokes. The man remained rigid, his eyes darting around as the dread in his chest grew. Olira could see the pain etched on his face, even though he was doing his best to remain still.

Once the wound was clean, Varelya lathered the leg in watered down *Gissuri* and *Etegon Thorn*. She wore gloves to keep her hands from going numb. She then picked up the flat needle and gave Olira a subtle nod.

Olira felt an unreasonable rush of nervousness as she stepped forward and said, "*Padlociatius.*"

All the tension drained out of the slave's muscles. His face relaxed. Olira could convince herself that he was peaceful if she ignored his eyes. They reflected the agony he was about to endure. The shudder that coursed through Varelya's shoulders suggested the young healer found the purebred's wakeful stillness just as creepy.

"Unnatural," Varelya said, drawing the Twelve's sign in the air. "Everything about purebreds is just wrong."

"You might want to hurry up."

Varelya took a deep breath and made the first incision, the scalpel slicing through the infected tissue. Nothing changed in the purebred's expression, but Olira imagined him screaming nonstop inside his head. Varelya worked quickly and confidently, draining the pus from the wound. The foul-smelling fluid seeped into the bowl she had placed beneath the leg, the air thick with the scent of infection.

Olira didn't wait for the subtle signs that signalled the paralysis fading. She counted in her head and kept repeating the First Word at intervals. She reminded herself that the First Word wasn't causing the slave any more pain, and that this was for his benefit. If he were to thrash and scream, it would only make Varelya's job harder. Besides, she had kept him paralysed before, only a few hours ago. She didn't have any problems with that then. Why did this bother her now?

Varelya continued slicing and squeezing the slave's flesh. One look at the gaping wound and the amount of blood and dark yellow pus made Olira nauseous. She couldn't imagine the horror of being trapped in a haze of pain, unable to scream for relief. She kneeled beside Varelya and put her hand on the man's suntanned arm. It probably didn't make much difference for him. She doubted he would even notice the touch while drowning in a torment like this. Not to mention the slave was a monster who had almost crushed Torren's neck just hours ago. Still, it felt like the right thing to do.

She lost count of how many times she repeated the First Word. Varelya continued to drain the wound, her hands steady and precise. Just as Varelya was making sure all the pockets full of pus were thoroughly emptied, Olira noticed the paleness of the man's hand.

"Umm, Varelya?" she said, pointing.

The healer glanced at the hand, then leaned over the man's face. "I can't tell when he's in this state…"

"You can't tell what?"

Varelya held her hand over the slave's mouth, feeling his breath. She then cupped her ear on his chest and listened to his heartbeat. She made a concerned noise.

"What?"

"Elevate his leg," Varelya said as she hurried with the poultice. "And wrap him in a blanket."

"Why?"

"Do it."

Olira didn't waste time with more questions. She scrambled into the next stall and grabbed a bucket and one of Warrior's saddle blankets. Running back, she slid the bucket upside down under the man's left leg and she wrapped his upper body with the blanket.

"Give him water. And try talking to him," Varelya grunted. "Keep him calm."

"His body is as calm as—"

"Keep *his mind* calm."

Olira grabbed a clean towel, soaked it in water, and slid a corner of it between his lips. She squeezed the towel slowly, letting the water trickle into the slave's mouth, and watching his throat bob as he swallowed. Leaning close to the man, she put her hand on his unusually clammy and pale arm. "It's almost over," she said with the most soothing voice she could muster under the circumstances. "You're gonna be okay. Just… just keep breathing." She doubted the man was listening, but she kept talking, because there was nothing else she could do. The man's muscles vibrated barely noticeably. If it wasn't for the uncanny effects of the First Word, he would have been convulsing.

When Varelya finished applying the poultice on the open wound, she wrapped the leg tightly with clean bandages. Slowly, colour started to return to the man's pale limbs. Olira removed the towel from his lips. Relief washed over her. She couldn't shake the feeling that they had just pulled the slave from the brink of death.

"Have you got any *Tusk Flower Root*?" Varelya asked.

"Yes."

"Bring all. He will need a very strong pain relief."

Olira didn't hesitate. She ran to the root cellar and grabbed the entire pouch of *Tusk Flower Root* from her storage. She returned to the barn just in time to witness the slave stirring.

"Let him," Varelya said as she lifted a hand to stop Olira. "But try to calm him down. He'll be confused and likely violent. Try to keep him from harming himself until the *Tusk Flower* knocks him to sleep."

The slave's fingers twitched, then his breathing became erratic. Olira knelt beside him, her voice more tired than gentle as she spoke to him. Meanwhile, Varelya started grinding the *Tusk Flower Root* into a drink, and mixing it with other powders from her bag. The slave's eyes sharpened with awareness, and a groan escaped his lips, quickly escalating into a muffled cry.

"Easy now," Olira said. "It's over, you're gonna be okay."

The man thrashed weakly, attempting to sit up, a growl-like scream spilling from his lips. He collapsed back down and shuddered with harsh, rugged breaths. Varelya moved swiftly, pinching his nose and pouring the drink down his throat. She pulled back just in time as the slave started flailing his arms. Olira kept talking to him.

Gradually, the man's screams subsided, and he slumped back, exhausted. Within minutes, his head dropped to the side, and he slipped into a restless sleep. Olira let out a breath. She gently brushed the man's arm in a calming gesture, then pulled her hand back.

Varelya stood, wiping her hands on a cloth. "I've done what I can for tonight," she said. The disapproval had returned to her face, evident in the tight lines on her forehead and the clipped tone of her voice. "Keep him warm and make sure he drinks plenty of water and gets enough food. Watch for persistent fever and chills. Rapid heartbeat. Confusion, disorientation, and odd behaviours."

"Odd behaviours?" Olira repeated. "He's a purebred. Everything he does is odd."

Varelya shrugged. "You'll have to figure what's normal for a purebred. If his condition doesn't improve by tomorrow, you will have to consider more drastic measures. Cauterising or severing that leg."

"Wait, me?"

"Yes. I will not be involved with that." She started packing her tools, her movements brisk and impatient.

"But you'll come back to check on him, right?"

"No. I don't care for slaves, Olira. Especially purebreds."

"How could you say that? Aren't you the one who always says *everyone* deserves the best care you can give? He needs help."

Varelya stopped packing her tools to give Olira a piercing stare. "What's going to happen to him when he recovers, Olira? What will you do to him?"

Olira pressed her lips shut. Varelya nodded like the silence was all the answer she needed.

"You're not saving his life. You're condemning him to a life of misery. He's better off dead." She put her coat back on, turning her back to Olira as she muttered. "I'm not going to go out of my way to save him, just so people like you can make a profit out of his flesh."

Olira took a deep breath. She tried to remind herself that Varelya had come all the way in the middle of the night and had spent hours in her barn to help her. She bit her tongue to hold back an angry retort and instead said, "Thank you for your time, Varelya."

Varelya gave her instructions on how she would need to keep expressing the pus over the next few days and apply warm poultice. She warned her that the next few hours would be critical, and that Olira should watch him closely. She gave her a list of herbs to speed up the recovery and help the slave regain his strength. Then she took her belongings and headed for the door.

Olira watched her leave, the healer's half-hearted warning echoing in her head. *Odd behaviours*. The first rays of the sun were beginning to rise outside. She felt a wave of exhaustion wash over her. Still, there was no time to rest.

She settled beside the man, adjusting the blanket to keep him warm. Her eyes were heavy with fatigue, but she forced herself to remain alert and watch over him. She couldn't stop thinking about Varelya's words. That saving the man would only condemn him to a life of misery.

14

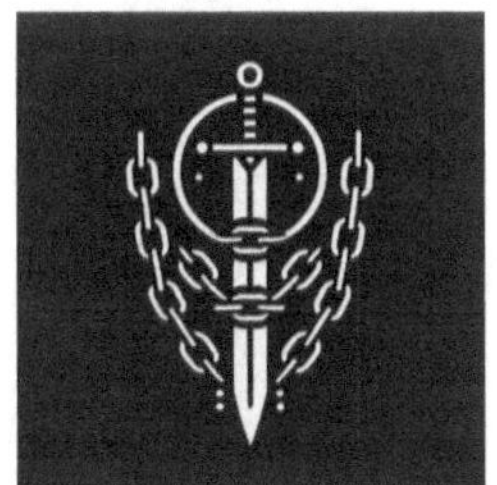

LION

"Let's do it again," the girl said, her voice cutting through the sound of Lion's heartbeat thrumming in his ears. "Look at me."

Lion trembled on his hands and knees, gagging and retching. Every muscle in his body locked up in anticipation of his Pain Word. Cold sweat broke out on his forehead and his vision blurred around the edges.

He was going to kill this girl. Tonight.

"Look at me," she repeated. She kneeled beside him, bringing her face close. She put a gentle hand on his arm. "When you're ready."

Lion shook her touch off. Squeezing his eyes shut, he forced himself to take a deep, shuddering breath. He clenched his stomach and braced for the agony.

Oddly, he saw no trace of malice in the girl's soft blue eyes. She wasn't doing this for her own amusement. This wasn't a twisted display of power. If anything, her eyes reflected a genuine concern as she offered him an encouraging smile.

He doubled over, an overwhelming surge of fear and pain coursing through him. The muscles in his neck and shoulders bunched painfully as he fought to regain control.

"It's going to get better," the girl whispered. "It has to."

She waited and watched as Lion pushed himself up to sit with his back against the wall. He was out of breath, weak and trembling.

The girl sat next to him, close enough that their legs nearly touched. She had tied the torn pieces of her dress together and somehow succeeded at looking decent in it. If anything, the tattered dress seemed more elegant than any of Queen Arasanara's jewel-clad, multi-coloured dresses. Her red hair spilled over one shoulder. She was silent for a while. It gave Lion time to shake the last of the lingering dread.

"Tell me something about yourself," she whispered.

Lion glanced at the door, then at the wall that divided his room from Badimar's.

"He's not back yet," she sneered. "I've been listening. Besides, we're barely even whispering. His hearing cannot be that good."

Lion rested his head on the wall, working himself up to push the exhaustion away. Earlier today, after the day's training, Lion had been resolute — he was going to kill the girl. The decision was final, and he had no other choice. But the moment he had stepped inside, and saw what she had done with the dress — and how breathtaking she looked in those rags — his resolve had wavered. The memory of tearing the fabric from her bare shoulders the previous night had surged back, making his blood rush. Next thing he knew, he was letting her torture him with those eyes.

"Tell me something about yourself," she whispered again. When Lion didn't answer, she added, "Remember, we made a deal. You'll look at me and you'll say something about yourself to me every night."

"I'm a purebred beast," Lion muttered, quieter than a whisper.

The girl shook her head. "Something your Owners and Masters don't know about you."

Lion crossed his arms. He couldn't help glancing at the door, hating how his stomach twisted with fear as he spoke. "They know everything." It was true. They probably knew more about Lion than he did.

"They don't know about that." The girl pointed at the bed, a sly smirk tugging at her lips.

Cold sweat ran down Lion's spine as he looked at the shadows under the bed. He swallowed. He would rather his Owners and Masters never knew about the map. White Tower. He would be sent straight to White Tower, no questions asked.

"Come on, tell me something about yourself. I'll even be more specific." She brought a lock of her hair to her mouth and started chewing thoughtfully. "Tell me your favourite food."

Lion rubbed his eyes. What kind of question was that? He shrugged. His thoughts were drawn to the bed again, but this time not to the shadows beneath it. He studied the bed and the pillow, memories of the previous night flooding his mind. His heartbeat quickened, but not from fear or the anticipation of violence. This time, it was something else entirely.

"Your favourite food?" the girl insisted. "What is it?"

Lion sighed and muttered under his breath, "I ate rye bread, roasted chicken and vegetables for supper."

"That's not what I asked."

Lion scratched his head and let out a quiet, frustrated growl. What did she want to hear? And more importantly, how was he ever going to sleep on that bed again without being haunted by the sensation of her soft body pressing, grinding, pounding against his? He pinched his arm and deliberately looked away to banish the images from his head.

"What's your favourite—"

"I don't have one," he grunted.

"Everyone has a favourite food."

"I eat what I'm given."

The girl sat up and scooted away from the wall, positioning herself so she had a better view of Lion's face. She crossed her legs underneath her, and Lion caught a brief glimpse of her skin before she adjusted her skirt over her knees. Propping one elbow on her thigh, she rested her chin on her palm, her eyes locked on his face with an expression of deep contemplation.

"What is the most delicious food you've ever tasted? The one that was so delicious, it felt like an explosion of taste in your mouth. Every bite is a bliss, and you are torn between devouring it as quickly as possible, and savouring each mouthful."

Lion felt heat rising to his neck. Was she still talking about food? He licked his lips and diverted his gaze from the bed. "There is no food that—" He stopped abruptly.

"What?" the girl perked up. She grinned. "You just thought of a food, didn't you? What is it?"

Lion shook his head.

"Come on, tell me. Tell me. What food is it?"

"Seafruit cake," Lion whispered. He wiped his mouth as if trying to get rid of the taste she had made him remember.

"Seafruit cake?" She arched an eyebrow. "So, your favourite food is Seafruit cake and your Masters don't know this about you."

Lion fidgeted restlessly. An odd guilt, mixed with fear, settled on his chest. If somehow Badimar knew that he had a favourite food, there would be punishment. Slaves were not meant to have preferred foods. It was a stupid notion. What was the point? He would eat whatever he was given.

The cake was nice, though. The fruit was common, and just the right mixture of sour and sweet.

He wiped his mouth again. He was done with this conversation. He sat up straight, ready to drag her to the bed and...

She put a hand on his chest and pushed him back down. She tilted her chin in a commanding manner and demanded, "Call me Saradra."

Lion blinked.

"Saradra," the girl said. "That's my name. Call me Saradra."

Lion scowled at the determined set of her lips. Her demeanour suddenly shifted, becoming serious and somehow desperate. He crossed his arms, his jaw clenching. He shook his head.

She scooted closer, her eyes narrowing with a mix of annoyance and something that resembled hunger. Lion could feel the heat of her presence, her closeness making his pulse quicken.

"Why not? That's my name," she insisted.

"No. You don't have a name. You're a slave."

Anger flickered across her features. Lion sensed this was important to her, though he didn't understand why. A stubbornness set into him. The tension between them thickened, her eyes pleading while Lion's were fixed on the wall across the room. Her frustration grew, making the air around them feel heavy.

"My name is Saradra," she said harshly. "Call me Saradra."

Lion stood, grabbing her arms and pulling her up with him. "Your name is what your Owner chooses to call you," he whispered and savoured that look of hatred and hurt. He dragged her towards the bed.

"My name is Saradra," she protested, a subtle quiver in her voice.

"You're a slave."

"You're a pig." She yanked her arm free and slapped him.

Lion touched his cheek, marvelling at the burning sensation her palm had left behind. Why was she so mad about his words? He wasn't even insulting her, or swearing at her. He was simply stating the truth.

He reached to pull her dress off, but she danced out of his grasp. She undid the tied pieces of the dress and shrugged out of it in a hurry, as if worried Lion would tear it again. She let him scoop her onto the bed and climb on top of her.

He froze before he went further than that.

Footsteps. He heard footsteps outside the room. From the way the girl's eyes widened, she had heard them too. They both recognised Badimar's heavy tread.

The girl's fragile body, still carrying the bruises left by Badimar's fists, seemed to shrink under him, burrowed between his arms. He saw a reflection of his own thoughts on her face; was he coming here? Had he heard them talk? Did he somehow find out?

Badimar's footsteps moved past the door, pausing for a moment before continuing into the room next door. Lion listened intently as the sounds of Badimar's routine filled the silence. First, the rustle of clothes being discarded, then the water jug being poured, followed by the faint splash of water. Each sound was louder than usual, magnified by Lion's heightened alertness.

He reminded himself that Badimar could not possibly know what the girl was making him do, because if he did, Lion would have already been punished. Still, he didn't relax until he heard the soft thud of boots hitting the floor and Badimar's bed creaking under his weight as he settled in for the night.

The girl let out a breath. The paleness of her face made Lion hesitate. She seemed shaken. Lion was torn between climbing out of the bed and giving her some time, or going ahead with what he was about to do. Frustrated and disappointed at himself, he moved to withdraw.

She wrapped her arms around his waist and pulled him back. Holding onto his shoulders, she lifted herself up, brought her mouth to his ear, and whispered, "Please, I need this."

Her request melted the knots in Lion's stomach. He didn't make her ask twice. He pressed his finger over her lips, warning her to be quiet as he slipped inside her. The bed was old, forcing them to move with deliberate care to avoid its telltale creaks. It infuriated Lion that he couldn't ravage her like he did the previous night. He had to restrain himself, move slow and tender, and be much more gentle than she deserved. It drove him insane.

The girl moved with him, her hands exploring him with an urgency that made Lion's blood rush faster. Lion felt out of breath, his muscles sore from the tension of holding himself back. A feral growl threatened to escape his lips. He buried his face in her neck to stifle that sound and he bit her shoulder, not hard enough to break her skin, but enough to leave a bruise. He clamped his palm over her mouth to muffle the delicious noise she made. He held her like that, pinned by his hand and his teeth, as she went over the edge. He savoured the violent shudders that rocked her body, thrusting himself deep and slow to draw out her pleasure. She clung to him, hungry and desperate, as he released himself.

They lay beside each other, spent and out of breath, their legs entangled. Lion stared at the mark he had left on her skin, glistening wet and slightly bruised. He imagined himself leaving marks like that on all over her body. He rested his eyes, relieved to hear the uninterrupted sound of Badimar's distant snoring.

Before he drifted into sleep, he came up with an excuse for not killing the girl tonight as well. Something about Badimar being next door, and not wanting to make any noise. Despite knowing it wasn't a great excuse, he still convinced himself. When he noticed the girl had fallen asleep between his arms, snuggled against his chest, he decided against turning her towards the wall like he did before. He let her sleep there, telling himself it was to avoid any unnecessary noise. He ignored the unexpected sense of peace her closeness brought him.

15

OLIRA

OLIRA STOOD BY THE counter, scraping the last bit of stew from the pot onto a plate. The background chatter of her brothers filled the room. They were arguing over something Olira wasn't paying attention to. She was focused on scooping the last bit of juice and vegetables from the bottom of the pot.

The living area of the farmhouse was cozy, the flickering light from the fireplace casting a warm glow over the furniture. Olira glanced at the sturdy wooden table, which was still cluttered with dinner dishes. "Torren?" she called to the boy who sat slumped on one of the five mismatched chairs. "Finish your food."

Torren looked up. "I'm not hungry."

Olira hated how Torren's voice was still hoarse and scratchy. His neck was bruised, and every now and then, he winced.

"Try to eat a bit more."

Torren looked down at his plate, his shoulders sagging. He forced a spoonful of stew into his mouth and winced as he swallowed. He put his spoon down, looking at Olira with a silent plea.

"Fine," she said. "Bring it over here."

Olira added Torren's leftovers onto the plate as well.

"Go to the root cellar and get me a pouch of *Numbleaf*."

Torren scowled. "But those are for selling," he whispered.

"Mix two drinks. One for you and bring the other one here." She pointed at the tray she was preparing. A pile of clean bandages, water, towels and a warm poultice filled half the tray.

"I don't need—"

"Don't argue, Torren. You sound like a croaking frog. Go."

Torren dragged his feet to the door. Olira took the pot to the large wooden basin, where the twins were squabbling over something instead of doing the dishes like she asked them to. "What's going on here?" she snapped.

"Andar's not scrubbing properly!"

"Yes I am!"

"I can still see grease there!"

"Well then, you do it!"

"I was on scrubbing duty yesterday. It's my turn to dry now."

Olira rubbed her forehead. Keeping up with the twins, even when they were standing still and just talking, required an effort that Olira couldn't spare tonight. She dumped the pot into the basin. "Stop squabbling and work faster. I want these done before I'm back."

"Can I come?" Kowas asked eagerly. "I wanna see him."

"No!" Olira said, her throat clenching. Kowas jumped at her tone, but Andar seemed unfazed. "You will both stay away from him. Do not go near him. Do you understand me?"

"Are we still gonna have to do the dishes once he's feeling better?" Andar asked, oblivious to how Olira's nostrils flared and the corner of her eye twitched.

"What?"

"Kantors have a slave and Tane says he never has to do the dishes or muck out the barn anymore."

Olira went cold with fury. "We're not keeping him."

"But Gilann says dad hated people who bought and sold slaves. But if we keep him and treat him nice, of course he still has to do the dishes, then we won't be—"

"We are not keeping him." Finally, Olira's frighteningly calm and low tone drew Andar's attention. The boy looked up, his eyes widening at Olira's expression. He bit his lips. Olira willed him to keep his mouth shut, but the boy didn't know how. When the words filled his mouth, he did not know how to swallow them back.

"But if we sell him—" Andar started, but Kowas elbowed his brother hard enough to make him yelp. Andar forgot what he was about to say, and the two of them squabbled over whether Andar's ribs were broken or not.

Olira walked away and praised herself for resisting the urge to dunk both their heads in the basin and slap them until they understood minding their own business. She resumed preparing the tray to take to the barn, her patience wearing thin. It was already dark and she would need a lantern too. She glanced at the armchairs positioned near the hearth, promising herself at least a few minutes relaxing by the fire after she was finished at the barn. She needed to just sit and think about nothing.

"That's not enough," Gilann said as he loomed over the plate, his expression grim. Olira sighed. She was wondering when he would come and talk to her.

"I know." She went to the pantry to get the man some more food. Gilann followed her. He crossed his arms, leaning against the doorframe, as he watched her with disapproval.

"You shouldn't have bought him."

"Gilann, I told you what happened," she hissed as she reached for a chunk of cheese and half a loaf of bread. "I'm sick of trying to explain myself. What would you have done? Walk away and forget about that money?"

"At least we wouldn't have another throat to feed," Gilann said. He thumbed over his shoulder at Torren, who had returned with the *Numbleaf* and was mixing it with two cups of hot water. "And we wouldn't have to use the stuff we put aside for selling."

"He's in a lot of pain. Would you prefer I let him suffer and starve?"

Gilann at least had the sense to blush. "That's not what I'm saying. It's just... You should have..."

Olira yanked him into the pantry and pulled the door closed, so the others wouldn't hear them. She pierced him with an icy stare, her voice dripping with anger. "Two hundred and fifty Blues, Gilann!" Gilann's expression darkened, though his eyes grew large. "That's what Gladwiel said he's worth. Two hundred and fifty Blues."

Gilann swallowed, shifting his weight from one foot to the other. He tried to hold Olira's gaze, but caved in and looked away. "This isn't right"

Olira had to soften her voice, because the look of shame on Gilann's face was heartbreaking. And she had been hiding that same look under a mask of outrage. "I know. But not only can we pay Master Tholthus, we won't even have to think about money for the next ten years!"

She paused for a moment to let Gilann imagine a future where they didn't have to stress about the next winter. She bit her tongue to stop herself from reminding him that with that much money, Gilann could finally marry Elara and move to Brinescar like he always wanted. She could see that Gilann was already fantasizing about that future, and feeling dirty and conflicted about himself.

"Two hundred and fifty Blues, Gilann." She squeezed his arm before walking back out. She added the bread and the cheese to the plate, and took the cup of *Numbleaf* tea from Torren. She sent the boy to sit and rest by the hearth, eliciting jealous protests from Andar and Kowas. Gilann came back out of the pantry just in time to help her balance the tray in one arm while holding the lantern in the other.

"It still feels dirty," Gilann said as he held the door open for her. He gritted his teeth, but at least the target of his resentment wasn't Olira anymore. "If Mum and Dad knew what we were doing, they would be—"

"Don't. Don't finish that sentence." Olira glared at him, though it was her turn to look away this time. Tears welled in her eyes, and a lump sat in her throat. She straightened her shoulders and composed herself.

"It's okay," Gilann said softly. He shrugged, trying to look casual, as he searched for something to grasp onto. "Well, at least he's a purebred."

"So?"

"It's not like…" Gilann shrugged again, scratching the back of his head. "You know… He doesn't know any better. It's just… I feel like it would have been worse if he was a freeborn or something."

Olira understood what he meant. If the slave was a freeborn, who had a family somewhere, who resented Olira for what she was doing, who hated the life he was condemned to, it would have been much harder.

"They say purebreds don't care, because it's the only life they know. You know?"

It didn't make her feel any better, it just kept her from feeling any worse.

"Just make sure Andar and Kowas finish their chores and get to bed."

Olira walked to the barn, the tray weighing heavy in her arms. The cold night air nipped at her skin. It was still early Autumn but felt colder than last year. She avoided thinking about how cold the barn was going to be soon. She focused on how well the slave was improving.

It had been three days since Varelya drained the infection. The purebred had slept through most of it, eating and drinking when Olira brought pureed food to his mouth, groaning softly when Olira tended to his wound. She drained the pus, applied warm poultice, and changed his bandages every day. The slave's eyes remained closed the entire time. His fever had reduced, and this morning Olira had noticed that the redness around the wound had started to recede too. He would pull through.

She pushed open the barn door, the soft creak of the hinges blending with the gentle rustling of the animals inside. She stepped in, the lantern's warm glow casting flickering shadows around the space. Warrior stuck his head out from his stall and greeted her. The mule at least seemed to be rested and happy.

As she walked to the slave's stall, she expected to find the man sleeping again. She froze abruptly, almost dropping the tray.

The slave sat with his back against the wall, his head down, his arms at his sides. It must have cost him an effort to sit up. He didn't move, but he slightly lowered his face as if the lantern's light disturbed his eyes. Despite his stillness, there was an air of intimidation about him. His broad shoulders and muscular frame seemed to fill the small space, making the stall feel cluttered.

He was still chained to the wall, the heavy iron collar snug around his neck. The chain lay slack over his shoulder, its length coiled beside him on the floor. Olira had turned the stretcher into a makeshift bed for him, piling it with heaps of blankets to keep him warm. Despite her efforts to make him comfortable, the sight of the chain was a stark reminder of what he was.

Olira took a hesitant step in, then forced herself to take a couple more steps. She deliberately avoided glancing at the hoop she had nailed to the wall. Putting the tray and the lantern down, she approached a couple more steps and looked down at the slave. She crossed her arms to hide her slightly trembling hands.

"Look at me," she said firmly.

The man slowly lifted his head, his eyes locking onto hers. In the dim light, they looked dark, almost black, and his stare was vacant. No emotion. No anger, no resentment for what she had done to him. No fear. His face was shadowed by a few days' worth of beard. The stubble and the dark circles that underscored his eyes added to his rugged appearance.

Olira held that intense stare for as long as she could, ignoring the chill that ran down her spine. She stood a bit straighter, her expression hardening. "I don't want to say the word," she said, her tone sharp. "Will you stay still?"

"Yes, Owner," the man said as he looked down at the straw covered floor.

Olira took a deep breath, reminding herself that the man was harmless. He was a purebred, for Twelve's sake. They were raised to obey. Since the day he attacked Torren, he hadn't displayed any other sign of aggression. She picked up the mug of *Numbleaf* tea and held it out to him. "This is for your pain. It's not as strong as the other one, but..."

The slave took the mug and drank it all without a complaint. He handed it back to her.

"I'll clean your wound and change your bandages, and then you can eat," she said as she brought the tray closer. The man didn't reply. Olira sat down, the straw crunching softly beneath her knees.

She set to work. She pulled the blankets off his lap. She had cut the side of his pants so she could access the bandages without taking his pants off each time. She carefully peeled away the old bandages, her fingers trembling slightly. The wound showed signs of healing. The swelling had reduced, and there was hardly any discharge. She cleaned the wound with the clean water and towel she had prepared, then reached for the poultices.

Her hands steadied as she worked, though her stomach still churned. She applied the poultices carefully, pressing the herbal mixture against the wound like Varelya had instructed. Olira's eyes flicked to the slave's face, searching for any reaction. The man didn't flinch, but she could see the subtle tightening of his jaw, the slight tensing of his muscles that hinted at the pain he was enduring.

She worked faster, putting the poultice aside and grabbing the fresh bandages. The tension that built on her shoulders and the knots in her stomach annoyed her. The purebred hadn't moved; his eyes still fixed on the floor, his hands relaxed at his side, his breathing shallow and controlled. He was perfectly still, doing exactly what she had asked him to do. Yet, there was something unnatural about him that made Olira want to hurry and get out of here.

"Stay still," she said, out of a need to fill the chilling silence, and also to steady herself. Even the animals were quiet in their stalls. Everyone but her felt calm and content, while her heart raced like she was alone in the woods and surrounded by a pack of wolves. Or trapped by a lone mountain lion.

She couldn't put her finger on why she felt so intimidated by the purebred. Was it the way he was built — a living instrument of violence — or his eerie calmness? She would have felt safer if he was yelling or sputtering threats and insults at her, or trembling in terror, or grumbling with resentment, or crying out in pain. Showing any emotion other than that vacant stare he fixed on the stray patterns of straw on the damp floor.

She finished up and gathered her things on the tray. She pushed the plate towards the man, noting how meagre the food looked now, compared to his size. Standing up, she brushed the straw and dirt from her skirt.

"I'll come back in the morning," she muttered pointlessly. The barn seemed to close in around her, the slave's silence growing heavier. She picked up the tray and the lantern, and nearly bolted out of the barn, leaving the slave in the dark.

The cool air hit her like a splash of water as she let out a shaky breath. Even after she settled on her armchair by the fire, she still couldn't silence the voice in her head, screaming at her that something was profoundly wrong about this purebred.

16

LION

"WHY ARE YOU BEING stubborn about this?" the girl whose name *was not* Saradra hissed. "My name is Saradra. Just call me Saradra."

Lion heaved, taking deep breaths to settle his stomach. He was slumped against the wall. He forced his rigid muscles to relax as he fought to shake that suffocating fear and sickness.

"Because it's not your name," he growled.

"I was born with that name."

"And you lost it when you were enslaved."

She made an angry noise that sounded more cute than intimidating. "Then look at me again."

Lion groaned, his shoulders sagging with dread. "Will you stop this if I call you that name?"

"Will you actually do it if I say yes?"

Lion made a noise that was half sigh, half growl. He breathed through the knot in his stomach, bracing himself for the discomfort, and looked up to meet her gaze. Just before he doubled over with a bout of nausea, he saw tears in her eyes.

Why was she crying over this? It was so stupid!

But shaking with the memory of a pain that wasn't really there was stupid, too. He swam through it and emerged on the other side, slowly regaining control of his trembling muscles. When he searched her face with a quick glance, he saw no trace of tears.

"Okay." She offered him a casual smile. She sat facing him, her knee touching his. She tilted her head, drawing Lion's gaze to the bruise he had left on her shoulder the previous night. "Tell me something about yourself."

Lion rolled his eyes. He rested his head back and stared at the wall. "What?"

"Tell me about the map."

Lion glanced at the bed like he wanted to bludgeon it with a war hammer. He cursed the day he first saw the map.

"Why did you draw it?"

"I don't know." He shrugged. "There is no reason."

"Which one is it? There is no reason, or you don't know the reason."

Lion let out a deep sigh. "I don't know."

She chewed her hair, staring at him like he was a puzzle to figure out, so she could smash it into pieces. "That's the map from the Throne Room, isn't it? The one on the floor?"

He nodded.

"When did you first see it?"

Lion shrugged. "A few years ago."

"What did you think when you first looked at it?"

"Nothing."

"Did you think it was beautiful? I mean, it really was exquisite."

"I didn't think anything."

"What did you feel..."

"Nothing."

She crossed her arms, one hand moving the rest on her chin. Her brows furrowed, and a frown played on her lips. "I'm just trying to understand why you drew it."

Lion didn't bother repeating himself, he had already told her he didn't know why he drew the map. Her relentless questioning wasn't going to suddenly make him realise the answer. He scratched his brand on his chest distractedly. It was still itching, though he hardly felt the ache anymore. And his shoulder, still bandaged snugly, only hurt if he strained it.

The girl was quiet again, her fingers drumming on her lips. Moonlight highlighted her features with a soft glow. Outside, the summer wind rustled the leaves, creating a lulling background noise. Lion eyed the bed eagerly. It was getting late. But the girl was still having fun with her odd little interrogation.

"Do you want to travel Chinderia one day?"

"I don't want anything," he said quickly.

"You're right, there's not much to travel. Just the same cesspit all around." She paused. "Maybe except Northern Chinderia. Especially West Kilrer. I've heard most people there don't keep slaves."

Lion didn't reply. There wasn't any question for him, so he was content letting her resume the conversation on her own.

"I've heard some countries don't keep slaves at all. Slavery is banned in the entire country. Can you imagine that?"

Lion shook his head. It sounded like a myth freeborns would trick themselves into believing. Like how their *rhoas* could still one day travel to Farhome and be free. Or how the Twelve Riders still watched over them if they prayed in secret.

"Do you want to travel to those countries one day?"

Lion shook his head again.

"Why not?"

"I don't want anything."

"Wouldn't you want to live a better life?"

"I don't *want* anything."

"Right." The girl paused, her eyebrows lifting with amusement. She smirked and rolled her eyes. "I forgot about that. Wanting is an Act of Defiance, isn't it? And it's the silliest amongst them." She chuckled.

Lion shot a glance at the door, clenching his fists. Was she trying to be heard? If Badimar or someone else walked in and started beating the girl... His throat tightened. At least she had the sense to cover her mouth and keep it down.

"When I first heard this one," she continued, whispering, but still with a mocking smile at the corners of her lips, "I thought they were *joking*. Like they can actually stop a person from wanting things. From feeling desire."

Lion clenched his jaw, staring at his lap. He didn't bother educating the girl about the training methods slave breeders used on young purebreds at the ranches. He knew for certain that they could scrape every drop of desire out of anyone.

"Even purebreds want things," she continued wryly.

"Not purebreds."

"No amount of beating can stop a person from wanting things. It's in our nature."

Beating. She thought, that's all they did. She had never been to a ranch. She was enslaved, and then probably only spent a few weeks tops at a slave merchant's warehouse. That wasn't the same.

Remembering Faychill Ranch invited that cold, hollow void inside Lion's chest. The gravity pulled him down into the harsh stone floor beneath him. "I don't. *Want*. Anything," he said flatly.

The girl quietened, noticing the change in his tone. She searched his face, her hands on her lap, and her head slightly tilted. That smug, confident grin vanished from her face, replaced by pity. She opened and closed her mouth several times before she spoke. "What about food? Drink? You want to eat when you're hungry, don't you?"

"I live to serve, I breathe to please."

"So?"

"I *live* to serve, I breathe to please."

She nodded slowly. "You eat and drink because you have to *live*. Okay, fine. What about survival? You want to survive. Why else would you fight and work so hard to be a good, obedient slave?"

"*I live to serve, I breathe to please.*"

"You *want* me to keep your secret, to stay quiet about the map..."

"I *need* you to stay quiet, so I can continue to *live to serve and breathe to please.*"

Her scowl deepened. "Don't you want a life without pain? Without chains?" Her voice dropped, quieter than a whisper. "Freedom?"

"No."

The stone wall behind him sent a chill through his clothes and into his bones. His eyes were still unfocused on his lap. His thoughts briefly drifted to the arenas, specifically to the moment when he wakes up from his Rage, victorious. The empowering weight of his weapon in his hand as he salutes his Owner on one knee.

"I live to serve, I breathe to please," he said numbly.

"What about last night?" she whispered. "And the night before?"

Lion shrugged. "I follow my orders."

"Your orders are to bed me. Not to make me moan and leave me spent and trembling with such intense pleasure that I almost forgot my name." She spoke in a hushed tone, and she bit her lower lip, as if barely keeping herself from saying more. Her cheeks flushed as she watched him with hunger. "You want that again."

Lion shook his head, but she shuffled closer. Her eyes were intense as they perused him from head to toe, lingering in places, not hiding her lust. "Go ahead and deny. You can't lie to yourself."

She reached and touched his chest, her palm flat over his heart. A thrill went through Lion's body. His heart raced and his breath hitched. She felt the strength of his heartbeat and smiled as if she had just proved a point. "You want it, don't you?" she whispered. "I know I do."

Her admission ignited a primal emotion inside his chest. He stamped it down. He grabbed her wrist and pushed it away. "I follow my orders."

"I think we already established what your orders are and aren't." She gathered his hand between hers and brought it to her mouth. She kissed his palm softly, her breath caressing his skin. Her soft lips brushed past his forearm and planted another kiss on his elbow. She continued up his arm and kissed an old knife scar from a fight several years ago. She kissed his bandaged shoulder.

Lion grabbed her arm to push her away, but couldn't. The girl's lips were gentle on his chest, almost hesitant, like savouring a new experience. Lion's eyes rolled back in his skull, his head resting against the hard stone behind him. She kissed her way up his chest, her mouth becoming bolder with each kiss. Her lips traced the line of his collarbone. Lion's throat bobbed. His fingers still trapped her arm, but he didn't push her.

Finally, her lips reached his neck, and Lion let out a soft groan. Her warm breath sent shivers through his body. She moaned quietly as she kissed his jaw, her lips brushing against his beard. She cupped his cheek, guiding him to face her.

Lion closed his eyes, though he couldn't unsee the desperate thirst and desire he glimpsed on her face.

"Do you want to kiss me?" she whispered. Her face was so close to his, her breath caressed his lips when she talked.

Lion pressed his lips tight and swallowed. The girl's mouth was right there, almost touching his. He wondered how she would taste. The memory of the other night, how those lips wrapped around his fingers, filled his mind. It was hard to distract himself from those images, especially with his eyes closed. But he couldn't dare open them, because the girl's eyes were right in front of his face. He felt vulnerable and powerless, despite still holding the girl's arm in his grip.

"Do you want to kiss me?" she repeated, her voice laced with need, and a hint of plead.

"I don't... want anything."

"Prove it," she whispered. "Prove it to yourself." Her lips brushed against his when she spoke, teasing him, sending a jolt of thrill down his core. *Struck by lightning.* He understood that lover's tale now, how Elrimandel felt when he first saw Galeahil. He inhaled a deep breath to steady himself, which turned out to be a mistake, because now the girl's scent left him teetering on the brink. With his eyes closed, his sense of smell was sharpened, much harder to ignore. Her sweet aroma, a mixture of soap and something uniquely her own, intoxicated him.

"Do you want to kiss me?" The girl's voice trembled slightly as she asked again, almost begging.

The vulnerability in her tone pierced through Lion's defences. Every inhale drew him deeper into the scent of her, making it harder to remember why he was resisting in the first place. He focused on his grip, willing his hand to push her away just enough so he could turn his head, open his eyes, and breathe air that wasn't tainted with her captivating scent.

She felt the weak but determined pressure of Lion's hand pressing against her, pushing her away. "Look at me," she said sharply.

Lion felt the desperate fear and nausea rising again. Then he decided maybe this was a good thing. The pain could help snap him out of this spell she put him under, remind him who he was, and why he had to resist. He opened his eyes.

The girl's eyes were filled with longing and disappointment. And their colour was such a bright blue, it made the rest of the room seem grey and dull. Lion's stomach churned, and his muscles cramped with pain.

The girl leaned in and crushed her lips against his.

A warm wave washed over him, countering that icy fear and pain. For a moment, Lion remained rigid, his hands still on her arms as if to push her away. He tasted the heat of her desire, so hot it melted his resistance. The thrill she ignited in him collided against the haunting memories of pain, not strong enough to completely wash them away, but enough to keep them from claiming him.

She kept the pain at bay!

When Lion leaned into the kiss, his resolve shattering to pieces, the warmth in his chest grew stronger. It was as if her kiss had reached into the darkest corners of his mind, pulling him out of the shadows and into the light. He pulled her in closer, deepening the kiss, and allowed himself to be carried away, like surrendering to a torrent. And the pain, and dread, and numbness, and fear... they were all left behind on the shore, unable to follow him.

She broke the kiss to gasp for air, her lips red and swollen, her cheeks flushed. She had somehow ended up on his lap, her legs straddling him. His arms wrapped around her, cradling her against his chest. Holding her like she belonged there.

"I want you to want me," she whispered, out of breath. She started landing small, hungry kisses all over his face, mouthing, sucking, nibbling. "I need you to want me." She hardly broke her kisses as she spoke. "Let yourself want me. Just for tonight. Allow yourself. Free yourself."

Lion groaned hungrily. His hands slipped down her back, trailing down her legs. They snaked under her dress, journeying up her smooth thighs. His fingers found her core, bare and drenched.

"Do you want me?" she whispered in his ear.

He stood up with her still on his lap. She clung to his shoulders and locked her legs around his waist. Lion spun and pressed her against the wall.

As he looked up and met her eyes, his stomach twisted, anticipating the familiar pain. That dread and discomfort would always be there; he doubted it would ever get easier. But he maintained her gaze, engraving that bright blue colour into his memory as the pain drew nearer, surging closer.

Lion leaned in and answered her question with a long, consuming kiss that left them both gasping for more. He let the desire in, freeing himself from the restraints. Ignoring the broken voice in his head screaming that this was bad, that this would be his demise, he surrendered to the moment.

And that little voice was right, because the next day at training, Lion started making mistakes.

17

LION

The Feline Yard was shaded by the Western walls, offering a welcome respite for the king's beasts who trained there vigorously under the afternoon sun.

Lion stood on a balance pole, his upper body bare, except for a pair of brass arm guards. Joharin walked around the pole with a basket full of hand-sized rocks. He threw them at him with a deceptive flick of his wrist, giving no hint and trying to catch him off-guard. Lion either dodged or parried the rocks with his arm guards, keeping his balance at the same time.

This was one of the easier exercises. He switched his feet and continued to trace Joharin's body language with quick glances. The older trainer was good at keeping his face blank. He picked up a rock, threw it up, caught it, inspected it closely, and then threw it at Lion with incredible speed. Lion deflected it with his right armguard and shifted his weight to keep his balance.

Piece of cake.

He wished the girl's tasks were this easy, too. Finding something new to tell her about himself was more difficult than he ever imagined. It had been three nights since he had discovered his desire for her. Three nights since he had admitted he wanted her with such intense craving, it horrified him. He was doomed. If his Masters knew how much he was looking forward to finishing this boring drill and heading back to his room so he could have her like his life depended on it, he would be screwed. He would be sent back to Faychill Ranch for some retraining for at least a few months. Or worse, straight to White Tower.

Lion dodged the next rock Joharin sent from his right, keeping his balance without breaking a sweat. This wasn't his *favourite* drill. He still found the concept of favourite stupid and pointless. The other night, they had a ridiculously long conversation that left them both frustrated and confused when the girl asked him what his favourite weapon was. She would not accept the answer that as a purebred, Lion was trained in multiple combat classes and styles, and was extremely efficient with a range of weapons. She had then asked which weapon he was most comfortable with, and Lion's answer was the same — that he was comfortable with many. And then she had rolled her eyes and asked if he was presented with a selection of weapons, which one would he pick. But when Lion asked perfectly reasonable follow-up questions — was he allowed an armour, or a shield? What was his opponent equipped with? Would he be Raged or Unraged? — she had seemed infuriated.

Eventually, they had discovered that Lion did have a preference. As foolish as it sounded, he did have a *favourite* weapon. It was a lor'qas paired with a tall shield. Not only he was extremely efficient, confident, and experienced with it, he also enjoyed wielding that weapon.

Every time he told her something about himself that his Masters didn't know, the cold fingers of anxiety strangled him. He knew he shouldn't harbour opinions. He shouldn't have favourites or preferences. He shouldn't desire. Desire led to wanting. Wanting led to taking. And taking was a gateway to defiance. He was acutely aware of what the girl was doing to him. She was eroding his purebred discipline, slowly breaking him. Yet he couldn't resist her. The moment he admitted his desire for her, he found himself addicted.

Every whispered conversation was concluded with hungry, passionate kisses that made Lion forget all about getting into trouble. The world outside the room stopped existing for a few hours. He was ever so thirsty for her body. No matter how many times he took her, he could never have enough. The way she touched and kissed him proved she longed for his body, too. Seeing how much she wanted him, how she shared his pleasure, was a thrill.

He swatted another rock with a lazy wave of his arm and switched his feet. What was he going to tell her about himself tonight? Her annoying game forced him to reflect on himself. Discover himself in a way he hadn't before.

He shuddered.

Moreover, there was the eye contact component of the game. She pointed out that he had at least stopped throwing up out of pain and fear. She acted like this was a victory, an improvement, but Lion's body was still convinced it was painful. Unless he distracted himself by kissing her immediately after, he still slumped against the wall, shivering with dread.

It helped that at least her eyes were beautiful to look at. He wanted to...

The rock hit the side of his head. He flapped his arms to catch his balance, failed, and fell.

He wasn't knocked out for long. It felt like he had only blinked, and Joharin was there, hovering over him, cursing nonstop.

"Injuries?" the old trainer barked between curses.

"No, Master," Lion blurted out without hesitation. He hadn't even finished mentally assessing his body, but the answer to that question was always 'no'. He couldn't have any injuries. He couldn't...

He jumped up to his feet — ignoring the disturbing pang on his elbow — and stood ready with his hands clasped in front of him. He discretely moved his fingers, confirming nothing was broken. Joharin looked him up and down, dismissed the bloody graze on his elbow, and nodded.

"Good," the old trainer snorted before punching him in the face.

Despite seeing the punch coming even before Joharin had curled his fingers into a fist, Lion didn't move to defend himself. He stood motionless, hands down, with not so much as a flinch.

If your Owners choose to inflict physical pain, you must receive it with respect, Breeder Astaldo had taught him. The slave breeder had beaten him regularly until he had learned not to raise his hands to defend himself, or flinch, or turn his head away.

Joharin's knuckles connected with his jaw, sending a jolt of pain. He blinked it away. The other beasts continued their drills, led by Doha and Caesh, without so much as a second glance. Joharin punched his stomach next, while Lion *received it with respect*. When the old trainer drew his fist back for a third time, Badimar stopped him with a hand on his arm.

"*Prihjtivaviula*," Badimar said.

Lion sunk into the pit of pain. Joharin and Badimar stepped out of the range of his thrashing legs. They waited coldly while he finished being tortured. As soon as the pain receded enough for him to regain control, Lion pulled his knees underneath, pressed his forehead on the ground, and wrapped his arms around his head, holding back a whimper.

"Up," Badimar ordered and Lion jumped up to his feet, his knees still shaking from the pain.

Badimar stepped closer until Lion could smell the staleness of his breath. "What is wrong with you, Lion?" Badimar growled quietly. The glimmer of fury in his eyes contrasted with the fake calmness of his voice. "You fucked up your steps yesterday. You let Crow land a blow on you the day before. You don't make mistakes. Ever. *What the fuck is up with you?*"

"I am well, Master," Lion said.

"We have three months left until the *Serpent's Grip*," Badimar continued. "Three months! Are you physically unwell?"

"No, Master."

"Then why the fuck did you fall?"

"The rock hit my head, and I lost balance, Master."

The veins on Badimar's neck bulged and his whole face flushed red. He closed his eyes, took a deep breath, then placed his hand on Lion's shoulder. It was surprisingly gentle. It made Lion's stomach churn with alarm.

"Tell me, Lion," he said with an eerie softness in his tone. "I'm listening. Tell me, why did you get hit by that rock?"

"I couldn't block or dodge it, Master," Lion answered weakly. He didn't trust this fake patience at all. Badimar was pissed and Lion had accepted he was fucked.

"And why didn't you block it?"

"I did not see it coming, Master."

"You did not see..." Badimar took another deep breath, visibly forcing himself to remain calm. "Why? Were you not looking?"

"I was looking, Master."

"And you still didn't see it?"

"No, Master."

Suspicion flashed across Badimar's face as he glanced at the fading scratch mark near Lion's left eye. It had almost healed completely. "Is there anything wrong with your eyesight?" he asked carefully.

"No, Master."

Vanalten had already checked his eyesight after the event, confirming there was no damage. Badimar already knew this. He nodded thoughtfully. His next question took Lion by surprise.

"Were you looking with your eyes, or with your mind?"

"With... my eyes, Master."

"Then, what was your mind looking at?"

Lion didn't want to confess what he was thinking. He shouldn't have been thinking at all. He should have been focusing on the drill, keeping his mind blank and ready. The lie slipped out of his lips without intention: "I don't know, Master."

Badimar's eyes narrowed. His intense stare raked Lion's face for any hint of deception, but purebreds didn't lie, and Lion's face was perfectly blank, though his heart was beating wildly. If he thought Lion was being dishonest, he didn't let it show. "Your mind was occupied with something," Badimar muttered, more to himself.

It wasn't a question, neither was it an order, so Lion remained silent.

Badimar casually put his arm around Lion's shoulder and rested his hand behind his head. The gesture appeared friendly and disarming, though it didn't put Lion at ease. If anything, it only made him more nervous. "You were distracted," Badimar decided, nodding thoughtfully.

Joharin's eyebrows shot up in surprise. Purebreds didn't get distracted. What could possibly distract them from a training drill? Badimar's statement still wasn't a question, so Lion resumed his silence.

Badimar grabbed a handful of Lion's hair in his fist and yanked firmly. It was a warning pain. "Tell me the truth," he ordered. "What is distracting you?"

An order and a direct question. It gave Lion little room to wiggle. He couldn't lie, but he was going to be punished, anyway. He just wanted to avoid getting a worse punishment.

He *wanted* to avoid pain.

"I don't know, Master," he said carefully, keeping his voice flat.

"It's that bitch," Badimar growled. His voice was still calm, but his grip tightened, sending a jolt of pain through Lion's scalp. "That bitch is distracting you."

Her name is Saradra, Lion thought unexpectedly, surprising himself. Standing next to him, Joharin's mouth gaped in disbelief. Badimar still hadn't asked a question. Despite his querying tone, he was only confirming what he already knew. Lion pressed his lips shut and once again took refuge behind the silence. He focused on the dirt floor beneath his feet, not letting himself witness the promises Badimar's face offered.

His scalp throbbed sharply as Badimar's pull intensified. Then, the Master of the Beasts pushed him towards the centre of the training yard. "Turn around. On your knees."

Lion did as he was ordered. He rested his hands on his knees, ducked his head between his shoulders, and braced. He focused on a spot on the dirt ground as he waited. *Not my body, it's their property*, he thought, willing his mind to crawl into *that place* before Badimar started.

It didn't work.

Lion swallowed, narrowing his eyes. Doha and Caesh had stopped to watch, not heeding any attention to the beasts. Purebreds continued their drills as if nothing was happening, but the two freeborns threw occasional glances at Lion. Behind him, he heard the crisp snap of leather as Badimar pulled his whip from his belt.

Not my body, it's their property, Lion thought furiously. *Not my body. Not... Not my body*. He even closed his eyes, which only made it worse, because now the girl's eyes flashed across his mind, and the memory of her body grinding against *his* body filled his thoughts.

Not my body. Not...

He blinked his eyes open, trying to shake the images out of his head and focus. He had to escape his body and go hide in *that place* before Badimar started...

The whip cracked in the air and landed on Lion's back. He held back a gasp and breathed out slowly. The first one was always more tolerable, a sharp and stinging pain that surprised more than it hurt. It usually started becoming too painful after the third.

Lion locked his muscles in place and concentrated on enduring his punishment in silence. *Not my body...*

The second strike lit his back on fire. He took a sharp breath and held it in, his fists clenched on his knees.

Why couldn't he escape? It wouldn't stop the pain, but it would at least help him tolerate—

Crack, whoosh, pain.

Lion stopped counting. He had discovered that counting somehow intensified the pain. Blood trickled between his shoulder blades, down his waist. His skin felt tight and on fire.

It was the girl. The girl was somehow stopping him from summoning that numbness. Another crack, followed by a jolt of pain spreading across his back. Lion smothered a grunt and kept his fists on his knees.

Badimar could have inflicted more pain if he had used Lion's Pain Word. There was no other torture or punishment that could compete with the agony of that half a minute. However, Badimar's intention wasn't just to punish Lion now. He wanted Lion to learn a lesson, and he wanted it to be learnt over time. The flogging was going to hurt for days, reminding Lion the consequences of getting distracted by that girl's stupid games. Inspiring him to be more careful.

Badimar was a good trainer.

The next strike nearly made him collapse. He clenched his core muscles, willing himself to stay upright. Sweat beaded down his forehead, stinging his eyes. He braced for the next one.

"Get up," Badimar grunted. "Get your ass back on that pole."

Breathe in, breathe out...

As soon as he moved, a scorching pain exploded on Lion's back. All he could do was to gasp quietly and keep his face neutral. He wiped the sweat from his face, doing his best not to flinch as he staggered to the pole. Darkness creeped in at the edges of his vision, as he fought to stay conscious.

Breathe in, breathe out...

His body swayed with every agonizing step as he hauled himself onto the pole. His knees buckled slightly, and he wavered unsteadily. He balanced his weight on one foot and slowly stood.

Breathe. Focus.

He raised his arm guards, fixing his gaze straight ahead. Badimar borrowed a handful of rocks from Joharin. Together, they started circling the balance pole and throwing their rocks at him. Lion tracked their movements through a haze of pain, his vision still blurry. He failed to deflect half the shots, but at least he didn't fall or get hit on the head.

After the balance pole, Badimar ran two more training drills with him, pushing him ruthlessly on each one. He almost seemed to test whether Lion would pass out or collapse. Several times, he came close to losing his consciousness, but he didn't.

After the other beasts were finished with their exercises, Badimar had Lion run laps around the training yard. It was only after the sun set that Lion was excused to go and have his dinner.

He skipped his bath. He couldn't imagine soaking his searing back in hot water. He put his tunic on, cringing at the friction of the fabric against the welts, and went straight to the kitchen. He forced himself to eat, despite having no appetite. His head down, he focused on his breathing; on not letting out any sound louder than an exhale.

Not until he returned to his room.

As soon as he closed the door behind him, he collapsed on his knees, letting out a strained cry.

"Merciful Alunwea!" the girl gasped. The smirk she had prepared for him was erased from her face. She rushed to his side, kneeling beside him. "What... What happened?"

When she placed her hand right in the middle of his back, Lion cried out in pain. He shoved her away, hard enough to send her stumbling into the wall.

No.

He ignored the look of shock and hurt on her face. He wasn't going to play her game tonight. No more. He squirmed to take his tunic off, recoiling every time the clothing brushed against his back. He walked to the basin and filled it with cold water.

Behind him, the girl gasped at the sight of his back. "What... Who did this to you?"

Lion didn't reply. He soaked the towel in water and reached back to dab it gently against his back.

"Here, let me do that for you."

When the girl tried to take the towel off him, Lion pushed her again. She tripped and fell onto the bed. Her eyes welled with tears as she gave him a wounded look. She didn't try to come near him again.

This was all her fault. She needed to stop what she was doing to him. She was compromising his training, his obedience, his focus. He couldn't let that happen. He didn't want to talk to her again. He didn't even want to be in the same room with her again.

He scowled at himself. There he was *wanting* and *not wanting* things. How was he ever going to undo what she had done to him?

He reached as far back as he could, dabbing the cold towel against his burning skin, desperately trying to ease the pain.

After watching him for a moment, the girl wiped that wounded expression off her face and replaced it with concern. She stood up hesitantly. She opened her mouth to speak to him, then changed her mind and sat back down, her shoulders sagged.

Pushing her away turned out to be the smartest decision Lion had made today. When Badimar barged into the room with no warning — no footsteps to give away his approach — they were at opposite sides of the small room, not even looking at each other's direction.

Lion straightened up to greet him, ignoring the jolt of pain on his back. The girl jumped to her feet.

The Master of the Beasts must have been hoping to catch them doing something they shouldn't have been doing — like chatting about Lion's *favourite* food or weapons — because his eyes flew between the two slaves, narrowed with suspicion. His gaze scanned the room next, dismissing the bloody towel in Lion's hand, before returning to the girl's face.

Lion's stomach twisted when Badimar walked up to her. Her bruises hadn't even fully recovered from the beating. Lion bit inside his cheek. If Badimar started beating her again... The fear sat like a rock on his chest, worse than what he felt earlier in the yard. He kept his head down, watching Badimar out of the corner of his eyes.

Don't piss him off, he thought desperately.

The girl looked at her toes, trembling slightly under Badimar's irritated gaze. After torturing them both with his silence for half a minute, "You will go to Vanalten first thing in the morning," Badimar finally growled. "Have him check whatever he needs to check to confirm you're with child. So I can get rid of you."

"Yes, Master," Saradra said without a beat. Her posture and her voice were submissive enough to please Badimar.

The Master of the Beasts scanned the room one more time, suspicion etched on his face. Not finding anything out of the ordinary, he stormed out.

The girl lowered herself onto the bed, shuddering and breathing heavily. When she glanced at Lion, he looked away and resumed trying to soothe his back, which felt like an impossible task. The more he tried to reach the welts, the worse it hurt. He gave up, feeling exhausted from fighting the pain all day. The towel slipped from his fingers as he sank to his knees. He was ready to pass out now. Just end the day. Take a break.

Her hands were gentle on his arm and she draped it around her shoulder to help him stand, and guided him to the bed. Lion collapsed on his stomach, breathing heavily. The searing pain made every breath a struggle. His muscles were tense, and an occasional shiver ran through his body. The girl soaked the towel in cold water and gently dabbed it against his back. Lion winced but didn't move. He was too exhausted. He wanted to sleep.

"This happened because of me," she whispered with sorrow. "I'm sorry."

Lion opened his eyes. Tears ran down the girl's face. She wiped them with the back of her hand and focused on cleaning the welts without causing more pain. Coolness of the towel at least gave him some relief.

"I'll stop," she said. "I promise. No more."

Something in the girl's voice pulled Lion back from the brink of passing out. He blinked, trying to focus on her words. *No more?* No more what? No more forcing him to talk and think? Good. That was what he wanted.

The girl started whispering calming words into his ear, telling him he was going to be okay, and that she was sorry. And she cried. Why? Why was she upset? Why was she backing off now? She dried her cheeks and dunked the towel in cold water again before gently pressing it, apologising over and over again.

No more talking. Good. He was better off left alone.

He closed his eyes, so exhausted, yet he still couldn't lose consciousness. Like his mind refused to drift. The girl's quiet sobs were still anchoring him. The meaning of Badimar's instruction finally hit him. What was going to happen once Vanalten confirmed that the girl was with child?

No more talking.

They were going to take her, and he would never have to talk to her again.

Lion shivered and groaned.

"It's okay," she whispered. "It's going to be okay. Try to sleep." She took his hand in hers and squeezed it. He squeezed it back.

No more talking.

He would never talk to her again. Never see her again...

"Saradra," he whispered.

She froze, the cold towel still in her hand.

"My favourite..." Lion turned his head and winced when the movement sent a wave of agony through him.

"No," she whispered. "You don't have to do this."

Lion looked at her, his gaze inviting hers. "My favourite... song... is *Galclad and the Coward*," he said. He didn't look away. If this was his last chance to look into those eyes, he would not look away.

"You don't have to do this," the girl — Saradra — shook her head. She kissed his hand, then leaned forward and kissed his lips. Lion surrendered to the kiss and everything seemed to fade away for a moment, his thoughts becoming fuzzy. He suspected he might have passed out briefly, as he didn't remember when Saradra pulled back.

"I first heard the song... at the celebration," Lion muttered. She rested her head on the bed, close to his. She brushed her fingers against his cheek as she listened intently. Lion continued, his voice rough and weak. "After the... Maiden's Kiss Tournament. A bard... A bard came from... Kaldoria. He sang *Galclad and the Coward*... It made people sad... I don't understand, but I liked the song."

Saradra chuckled softly. He focused on the soothing sensation of her fingers on his face. "It's a sad story," she said.

"Because he dies?"

"Because his brother betrays him at the end, when he needs him the most."

"Oh... Well... It's my favourite song."

"It's a good song."

"But you said... it makes people sad?"

"It's a good song because it makes people sad."

Lion closed his eyes. Saradra caressed his head, stroking her fingers through his hair.

"Why?" Lion asked, his eyes closed.

"Why does a good song make people sad?"

"Why do this? To me?" He squeezed her hand again, holding her delicate fingers securely in his palm. He just needed to know. "Why?"

Saradra's fingers played with his hair. She leaned in and kissed him again, softer this time. "If I give them a son," she whispered, her voice quivering, "They will send him to a slave ranch, to be raised by slave breeders, and they will do to him what they did to you. They will raise him to be like you. I need to see if what they do can be reversed. If my child can ever be free."

Lion opened his mouth to tell her the boy would be lucky to have a life like his. He was well-fed, dressed, cared for. He worked out with the best trainers in the country. He slept in a real bed! Even his punishments were fair, including the flogging he endured today. He had made a mistake, became distracted during his training. He deserved the punishment. It was his fault. Not Saradra's. Lion's.

Instead, he whispered, "He can be free. If he's good enough to win Twilight of Infinity."

Saradra lifted her head. "Is that a tournament?" She sounded so excited. Hopeful. Not for herself, but for her child. The baby wasn't even born yet, didn't exist. And yet, he was already blessed with Saradra's relentless affection.

Lion nodded, his eyes still closed. The exhaustion was rolling in to claim him. He wondered if she knew she wasn't even going to spend a minute with the baby. That he would be taken from her straight after birth.

"Have you ever met anyone who won it?" Saradra asked. When Lion nodded again, she whispered eagerly, "What was he doing?"

Somehow, Lion sensed she wasn't going to like the real answer to her question. The freed slave — a purebred beast — who had won the last Twilight of Infinity was still serving the same Owner. He was still following orders and keeping his eyes on the floor. It was a good thing the tournament was only held once every four years. Freeborns never won it, and the purebreds who did never knew what to do with their freedom.

"His tattoo was removed," Lion whispered, his words slurring. He winced as another wave of pain shot through his back.

Saradra kissed him again. "It's okay," she whispered. "Go to sleep." Her hand trailed down his neck; her fingers circling the faded lines of Lion's tattoo.

With a soft groan, Lion finally succumbed to exhaustion and passed out. Saradra stayed up all night, soothing his back with the cold towel, whispering comforting words into his ear, and kissing him every time he woke up shivering and groaning with pain.

18

OLIRA

Olira fixed her hood, making sure it kept her face hidden, before she walked through the open doors of the Chamber of Twelve.

The Chamber, a modest, circular building overlooking the town square, was made of weathered stone and sturdy wood. Its thatched roof rose gently, and the round windows along the walls welcomed the last rays of the evening sun inside. The Underlings had already lit torches around the entrance, expecting the meeting to last until after sunset and ensuring there was enough light outside.

Olira stepped through the arched doorway into the main area, her eyes adjusting to the dim light. The central circular room was alive with the hum of conversation. The entire town must have been in attendance, filling the space between the twelve statues representing each Rider and their dragons. The statues were arranged in a large circle, with a smaller, hand drawn Prayer Ring in front of each one. Olira felt a pang of guilt as she glanced at Alunwea's simple but beautiful statue. She hadn't been to the Chamber of Twelve for nearly a year. She had drawn a Prayer Ring devoted to Alunwea in her room, and she held her own rituals in private. She didn't remember the last time she attended to a Long Ritual, or a Sending led by the town Pyre.

She added Pyre Aldric as another figure to avoid tonight.

She crossed her arms as she stood along the wall and scanned the gathered faces. Elderly townsfolk occupied the simple wooden stools placed around the room. All the straw-filled cushions were in use, providing a bit of comfort to those seated on the cold stone floor. Most people, however, sat cross-legged on the floor or stood along the edges, forming a dense ring of bodies around the central space.

Olira wondered if coming here really was a good idea, considering the number of people she didn't want to talk to. But the size of the crowd eased her worries, as she could easily go unnoticed if she was careful enough.

She spotted Master Tholthus in exactly where she expected him to be, right near the centre with the Bailiff and the Agha. Sitting on a stool with his arms crossed, he was focused on Bailiff Zerla's speech.

"... but with the ongoing unrest, his resources are divided," Zerla finished, and his words evoked a loud protest from the townspeople.

Master Tholthus's scowl deepened, though he didn't offer any protests. Zerla raised his voice, trying to maintain order as he continued with his explanation: "As I've said, I have notified Lord Rhuagh—"

"Lord Rhuagh doesn't give a shit about us!" a young man called out from the edge of the crowd. "We need to fend for ourselves!"

Olira spotted Jygan near the man who spoke. He was the second person he wanted to avoid tonight. Jygan stood isolated between the statues of Kyrus and Kahil, his arms crossed, his face set in a grim expression. Jygan's isolation wasn't by choice or by character flaw; it was his occupation. Being the town's tanner came with the odour. Despite bathing every day and using scented oils and incenses he bought from Olira, Jygan had a persistent smell that deterred townspeople from standing near him. Jygan didn't take offense. The smell never bothered Olira. Jygan was the kindest, most easy-going person in town, and yet when he spotted Olira across the crowd and offered an uncertain smile, Olira gave a curt nod and looked away.

In the centre, the argument continued, people claiming Lord Rhuagh only cared for his city and failed to even keep the roads safe. As the townspeople raised their concerns and discussed the riots all over Chinderia, Olira fidgeted with her hood, feeling Jygan's gaze on her.

Things had been awkward between them since Jygan returned empty-handed from *The Wicked Mirror*. The bags of supplies Olira had stashed near the inn and left behind were gone. Stolen. Jygan had apologized, looking genuinely sorry, though it wasn't his fault. And Olira wasn't angry at him, neither did she blame him. She was just upset, and she didn't want Jygan to feel sorry for her. It didn't change the fact that her root cellar was still empty and she had one too many mouths to feed.

"Lord Rhuagh's men don't even patrol the roads past Attlecana Grove anymore!" Master Tholthus raised his voice over everyone else's. His words elicited more complaints from the townspeople.

"As I said, his resources are tied…" the Bailiff yelled to be heard.

Olira shuffled along the edge of the crowd, still scanning the faces. She found Mistress Aeliana sitting on one of the stools near Zaon's statue. Like she expected, the old woman sat isolated too, but unlike Jygan, she did so out of choice and character flaw. Olira started making her way there.

"As soon as the riots in Kilrer settles…" Bailiff assured the crowd.

"Riots won't settle until justice is served in Brinescar!" Grollen, the town's baker, yelled, raising his fist in the air. He was bold enough to wear black and gold, clearly not fearing the Bailiff's wrath. He didn't need to, as he had a large group of people sitting close to him in an unspoken show of support. Besides, no judgement against any person could be made by another person inside the Chamber of the Twelve. This was the Twelve Riders' sacred home, and anyone could speak their mind without fear of repercussion.

"There is no injustice in Brinescar!" Bailiff said, his face red.

Olira creeped past Zaon's statue and sat right next to Mistress Aeliana's stool. The old woman, watching the discussion with boredom, didn't spare her a glance.

"How do you not call what happened injustice?" Grollen shouted.

"The king exposed their heinous plans! Do you not fear Darkhome?"

"All lies! There is no proof!"

"Enough!" the Agha finally spoke.

Despite the Bailiff being Lord Rhuagh's official in town, the Oxreach's recognised leader was the Agha. The title was mostly used in Northern Chinderia towns and was given to the family who owned the most land. The Agha consulted with the Bailiff but made their own decisions.

"This isn't Brinescar," the Agha said. "We have our own concerns, like the safety of our roads and the crimes committed near our town. Someone murdered an inn full of people."

"An inn full of traitors!" Grollen objected, though he kept his voice in a respectful tone.

Mistress Aeliana scoffed. Olira glanced at her, thinking a clever way to start the conversation. Mistress Aeliana, who blatantly ignored everyone around her, didn't make it easy. Most of the townspeople muttered their satisfaction with the Agha's decision to start patrols themselves, though more than a few seemed concerned. Master Grollen was amongst the people who was openly displeased.

"Agha, we need to do more than simply patrol the roads."

"What do you suggest, Grollen? We march to Brinescar with our pitchforks and your rolling pin?"

"Are we not any better than a mere purebred?" Grollen said, and Olira's heart skipped a beat. This was her opening.

"Are you comparing yourself to a rabid animal?" Bailiff spat. "He's a broken thing."

"It's pretty scary, isn't it?" Olira whispered, leaning towards Mistress Aeliana. "All that talk about a rabid purebred."

Aeliana levelled her with a hard gaze. Her eyes narrowed slightly, and her mouth pressed into a thin, stern line. Olira hardly kept herself from biting her lip or looking away. She tried to smile, but her attempts at sociability couldn't melt the suspicion from Aeliana's face.

Olira was about to conclude this was a stupid plan, when Aeliana returned her gaze back to the argument at the centre. "Disturbing indeed," she muttered, leaning slightly towards Olira. She huffed disapprovingly as she shook her head. "And Leonis has no one but himself to blame."

She hadn't raised her voice, neither had she lowered it sensibly. One of the men who flocked around Grollen glanced at Aeliana, and almost immediately looked away.

"Oh?" Olira said. She kept her eyes at the centre, though she hardly followed the argument. "What do you mean?"

"Rumours say Leonis spoilt that thing," Aeliana said. "Pampered him. Even gave him a private room and women to sleep with."

Olira made a noise that she hoped matched Aeliana's contempt. She worded her next question carefully, trying not to sound too eager or odd. "So it is possible? Purebreds being disobedient? Dangerous?"

"Of course it's possible. They break, just like any tool."

"How can you tell?"

"Tell what?"

"When a purebred is... you know... broken?"

Olira blushed under Aeliana's suspicious stare. "They behave oddly," Aeliana said slowly.

"Aren't they always odd? I mean, I've heard they're odd. How do you know when they're *odder?*" She grimaced. Aeliana kept staring at her like she was seeing through her.

"Why suddenly interested in purebreds?"

Olira shrugged and nodded towards the centre, though they had long moved on from the topic of the king's mad purebred. "It's just all that talk about disobedient purebreds making me nervous." She didn't have to sell the nervous bit. "And you're the only one in town who knows a lot about purebreds."

"Because I keep two," Aeliana said, drawing Olira's gaze to the far corner of the room, to the man who stood apart from everyone else. Mistress Aeliana's purebred house slave stood perfectly still, his head down, his hands clasped in front of him. She must have left her other purebred at home.

"And I will continue to keep them," the old woman said through gritted teeth, "despite your father spending years shaming me for participating in slavery."

Olira blushed again, fumbling with her skirt. Her fingers trembled slightly, and she could feel the full weight of Aeliana's grudge. Aeliana was one of the few people in Oxreach who kept slaves, and the only one who kept purebreds. Majority of the town shared Vakko Aryanna's dislike for the Domestic Assets Trade Union and the slave trade, and for years, Vakko had tried to convince Aeliana to see his ways. But the old woman was stubborn. She rejected the town's opinion of her and sat in her expensive manor at the town square alone, in the company of her two purebreds, not even bothering to hide them.

Olira didn't think she could squeeze more information from Aeliana, not without revealing her concerns about the slave in her barn. She prepared to leave. Agha Fenric was now concluding the meeting, asking for volunteers to come join patrols. She glanced at Jygan, expecting the tanner to be amongst the volunteers, but he had already left.

"I would be most concerned about fiends," Aeliana muttered reluctantly.

"Fiends?"

"Purebreds don't have *rhoas*, as everyone knows, which makes them perfect hosts for fiends."

Olira glanced at Pyre Aldric. "Umm, fiends are locked away in Darkhome. They don't—"

"I would check for any fiendish influences," Aeliana continued. "Fiends can't enter a Praying Ring when a believer is in it. It's always safe to check that."

The memory of the slave's face as he strangled Torren sent shivers down Olira's spine. And that eerie stillness every time she walked into the stall to change his bandages or bring him food. She couldn't get out of there fast enough. "Do you really think that's possible?"

"I would check that," Aeliana repeated sternly. "And if that's not the case, then I would check their discipline. That's how you understand if they're broken or not."

"How do we..." Olira glanced at Aeliana's purebred, who stood motionless by the wall. The man in her barn often stood still like that, too. She didn't see any difference.

"Check for any display of emotion," Aeliana continued. "There are many ways to do that, depending on what your stomach can handle. I prefer giving them pointless, tedious tasks. You know, tasks that would annoy or frustrate any normal person. And I would watch for a reaction. Boredom. Annoyance. Resentment. Any emotion. And then I would make them talk."

"I thought they don't talk a lot."

"Not unless you make them. I would listen for any opinions. Any thoughts, beliefs, preferences. Desires."

"How do I get him to reveal those?"

Aeliana smirked. "You must be clever with words, which you clearly aren't. Now tell me, how did Vakko, Aryanna's daughter, end up with a purebred?"

Olira glanced at the nearest people, which made Aeliana chuckle. "Thank you for the conversation, Mistress Aeliana," Olira said as she stood. "Have a good evening."

"If you're looking to sell, don't bring him to me. I have no desire for a broken purebred."

Olira didn't reply. She had made the mistake of looking towards the centre as she stood, and her eyes just met with Master Tholthus's. She looked away instantly and started making her way towards the door. Agha Fenric had just concluded the meeting, so everyone began to rise. The room was filled with the murmur of voices as some people moved towards the door and others gravitated to the Agha. Olira kept her hood down, trying to blend into the crowd. She sidestepped an older man who was lingering to talk to his neighbour and nearly stumbled over a stool. Someone grabbed her elbow to steady her.

"Thank you," Olira said, then paused when she recognized who it was. She had done a terrible job at avoiding all three people she didn't want to be seen by: Jygan, Master Tholthus, and now Varelya.

Varelya pulled her hand back and studied Olira with a tight-lipped frown. She blinked slowly and sighed. "How is he?"

Olira crossed her arms. If Varelya was so curious, she should have come and checked on the slave.

Varelya sighed again, shaking her head. "I'm assuming you are changing his bandages and applying poultice regularly, so the infection should have cleared by now. Is it starting to look swollen and stiff?"

Olira nodded slowly. She had noticed the stiffness and wasn't sure what to do with it.

"Get him to move the leg. Slow and gentle at first." She lowered her voice and leaned in. "You'll have to let him out of that stall. Fresh air. Clean environment. Warmth."

"I keep the stall clean, and he has plenty of blankets."

Varelya rolled her eyes and shook her head. "Let him move," she muttered before walking away.

Olira glanced back at the centre, expecting to see Master Tholthus making his way towards her, but people blocked her view. She hoped they blocked his view of her as well. She pushed through the last knot of people, almost knocking a table with items dedicated to Ara, the Goddess of Nature. She steadied the table, then hurried out the door.

The cool evening air hit her face like a splash of water. She sighed in relief, the tension of the meeting slowly dissipating, and her thoughts already drifting to ways she can use the information Aeliana shared to test whether the purebred was normal or not. As she turned to leave, she nearly collided with Master Tholthus.

"Mistress Olira," Master Tholthus greeted her politely.

Olira's heart sank. "Oh, Master Tholthus. I... didn't see you there."

He gave a slight nod, but didn't speak, giving her a chance to talk first. Olira shifted uncomfortably, glancing around as the townsfolk walked past them, heading home. The darkness of the night settled in, the only illumination coming from the torches and lanterns lit outside the Chamber of Twelve.

"I know I missed your deadline to make a payment," Olira squirmed. She hated feeling the heat of her embarrassment rising to her cheeks. "I just encountered some problems collecting payment from someone else."

"I feel your pain, Mistress Olira, when it comes to dealing with people who are excessively late in making payments."

Olira wished the ground would swallow her. "I have every intention of paying you. I'm just waiting for something." *Waiting for the purebred to hurry up and heal, without attacking any more of my family members,* she thought furiously in her head. "I'll have more than enough to cover what I owe you," she added.

Tholthus simply watched her, his silence pressing her to continue.

"I know you have been very patient with me, Master Tholthus. I—"

"How long?" Tholthus's expression remained neutral, his eyes steady on her.

"Four months." Olira nearly shrunk as she said the words. Four months was barely enough to ensure the slave's full recovery, and it gave her just enough time to go sell him. She didn't dare look at Tholthus's expression. She bit her lip, her frustration bubbling up despite her efforts to stay composed. "I know it's not ideal and I really appreciate your patience. I'm not trying to avoid paying you, Master Tholthus. It's just... things don't seem to go as planned."

Tholthus remained silent, his polite demeanour unchanged, which only made Olira more uncomfortable. The townsfolk continued to pass by, some glancing curiously at the pair.

"So, four more months?" she asked, her voice almost pleading.

Tholthus finally nodded. "I know things haven't been fair to you and your brothers since your parents' accident. I felt a duty to help you, out of respect for the friendship I had with your father. But every time I give you a hand, I seem to lose an arm."

Olira crossed her arms tightly over her chest, her cheeks burning with embarrassment. Her eyes darted after the last of the attendees heading back to their homes.

"Maybe this isn't the type of help you and your siblings need?"

Olira's skin prickled with unease. "What does that mean?"

"I will have to apply another interest to this extension, and I expect a full payment in four months. Good night, Mistress Olira."

Olira muttered a dull reply as she watched the old man walk away. The discomfort still gnawed at her. Despite the extension she had just secured, allowing her more time, she was far from feeling relieved. Her family's future depended on the purebred, and she loathed the sense of helplessness it brought.

19

LION

Hopper was one of King Leonis's freeborn beasts.

He was more agile than would have been expected from someone his size. He was clever enough to use his appearance to mislead his opponents in battle, make them believe he was slow, then prove them fatally wrong. His little strategy didn't work on beasts who were familiar with Hopper's actual agility.

Lion was one of them.

He was wielding a lor'qas against Hopper's battle axe, both weapons blunted for training. The weapon, despite being his favourite, gave him a clear disadvantage. He wasn't given a shield to complement it, and neither were wearing any armour. Not to mention, Lion was severely fatigued. His back muscles wouldn't stop spasming and limiting his movements, and the pain relief Master Vanalten reluctantly gave him this morning was wearing off. Salty sweat trickled down Lion's back, leaving a trail of fire behind them. Some of the welt marks had started bleeding again, and his entire back felt sore and swollen.

Still, Lion leveraged the pain to keep his focus on the fight.

The other beasts had formed a circle, sitting on the ground. Joharin was supervising the fight, while Badimar and the two trainers stood behind, studying. The Master of the Beasts crossed his arms as he tracked Lion's movements, a scowl darkening his expression. He didn't seem to take any pleasure from Lion's suffering. Lion knew him enough; Badimar wasn't one of those who enjoyed torture and power displays. If anything, he genuinely wanted to test what Lion could do in this state, and his intense stare suggested he wanted to see Lion succeed. Why else would he allow Lion to go see Vanalten first thing in the morning?

Lion didn't want to fail Badimar. He wasn't angry at the Master of the Beasts for what he had done to his back. He was just angry. And he didn't want to lose.

Joharin shouted instructions now and then; "Where's your bloody defence?" or "Don't you see he's bloody open?" or "You're staying in his range for too long. Keep your bloody feet moving!"

'Bloody' was Joharin's favourite word.

Favourite words. That could have been a conversation topic to discuss with Saradra. Except she would not be there when he returned to his room tonight.

When Hopper lunged forward like a viper and swung his battle axe low, Lion barely dodged it. Without losing any more ground, he countered immediately, forcing Hopper to retreat.

Hopper had a habit of staring at his opponent's eyes. It was another one of his silly little strategies. He would use it to intimidate his opponents. However, the technique rarely worked on purebreds since they didn't participate in eye contact.

Another topic he could talk to Saradra about: combat strategies. His favourite strategy, which weapons worked well against which combat style, how having a shield could entirely change the pacing of a combat, the importance of footwork, clever ways of using a handguard. He was certain Saradra would find the topic so interesting! He could imagine the fascination on her face when he told her all about how some weapons were only useful when paired with a shield, but others were designed for solo combat.

He suddenly found himself willing to talk to her for hours. And she wouldn't be there tonight.

Saradra was asleep this morning when he woke up from his restless, half-conscious state that he couldn't really call sleep. Not knowing what else to do, Lion had crawled out of bed, dressed, and left.

He had left. What else could he have done?

Being in that room with her, watching her peaceful face, knowing it would be the last time he would ever look at her, was a torture. He had just wanted to get out of there before she opened those beautiful eyes and forced him to confront his helplessness.

He had lost her. The searing pain on his raw, swollen, bleeding back could not compete with the ache he felt in his chest. He wanted to scream. He wanted to hit. He wanted to win.

Lion stared at Hopper's eyes, and the freeborn beast flinched. The flash of rage he saw in Lion's eyes made him hesitate.

Lion charged at him with a furious howl. His lips were pulled back in a snarl. Hopper stepped back, swinging his axe at Lion's head. Lion raised his lor'qas sideways, parrying the strike. He hooked his weapon under the blade of the axe, pulled, twisted, and kicked Hopper's wrist at the same time, disarming him.

Throwing both weapons aside, Lion grabbed Hopper's ears and buried his knee in his stomach. Hopper doubled over, gasping for air and holding his stomach. Lion brought his elbow down on the back of Hopper's head. The blow sent Hopper sprawling onto his hands and knees, gasping for breath and disoriented.

Rage was roaming inside Lion, like an out-of-control bushfire. He was bloodthirsty. He wanted to win. He wanted to hurt. He wanted to stop feeling so helpless. When Hopper attempted to get up, Lion knocked him down and kept kicking repeatedly.

Hopper grappled Lion's leg, rolled, and pulled him down with him. He punched Lion's back, causing the welts to flare up. Lion screamed, blinded by the white-hot pain. Hopper attempted to roll away and stand, but Lion tackled him. The focus of his vision narrowed, and the rage obscured his thoughts. He pulled Hopper in a headlock.

"This is not a *bloody* wrestling drill!" Joharin yelled, getting ready to stop the fight.

"Leave them," Badimar grunted, an amused grin on his lips.

Hopper wrestled his way free and attempted to lock one of Lion's arms. With his free hand, he slapped Lion's back, trying to distract him with pain. There were no such concept as cheap moves for beasts. Especially for freeborns when they versed purebreds. They fought dirty and did whatever it took to win. But all Hopper succeeded instead was to piss Lion off more.

Lion growled like a beast, reached forward, and bit Hopper's leg. The freeborn was surprised enough to flinch, curse, and loosen his grip. Lion pulled his arm free. After elbowing Hopper's jaw, dazzling him, he straddled his chest. He started punching.

Hopper scowled at him, murder in his eyes. Lion glared back. The nausea and the anticipation of pain started building in his chest. He hated the feeling, but he hated losing more.

He hated Hopper's eyes. He hated how the freeborn was flaring his nostrils and looking at him like he wanted to kill him.

He hated how helpless he was.

He hated how much he wanted to avert his gaze.

He grabbed Hopper's face and placed his thumbs over his eyes.

"*Padlociatius.*"

Lion collapsed on Hopper. The other trainers exclaimed and swore, only just realizing what Lion was about to do. It was lucky Badimar had read his intentions and acted before Lion put enough pressure to pop Hopper's eyes out.

They were both lucky.

Hopper pushed Lion's paralysed body off him. He shook his head, blinking and rubbing his eyes as he stumbled to his feet. Comprehension of what Lion was about to do came to him in waves. He swore under his breath, then roared like a wild boar and threw himself at the purebred, kicking and punching Lion's helpless body.

"Enough!" Joharin grabbed Hopper from behind and yanked him away. "I said enough! Back off!"

Hopper didn't back off until he received several lashes from Joharin. Breathing heavily, he went back to sit with the other beasts, his snarl promising Lion revenge.

"What the fuck were you thinking?" Joharin turned to Lion. The whip cracked at his side threateningly.

"Joharin, cut it out," Badimar said. His lips twitched. "He fought well. Set up the next fight."

Two beasts dragged Lion's limp body to the side. The effects of his First Word didn't last long, but that was enough time to contemplate what Lion had almost done. If Badimar hadn't acted in time, Lion could have ended Hopper's life.

Worse. Death would have been a mercy when compared to the fate of a damaged beast.

How had he lost control like that? He had never carelessly caused a permanent injury to another beast. Not in training, not even at a Duskblood Fight. Injuring a beast like that, condemning them to a fate worse than death... He shivered.

He watched the rest of the fights, feeling Hopper's vengeful gaze on him. When the sparring session was over, Joharin ordered the other beasts to clean up the yard. Badimar dismissed Lion to go have an early supper, then get Vanalten to patch him up again.

His meal was roasted lamb with rice, potatoes and Seafruit cake. He felt a devastating twinge as he looked at the Seafruit cake. A lump sat in his throat. He hardly swallowed his food before he dragged his feet to Vanalten's office.

The old physician muttered disapprovingly after reviewing the state of the swollen welts. He ordered Lion to lie on his stomach as he rubbed a cold paste on them, which numbed the throbbing within seconds. Lion's eyelids fluttered shut, but as soon as he closed his eyes, Saradra's sleeping face flashed in front of him. So he forced himself to stay awake.

She had been here, in this office, earlier in the day. Lion could smell her unique aroma still lingering in the room.

The lump in his throat grew larger, to the degree it was hard to talk. Vanalten only became more agitated when Lion struggled to speak and answer his questions. The physician mumbled under his breath, swearing at Badimar for not heeding his recommendations about the beasts' well-being, and that he would end up injuring them and costing Vanalten his position. He snapped his ledger shut as he ordered Lion to return to his room and rest for the next few days.

Lion's feet felt heavy as he trudged along the corridor leading to his room. He froze with his hand on the doorknob, dreading finding his room empty. His chest hurt. Closing his eyes, he pressed his forehead against the cold wooden surface.

And he heard a soft rustle behind the door.

He opened it and his heart did a somersault at the sight of Saradra's sky-blue eyes. He staggered forward, blindly closing the door behind him.

Saradra stood from the bed, an uncertain smile touching her beautiful face. "Master Vanalten said it's still too early to tell—"

Lion tackled her into a hug and cut her off with a kiss. Saradra matched his passion. Her arms came around him at first, then fell back on her sides when she remembered the welts on his back. Lion held her tightly, afraid to let go. He broke the kiss to gasp for air, then continued kissing all over her face; her eyes, the side of her mouth, her jaw, her cheeks. He tasted tears.

He held her in his arms for hours. He didn't know what she had done to him, but he knew there was no taking it back anymore. He couldn't go back to what he was before. And he couldn't let them take her.

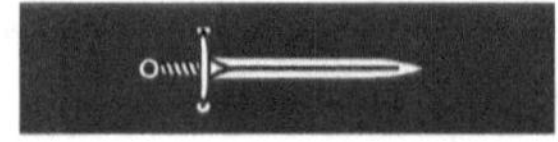

MOONLIGHT DRIFTED THROUGH THE window and gave Saradra's hair a faint glimmer.

Lion lay still, not moving, his breathing calm and quiet. For once, he was grateful for the small size of the bed. Saradra was lying in his arms, her bare body resting against his chest, their legs tangled. The steady thumps of her heart were in unison with his. She slept so peacefully.

It had been four days since Vanalten sent Lion to his room and ordered him to stay there and rest. The old physician was ready to battle Badimar to let him excuse Lion from any training for a few days. Badimar didn't take long to convince. It was agreed that Lion would stay in his room and only go out to eat his meals under the trainers' supervision and to visit Vanalten for regular checks. He wasn't even expected to show up and watch other beasts spar.

Four days of strict rest.

Four blissful days he spent in bed with Saradra, wrapped in each other's arms, lost in her warmth and softness. They exchanged intimate whispers and kisses, made love lazily, passionately, hungrily. The way her body moulded into his arms so perfectly suggested they were made to be together. Now that his skin was mortally addicted to hers, Lion couldn't imagine sleeping alone anymore. He couldn't go back to the way his life was before. He was too far gone by now.

Despite the perfection of this moment, all Lion could feel was fear and dread. Every speck of peace and happiness that attempted to infiltrate inside his heart was shot down by hopelessness. Sooner or later, Saradra was going to be sent back to her Owner. They were going to take her from him.

His muscles tensed at the thought. He hugged her closer. The movement almost woke her up. She fidgeted, rubbed her cheek against his chest, inhaled deeply, and settled again.

Lion expected tomorrow he would be called back to resume training with the other beasts. Vanalten's mixtures, which he kept complaining about how rare and expensive those herbs were and how Badimar shouldn't have gone this far just to teach a lesson, had worked wonders. The swelling had reduced and although his back still appeared like a patchwork of purple bruises and scabbed over welts, the pain had dulled to a persistent soreness that he could mostly ignore, with occasional sharp twinges if he moved wrong. He doubted if he could get another day of rest from Badimar.

Once he returned to training, Lion had to be very careful to avoid making another mistake. Badimar was going to watch him closely. Lion would continue to spend his nights with Saradra for another week or two. After that, it was a matter of time before they confirmed she was with child and sent her away.

Lion brushed his fingers over the faint bruise he had left on Saradra's shoulder many nights ago. A strange blend of guilt and pride crossed his face. She had left a similar one on his neck. It marked him as hers, just as the one on her shoulder marked her as his. She was his, and he had to find a way to keep her here. He caressed that bruise, circling it lightly with the tip of his finger. Every course of action he could think of ended with him being dead — after a severe punishment — or him being sent to White Tower — also after a severe punishment.

He could not go to White Tower.

He could not live without her, either.

That only left him one other option.

Somehow, the decision lifted the tightness off his chest. He felt lighter. Almost peaceful. His eyes closed.

He was in that sweet place, just on the verge of drifting into sleep, when he heard the hushed voices from the yard just outside his window. He lifted his head off the pillow, straining to hear. Was there someone outside? He listened for nearly a minute, but didn't hear anything else.

When he rested his head back on the pillow, he found Saradra watching him. Her smile was glowing. "Can't you sleep?" she whispered, stifling a big yawn.

Lion shook his head.

She shifted up, propping her head with a hand. Concern creased her face. "Is it your back?"

Lion shook his head again.

Saradra lowered herself back on the pillow they shared. Her long eyelashes fluttered. Their lips were so close. A temptation.

"Tell me something about yourself," she whispered.

"No." Lion's lips brushed against hers. His refusal raised an eyebrow. "You do," Lion requested.

A playful glimmer flashed in Saradra's eyes. "Are you asking me to tell you about myself?"

When Lion nodded, she couldn't contain her smirk. "I was wondering when you would just stop talking about yourself all the time." Lion's heart melted at the sight of her smile. "Let's see..." Saradra continued, tapping her finger on her lips, thinking. "I'm from Bellmouth. It's a town by the coast, near—"

"Ascain."

"How do you know that? Have you been to Ascain before?"

Lion shook his head. "Map."

"Ah, that's right. You're fascinated with maps," she whispered. "I still don't know why?"

Lion offered her a shrug. He didn't know it either. He watched her expectantly until she remembered it was her turn to speak tonight. She giggled softly. "Right. Something about myself... Well, this is hard!"

After seeing the look on Lion's face, she broke into a silent laughter. Lion covered her mouth with his palm, muffling her voice. A fluttering warmth filled his chest and he couldn't keep himself from smiling. He pulled her in tighter. When she was calm enough, he moved his hand and he brushed her hair back from her face.

"You're smiling!" she gasped. "I don't think I've ever seen you smile! What a special occasion!" Saradra leaned closer, her fingertips lightly grazing his lips, feeling their warmth and softness. He caught her hand, bringing it to his lips and pressing a tender kiss to her fingertips.

"You look so different when you smile," Saradra whispered, her fingers now threading through his hair. When Lion scowled, she added. "It's a good thing. You look like…" She bit her lips and went quiet.

Lion squirmed with a sudden curiosity. He needed to know her thoughts. "Like what?"

Her gaze flicked to his neck. Although it was too dark to see it clearly, he knew she was looking at the dark spot on his neck. His tattoo. "You look free."

Lion didn't like that word. It gave him a shiver, which he disguised by shifting like he was trying to get more comfortable. He didn't let his smile falter. It seemed to make her happy. His hand found its way to her cheek, cupping it gently. "Your favourites," he prompted her.

Saradra chuckled. "That's right. I can't get out of this, can I?" When Lion shook his head, she sighed with resignation. "Well, my favourite food is grilled salmon. Marinated in butter and garlic. Served with roasted sweet potatoes. Mmm."

Lion's thumb traced the soft lines of her jaw. In the dim light, her eyes appeared almost black. He hardly noticed the discomfort in his stomach as he gazed at them, wishing he had more light to appreciate their distinctive blue hue.

"My favourite colour is grey," she continued after kissing the base of Lion's palm. "It reminds me of the sea after a storm. I love watching a storm roll in."

Lion leaned in closer, his breath mingling with hers. Her cheeks flushed with desire as she continued: "My favourite time of the day is night. Especially on clear nights when you can see all the stars."

A look of hunger flashed across Lion's face, filled with longing. Saradra's breath hitched when she read his intentions, which Lion made no effort to disguise. She shuffled closer, her lips brushing his as she spoke: "My favourite—"

Lion pressed his mouth against hers, muffling her words. She responded by parting her lips, inviting him in. Lion snaked his arm around her waist and pressed himself against her, enjoying the thrill that surged through her body. He pulled himself over her. She tilted her head back when he kissed his way down her jaw, neck, and below. Her hand found the back of his head, urging him to take her.

That's when the alarm bells at the Castle Brinescar began to sound.

20

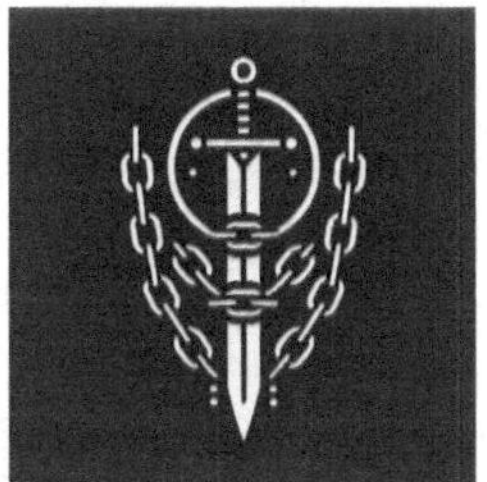

LION

The alarm bells shattered the stillness of the night, their urgent clanging echoing through the castle walls. Lion's head snapped up, his instincts instantly on high alert. He swung his legs over the side of the bed and hurried to the window.

"What's going on?" Saradra whispered, her eyes wide with concern.

The yard below his window was still dark. Lion grudgingly noticed this wasn't the kind of nights Saradra favoured. The clouds kept the stars and the moon hidden, obscuring the ancient collection of structures and courtyards that made Castle Brinescar. His eyes narrowed when he spotted figures running across the yard, but they were too quick and it was too dark to identify them.

"Fire," Lion said, as he traced the direction the figures were running to. Somewhere near the Upper Keep, flames were licking the sky. The alarm bells continued to ring through the night, now confused sounds of people mixed with the noise too.

Saradra came over to his side, the blanket draped over her naked body. "Merciful Alunwea," she gasped, with her hand over her mouth. "What do we do?"

Lion scowled, like she had asked a silly question. "Nothing," he said, reaching for his clothes. Saradra copied him, finding her dress and slipping it on.

"What do you mean nothing?"

"We stay here until someone comes and tells us what to do."

"What? We can't just…"

Lion finished getting dressed and shrugged. "We're not allowed to leave this room until dawn."

Saradra opened her mouth to say more, but a loud scream from outside cut her off. They both hurried to the window as the bone chilling screams continued, now joined by alarmed shouts. More figures ran across the yard, a few of them carrying lanterns, the flickering light reflecting from their armours.

"This doesn't seem right," Saradra whispered.

"They'll put out the fire."

"Those screams. We should see what's happening." She dashed to the door, but Lion grabbed her arm before she took two steps.

"No. We stay here."

"I just wanna—"

"We're not supposed to be outside, and it's safer here."

A series of loud thumping noises echoed through the building, growing louder with each impact. It was close. The sound elicited panicked and confused shouts. Lion's argument faltered, his attention shifting to the noise. The thumping ceased after a deafening crack, the obvious sound of solid wood breaking in half, followed by more shouts.

Saradra seized the moment, yanking her arm free. She bolted for the door. Lion reached out again, but this time, he missed. She slipped through the doorway and into the corridor.

"Saradra!" Lion hissed. He hesitated for a moment before chasing after her.

Saradra had a head start, her figure already disappearing down the corridor. The alarm bells blared louder now, mixed with the increasing sounds of screams and shouts. People screamed, confused and scared.

Lion sprinted down the corridor, wincing at the sudden sharp pain on his back. He pushed through the pain. He had to get to Saradra. Her light shoes echoed off the stone floor ahead of him. As he turned a corner, he caught a glimpse of her at the far end, her pace not slowing down. He pushed himself harder and caught up with her halfway through the next corridor.

"We need to go back to our room," Lion hissed, gripping her arm tightly.

"Something bad is going on. This isn't just a fire."

Lion clenched his teeth. "That's exactly why we need to return." He could hear the familiar sounds filtering through the alarm bells; clash of steel, thud of boots, and the distinct cries of battle.

"Is someone..." Saradra's question was interrupted by panicked screams coming from the corridor ahead. Lion pushed Saradra against the wall, both to shelter her and to keep her still. A male voice barked orders, and a door broke open. More screams echoed through the corridor until they were silenced with wet sounds of slicing and hacking. Lion could not mistake that distinct sound blade made against flesh. Another door broke open, closer this time, and more screams were quietened violently.

Lion ran back the way they came, still clutching Saradra's arm tightly. He was ready to toss her over his shoulder if he had to. Fortunately, she had the sense to keep her mouth shut and keep up.

When he reached his room, more sounds of conflict and murder were approaching from the other end of the corridor. They were sweeping the floors systematically. He shoved Saradra into the room, then hurried to Badimar's door. He slammed his fist against the door.

"What are you doing?" Saradra gasped from the doorway, though she was smart enough not to come out.

Lion didn't reply. He had to warn Badimar about the intruders. He couldn't let the Master of the Beasts be caught unaware. He knocked again, louder this time. The sounds of violence were drawing closer from the adjoining corridor. He heard nothing but silence from Badimar's room, so he ducked back into his, closing the door behind him.

"What are we going to do?" Saradra asked, her voice quivering. She hugged herself as she paced the room. "We... we need to hide."

Lion grabbed her shoulders and kept her still. "When they break the door, we kneel."

"Someone's attacking the castle! Where are the king's soldiers?"

"Saradra, listen to me!"

"I don't understand! Who would do this?"

"Saradra!" Lion flinched at another sound of a door breaking in, closer this time. Only a few doors away.

"Aren't these the servants' quarters? Why are they killing servants?"

Lion positioned her so they both faced the door and forced her to kneel with him. "Keep your hands on your lap and lift your chin up, so they see your tattoo."

"What? No…"

Lion squeezed her hand as the next door broke open, screams spilling into the corridor. "Saradra! Trust me! They teach us what to do in situations like this."

"Situations like this? What is this?"

"In an unforeseen conflict, unless we are ordered otherwise, we surrender. They won't kill us."

Tears welled up in Saradra's eyes. She stifled a whimper when another shrill scream filled the corridor. "How can you be so sure? You don't even know who—"

"They *won't* kill us. Slaves are valuable property. Whoever they are, they'll take slaves alive."

Badimar's door slammed open. Lion held his breath as he listened to the sound of boots stomping around the room, kicking and pushing furniture. No screams or shouts. Like he had hoped, Badimar wasn't in his room.

"Chin up. Don't look. Don't speak. Don't even flinch."

Saradra's fear was palpable, her breathing quick and shallow. Lion leaned in and crushed his lips against hers in a desperate kiss. He pulled back and let go of her hand mere seconds before their door was kicked open.

Saradra flinched despite his warnings, but she raised her chin, exposing her neck and displaying her slave tattoo. Lion did the same, trying hard not to doubt what he knew. All free men were greedy, and nobody gained anything from butchering expensive slaves. Saradra's hands trembled on her knees, yearning to hold Lion's, but she kept them where they were.

Two men stormed into the room. They wore unfamiliar uniforms; silver and blue tabards, chainmail, short swords, suitable for combat in close quarters. Their blades glistened red with fresh blood. The men raised their swords as they stepped forward. Saradra closed her eyes, but Lion kept his open. A terrible suspicion slammed him like a sledgehammer; there was no light in the room! What if they couldn't see the slave tattoos?

The nearest of the two men grabbed Lion's hair and pulled his sword back. Lion imagined the cold steel slash through his flesh, ripping his midsection open, yet he still didn't flinch. But when he saw the second man go for Saradra, his muscles tensed. He was a heartbeat away from springing into action and killing both men, when the first attacker spoke.

"Slaves!' he yelled over his shoulder. He still didn't let go of Lion's hair, nor did he lower his sword, but at least the man who was going for Saradra hesitated. He lowered his sword and tilted Saradra's head back roughly to check her tattoo. A jolt of rage rushed through Lion's body at the way he manhandled her, but he kept himself perfectly still.

Another man stepped into the room. The insignia on his shoulders showed rank, and his tabard displayed a coat of arms; a brown bear, standing on its hind legs and fighting.

House Vogros.

Even slaves who knew nothing about nobility could recognise the coat of arms of the second largest dynasty in Chinderia. House Vogros was a very frequent guest at King Leonis's grand events. What were House Vogros soldiers doing at Castle Brinescar?

The officer squeezed past the other soldiers, the room now crowded with five people. He glowered at Lion and Saradra.

"This one's a purebred," the one who held Lion said. He yanked Lion forward, tilting his head back roughly to see the tattoo in the flickering light of torches held by the men outside.

"Why are they here?" the officer grunted. "I thought all the slaves were kept in the slave barracks downstairs."

His soldiers shrugged and waited for their orders. Seconds stretched like hours, the doubt gnawing at Lion as he kept repeating silently; *all free men are greedy, all free men are greedy.* Finally, the officer barked: "You two, take them downstairs and join us near the southeast stairwells."

"Yes, Sir."

Lion released his breath quietly. Breeder Astaldo was right. He was always right.

The two soldiers pushed them out of the room and started herding them down the corridor. The man who walked behind Lion gave him a needless push now and then. The other man kept Saradra's elbow in his grip, as if she would dare to run. Their swords were still unsheathed, but the men seemed more relaxed now. They had no reason to expect trouble from a couple of slaves, and Lion had no reason to give them trouble; although he could think of a dozen ways to overpower and kill them both even before they could blink.

After the next turn, one of the men tapped his friend on the shoulder. He nodded towards a room on the left. The door was open, revealing a ransacked room and the bloody body of a servant sprawled on the bed. The other man shrugged and nodded his agreement. They shoved the two slaves into the room.

His captor pushed Lion towards the middle of the room. "Move that body out of the bed."

The other man, who held Saradra by her arm, glanced at the hallway and closed the door behind him. Lion caught the look on the man's face as he turned his attention to Saradra.

The first man smacked Lion's head. "Are you deaf?"

Lion tucked his head between his shoulders and dragged the corpse off the bed, leaving it next to a chest on the far side of the room. When he was done, the first man pushed him towards the corner. "Face the wall, on your knees. Don't move."

Lion's eyes locked with Saradra's. With wide eyes and a paler complexion than the corpse, she looked horrified. The man beside her still watched her with that expression which left Lion's stomach churning. The first man was glaring at him, so Lion faced the corner and slid to his knees. The hurt and disappointment that flickered across Saradra's face, just before he turned his back on her, nearly made him sick.

"Stay there," the man growled before stepping away.

Lion's hands and feet grew cold, as a numbness filled his chest. Behind him, a scuffle broke, and one of the men grunted in surprise. Saradra's strong voice rang in the room as she backed away from them. "Don't touch me!"

"Bitch bit me," the man said. "I thought she was a fucking pleasure slave."

"Get on the bed, whore."

"Fuck you!"

"What did you say?"

Lion's ears thrummed. His eyes found a little crack on the stone wall in front of him and he focused on that, everything else on the edges of his vision blurring. The scuffle in the room went on, and Saradra screamed.

Don't move. Stay there.

He was given clear orders. By free men. A chill settled in his chest. His arms weighed heavy on his thighs, like being pulled down by cold, cruel shackles. His training bound him more tightly than any chains could. Obedience and learned helplessness held him in place, forcing his muscles to stay rigid while he listened to Saradra fight the men alone.

Don't move.

One of the men yelped and cursed. "She fucking raked my face!"

The other man laughed. "Playing hard to get huh? Fine."

"I'm gonna cut your fingers off, stupid bitch!"

Saradra spat. The man growled as he moved through the room. Lion's jaw twitched as he listened to the sounds, unable to keep them out of his ears; a slap, a thud, Saradra's scream, and a body slamming against the furniture, followed by a crack.

Stay there.

The bed creaked when they tossed Saradra on it. A fabric ripped and she sobbed.

Blood seeped from Lion's clenched fists. As he stared at the crack on the wall, he felt himself dissociating from his body. Except this time, he wasn't going to *that place*. He was slipping into a state that felt akin to Rage.

When he found himself on his feet, Lion wasn't surprised. Deep down, he had known how this was going to end the moment that man had ordered him to face the wall. With bitter amusement, he realised what he was about to do wasn't even a choice. Those free men had made this decision for him, when they thought they could force themselves on Saradra. And now, Lion was simply following the path set before him.

The two men leaned over Saradra, one holding her down, the other wrestling her clothes off, while Saradra still fought and kicked. Lion moved like he was in a dream, seeing himself, but not quite in control. He snatched the sword one of the men had carelessly left by the bed. He grabbed the man by the scruff of his neck, and plunged the sword through him. The tip of the blade poked out from the man's stomach, and when Lion pulled it back, blood gushed out, spilling all over the bed and Saradra.

The second man jumped to his feet. Lion tossed the dying man away from the bed so he didn't crush Saradra, and kicked the second man against the wall. The man reached for his sword, but Lion had already slashed his throat before he could raise it.

He expected Saradra, sprayed with the blood of her attackers, to scream. He knew he should go to her and comfort her, but he couldn't move. He stared at the two dying men.

Free men.

A cold, black emotion filled his chest. Saradra pushed off the bed, trying to cover herself with her torn dress. She shuddered with deep breaths, shaking, but still managed to stay in control. Which was great, because Lion was about to break.

The sword slipped from Lion's fingers. Bending over, he retched and emptied his stomach.

"Merciful Alunwea," Saradra gasped. "Are you okay?"

Realisation struck him in waves, each one wringing his chest tighter. His breathing became shallow, and dark spots started flying across his sight. He found himself on the floor, his back against the wall, struggling to breathe.

"Killed... killed free men... I killed.... free men."

Saradra kneeled with him, her lips moving, but Lion's ears were ringing. He couldn't hear anything but his rapid heartbeat and his own thoughts.

He had killed free men. Free men! He had committed the greatest Act of Defiance.

Panic sat on his chest, heavy, strangling him. Stealing his air.

Killed free men...

His head was spinning.

I killed free men...

Saradra's palm exploded on his cheek, hard. It snapped Lion out of his panic. He blinked.

"Get a hold of yourself!" Saradra yelled.

"I... I killed... free men." Without orders. If he had been ordered to do so by his Masters, it was a completely different story. But he had killed them on his own. There was no turning back from this.

"You killed pigs," Saradra snarled.

"Wh... White Tower. They'll send me to White Tower." His chest tightened. Air escaped from his lungs and refused to return. He dipped his head between his knees, dry heaving.

"Fuck White Tower," Saradra said fiercely.

Lion's head snapped up. He opened his mouth, but no reply came out.

A dangerous glint settled in Saradra's bright blue eyes. Determined. "We're running," she decided.

Lion shook his head. "We can't. Hunters always—"

"Fuck Hunters too."

She was out of her mind! Lion gaped at her, shaking his head furiously, but she was already on the move.

She slipped out of her torn, blood-stained dress and went over to the cabinet in the corner. She rummaged through the clothes until she found a pair of baggy pants and a shirt.

"Whatever this is, whatever is happening at the castle, things will settle. One way or another. And you're right; they will figure out what we've done, and they will send us both to White Tower." She pulled the pants up and glanced at him over her shoulder. "So we've got nothing to lose. I'd rather take my chances with the Hunters."

No. She didn't understand. Hunters weren't human.

But... she was also right. They had nothing to lose.

"Besides," she continued after putting the shirt on. "This is the perfect time to escape. By the time they realise two slaves are missing — if they ever do — we'll be out of Brinescar. Hunters can't start searching until someone reports us missing, right?"

"They don't need someone to report... They will know." She didn't understand. *Hunters were not human.*

Saradra picked clean clothes for Lion and sat with him. Her eyes were sparkling with excitement. "We have to try. We'll go to Kaldoria."

"Kaldoria has an extradition treaty for escaped slaves..."

"We'll seek refuge at a Chamber of Twelve. One that's devoted to Alunwea. Pyres of Alunwea are the most merciful, they won't surrender us."

Lion allowed her to change his clothes. "Hunters are not human," he tried to explain. "They won't stop at the border. They'll find us anywhere."

"And Alunwea is the Goddess of Mercy," Saradra scoffed. "Her Pyres won't give us up, and her mercy will protect us." She pulled Lion up to his feet and went to search for a pair of travel cloaks. She shot him a dark gaze over her shoulders. "What other choice do we have?"

She was right. White Tower stood at the end of either option. At least this way, he was going to have the extra time to spend with Saradra. And if Hunters came too close... A sharp knife was all he needed for a painless end.

Saradra could only find one cloak and it was too small for Lion. She swung it over her shoulders and brought the hood down until her face and neck were concealed. She pushed the door ajar, peeking at the corridor outside. The sounds of battle were not nearby. Grabbing Lion's hand and tugging him behind, she slid outside.

As soon as Lion stepped into the corridor, he yanked his hand free, returning to the servant's room. Saradra opened her mouth, disappointment weighing on her features. She let out a relieved sigh after noticing Lion's intention. A sword would attract too much attention, but both soldiers had daggers. Lion pulled one free and hid it inside the sleeve of his shirt, blade against his wrist. He met Saradra at the door. She smiled at him encouragingly and took his hand.

After looking in both directions, Saradra turned to Lion. "Take us to one of the outer yards, somewhere we can escape into the city." When Lion didn't move, Saradra scowled. "I don't know the castle as well as you do. I've hardly even left the room. You have to lead. Take us through less used hallways."

She spoke like a free woman, and as pathetic as it was, it helped Lion. Her confidence and authority steadied him, and the last trickle of panic subsided. He scanned the corridor for a reference point, then turned left and led the way.

Saradra fell in step right beside him, her shoulder brushing against his elbow. She held her head high, but not high enough to reveal the tattoo on her neck. She walked confidently, as if she owned the castle. They stopped to listen and peek before turning each corner. Sounds of conflict echoed in every direction. It was difficult to pinpoint which way the Vogros soldiers were.

Once, they stumbled upon a young servant, running with a pile of jewellery in her arms. Lion tensed, clutching his knife, but Saradra didn't budge. Her steps never even faltered. She glared at the servant until the young woman averted her eyes, giving them a wide berth as she ran past, pretending not to see them.

They entered a landing which led to a less used set of stairs. When they heard a group of heavy footsteps climbing from the lower levels, Lion ducked under a windowsill at the back, pulling Saradra with him.

Half a dozen soldiers in Zarall uniforms appeared, led by Sir Dramesh. They ran past towards the way Lion and Saradra had come from, without even glancing at the shadows under the windowsill.

Saradra waited until they couldn't hear the soldiers' footsteps anymore, and sprinted for the stairs leading below, only to be stopped by Lion who yanked her back. He nodded upstairs.

"Why are we going up?" Saradra whispered as she trailed behind him.

"Lady Wharton's room," Lion said simply, as if that explained everything. "She cheats on her husband."

"Uh... What?" She narrowed her eyes, no doubt suspecting Lion had finally lost his marbles. Grabbing his forearm, she forced him to stop and look. She spoke tenderly, as if talking to a confused child. "We need to get to a courtyard."

Lion didn't move. The cooks in the kitchen gossiped all day. Everyone knew Lady Wharton cheated on her husband every time she stayed at Castle Brinescar. She always insisted on staying in the same room, even though the room was colder than the others in the winter.

She has other means to warm herself anyway, one of the scullions had commented snidely.

"There's a tree underneath her balcony," Lion explained. "We can climb down to the garden. And... there's a servants' entrance near the East Wall."

"How do you even know this?"

"The servants' entrance is–"

"No, how do you know about the cheating lady?"

Lion shifted his weight. "I listen." It was hard not to know about every rumour. The kitchen staff and Caesh loved to gossip.

Saradra's eyes grew large. She let go of his forearm. "Are you sure you haven't planned your escape before?"

"Never!"

"You memorize a map and you know exactly how to get out of the castle without being seen." When Lion simply shook his head in denial, she nudged him. "Never mind, let's go!"

Lion had only been to the guest wing of Castle Brinescar once. He vaguely remembered it was somewhere on the second level, facing East. He kept his eyes open for any clues to let them know they were headed in the right direction. They walked into a wide corridor with doors on one side and windows on the other.

Lion halted, causing Saradra to bump into his back. "What is it?" she whispered, following his gaze to a window.

She stepped closer; her expression darkened when she looked down into the courtyard below. She frowned at Lion. "We have to go," she said firmly, tugging at Lion's arm.

When he didn't move, Saradra cupped his chin to tear his gaze from the scene below. "There's nothing you can do. We have to go. Now."

Badimar and the trainers were cornered in the training yard below. They were joined by a handful of Zarall soldiers, the weaponsmith, and a pair of apprentices, and yet they were still painfully outnumbered against dozens of Vogros soldiers. They must have had the chance to raid the weapons shack near the training yard, because each one of them was equipped with weapons and even some armour.

Lion had never seen Badimar fight before. The Master of the Beasts was a better trainer than he was a fighter. Even so, Vogros men couldn't be cautious enough within his sword's reach. His steps were calculated, precise. He only struck when there was a clear opening, never wasting an attack. He was not bold, but neither was he timid. Despite the growing number of the enemy, he wasn't withdrawing. He was...

"Stalling," Lion muttered.

Almost as if they were waiting for something. Or someone.

"We have to go," Saradra urged him again.

Lion was overwhelmed by an immense urge to go down there and help them.

"You can't possibly be serious!" Saradra hissed, as if reading his mind. "Forget about them! He's a ruthless man. Don't you remember what he'd done to you?" To remind him, she pressed a hand against Lion's back, causing a jolt of pain.

She didn't understand. Badimar was a great trainer. He was not merciful, but not cruel, either. He never punished him without a solid reason, and the magnitude of his punishments always matched the mistake. They always made Lion a better fighter. He had spent the last three years training with him every day. He respected him. He had to go there and help. He had to fight beside him. He wanted to see the look on his face — surprise, gratitude, pride — when Lion rushed to save him.

"Please," Saradra begged. "Look at me."

She stepped between Lion and the window, but he pushed her aside with a frown. He was noticing two things now. First, the fighting bear of Vogros was not the only coat of arms on the enemy soldiers. Some coat of arms Lion didn't recognise, but some he did from guests he had seen at the feasts. Vogros soldiers had allies. Moreover, some men fighting against Badimar were wearing the black and gold uniforms of House Zarall!

There were traitors amongst Zarall soldiers. That explained why there wasn't much of a resistance from the king's soldiers.

The second thing he had noticed was how one of the Zarall traitors was flanking Joharin.

The older trainer didn't see him and he didn't get any time to regret his mistake. Zarall traitor stabbed Joharin's midsection. Caesh pulled him back, while Badimar gave them cover, but Lion had seen the angle the sword had gone through.

Joharin was giving his last breath.

Lion's chest hummed. That was his team. His team was fighting and dying.

Saradra's slap brought him back to himself for the second time that night.

"Look at me!" Saradra commanded harshly. "You can't do anything for them. We have to move!" She shoved him away from the window as if to make her point.

Lion melted under her gaze. He embraced the nausea and the faint pain that soared through his body, just so he could enjoy those eyes for a few more precious seconds longer. He was itching to have one last look at Badimar, but if he did, he knew he wouldn't be able to look away again. So, he took Saradra's hand and led the way.

He was too aware of the windows lined on the right side of the corridor. His skin was prickling. He wiped his forehead, suddenly remembering Sir Dramesh and the group of soldiers heading in the direction of Lion's room. Were they sent by Badimar? Was he stalling for Lion to join the fight? As overwhelming as their odds were, a Raged purebred could change the course of that skirmish. What would happen to them when Sir Dramesh found Lion's room empty?

Saradra's fingers squeezed his hand, reminding him of her presence. His priority was her. He belonged to her now, the same way she belonged to him.

After the next turn, Lion immediately recognized the familiar clues indicating they had arrived at the guests' quarters. The corridor was wider and cluttered with decorations; flowers, paintings, statues, and other useless ornaments. The air was heavy with the sweet smell of fresh flowers and scented candles. Lion's sense of direction told him the doors on their left had a view of the royal garden. They just had to find the right one.

"It's one of these rooms," he pointed at the doors.

Saradra let go of his hand and hurried to the first one. She turned the knob, but it was locked. She moved to the next one. "How do we know..."

Heavy boots began approaching from the other end. They were fast.

Lion's head snapped back and forth, trying to decide between hiding or pulling his knife out. Sweat trickled down his back. He had already killed two free men. What difference would a few more bodies make?

"Here!" Saradra whispered victoriously. The next door she tried was unlocked. She darted to grab Lion's hand and tugged him inside the room with her. She closed the door as quietly as possible.

Lion only had a couple of seconds to notice the burn marks on the doorframe before Saradra shut the door, leaving them in the dark. She stepped back, her eyes fixed on the door. Someone gave a muffled command outside, and the boots approached. Lion hooked his elbow around her waist and pulled her close. He turned his back to the door, his eyes scanning the shadows in the room, looking for a place to keep her out of harm's way as he faced whoever came through that door. He smelled something wet and burning.

They were not alone.

At the back of the room, a dark shape towered high, the top of its head grazing the ceiling. A deep, guttural growl filled the room, chilling Lion's bones. The thing resembled a dog, maybe a hound, but was unnaturally enormous. Its pointy ears were tilted back, mouth pulled into a snarl. Its neatly lined, sharp teeth were shining with spittle. Its black coat was patchy and wet. Molten red eyes focused on Saradra's back.

Lion pulled Saradra closer to him as the hound flared its nostrils. It breathed out a growl, which reverberated through the room, making Saradra yelp. With another low growl, the hound's coat was lit on fire, flames licking its head and upper body. Saradra covered her mouth with both hands, eyes wide with horror, as a whisper escaped: "Merciful Alunwea."

Liquid fire dribbled down the hound's teeth, singeing the carpet-covered floor. Its coat was on fire and it didn't even flinch, like the flames were an extension of its fur. It crouched on its thick, muscular legs, ready to leap.

Lion pushed Saradra between him and the door, readying his knife, his mind already going through combat strategies for fighting large animals, assessing his environment, looking for things he can use. Animal... This thing wasn't even an animal. What was it? How did it move? How did it think? How was he ever going to get through those flames to...

His thoughts were distracted by the sounds of the men right outside the door. The hound's molten eyes were drawn to the door as well. *It can be distracted*, Lion noted as he started planning ways he could use deception. One of the soldiers outside — he knew they were soldiers as he could hear their chainmail as they moved — barked out instructions: "This is the one. Break the door!"

They were about to get caught between a burning monster and a group of Vogros soldiers. Lion knew which enemy he could defeat. He grabbed Saradra's arm, ready to bolt for the door, when he spotted the man crouched behind the hound. The monster dispelled enough light to let Lion recognise the man's face at first glance. He had seen him at King Leonis's latest feast; he was the stranger who was sitting at the head of the table with Leonis's head physician.

Still dressed in his plain black robe, the man was slumped against the wall. He seemed unfazed by the flame-dribbling monster beside him. His eyes were fixed on Lion. Grasping the bed for leverage, the man in the black robe dragged himself up to his feet. His gaze trailed down to Lion's neck and his eyes narrowed. His face looked older or simply tired, then Lion remembered. The left side of his robe was soaked in blood. A small object attached to a leather string dangled in the man's free hand.

The man's eyes widened as he stared at Lion's neck. Then, he smiled. It was a smile that made Lion's skin crawl with unease. The man moved his lips and mouthed two words: *Purebred. Perfect.*

Multiple things happened in quick succession.

First, the man in the black robe staggered to his knees. The burning hound hissed, then disappeared in a puff. Before the last sparks of its flame coat died, the door behind them broke open and a horde of Vogros soldiers filed in, swords raised.

The black-robed man pointed a finger in their direction and yelled, "*Dracistuecto!*"

Lion didn't have the time to wonder how the man knew his Kill Word.

Rage surged into his mind, claiming control. A shudder soared through his muscles as he looked at the armed men from behind a haze. A deep growl rose out of him. His last act was to push Saradra away from himself, hoping she would stay out of his sight until the Rage passed.

21

LION

LION WOKE WITH AN itch on his face.

He scrunched his nose, but it didn't provide relief. His own hair and beard were brushing against his cheek. He raised a hand to push them away, but his sense of direction had gone awry. Up was down and down was up and he couldn't move a finger. He couldn't even open his eyes.

He was floating in a red darkness. His clothes were soaked. He smelled blood. There was too much blood...

Saradra!

He shot his eyes open with some difficulty. Dried blood was stuck on his eyelashes, gluing his eyelids together.

He was hanging in the air upside down, his arms dangling past his head. He tipped his chin to his chest, gazing at his feet. His body was coated in a thick layer of blood. Some of it belonged to him. Warm blood trickled down his shoulders, painting his blond hair and beard red, before dripping to the floor beneath him.

A pulsing, black rope, thicker than his wrist, was wrapped around his ankles, keeping him in the air. Lion's eyes traced the rope to the ceiling, where it disappeared in the shadows.

A single eye blinked at him from those shadows.

Lion shouted. When he flailed his arms weakly, a second rope reached out from the ceiling, snaking around his knees to steady him.

Lion screamed again.

Pain jolted in his abdomen when he struggled, and more blood spilled from the wound that he had just discovered. He panted, craning his neck to see the room beneath him.

The man in the black robe was right underneath him. He didn't look up. He was drawing a large circle on the floor, using Lion's blood as ink. He was scribing fine details along the inner lines of the circle. Shapes that looked like letters, but nothing Lion had seen before.

In the middle of the circle, there was the strangest necklace Lion had ever seen. It was a single, large animal tooth at the end of a black leather string. The tooth was larger than his hand. Lion couldn't picture any animal that was humongous enough to accommodate a tooth that size in its mouth.

Panic started clawing at Lion's chest. Nightmare. He was having a nightmare. But everything felt so real; the smell and taste of blood, the pain in his gut, even the battle soreness he felt in his muscles, were all real. He brought one hand down — or up — to his stomach, pressing against his wound. Still groaning and wheezing, his gaze flickered between the blinking eye in the ceiling and the black-robed man. Was the man even aware of the creature lurking over his head?

Nightmare. He was in a nightmare.

Where was Saradra? Where was this place, if not a nightmare?

He could see tall windows and a round-shaped room. He glimpsed at an upside-down view of the castle walls outside. It was still dark. Was this still the same night?

The door burst open and another group of Vogros soldiers charged in. This time, they were mixed with several Zarall traitors.

The man in the black robe hardly even glanced at them. He made a sharp gesture with his hand, pointing at the newcomers and speaking Lion's Kill Word once again.

The living ropes around Lion's legs tensed, swung back slightly, and flung him towards the attackers. Lion hit the first two hard, knocking them down. He screamcd in pain.

He was almost glad the Rage took over his mind, putting an end to this horrific nightmare.

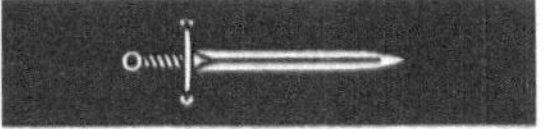

When he opened his eyes again, the nightmare kept going.

Lion was lying on his back. The man's face, looking even more tired and aged, hovered over him. His eyes were closed, mouth moving, speaking an unfamiliar tongue. He gripped the necklace in one hand, and a knife in the other. His skin was pale and wrinkled as if he had aged thirty years in the last... how long was Lion out for?

The man opened his dark eyes and plunged the knife into Lion's chest.

Lion gasped, more surprised than in pain. He lifted his head up, staring at the knife protruding from his chest. Right in his heart.

The man had stabbed him right in his heart!

When the man moved the knife, cutting his chest wide open, Lion's heels kicked the floor weakly. His head felt heavy, and a cold shiver took over. Blood filled his mouth. He coughed it out. His head fell to the side, and he noticed the circle of blood around him. The letters and shapes the man had drawn were moving, crawling like squiggly worms. Towards him.

The man raised his voice, chanting, almost yelling. He threw the knife away and dipped both hands into Lion's chest, causing him to jolt upright, only to fall back again. All his strength drained out of his muscles.

A cold darkness creeped in around the edges of his vision. All he could hear through the ringing in his ears was the weak sound of his slowing heartbeat.

He was dying.

The man's hands cupped his heart, something sharp pressing against it.

A cold, pure darkness invaded his mind, obscuring his thoughts and senses. With a detached sense of amusement, he noticed dying was pretty similar to surrendering to his Kill Word. Except he wasn't going to wake up from this.

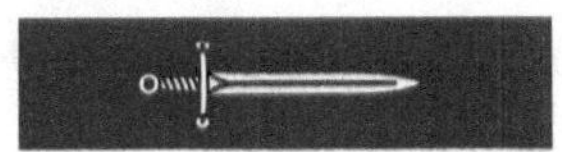

LION WOKE UP WITH a start, his body jerking upright from the cold stone floor. His mind was a haze of jumbled memories and fragmented images, with one horrific moment standing out.

He had died.

He remembered the agonizing pain of the knife plunging into his chest. Instinctively, his hand flew to his chest, expecting to feel the gaping wound. He must have lost so much blood and had to find something to stop the bleeding...

Nothing. There was nothing. No blood, no wound, not even a scar.

He lifted his shirt, examining the perfectly intact — blood-stained but un-broken — skin beneath. He scrubbed the dried blood off and pressed his fingers against his chest and his stomach, where he remembered another wound had been. Just smooth, dirty, but perfectly healthy skin.

Nightmare. The memories felt so real, but they couldn't be real, because his body bore no evidence of it. So it must have been a nightmare.

He rose to his feet, his head swimming with disorientation. He shivered with the memory of the man's fingers crawling inside his chest. He rubbed his temples, trying to make sense of it.

He had died. He remembered dying.

He stumbled back onto his knees, black spots flying in his sight. He swiped his hand across the stone floor beneath him and stared at the dust on his fingers. The intricate drawings he thought he saw — odd signs and patterns scribbled with his blood — were gone. Not even a drop of blood. Just dust.

When he blinked, the image of crawling red letters and signs flowing into his body flashed in his mind. He shook his head. No, none of those things he saw were real. The crawling letters, knife plunging through his chest, and the shadows on the ceiling...

He jumped back to his feet, staggering as he craned his neck to see the ceiling above. Had he imagined the monster as well? The thing with a single blinking eye and rope-like tendrils that reached from the shadows. Nothing. No shadows, no tendrils. Just a grey stone ceiling with soot stains and mould.

He groaned, barely keeping his balance. He couldn't shake off the lingering sense of dread. The possibility that it had all been a dream seemed both a relief and a source of deeper confusion. What had that man done to him? He looked around. Where was the man? His black robe was bunched up in a messy pile, but the man himself was nowhere to be seen.

Lion shuddered. His head was hurting. He had to get out of this place before the man returned and spoke his Kill Word again.

Before he stabbed his heart again.

He was in a round room — one of the tower rooms — of the castle. The room was dimly lit by the morning light filtering through the windows, casting long shadows across the floor. Lion looked for the door, and he saw the bodies.

A dozen soldiers lay scattered near the door. The sight of their mutilated bodies chilled Lion's blood. He recognised his own work. He had done this. Smashed heads, twisted necks, broken limbs posing in unnatural angles. Some others were disarmed and killed by their own weapons. Lion wasn't disturbed by the aftermath of violence; he was horrified because this part of the nightmare — being Raged and unleashed at the intruders — was true.

Then did that mean...

He rubbed his face with his palms, trying to push back the nagging questions and the headache they caused. He tried to focus on the single, most important question he needed to explore.

Where was Saradra?

He staggered towards the door, leaning against the wall and carefully treading between severed limbs and spilled guts. As always, Lion had no memory after the Rage took his mind. A cold doubt grasped his heart. What if he killed Saradra too?

He swallowed. No, he would have remembered Saradra. He would have stopped himself. Even under the iron grip of Rage, Lion would never harm Saradra. He tried to swallow the lump in his throat, hating the doubt that tangled his heart. He forced himself to breathe and move on. He had to get to the guests' quarters. Saradra was smart. She would have stayed hidden, out of Lion's sight.

Outside the round-shaped room, Lion found a set of stairs spiralling down. Small, square windows lined along the right wall of the stairs. The fire from last night was out and an eerie silence hung over the castle. In these early hours of the morning, courtyards would have been bustling with noise and activity. Everything was dead silent.

He wondered how long it had taken for the king's men to repel the intruders. He found his answer at the bottom of the stairs; they hadn't.

A group of Vogros soldiers were patrolling the corridor downstairs. When they spotted him, they drew their weapons and charged.

Lion dropped to his knees without hesitation. Tilting his head back, he revealed his neck and rested his hands on his lap. He didn't even consider resisting the men or trying to break free. Because he knew Saradra wouldn't have escaped without him. If she was alive — if Lion hadn't killed her amidst his Rage — there was a high chance she was captured and taken to the slave barracks. There was no reason to attempt an escape or fight these men without her.

The Vogros men didn't slow down.

Lion's eyebrows twitched, though he tried not to look or flinch. *All free men are greedy.* Why were they not lowering their weapons? Sweat ran down his spine when he remembered he was coated in blood. Was his tattoo even visible?

He clenched his fists. A survival instinct that wasn't there before urged him to stand up and protect himself. He didn't want to die without knowing what happened to Saradra. Yet, his slave training took over promptly, and he sat still. Helpless by choice.

A gauntleted fist landed on the side of his face, sending him sprawling to the floor. Next came the kicks of heavy boots. He curled into a ball, wrapping his arms around his head and enduring until they decided it was enough.

He didn't remember the last time he received such a beating; Badimar wasn't a big fan of risking permanent damage to the king's precious Lion of Zarall. He predominantly used a whip or his Pain Word, and he would use them sparingly. This beating felt different, though. It didn't serve to punish or discipline. These men were angry, and they wanted to bleed him.

Someone called to a halt, and the men complied reluctantly. The same person ordered two of them to climb to the top of the tower and see what was up there.

Lion remained motionless; still curled up and covering his head. He kept his eyes on the blood-soaked floor. The heavy boots remained at the peripheral of his sight, ready to strike again.

Within a few minutes, the two men came back from the top of the tower. One of them leaned against the wall, throwing up, while the other one reported the scene upstairs, his face grim and green.

Lion could feel their eyes on him, piercing his back with their hostility, blame, and promise of vengeance. His body tensed with the prospect of more kicks. But their leader's decision almost made him smile.

"Take him to the slave barracks."

Saradra was there, Lion was sure of it. If he could hug her one more time, everything was going to be okay.

However, his triumph melted like snow on a summer's day at the man's next words: "Stick him in a cell. No food or water until further notice."

Two men moved forward to yank him up to his feet. They paused when their leader added, "And be gentle with him. He's the Lion of Zarall."

22

OLIRA

THE MIDDAY SUN CAST long beams of light through the gaps in the barn's weathered wooden walls. Olira stood in the centre of the barn, watching the motes of dust that danced lazily in the air, waiting. Procrastinating.

She had changed the slave's bandages earlier and given him some food. Then, she had kept herself busy pushing the bales of hay aside and clearing some space while she waited for the slave to finish eating. She was going to need a lot of room to do what she had in mind and doing the tedious work of pushing the bales gave her a moment to steady her nerves.

As if sensing her hesitation, Warrior brayed from his stall, telling her to stop being a coward and go through with it. She rolled her eyes at him. She grabbed the makeshift crutch she had left against the wooden wall. Then she took a deep breath before returning to the slave's stall.

The purebred lay on the makeshift bed, his eyes open but staring at nothing in particular. He had pushed the empty plate aside. As she entered, he sat up slowly, not meeting her gaze or speaking a word. His hair was unkempt, and a rough stubble covered his jaw and cheeks. *Look for a display of emotion*, Mistress Aeliana had said, but the man's face offered her nothing.

"I'm going to take that chain off," she said before she approached him. She found herself giving him a warning every time she needed to approach him for something, as if soothing a wild animal so it doesn't bite her hand off. She pulled the keys out from her pocket and knelt beside him. She carefully unlocked the collar, stood up, and handed him the crutch. "Stand up."

The slave gripped the crutch tightly and pulled himself to his feet. His leg was healing well, but Olira suspected it still pained him. It was hard to tell. Every time she asked whether he was in pain, he said he was well, but the flesh was still swollen and stiff. So she still gave him *Numbleaf*, and he drank every drop of it. Leaning on the crutch, his muscular forearms bulging beneath his sleeves, the purebred waited for his next instruction.

"We need to get you moving again," she said. "It will help with the stiffness." She nodded towards the centre of the barn. "Walk back and forth. Take it easy."

The slave complied without complaint. He took a tentative step, leaning heavily on the crutch, and began to walk. Olira stood aside and watched him for a moment, then she got to work. Still watching him out the corner of her eye, she picked up the chalk she had brought earlier and started drawing a Praying Ring on the dirt floor.

The purebred was focused on his task, his gaze fixed on the ground ahead of him. His worn-out shoes made a soft scuffle on the dirt floor as he hobbled and dragged his foot. Olira finished drawing the circle, then dusted his hands, still glancing at the slave for a reaction. Nothing. She stepped into the Praying Ring and kneeled in the centre.

"Hey," she called out to the slave. He stopped and looked in her direction, his eyes fixed on the circle. "I need something red."

The slave didn't move, still staring at the circle, blinking.

"I'm praying to Alunwea," Olira said impatiently. "I need to hold something red." When he still didn't move, she pointed at the apple she had brought from the pantry and left on a bale of hay. "Can you bring me that, please?"

The slave hobbled to the bale, picked up the apple, then approached her. He stood outside the Praying Ring and reached over the line to hand her the apple. Olira glanced at the slave's feet, firmly planted outside the chalk line. Her heart raced. Was he avoiding stepping into the ring? Was Aeliana right about fiends taking over purebreds? She needed him to step inside.

And what if he was possessed? Would he become violent if she forced him? Well, as long as she stayed inside the ring, she was safe. She could paralyse him, drag him back inside the stall, chain him, then decide what to do with him.

"Are you expecting me to get up?" she snapped. "Bring it over."

The purebred tucked the apple under his arm, then steadied himself with both hands on the crutch. As he stepped inside, his feet smeared some of the chalk away and broke the circle. He handed her the apple, then turned and limped back outside.

Olira stared at the disrupted line, her hands gripping the apple so tight, she almost bruised the fruit. She had to know for sure. She dug out her chalk and quickly fixed the line. Sitting back in the centre, she ordered, "Come pray with me."

The purebred froze with his back to her. She wished she could see his face. Tension coursed through her muscles as she watched for the slave's reaction. When he still didn't move, Olira huffed. "I'm praying to Alunwea, the Goddess of Mercy. You could really use her favour right now."

The purebred stood like a statue, his messy blond hair catching the light that filtered through the gaps in the barn walls. Olira narrowed her eyes at the man's back, her heart pounding in her ears. "What's the problem?" she asked carefully.

"Purebreds don't worship, Owner." The purebred's voice was quiet but clear, with no hint of any emotion. "We don't have *rhoas*. Riders forsake slaves."

This was the most words he had spoken in the last few weeks. Olira huffed. "Twelve Riders don't forsake anyone. I'll do the praying. You come sit." She held her breath. Seconds stretched to hours before the man finally turned and complied, his face devoid of any emotion. She couldn't help but feel a flicker of disappointment, even though this was exactly what she had anticipated.

"And watch the line," she warned him firmly as he approached the Praying Ring. He hesitated for a moment before lifting his foot over the line and walked into the Praying Ring.

Olira didn't know what she had been expecting, and she couldn't quite explain the conflicting feelings of relief and frustration as the slave carefully settled himself beside her. He extended his right leg in front of him, moving slowly, and sat with his hands on his lap, staring straight ahead. She cast a quick glance at the chalk line to make sure it was unbroken, then composed herself, keeping the apple close to her heart, and started praying.

She held the Long Ritual, speaking twelve prayers each to the Twelve Riders and ending with a last prayer for the lost *rhoas*. Then she devoted a separate prayer to Alunwea, asking for mercy and forgiveness, and a quick recovery for the slave. The purebred sat without a stir the entire time. As soon as she was done, he stood and limped back into his stall, leaving Olira simmering with an unexplainable irritation and embarrassment.

23

LION

LION'S EARS PICKED UP footsteps approaching his cell again.

His hearing had become much sharper than before, very quickly. His heart skipped a beat as he covered his head and drew his knees to his chest. No matter how much he braced, he could never prepare for this.

The grill on his cell door slid to the side, and a guard peeked in. The torch-lights from the hallway outside spilt onto the floor of his cell, breaking the thick darkness.

"*Prihjtivaviula*," the guard muttered dully. He watched Lion's quiet suffering for several seconds, his face a mask of boredom, then slid the grill closed and walked away.

An eternity later, when the pain receded, Lion rolled on to his back. In the small, dark cell, he had lost his sense of time. Each time he came out of his Pain Word, his mind went foggy as his thoughts raced, disoriented. In those few seconds, he couldn't remember where he was, why he was here, what happened. And then it would all come to him, and he would cry and hyperventilate, because that moment when he acknowledged the possibility that he might have killed Saradra was worse than the pain itself.

No, he thought desperately. *No, I wouldn't. She would get out of the way. She would hide.*

The other slaves were held in three larger cells together. Lion had searched for Saradra's face amongst the vacant faces of the slaves, but he only had a split second to look. He was dragged past through the slave barracks quickly and was stuffed in his cell, alone. At first, he was starved for several days. Then, food and water started to come, but irregularly and in pitiful amounts. Just enough to ensure his survival but still leave him starving continuously.

He blinked at the darkness numbly. He had lost track of time and had no way of knowing how long had passed since that night. The cell had no windows. He lay in darkness, in a state of deprivation, flinching every time the grill slid open and the light broke the shelter of his shadows. He even gave up on trying to understand whether they were coming to bring food or torture or both.

Nothing they did to him mattered. None of these were more unbearable than not knowing what had happened to Saradra.

He had nightmares. Every time he closed his eyes, he saw the images of the massacred corpses at the top of the tower. He never had any nightmares about any of the slaves he killed in the arenas before. He never even thought of them. However, each of those nightmares ended with him discovering Saradra's cold body amongst his victims at the tower. Her bones were broken, her skull bashed in with blunt force, her face was bitten off... The only recognisable part of her body was her flame-coloured hair.

He would wake with a scream each time, the noise drawing the attention of the guards, who never missed an opportunity to torture him.

He was desperate to know what happened to Saradra. The uncertainty ate him up. He couldn't rest until he confirmed that she was unharmed. Lion pressed his palms over his eyes, breathing deeply, trying to stay calm. If he had hurt her... The mere thought sent waves of sickness coursing through his body. The guilt was an unbearable weight pressing down on his chest. He almost wished the guard would return to speak his Pain Word again.

He dropped his hands to his sides, a scowl creasing his forehead. He still didn't know how that man in the black robes knew his Kill Word. Lion thought he was just a guest, not even a castle staff. Even amongst the castle staff, only a few knew Lion's Words: Badimar, the other trainers, Vanalten, and Raydon.

Now, he was certain half the Vogros soldiers memorised his Pain Word.

They made a habit of speaking it every time they'd walked past his cell. Who-ever was patrolling the cells would speak the word each time he passed his door. A few of them, whom he now recognised, appeared to be enjoying themselves as they watched with fascination. Once he heard them play a drinking game with his Pain Word.

Lion suspected it was the officer who first discovered his Pain Word. The man who raided his room that night and ordered his two soldiers to take Lion and Saradra away. He had discovered the corpses of his men and knew Lion had done that. He had charged into his cell and beat him bloody, yelling his Pain Word repeatedly. Lion had expected to be on his way to White Tower the next day.

And yet, days had passed, and he was still here.

He was growing more and more nervous each day, especially since he received a visit from Karhad, the new Master of the Slaves. Master Raydon's replacement had short brown hair, a young face, and a large earring dangling from his right ear. The heavy, leather-bound book he carried contained Master Raydon's slave records.

After examining Lion against the records, Karhad had recited the change of ownership statement to Lion: "You are now the property of King Kastian Vogros, the first of his name, the ruler of Chinderia. At your Owner's request, your name will remain Lion of Zarall. Acknowledge."

Staggering to his feet, Lion had faltered, almost making the mistake of gawk-ing at the new Master of the Slaves. Guards talked a lot, and he had already learned that King Leonis and Queen Arasanara had been killed on the night of the coup. The guards had also laughed about how Prince Lygor Zarall, who had been on a diplomatic mission at Kaldoria for the last five years, was simultaneously assassinated. Even the distant relatives who carried the Zarall name were taken care of.

"King Kastian has a strong distaste for the Zarall name," one of the guards had laughed. "Next, he'll make sure the name will be erased from all the history books."

"Not that you know how to read 'em," his friend had mocked, before they had resumed Lion's torture.

Therefore, when Master Karhad declared Lion's name to remain the same, a sense of foreboding overwhelmed him. He obediently recited the memorised phrase and acknowledged his new Owner, knowing this could not be good.

When the physical beatings had stopped after that, Lion's unease had only grown more.

They never asked him anything about the soldiers he had killed. They never asked what he had been doing in that tower, or what had happened to that man in the black robe. He even had a visit from a new physician once, making sure the guards hadn't taken their hospitality too far.

There was only one explanation why Lion was still alive, still at Castle Brinescar, and still carried the Zarall name; King Kastian had plans for him. And those plans involved a very public, humiliating, and slow death for the late King Leonis's beloved, famed Lion of Zarall.

When he heard a group of approaching footsteps again, Lion turned to his side, curling up on himself. He wasn't afraid of dying. He didn't even care about the torture. He just didn't want to die without knowing what had happened to Saradra.

The grill slid to the side with a metal screech. Lion tensed. Instead of his Pain Word, the next sound he heard was keys sliding into the lock and the cell door opening with a creak. The light dispelled the darkness of his cell. Since taking up residence in this cell, Lion had developed a distaste for the light. The darkness was safe. The pain always came with light.

Lion knew his time in this cell was up even before two pairs of strong hands yanked him. His stomach growled, his head spun, and he swayed on his feet. When the guards dragged him out into the hallway, he was struck temporarily blind by the torches on the walls. He hung his head low, blinking his eyes furiously as he staggered forward along the hallway between the two guards.

He almost sensed her.

As he walked by the spacious open cells where slaves slept, he somehow felt her presence among them. He whipped his head up, digging his heels to the ground. However, his sight was still impaired by the light. One of the guards kicked behind his knee and dragged him forward. Lion kept craning his neck back. He knew she was there. He just wanted to look at her bright blue eyes one last time. He wanted to break free and run back.

As if sensing his intention, one of his guards buried a punch below his ribs. The blow stole his air. By the time Lion caught his breath, they were already out of the slave barracks.

Master Karhad was waiting for him in a room he recognised by the rows of clothes hanging on racks and the tables scattered with combs, jars of oil, powders, and various accessories. This was where Raydon had prepared him before every appearance at King Leonis's feasts and banquets.

They dropped him on a chair and pushed a plate in front of him. Lion hardly even looked at the food, shoving it in his mouth with his eyes half-closed. He tasted bread, cold meat, and some sort of gruel.

Next, Karhad ordered him to get into a wooden tub filled with hot water. Already feeling stronger and steadier on his feet, Lion complied without help. Two house slaves approached to scrub the blood and dirt off his skin. One of them was a familiar female slave who worked on his appearance before every battle. Lion wondered what happened to the old slave with the weathered face and bony fingers.

After the bath, Lion climbed on the low pedestal and stood still. He knew the drill. The slaves brought the outfit he wore at the last feast: a pair of black pants and boots, and a black half-cape. He scowled when they slipped the golden greaves and the golden belt on; the Zarall symbol was openly engraved on them both.

He wasn't surprised when he didn't receive any weapons. The slaves spent most of the time brushing his hair; the whole process was almost comparable to having his skin flayed off alive. They slapped a grey liquid on his hair, giving it more volume. He looked exactly like he did at the last feast; King Leonis's proud Lion of Zarall.

After a final inspection, Karhad led him back outside, with two guards bringing up the rear.

Lion couldn't help but feeling like a lone cat in a house full of hungry dogs. Or bears. He had no loyalty for the black and gold lion of House Zarall he carried on his accessories, but the fighting bear of Vogros evoked hostile feelings in him.

He shouldn't even have been feeling anything for any of his Owners. This was Saradra's doing. She had awakened something inside of him. She had made him desire and want and wonder. His world had been black and white prior to meeting Saradra. Now it was coloured with thoughts and feelings he couldn't control. His mind was a whirlwind. Part of him missed the emptiness, but he doubted he could ever go back to being that mindless slave again.

They reached a small service yard behind the upper kitchen. It was night outside, and the yard was lit with torches on the walls. The kitchen sounded busy. The new king was giving a feast and Lion was going to make an appearance. But for what?

A cage waited just outside the large doors leading to the inner keep. It was tall enough to stand inside and it was placed on a cart pulled by two slaves. Two beasts. One was Hopper. The other was Crowseye, a purebred. They were both wearing Vogros colours now. Lion wondered if they kept their names too or they were given new names. If they were wearing Vogros colours, then the king must have decided to keep them. Lion clenched his jaw, ignoring that odd mixture of relief and jealousy. He wanted to ask Hopper about Badimar. Did Badimar and the others make it? He knew it had been a bloody coup. Almost all servants and castle staff were killed without being given a chance to surrender. So if Badimar hadn't escaped, he was dead.

Lion tried to catch Hopper's gaze, but the freeborn stared straight ahead, behaving perfectly disciplined in front of the new Master of the Slaves. Karhad unlocked the cage and stood aside. "Get inside."

Lion didn't move, watching Hopper out of the corner of his eyes.

"I said, get inside!" Karhad ordered, louder.

That caught Hopper's attention. The freeborn beast glanced in his direction. Beneath his frown was curiosity, and a pinch of annoyance. Hopper still fostered a hatred at Lion for nearly gauging his eyes out. His scowl deepened when he read Lion's unspoken question.

The hilt of a sword landed hard between Lion's shoulder blades. He staggered forward, swallowing a groan. Ignoring the brewing growl deep in his chest, Lion climbed inside the cage before the guard struck him again.

"Stay standing and face forward," Karhad instructed. "Eyes on the floor."

Lion complied. Karhad and the guards pulled a black curtain over the cage. Just before the curtain shrouded Lion from the outside world, Hopper's chin dipped vaguely.

Lion's heart skipped a beat. The Master of the Beast had survived. He closed his eyes and let out a breath.

With the thick curtain draping over all four sides of the cage, Lion was left in semidarkness. He could still hear outside and see the dark silhouettes of anyone who was near enough, but nothing more.

He stumbled back when the cart moved forward. He steadied himself by holding on to the bars on two sides. Anxiety was like a giant animal trapped inside the cage with him. It filled every bit of the empty space surrounding him, strangling him and stealing his air. He couldn't shake the feeling that this cart was taking him to a painful death.

For the millionth time, he wished he could see Saradra one more time before he died.

The fear must have been playing tricks on his mind, because he started hearing violent growls. Lion's skin prickled and his muscles froze. The image of the burning hound flashed in his mind, followed by the image of the monster on the ceiling. Lion shook his head, trying to focus on the present. But the sounds were getting louder and closer.

The man in the black robe! He was outside, along with his monsters!

Was this the painful, humiliating death Kastian Vogros was preparing for the Lion of Zarall?

The cage rattled and Lion stumbled to the side. He didn't dare closing his eyes for the fear of reliving the events of that horrible night. In his dark cell, he had tried so hard to forget about the man in the black robe. His pale, sunken face. What he did. How he stabbed his heart and killed him!

The cart stopped.

Lion heard a muttered speech from outside, but the low rumble of the monster blanketed it. As the time stretched, the fear continued to gnaw on him.

Not my body, it's their property, he thought desperately, despite knowing it would not work. Not anymore. He was trapped in his body, drowning in fear.

He heard large doors creaking open, and the cart started moving again.

More speech, excited whispers. Echoes. Lion's eyes narrowed as he listened. Were they in the banquet hall? It sounded crowded. The monster's growls broke away, but it was still nearby. And it roared louder now. Silhouettes of people glided past behind the curtains. The cart slowed down, stopped, and turned right. Lion's heart thrashed wildly in the cage of his ribs.

After a moment filled with the excited chatter of people in the room, a male voice spoke.

"You are the most fortunate descendants of your families," the man said with a strong, tenor voice that Lion clearly heard despite the thick curtain between them. "Because you are here, in this hall tonight, to witness the beginning of a new era for Chinderia."

"Long live King Kastian!" someone yelled and others repeated.

King Kastian gave a brief pause. The buzz of excitement subsided. Lion didn't have to see to know that every pair of eyes in the hall was now firmly fixed on the new king.

"This country had an illness," King Kastian said gravely. "A taint. For a hundred years, we have been striving to be free from this stain. This sickness called Zarall." He paused to let the murmurs of agreement heard, then continued: "I would like you to listen to what Pyrearch Mendrich has to say. I know you all are loyal followers of the Twelve Riders. And in days like these, it is even more critical that we heed the Twelve's teachings. It is important we remember the *Dividing of Homes*."

A pause, a shuffle of feet, low murmurs. Lion imagined King Kastian greeting an old man in pyre robes up the platform in front of the long table where King Leonis used to sit. The Pyrearch spoke with a voice that sounded older than what Lion imagined.

"Kiejain, the first Rider, the first warrior, the first husband, the mightiest," the Pyrearch bellowed enthusiastically. "We have wandered from your path and came to confess our sins. We seek redemption and—"

"It is important we remember the *Dividing of Homes* tonight, Pyrearch Mendrich," Kastian interrupted. There was an impatient edge to his voice. "I'm confident everyone here will attend to the first sermon at the Grand Chamber of Twelve in the city first thing tomorrow morning."

The old man cleared his throat. If he was offended by the interruption, he didn't show it in his voice. "I will recite you *Dividing of Homes*, word by word, from the Book of Twelve." He paused to take a deep breath, then spoke again.

"In the dawn of creation, the world was whole and cloaked in darkness. Before the advent of humankind, two mighty races vied for supremacy. Both were offspring of the sacred fire. The dragons, defeated in battle, retreated into the hidden depths of the Frozen Caves. The fiends, triumphant, became sovereigns of the darkness."

Lion crossed his arms and leaned against one side of the cage. What was going on? The monster was still growling lowly somewhere behind the curtains; he wasn't imagining it. King Kastian was giving a feast, had invited guests, and brought Lion over, for what? To make them listen to the origins of religion?

"There were thirteen High Fiends, each wielding dominion over legions of fiends and fiendish creatures. In those times, no human nations or kingdoms existed to stand against the swarms of fiends. Humanity lived in tribes, led by half-fiends, born of heinous mating rituals between the High Fiends and human whores. These tribes were forced to serve, to worship, and to offer human sacrifices. The fiends feasted upon their flesh in life and consumed their *rhoas* in death."

Lion started pacing back and forth. Even though he had nothing to do with religion, Lion still had heard bits and pieces of this story from the castle servants and soldiers. What was the point of...?

His steps faltered. Was the burning hound he had seen that night — and the one who was snarling out there — a fiend? Did Kastian have a fiend here tonight? Is that why he was making that Pyrearch talk about fiends?

Was this the death he had prepared for Lion of Zarall?

"Then, on a fateful day, a nameless Pilgrim embarked on a quest for aid. He journeyed the shadowed paths of the dark world alone until at last he reached the Frozen Caves. With a heart full of hope, he ventured deep into the caverns and discovered the twelve dragons, the last of their kind, slumbering in the deepest, darkest recesses of the caves."

Lion shivered. An absurd laughter was building up inside his chest. He pressed his palm over his mouth to muffle his loosening nerves. A fiend! He was going to fight a fiend!

"The Pilgrim implored the dragons to emerge and aid humanity in a battle against the High Fiend. Each of the twelve dragons refused his plea, advising him to leave. Yet, he remained steadfast, beseeching them for twelve long years."

So, man found sleeping dragons, woke them up, and pestered them for years. And that was how religion started? Lion covered his mouth with his palm to suppress a sudden need to laugh. He breathed through his nose, trying to muffle the laughter. Where did this come from?

"The Pilgrim died in the Frozen Caves, still pleading them with his last breath."

Or maybe the dragons had finally had enough, and the fellow was just begging not to be eaten alive! A chuckle escaped Lion's lips. He took a sharp breath, held, and pricked up his ears. Even if someone had heard him, there was no way of knowing. The Pyrearch continued passionately.

"The Pilgrim's unwavering dedication and righteousness moved the hearts of the twelve dragons. Each shed a tear over his lifeless body. Then, they emerged from the Frozen Caves, unfurling their enormous wings for the first time in centuries. They soared above the clouds and vanished behind the moon."

Looking for another place where they could sleep without being disturbed by noisy missionaries. Lion slid down to his knees, shaking with silent laughter. He was going to be slaughtered by a fiend! A fiend! There was nothing funny about this! Why was he laughing?

"The next morning, the dragons returned, each bearing a rider on its back. These were the twelve gods and goddesses, who united all of humanity under the protection of their dragons' wings and waged war against the High Fiends. Leading them was Kiejain, the God of Warriors, astride Karaalev the black dragon. Beside him rode his wife Alunwea, the Goddess of Mercy, on the back of Alnara the red dragon."

Please tell me he's not going to name all twelve gods and goddesses with their dragons and colours. Please...

"Beside her rode Sharrap, the God of Pleasure and Wine, riding Ahzu the silver dragon. Beside him, rode…"

Lion rolled his eyes and listened to the screeching voice of the Pyrearch distractedly. There was the God of Shadows, Kyrus, riding a grey dragon. He was brothers with the God of Craftsmen, Kahil, also riding a red dragon. There was a woman and a man, twins, each riding a golden dragon. They were the God of Art and Goddess of Nature, or the other way around. There were even useless sounding gods, like Zaon, the God of Roads, who just travelled the roads. He was riding a bronze dragon named Yolgezer. Why would someone bother with roads where they could simply fly on their dragon? It didn't make sense.

Nothing made sense.

Lion wiped a tear, still laughing silently, as he listened to the end of the story.

"The fiend wars raged on for years, and the Twelve Riders vanquished the thirteen High Fiends one by one. Yet, countless lesser fiends remained, and too many *rhoas* lingered for them to feed upon.

"At last, the gods and goddesses resolved to divide the world into three realms. They created Darkhome, banishing all fiends there. They then built Farhome, a sanctuary where all *rhoas* could find peace after death. What remained was Earthome, where humans would dwell and flourish under the light.

"In honour of the Pilgrim's sacrifice, the Twelve Riders remained with us. They initiated the Thrive, an era where humanity prospered under their guidance. To this day, our civilisations continue to Thrive in the light of the Twelve Riders."

"Thank you, Pyrearch Mendrich," King Kastian said as soon as the Pyrearch stopped talking. The old man mumbled a response before shuffling down the platform. Lion stood up. His cheeks still ached, but the gravity of his situation was now settling in his chest like a rock. His unwanted mirth was leaving its place to nausea. He held his breath as Kastian continued speaking.

"Some of you have known Leonis Zarall's unhealthy obsession with ancient artefacts. Some of these artefacts were family heirlooms handed from father to son. What you did not know was a lot of these artefacts he collected with pride were tainted by Darkhome magic!"

His dramatic pause was filled with shocked gasps and shaken whispers.

"Yes," Kastian raised his voice to be heard over the dismayed chatter of his guests. "House Zarall had their hands deep in Darkhome magic up to their elbows!"

He gave another pause to let the guests work themselves up to near panic. He savoured their fear before continuing with an angry, vengeful voice.

"We have been scaring our children to behave, to be loyal followers of the Twelve Riders by telling them of the horror tales of Black Stain in the far south," he said. "Some believe that the Thrive ended the day Black Stain appeared.

"Then there is the Forbidden District in the city of Varostan, just beyond our eastern borders. Two places of darkness, created by blood and massacre of innocents. Created by wicked experiments using Darkhome magic." He lowered his voice to a whisper, following a brief pause. "In a few years from now, our neighbours would have been scaring *their* children with the horror tales of Brinescar!"

Shouts of anger and denial filled the hall.

"With all due respect, Your Majesty," someone in the crowd raised his voice to be heard. Lion imagined an old, cranky looking lord in his late fifties. "These are frightful and truly disturbing accusations. I am an old, foolish, and nearly blind man, and it doesn't take Kyrus's wits to deceive someone like me. But there are lords and ladies in this hall who are far better judges of character than myself. I'm sure they all must be wondering, what are you basing these accusations on?"

"You are neither old, nor foolish, Lord Rhuagh," Kastian replied. "And looking at your lady by your side, I vouch your eyesight is as good as any of us." There was a patient smile beneath Kastian's words, as if he was expecting the question. "However, when it comes to mages, one cannot trust their senses and judgements.

"House Zarall was hosting a mage here in Castle Brinescar; one who had been expelled from the Eternal Pillar because of his secret experiments. Experiments involving fiends and Darkhome; the kind of *experiments* that gave birth to Black Stain and Forbidden District in the past."

The way Kastian emphasised 'experiments' created another ripple of fear in the crowd.

"Yes," Kastian raised his voice. "House Zarall have been aiding this rogue mage, Belandir Malderan, in his research to bring the nightmares back from

Darkhome. Leonis Zarall was giving him access to his collection of magic arte-facts. I have information revealing how Lygor Zarall was importing more artefacts and enchanted items over the Kaldorian border to support his father's corrupted plan. The name Zarall is an ailment, a curse on this country."

He was manipulating the emotions of the crowd like a slave master command-ing his slaves. He had fed their anger with fear and now, the lords and ladies in the hall were thirsty for blood.

Kastian was still speaking, but Lion's ears had started ringing after hearing about the mage. *A mage...* Was he talking about the man in the black robe? The thought made Lion's hair stand on end.

He had seen other mages at King Leonis's court before, but they all wore white robes, and they did nothing other than talk to the king. They certainly didn't go around stabbing people in the heart and fiddling their hands in their chests. But what that man in black robe did couldn't have been explained with anything other than magic. Kastian must have been telling the truth. The things he had seen that night... The burning hound, the monster on the ceiling, blood crawling on the floor, even the stabbing... He didn't imagine any of those. It was all Darkhome magic!

"Three weeks ago," Kastian raised his voice. "On the night of the Uprising, the great houses of Chinderia gathered together to save our country from this darkness called Zarall. I have personally attended to the Sending Ritual of Leonis Zarall's *rhoa*. People of Chinderia are now ready to leave the name Zarall behind and embrace a time of new Thrive. But..."

Lion shifted his weight as he fixed his eyes on the curtain ahead. He could almost see the smirk touching Kastian's lips as he continued in a softer voice. "There is someone who's still carrying the name Zarall, although it was never his. Someone you all have seen, maybe cheered for, no doubt."

They never cheered for me, Lion thought. *They cheered for blood. They always cheered for blood.*

The curtain twitched as someone prepared to pull it off. Lion braced himself.

"And tomorrow, you will watch the Lion of Zarall fall to the Bear of Vogros!"

Hopper and Crowseye pulled the curtain off the cage.

The hall was so quiet, Lion could hear the rustle of the curtain as it fell. After the darkness of the cage, he was blinded by all the light in the banquet hall.

The brief silence was followed by an uproar. The guests cheered and clapped. Several women yelped, but most were laughing, amazed.

As he blinked to restore his sight, Lion was confused by the admiration in their tones. It wasn't like they were seeing him for the first time, and he certainly deserved nothing less than detest after Kastian's speech.

Then, his eyes finally adjusted to the light, and he saw the second cage across from his. Its host stood up on trunk-like hindlegs and roared.

It wasn't a fiend.

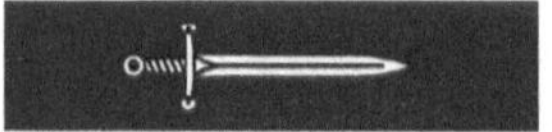

THE BEAR OF VOGROS stood nearly three meters tall on its hindlegs. He must have weighed at least ten grown men. He was covered with brown fur, thick as armour. Muscles rippled under his coat when he moved. His mouth was pulled back to show a set of sharp teeth. He could bite a man's face clean off without even opening his mouth to the jaws. Lion couldn't tear his eyes off the bear's black claws, quick and sharp as any weapon he had ever yielded.

Still, it wasn't a burning fiend hound as Lion had feared. He exhaled slowly.

King Kastian's guests were clapping with excitement. Their sounds made the bear angrier. He threw himself to the bars, sticking his arm out and swiping at the nearest guest, a young lady in an emerald dress. It fell way short — Kastian's men were keeping anyone from getting too close — but the woman screamed and the man next to him grabbed this opportunity to pull the woman in his arms. The lords and ladies, including the woman and the man, laughed at this little excitement. Lion, on the other hand, couldn't see anything to laugh at in those claws.

A frown creased his forehead. He rummaged through his memories to find what knowledge he could remember about beast versus animal fights. Badimar hadn't bothered training him on the Apex Contests. He hadn't need to. Animal fights were way beneath the king's famed champion beast. Lion predominantly fought in Grand Tournaments, while others in the team competed in Dawn-bloods, Duskbloods, Apex Contests, and lesser tournaments.

Breeder Astaldo, however, did teach him how to fight animals using various weapons. Purebred beasts needed to have a baseline knowledge in every fight class and against every opponent. He reviewed his knowledge about bears but he couldn't form a strategy yet. Everything would depend on the weapon he would be given. Against bears, he needed a quick and long-range weapon, like a spear or lance. Would he be allowed armour? Shield? What would the arena placement look like? Setting and decorations made Apex Contests all the more interesting. Could he hope for a bow and an arrow, lots of obstacles to hide and take cover, and a high a place to stand? Until he knew what weapon they were going to give him, he couldn't strategize.

"Fancy your eyes with tomorrow's champion and enjoy the feast," King Kastian concluded and motioned towards the feast tables. "Oh, and do not feed the contestants before the fight. Lion does not have any stomach for food right now and Marzul is on a strict diet for beasts."

His insult elicited more laughter from his guests, and it drew Lion's gaze to the new king. His new Owner. Kastian Vogros.

The king had a hard-set face. Creases around his eyes and mouth were putting at least forty years on his shoulders. A short-trimmed, salt-and-pepper beard and hair surrounded his face. The ornate, golden crown Lion had seen on Leonis's forehead countless times adorned Kastian's head now. Although it sat perfectly even on his head, somehow it didn't fit him.

Kastian's jaw popped from side to side as he scowled at Lion with his poisonous green eyes. Lion didn't avert his; at least not immediately. The king seemed to be disappointed, even frustrated, by Lion's reaction. After expecting to fight a fiend, Lion was observably relieved at the sight of his rival. That clearly wasn't the response King Kastian wanted to see.

What had he expected from a purebred, anyway? It wasn't like they displayed a range of emotions.

Although it was intended to be an insult, Kastian's judgement wasn't far-fetched. Lion had lost all his appetite. The bear, on the other hand, looked like he could take a bite from everyone in the room and would still be hungry. He kept snarling at the people and gnawing on the bars. His teeth made an ear-scratching grinding sound against the iron bars. When he shook his head, the bars bent just slightly.

Lion imagined the bear breaking free and slaughtering all the guests and the king, while he sat in the safety of his cage. The thought brought a grin to his lips, which he dismissed promptly after seeing the king's frown deepen.

Kastian curled a finger at Karhad, who hurried to his side. The king whispered an instruction in Karhad's ear, which made him glance in Lion's direction and nod.

Excellent. He had just made his already fucked-up situation worse.

He pried his eyes off the king and studied the faces of the others sitting at his table. The king's family. A short-haired woman, who was wearing the late Queen Arasanara's elegant crown, sat next to Kastian. Lion's eyes lingered on the woman's hair. He had rarely seen women with short hair, unless they were female beasts or free warriors. A striking choice of fashion for a queen.

On either side of the king and the queen sat two younger men. The older one had chestnut hair like the queen, and the younger one had Kastian's venom green eyes. The seat next to the younger prince was empty, but apart from that one, other seats were given to the lords and ladies from the most influential houses. A great many of them Lion recognised from Leonis's feasts. They had raised their glasses for another hundred years of Zarall reign not long ago.

The other guests took their places at the long tables of the banquet hall. House slaves served the food they carried on large trays. The smell of roasted meat made Marzul the bear even more enraged. They must have had been starving him for this fight.

Great.

Lion's eyes scanned the house slaves, searching for a flutter of red hair. He found several, but none were Saradra. His heart skipped a beat when he saw another pair of eyes scanning the horde of slaves. It took a moment to recognise him.

Lord Hooten, Saradra's Owner.

Although Lord Hosten participated in conversations with other guests around him, his smile faltered every now and then when his eyes swiped across the faces of the slaves. He was looking for Saradra.

An uncertain smile lifted Lion's lips. Did that mean Saradra was alive? Lord Hosten clearly believed she was. And he believed Kastian had her here.

Unless... Unless Saradra escaped without alerting anyone!

Lion's heart fluttered in his chest until he saw Kastian's death stare. He wiped his smile. Maybe he should have feigned fear, just to keep his Owner in a good mood. But then, what could Kastian do that was worse than being starved in a cell and tortured with his Pain Word for three weeks, and then pit him against a full-grown bear? Lion was as good as dead anyway.

Towards the end of the feast, Kastian announced that tomorrow's contestants would have to leave early tonight, in order to get a good night's sleep.

"Although I doubt if one of them could get any sleep at all tonight," he added, smirking at Lion.

Lion felt a surge of outrage. Why did he care how Kastian mocked him? Words shouldn't have bothered him, as long as they were not his Words. He contemplated on plastering a cocky smile on his face. But there was no reason to *poke the bear*. He bit inside of his cheek to suppress another laughter. He had to pretend to wipe his mouth and keep his head down until he could regain his composure. He stood straight, keeping his face blank. Unfazed and indifferent. His display of courage neither lessened the guests' laugher, nor made the bear look less intimidating.

This animal was still going to rip his head off tomorrow. It wasn't a flame-coated fiend from Darkhome, but it was still a full-grown bear.

Hopper and Crowseye returned, hitching themselves to the handles of the cart. Four other slaves — all beasts from Badimar's team — did the same for Marzul's cart. They pulled the two cages through the tables; Marzul's cage at the front, and Lion's bringing up the rear.

The bear roared and swiped at people as the cage slid between them. Lion could feel their judging eyes at him; calculating not only his chances of survival, but how many minutes he would last tomorrow. Still holding on to the bars on each side, Lion tilted his chin up and kept his eyes at Marzul's cage.

Once they were back at the service yard behind the upper kitchen, Karhad let Lion out of his cage. The slaves dragged Marzul's cage towards an archway leading to the outer courtyard.

As Karhad and a group of guards escorted Lion back to the dressing room, where he changed into a plain tunic and pants, his thoughts were already occupied with the fight tomorrow. Although he expected to be taken back to his cell, he wasn't surprised to find out that tonight's entertainment was not yet finished.

Karhad took him to the outer courtyard where Marzul's cage was placed right next to Lion's.

He spent the night as Marzul's neighbour, their adjacent cages only separated by a set of bars.

Lion pressed his back against the bars opposite to Marzul and sat down carefully. Half of his space was within the bear's range. Marzul stuck his arms through the bars and tried to reach him all night. His claws left long marks on the cage floor. He threw himself against the bars and gnawed at them. Lion dreaded the moment he would have to face those claws and teeth without the bars between them. No armour would protect him against those.

He tucked his knees under his chin, hugging himself tightly. If he allowed himself to relax just a little, he would wake up with Marzul's claws hooked in his flesh, dragging him to the other side of the cage.

Kastian's mockery turned out to be justified at the end. Lion didn't sleep at all that night.

24

OLIRA

Olira crouched low in the root cellar, inspecting the dwindling food supplies with a growing sense of dread. She felt hot, despite the cool and damp air in the cellar. Shadows flickered in the dim light of the lantern, casting eerie shapes on the stone walls. She sighed with defeat. Sacks of potatoes were fewer than she remembered, and the jars of preserved vegetables were down to fifteen.

As she counted the remaining provisions, her mind raced with worry. There wouldn't be enough to last the winter, not with another mouth to feed. Master Tholthus's deadline, though still months away, was drawing near, and she feared what would happen if she didn't make the payment. With her root cellar empty, and the winter at her door, she could lose the farm. All her hopes hung on the slave's recovery and sale. She had to know for sure that he wasn't broken or dangerous.

The slave, as silent as ever, sat in a corner, a large blanket sprawled in front of him. He was counting the grains in a sack of barley. It was a pointless task that she gave him simply to observe his reaction. He had poured all the grains into a pile on the left side of the blanket and had been making another pile on his right side as he counted them. He scooped a handful from the left, then dropped them on his right one by one, as he counted quietly.

She had been giving him these pointless, tedious, and frustrating tasks all week, watching for any sign of emotion. He hadn't given her anything yet. He hadn't raised any complaints when she got him to muck the stalls, then poured the dirt back into the stalls and got him to start all over again. Five times. He hadn't rolled his eyes when she got him to sort through piles of straw. He hadn't even sighed when she asked him to transfer water from one trough to another using a spoon. She was running out of ideas and nothing seemed to elicit any response from the purebred.

She should have been satisfied, but instead, she found the man's indifference was irritating her. Why did she want to see a reaction? Purebreds were supposed to be mindless things who didn't react to bothersome and meaningless requests. Why did her instincts keep telling her the slave was more than what he seemed?

She hovered over him with her hands on her hips, watching the pile on the right side grow bigger as the purebred counted them. He didn't look up.

"Stop," she said sharply. "How many?"

"Sixty two hundred. And fifty five. Owner."

Olira was impressed that the man even knew how to count. She sized the pile on the right, wondering whether he could have made up the number. It looked about right.

"Start over," she ordered, watching the purebred's face carefully.

The man pushed the pile to the left, combining them into one. He scooped a fistful, then started counting again. Olira waited, watching the man's lips move subtly as he dropped the grains into a new pile.

"Stop. How many?"

"Eleven, Owner."

"Start over."

The slave swept the grains to his left again and started over. Olira repeated this several times over the next quarter of an hour. She even called out random numbers to try to distract him. The slave's face remained flat. Like a perfect, mindless purebred. Her frustration gnawed at the bottom of her stomach. She needed to see something — anything — that hinted at his true nature.

"Start over," she ordered again. "Line them up. One by one."

The slave began picking up individual grains and meticulously placing them in a line on the blanket. His movements were precise, almost mechanical. After a few minutes, when he had arranged a long line of grains, Olira stepped forward. With a swift motion, she scattered the grains across the blanket.

The man paused, his eyes following the mess, but his face remained impassive, giving nothing away.

"Start over," she commanded.

Without a word, he began again, picking up each grain and lining them back up, just as methodically as before. Olira sighed, feeling the weight of embarrassment. She felt like a mean child, prodding a defenceless animal, just to see if it will turn back and bite. "That's enough. Leave it. Just pack it away, please."

The slave retrieved the burlap sack and started scooping the grains back inside. Olira bent down to help him, but she froze, her attention caught by a faint noise from outside.

Leaving the slave to his task, she climbed the narrow, creaking steps that led out of the root cellar. The sunlight was harsh after the dimness below, and it took a moment for her eyes to adjust. The root cellar was built a short distance from the main farmhouse, nestled into a small hill to keep it cool year-round. The farm spread out before her: fields of odd-looking, exotic plants, vegetable patch, farmhouse and the barn, and beyond that, the dense woods that bordered the property.

As she stepped outside, she nearly collided with Gilann, lingering just outside the cellar. Gilann's posture stiffened, and his face betrayed an attempt to appear casual.

"Gilann?" she called out, her voice firm. "What are you doing here?"

Gilann's eyes flickered to the root cellar door before meeting hers. He wasn't good at lying. He could not hide his guilt if his life depended on it. "Just checking on things," he mumbled, kicking at a loose stone with his boot. "I thought I'll... umm... check the walls for cracks and moisture. You know, before the rain season."

"Rain season isn't until at least two months."

"And the beams. One of the beams looked worn out the other day. I was gonna check if the wood is rotten."

"Yes, it is. And I'm getting it fixed next month."

"Right. Should I have a look and—"

"Gilann." Olira took a step closer, her voice lowering to a tone she resolved for scolding her brothers. She hadn't used this tone with Gilann in years. She didn't say anything else, just let the silence force a confession.

Gilann shifted his weight, glancing over his shoulder toward the path that led away from the farm. "I thought you would be busy at the barn, tormenting the purebred or something."

"Tormenting?" Olira went cold with anger.

"What else do you call what you're doing with him? Getting him to carry pebbles and sticks from one side of the yard to the other, then back, over and over again."

"He needs to move, to speed his recovery, so we can sell him and avoid losing our home. And I'm letting him outside, so he could get fresh air and..." Olira stopped sharply, narrowing her eyes. She had to admit, Gilann almost succeeded in distracting her by changing the topic. If he could have kept that tiny smirk clear from his face, he could have gotten away with it.

"You're obsessing over him," he said, still trying to herd Olira away from the topic.

"Gilann. Why are you here?"

Before she could press him further, she noticed movement in the distance, down the path. A figure was approaching, leading a horse with a mountain of sacks and crates on its back. As they approached, Olira recognised Jygan's confident gait. The tanner's face flickered between Gilann and Olira, then back to Gilann. His steps faltered briefly before he resumed, his face set with determination.

Olira's anger flared up to her cheeks as she turned to Gilann, who was now avoiding her gaze altogether. "Gilann," she muttered. "What have you done?"

Gilann didn't reply. Olira's heart pounded as she pieced together the situation. Jygan guided his horse towards them. The saddlebags were bulging with what looked like provisions.

"Gilann! What did you tell him?" Olira snarled, but Gilann was still quiet, and she couldn't press any further, because Jygan came to a stop beside them.

"Hey," Jygan said awkwardly, his deep brown eyes searching Olira's face for a reaction. His presence only made her frustration boil over.

"What did he offer you?" she asked Jygan.

Jygan glanced at Gilann. "Olira," he said cautiously. "Your supplies—"

"My supplies were gone, and it wasn't your fault."

"I should have got there quicker."

"You don't know if they would still be there. For all I know, they were stolen within ten minutes after I left them."

"I should have still—"

"What did Gilann offer you, Jygan?"

A tense silence hung between them, the weight of an unspoken resentment pressing down like a heavy blanket. There was a time she believed she was going to marry Jygan. The tanner had always been there, hovering on the edge of her life, but never taking a step forward. She hated the way Jygan made her feel.

"I know you wouldn't dare the audacity to offer us a handout, so I know Gilann must have offered something to you for all this. What did he offer?"

Finally, Jygan raised his hands in a calming gesture, the muscles in his forearms flexing slightly under his rolled-up sleeves. "Don't take it out on Gilann. This trade was my idea."

"Incense and scented oil?"

Jygan shrugged and flashed her a smile that was barely noticeable beneath his beard. It made Olira's heart prance like a playful lamb. "Those, and also your mum's Crimsonplum Harvest Tart recipe."

Olira rolled her eyes. Growing up, her mum had always invited Jygan over whenever she baked the tart, knowing it was his favourite. Olira always resented that there would never be leftovers.

"You can't handle that recipe." She shook her head.

"I guess I'll have to try."

"You'll butcher it. It'll turn out like mud."

"Then I'll eat mud."

Olira tilted her head back, sighing deeply. She wanted to appear like she was considering, though she also needed a break from Jygan's intense gaze. "Three years," she said finally, eyeing the packed provisions. "Three years' unlimited supply of incense and scented oil and whatever herbs you need. And come over for supper before the final harvest. I'll bake you the damn Crimsonplum."

She left Gilann and Jygan — who was smiling like a donkey — to unpack the supplies, while she returned to the root cellar. Stepping into the cool, dimly lit room from bright daylight, she had to stop to let her eyes adjust.

The slave was sitting in the same spot she had left him. The burlap sack lay beside him, now filled with the carefully packed grains. His hands rested in his lap, his gaze unfocused, as though he were somewhere far away. For a brief moment, Olira felt a chill crawl up her spine. She couldn't tell if he was simply being vacant, or if he was lost in some deep thought.

A strange impulse took hold of her. She found herself creeping forward silently, without thinking. She wasn't sure what she was planning to achieve, sneaking up on a deadly, mindless weapon like this. Her third step scuffed the floor softly, and the slave recoiled.

Olira cursed the fiends. She thought she saw something in the look the purebred gave her, but her eyes were still adjusting to the dim light, so she wasn't sure. She blinked rapidly as the slave rose to his feet, favouring his injured leg. He stood ready, his head down, projecting nothing but respect and obedience.

"Help the others carry the supplies inside, please," she ordered, her voice firmer than she felt.

"Yes, Owner." Then he turned, his crutch tapping lightly on the ground as he made his way toward the bright daylight.

25

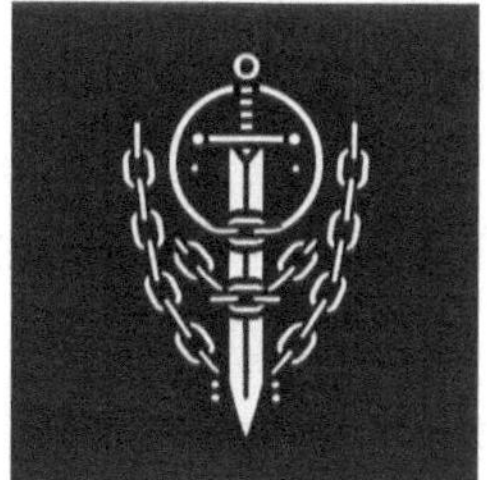

LION

LION WAS ALONE IN the launch room behind the Gates of Life of the Switchblade Arena. And he was trembling.

There was no one to give him instructions, to talk strategy, to calm him down, or to whisper his Kill Word as the gates opened.

There was no weapons rack to choose from.

There was not even a piece of armour on him.

The announcer's voice projected through the arena, getting the crowd hyped up. He was saying something about the Lion of Zarall and the Bear of Vogros, but Lion couldn't listen to anything but his own heartbeat.

He was dead.

No weapon, no armour... He had no chance.

Kastian had made sure the Lion of Zarall would die with no respect. He was naked, except for the few pieces of accessories to make him look like a kitten instead of a lion. He was wearing a belt with a yellow tail attached to its back. His hair fell down his shoulders in two neat braids, and his beard made a third one. Triangular wooden ears were protruding from a hairband on his head. All his body was coated in a shimmering, golden paint. Lastly, he was wearing his lion mask, but a black nose and whiskers were drawn on it.

The only part of his accessories that had a remote resemblance to any sort of weapon were the gloves. He was given dark brown leather gloves with metal fingertips. Cat-like claws, short and pointy, extended from every fingertip. Although they looked sharp enough, they couldn't possibly leave a scratch on Marzul's thick brown fur.

He could not survive a clawing contest with a bear.

He had been repeating Breeder Astaldo's lectures about Apex Contests and animal fights in his head all night. Specifically, what the breeder had said about bears.

"They run faster," his rough voice bellowed inside Lion's mind. *"They climb faster and swim faster..."*

One more thing... There was one more thing a bear could do better than humans. What was it? What was it?

He knew the information would come to him, but when it did, it would be too late.

The audience was built up, cheering and stomping their feet impatiently. Lion took the mask off, careful not to cut his face with the claws.

He didn't care about the other accessories; not even the ridiculous tail. In fact, having his hair braided like this was less distracting than getting it in his eyes all the time. But the mask's slits were too narrow and if he was going to die, he at least wanted to see where his death came from.

It wasn't like they could punish him after the fight for taking his mask off, anyway.

"And now, let the fight begin!" was the only part of the announcer's speech he had been waiting — and dreading — to hear.

The Gates of Life slid apart slowly. The sunlight reflected from the golden sands and cut through the darkness inside the launch room. Lion blinked, forcing his eyes to adapt to the light as quickly as possible. The slim slice of light between the gates grew wider.

Then, he saw something in the middle of the arena; an advantage that might maybe, potentially save him.

He squeezed past the gates even before they were fully open, and he broke into a mad run.

The sound of the crowd hit him like a wall. The golden sands, heated by the sun all day, burnt his bare feet, and the stupid piece of tail floated awkwardly behind him as he ran. He couldn't imagine how ridiculous he must look to the audience; gleaming golden under the sun, his braids fluttering in the wind, and his privates flopping against his thighs with each step.

Without breaking his run, he took his right hand to his mouth and pulled the glove off. Muffled by the crowd's laughter, he could hear Marzul's confused growls, and knew that the bear had been released into the arena as well. He didn't stop to look.

He kept his eyes on the steel pole erected in the middle of the arena and ran like he had never run before.

The pole was thicker than a tree trunk, and gleamed a menacing grey. Odd-looking, neat shapes and symbols were carved along one side from bottom to top. He didn't care how or from where they found a steel pole like this and brought it into Switchblade. All he knew was that the pole was his salvation, because there was a flat platform at the top.

Marzul let out a sharp, angry growl and Lion knew the bear had spotted him. The crowd's excited screams told him Astaldo was right about the bears' speed. He was still ten seconds from reaching the pole, and Marzul was going to get to him in five.

Lion dropped the glove behind him, then pulled the left one off.

"*Drop something,*" Breeder Astaldo had said. "*Bears are curious animals. They will pause to sniff it, which will buy you the few precious seconds that might save your Owners from losing their property.*"

It worked.

Sort of.

Marzul paused briefly to sniff the glove, but he resumed running almost instantly. This earned Lion only a handful of seconds.

Lion dropped the second glove, hoping but not really expecting to trick the bear again. Marzul didn't disappoint him.

Lion threw himself at the pole, wrapping his legs around it, the impact almost crushing his balls. With his feet locked at the ankles, he pulled himself up swiftly.

The steel pole was heated under the sun and burnt his bare flesh. However, being naked worked in his favour; it prevented him from sliding down and helped him climb faster.

But not fast enough.

When the crowd gasped in unison, Lion braced himself for the strike.

He was a few meters off the ground, but not high enough to escape from Marzul's reach, when the bear stood up on his hindlegs. The swipe of his claw landed on Lion's back and he felt four sharp claws slicing his skin from shoulder blades to waist.

His scream was lost in the delighted cheer of the spectators. His grip weakened, and he slid down half a meter. He didn't know if he was lucky, or if it was because they had kept the bear too hungry for too long, but Marzul stumbled. Unable to stop his charge, he hit headfirst on the pole, releasing his grip.

Blood gushed from Lion's back. The pain blinded him, threatened to steal his consciousness. He pulled himself together and used his only chance to get away from Marzul's next strike.

Wrapping his legs around the pole again, he climbed.

Marzul stood up on four legs and shook his head in a comical way. The crowd laughed and Lion felt a vicious jolt of satisfaction at the humiliation of the bear of Vogros. Then, the bear fixed his attention back at Lion and stood up on his hindlegs for another strike. This time, Lion was out of his reach and the only thing Marzul could get his claws on was the tail, which ripped off easily.

He came so close to fainting and only stayed awake by pure willpower. Blood soaked the pole, making it slippery between his legs. The skin on his chest, arms and inner thighs burnt from the heat and friction. He allowed himself to groan and cry out as loud as he needed to, while forcing himself to keep climbing. His movements were methodical: support himself with his legs, reach with his hands, ignore the pain on his back, pull himself up, curse at the burn, repeat.

When he reached the top, he was growling and panting almost as loud as Marzul.

The platform at the top of the pole was barely wide enough to stand on two feet. Lion pulled himself up on it. As soon as he stood, the arena started swirling around him. He crouched low, his hands grasping the sides of the platform hard enough to drain his knuckles white. The height and the blood loss were making him dizzy.

Marzul rose on his hindlegs. He hugged the pole with claws the size of a man's face and lifted himself in an attempt to climb.

Lion held his breath.

They are good climbers, Astaldo had lectured the young purebreds. But this was a steel pole with a smooth, blood-soaked, slippery surface. An animal that size shouldn't have been able to climb it...

Marzul lifted himself off the ground, his hindlegs clawing the pole frantically, before he slid down helplessly. Next, the bear crouched down and jumped. This time, he reached higher, but no matter how much he hugged and clawed the steel, he slid down on his bottom again. His third try was half-hearted.

Lion's shoulders sagged as he exhaled slowly. The arena masters placed this pole here because they were certain that Marzul couldn't climb on it. They wanted this fight to last longer than five seconds.

Marzul stood up one more time, but instead of another climbing attempt, he leaned against the pole with his front claws and threw his weight at it.

Lion mouthed one of Joharin's favourite curses as he threw himself flat on his stomach, wrapping his arms and legs around the platform. The spectators let out an amused laughter at the sight of him clinging to the pole like a scared cat, his bare ass to the crowd. They could go to Darkhome. Lion couldn't care any less about his image.

Marzul continued shaking the pole by using the force of his considerable weight. The pole swung violently, causing Lion to exhale sharply as the air rushed out of his lungs. He bit his tongue and tasted blood. For a terrifying moment, he imagined Marzul ripping the steel off the ground. The golden sands gaped around the root of the pole. Minutes dragged like hours while the spectators jumped up and down with excitement. Their screams pierced Lion's ears. He didn't remember ever hearing them this frantic. They were thirsty for his death.

Marzul eventually surrendered and dropped down onto all fours with a disgruntled sound. Lion climbed back up on the pole and crouched, holding onto the sides tightly. Although he was far from being relaxed, he allowed himself to take a moment to assess his situation. When he scanned the arena, he spotted the weapons scattered across the outer edge of the battlefield, opposite to where

Lion had entered. Okay, so he was not completely unarmed. He was just at an impossible distance away from the nearest weapon.

Also stranded at the top of a pole and bleeding heavily.

The only feeling he had on his back was wetness. Fear and adrenaline had numbed the pain momentarily. Blood seeped down his back, dripping on Marzul's face and driving him even more enraged. Lion was on the brink of unconsciousness. He had to stab his nails at his legs to keep himself from fainting.

Weapons. He needed to get to those weapons…

Marzul circled the pole, giving it an occasional swipe or a shake. Despite the noise, Lion could hear the sound of Marzul's claws as they grinded against the steel. Although the bear hadn't given up, his attempts to get to his prey were subsiding, and this reflected on the spectators immediately. They tolerated this idleness for only about five minutes before yelling their disappointment and frustration.

They could suck it. Lion was nowhere near tired. Badimar used to run stamina exercises on balance poles, far more straining than this. He could remain here for at least several hours; unless Marzul finally ripped the pole out, or he fainted from blood loss.

Still, it didn't mean Lion was *willing* to stay here for several hours. No, he had to find a way to get to those weapons. If only there was a way to distract the bear. He calculated the time he needed to slide down, run, and grab a weapon. He would need at least half a minute of distraction. How was he going to do that?

A brilliant but not so hopeful idea flashed in his mind: His Kill Word. What if he could Rage himself?

He never tried using one of his Words on himself before – never had a reason to try. He would have a fighting chance against Marzul if he could put himself in Rage. And if he still died, at least it would be painless.

"*Dracis…*" he started, but his throat tightened and the rest of the Kill Word didn't come out.

He coughed, cleared his throat. He could say the Word clearly in his mind. Closing his eyes, he tried to pronounce it out loud again and again, just to get stuck in the same syllable. He even tried breaking the word in two and vocalising it in two parts, but the result was the same. His throat tightened each time, not letting the Word out.

So, he couldn't Rage himself then. *Shit.*

Meanwhile, the crowd was continuing their futile attempts to convince him to 'get down and fight like a man.' Lion looked at Marzul and his teeth and claws. Fighting like a man? Against a bear? Not until he could get a…

A sudden pain in his left arm shattered all his thoughts.

He lost his grip. The force of the blow pushed him forward and cost him his balance. He swung his right arm and grabbed the top of the platform just as he fell.

Marzul and the spectators roared at the same time as Lion hung from the platform with one hand. His fingers were sliding on the platform, which was wet with his blood. He kicked the air desperately, trying to wrap his legs around the pole. Pain had numbed his left arm. He couldn't move it.

An arrow! An arrow was sticking out of his upper arm!

Fairness was the last thing he expected from this fight, but *this*? They shot an arrow at him! Because he was taking too long to fall?

Marzul backed away from the pole and crouched on his hindlegs.

"Shit!" Lion cursed and pulled his legs up just in time.

They jump! That was the other thing Astaldo had said bears could do better than humans. *They can jump higher.*

Marzul gained speed and jumped, almost running the length of the pole and swinging one of his claws at where Lion's legs had been a second ago. The bear fell back on his four with a loud thud, almost shaking the whole arena.

Lion released his legs while Marzul prepared for another jump.

As he struggled to hold on, the crowd did something odd: they started booing. At least half of them were on their feet, shaking their fists and yelling how cheap this fight was. They still wanted to see Lion dead, there was no doubt about that. But not like this.

Good. The crowd's reaction suggested that there wouldn't be a second arrow. Not that it mattered, because Lion's fingers were starting to lose their grip one by one.

With a laboured groan, he lifted his left arm through the pain to grab the edge of the platform. He swung his legs back and forth and wrapped them around the pole just as Marzul jumped again.

The bear missed by a hair.

It took an excruciating amount of time to pull himself back up on the platform, with the pole constantly slipping between his legs and the jolt of pain scouring his arm. Not trusting his balance, he lay on his stomach, locking his legs under the platform.

Blood dripped down the pole, painting the sands below. Marzul roared in fury and resumed shaking the pole violently.

Somehow, Lion managed not to pass out. The arrow had punched through his arm, but it seemed to have missed the bone. Otherwise, he wouldn't be able to move it at all. Leaving the arrow there seemed like the easiest option; trying to pull it out would have cost too much blood.

If only he had a bow... Then it would have been worth the risk of pulling the arrow out. One shot at one of Marzul's eyes. That was all he needed. It may not have killed the bear, but it would certainly give Lion the distraction he needed to get down and...

He raised his head and calculated the distance to the weapons again. A plan had started to shape in his head. It was a terrifying plan and he couldn't help but chuckle at its chances of success. But it was the only plan he had.

"Merciful Alunwea," he prayed, not because he believed in the Twelve Riders, only to feel himself closer to Saradra.

With his right hand, he reached for the belt around his waist. He unbuckled it with blind fingers and tied it just above the arrow wound. He used his teeth to tighten the belt, so it cut the blood flow.

That was the easy part. Now came the fun bit.

The arrowhead poked out at the front of his bicep. He wrapped his fingers around it, took a deep breath, and pulled.

He howled.

Marzul roared and rounded the pole frantically.

Lion cursed, screamed, spat, and cried out, yet kept pulling until the arrow came out. Despite the belt, a surge of blood gushed down his elbow.

He was exhausted. Dark spots appeared in his sight. He was passing out…

The arrow…

He tucked the arrow under his stomach as he lay on the platform.

He couldn't afford to drop the arrow…

If he did…

Everything would be…

He flinched awake. He must have passed out just for a split second, and somehow, his body had stubbornly held on. He was still lying on his stomach, his arms dangling from one side of the platform, and his legs from the other. The arrow was still safe under his stomach.

He shook his head, trying to regain his strength. He retrieved the arrow and placed it between his teeth. Carefully, he climbed back up on the platform. To get himself used to the pain, he moved his left arm up and down. If there was any chance of his plan to work, he was going to have to use this arm.

Marzul pressed his front paws against the pole and raised his muzzle up at Lion. His wet, black nose twitched as he tried to sniff Lion's intentions.

Lion took the wooden hairband off his head and held it with his trembling left hand. When he grabbed the arrow with his right and straightened up, the crowd anticipated what he was planning to do. They started cheering madly, inviting him to go ahead and do it. Although they sounded divided — half cheering for the bear and half for Lion now — they all were desperate for some action.

And Lion was ready to finally give them what they wanted.

He pointed the sharp end of the arrow at the bear. Holding the hairband from one of the wooden ears, he dangled it in the air.

Marzul opened his mouth.

Taking a deep breath, Lion dropped the hairband. Then jumped right after it.

Marzul's teeth clamped around the hairband. It broke with a sharp crack.

Lion landed on Marzul's shoulders before the bear could open his mouth again. He stabbed the arrow in the animal's eye.

The bear stumbled down with Lion's sudden weight and roared. He spat the pieces of the hairband out of his mouth, grabbed Lion with one of his claws and flung him away.

Lion lay in a surge of blackness. Soft, hot sand cradled his body. He could still hear Marzul stumbling and roaring in pain in the distance. Although the spectators made more sound than him, Marzul's was the only one he heard.

He fought to disperse the darkness. He had to get up. He had to get up now.

He rolled to his side, shaking his head, shaking the dizziness out of his eyes. He was noticing a new pain on his side. Blood was pouring out from a new gash. Sand and blood coated his body.

Marzul was shaking his head, trying to get the arrow out. Lion had lost his sense of direction and had to look around to spot the weapons. For a few fearful seconds, he couldn't see anything but blood and sand. Then he spotted them and climbed up on his feet.

Blood poured from his newest wound when he stood. He took two steps and stumbled on his knees, fighting madly not to faint again. Putting a hand over the side of his stomach, he broke into something between crawling and running.

The crowd was raving, quite a lot of them cheering for Lion to get up and run. The inflection in their excitement told him that Marzul had just taken the arrow out and was trying to locate him with his one good eye. The bear roared in triumph and Lion didn't need to look over his shoulder to see him charging on all fours.

The nearest weapon was a crooked short sword: a lor'qas, his *favourite* weapon, as he had told Saradra one night. This was the weapon he was most experienced and confident with. He ran past it. His eyes were fixed on another weapon.

Lion grabbed the net and the trident seconds before Marzul was on him.

He barely had enough time to fix the net before throwing it at the bear. He rolled out of the way while Marzul fell headfirst, tangled in the net. The weights were not heavy enough to keep the bear down, but they were enough to distract him while Lion claimed the only opportunity he could ever get.

With a strength he had no idea he possessed, he jumped up and stabbed the trident in Marzul's neck.

He had just enough strength left to avoid the dying animal's blind strikes. He pulled the trident free and stabbed again, just for good measure. The third strike ended Marzul's last convulsions and Lion realised he had been screaming, roaring, at the top of his lungs.

He fell on his back, next to the dead bear. His victory was going to be the shortest one in the history of Switchblade Arena. Blood poured out of his wounds, already creating a dark red puddle around him. He felt weak and cold, his breathing getting rapid and shallow.

There was something odd about the crowd. They were cheering for Lion now. And they sounded so angry. Striking words and phrases such as, 'Zarall', 'Leonis is the true king', 'Usurper Vogros' and 'false king on the throne' were reaching to Lion's ears. There was turmoil among the seats as well. As his sight darkened, he recognised the sounds of fighting.

Riot, was his last thought before he passed out. *I've started a riot.*

26

OLIRA

Olira lay in her bed, staring at the wooden beams above. The familiar creaks and groans of the old farmhouse blended with the howling wind outside.

The night was bitterly cold, colder than it had any right to be in mid-Autumn. Frostbringer's Eve arrived earlier than Olira had expected this year. The air turned unnaturally cold, and the violent winds carried a biting chill on the night of the Frostbringer's Eve. The weather softened for the remaining of the Autumn, with occasional light rains, before the winter rolled in with its full intensity. The folks in Oxreach rightfully believed Frostbringer's Eve was a prelude to winter and foretold how harsh it would be each year. By the sounds of the howling winds outside, this was going to be a tough one.

Olira curled tighter beneath her heavy quilts, drawing her knees up to her chest. Under the layers, she could feel the warmth of the heated rock nestled at the foot of her bed, a trick passed down through generations to stave off the night's chill. But even that warmth wasn't enough to calm her restless mind. Her thoughts kept drifting back to the slave in the barn.

She had prepared him for the harsh night, providing every blanket and coat she could find in the house. She also arranged a heated rock for him as well, but she couldn't deny the fact that if she was shivering in her warm bed, the barn must have been freezing.

The preparations for the Frostbringer's Eve had consumed her thoughts all day. She had spent hours in the garden, gathering what she could in an early harvest. The hardy roots — carrots, turnips, and parsnips — had been pulled from the earth. The more delicate herbs, those that wouldn't survive the night's frost, had been clipped and bundled, hung to dry in the kitchen. Tarps had been stretched over the remaining plants, their edges weighed down with stones to keep the biting wind from tearing them loose. She had secured the most valuable of them all — the Palleogano plant — with a sturdy, overhead box that she had custom made a few years ago. She had even set aside seeds for radishes, leafy greens, Crimsonplum, *Siglesil Weed*, and other fast-growing herbs to plant the next morning, to take advantage of the short window of warmth that followed Frostbringer's Eve. If she could squeeze in one last harvest before the Winter truly took hold, and with her root cellar nearly full thanks to Jygan's help, she could finally ease her mind about the winter, regardless of if she sold the slave or not.

She frowned. Of course she would sell the purebred. She needed the money. But it still felt good to know she had a full root cellar for the winter, and more produce to harvest. It took some of the pressure off.

Despite the exhausting work of the day, sleep remained elusive. Olira turned on her side, pressing her face into the pillow, but it was no use. The image of the slave, chained to the stall and shivering under his blankets, haunted her thoughts.

With a frustrated sigh, she sat up, the cold air biting at her through three layers of her nightgown, chemise, and leggings. She couldn't shake the nagging feeling that she had to do something. Dangerous or not, purebreds got cold too. She couldn't let him spend the night of the Frostbringer's Eve in the barn. It wasn't right.

Throwing off the blankets, she swung her legs over the side of the bed, gasping when her feet met the cold floor she could feel through the thick rug. She quickly dressed. She pulled the heated rock out of her bed on her way out and placed it in the hearth in the living quarters. She fed the fire with more firewood, moving quietly, though the floorboards still creaked softly under her feet. There was no need to be sneaky. If her brothers could sleep through the howling wind that rattled the windows and pounded at the walls, they weren't going to wake up to the sound of her footsteps.

She lit a lantern, then she braced herself with a deep breath, before pulling open the heavy door. As she stepped into the night, the cold hit her like a wall. The sky was clear, the stars glittering like shards of ice, and the moon bathed the farm in a pale, ghostly light. She wrapped her shawl tightly around her shoulders and started toward the barn, her breath puffing out in clouds before her.

She hesitated at the barn's door, her hand resting on the rough wood. She had to know. She had to know if she could bring the slave inside her house and not see him strangling one of her brothers again. She pushed open the barn door; the hinges groaning in protest. The light of her lantern filled the space, casting fiendish shadows across the floor. When she stepped inside the stall, she found the man lying on his side, facing the wall, buried among the blankets. His large form was barely visible in the darkness. A pang of guilt took over her.

She stood with her back against the stall wall, watching the faint rise and fall of the purebred's bulk. She hadn't been overly quiet, and the light of the lantern was surely bright enough to disturb him from his sleep, but the purebred didn't sit up. Was he pretending to sleep, or ignoring her? She waited for nearly ten minutes before she finally spoke. "Sit up, please."

The purebred didn't stir, nor startle. He simply rose from beneath the mound of blankets like a mythical sea monster. He sat with his back against the wall, facing Olira, though he kept his head down as usual. He pulled the blankets over himself to cover as much of his shivering limbs as possible.

"You're not used to Frostbringer's Eve," Olira observed. "You're not from West Kilrer, or Northern Chinderia."

The purebred didn't respond. The light of the lantern barely reached his face. Olira stood over him, her heart pounding in her chest as she still tried to read the man's face.

"My guess is South," she said. "Or West, somewhere beyond the Savage Mountains. I've heard the weather is warmer by the sea, near Ascain."

Still no response, but he slowly bent his legs and propped his arms on his knees, his head sagging between his shoulders.

"I'm going to ask you questions," Olira said firmly. "Convince me you are no danger to my family, or I will let you freeze here the rest of the night. Do you understand me?"

The purebred nodded. Olira placed her lantern in the space between them, causing the man to squint with discomfort. She wanted a clear view of his face before she resumed her questioning. *Try to make him talk*, Mistress Aeliana had suggested. *Listen for any opinions and preferences.* This was the only thing she hadn't tested yet.

"Why did you attack my little brother?" Olira held her breath, her focus entirely on the purebred's face.

"The pillow," the purebred said, flatly. "He held a pillow over my face, Owner."

Olira breathed through her nose. "Torren said he was just trying to make you more comfortable."

"I was having a nightmare, Owner," he said, his tone matter of fact, with no hint of an apology.

"About someone smothering you with a pillow?"

"Yes, Owner."

"Really?"

"Yes, Owner."

"So, you just happened to have a nightmare about someone smothering you with a pillow, right at the same moment my brother was fixing your pillow. Isn't that a convenient coincidence?"

"No, Owner."

"No?"

"No, it is not a convenient coincidence. It is how Master Gladwiel tried to kill me before you arrived, Owner."

"*What?*"

"It is how Master Gladwiel tried to kill—"

"I heard what you said," Olira snapped. Colour drained from her face as she pictured what the man described. "I meant, why would Gladwiel do such a thing?"

"I am not privy to my superiors' thoughts."

"I know Gladwiel has a physician and all the resources to save your leg. I sold him those resources. Why wouldn't he save you?"

"I am not privy to my superiors' thoughts," he repeated.

Olira gritted her teeth. Her hands trembled from the cold and from the fury that warmed her blood. That greasy, sneaky piece of fiend turd called Gladwiel was up to something. Why was he desperate to get rid of the purebred, despite boasting about his worth? She glanced at the purebred's injured leg, hidden beneath the blankets. "How did you get that injury?" she asked. "Earlier when I asked you about it, you made yourself pass out just to avoid talking about it. Why?"

"I did not have the strength to answer your questions then, Owner."

Olira narrowed her eyes. "And you're still avoiding my question. How did you get that injury?"

"From a fight, Owner."

"Details," she growled.

The purebred took a deep breath. His gaze drifted briefly, as if recalling a distant memory. "It was a tournament fight in a sand-based arena. I versed a purebred beast who was Raged and equipped with full plate armour, lor'qas, and a Kallakal shield. He was predominantly Stonewall class trained for Slayer's Pit fights, but competent with Ironshield style for tournaments. I countered a blade catch and withdrew, followed with a draw cut, and then a gale slash, which he shield-bashed. He then feigned a cleave, pivoted and—"

"Enough," Olira snapped. She scrutinised the purebred's face for any sign of a mockery. She hadn't understood half the things he had described. The purebred stared straight ahead, his face dead serious, his breath clouding in the cold air. "So, it happened in a fight?"

"Yes, Owner."

"And your Owner didn't bother patching you up."

"He did, Owner."

"Then why did it get infected so badly?"

"I do not have medical knowledge, Owner."

Olira craned her neck, trying to relax her stiff muscles, as she took a deep breath. "So, you get injured, your Owner patches you up, your wound still gets infected. And then what? He figures you'll die and decides to sell you to Gladwiel?"

"Yes, Owner."

Olira rubbed her jaw. "I'm guessing Gladwiel didn't know how badly you were injured when he bought you."

"No, Owner."

She drummed her fingers as she kept thinking. "Gladwiel must have overpaid for you. And rather than trying to save his profit, decided to cut his losses by killing you." She shook her head. "I arrive just at the right moment, and he decides to palm you off to me instead and get rid of a debt, too."

Her jaw ached from gritting her teeth. As she studied the man's relaxed shoulders and casual expression, a strange sense of reassurance slowly blossomed, like a stubborn knot slowly untangling.

She went over everything she had heard from the slave and although some parts still didn't sit well with her, most of it made sense. Even his explanation about attacking Torren matched with what her little brother had told her. Torren had said the purebred had looked terrified, not malicious, as he lashed out. She sighed. She was tired of suspecting the purebred's every action. She wanted to be convinced that he was harmless.

"Are you hiding anything from me?" she asked carefully.

"No, Owner." There was no hesitation, no hint of malice in the purebred's voice.

"Would you tell me if you did?"

"Purebreds don't lie, Owner."

"One last question," she said softly. She took a deep breath. "If I bring you inside, would you ever become a danger to me or my family?"

"No, Owner."

"Look at me when you answer."

The purebred's dark eyes met hers. "I will not become a danger to you or your family, Owner."

She nodded slowly, feeling overwhelmed with an unexpected relief. She reviewed the conversation one more time in her head, confirming that the man hadn't expressed any opinions, ideas, or resentments. She pulled the keys out of her pocket and unlocked the slave's collar.

"Gather all the blankets and follow me."

They made their way to the farmhouse in silence. The purebred carried the blankets in one arm while leaning on his crutch with the other, though he had been relying on it less every day. Olira led him inside, the warmth of the hearth a welcome relief from the bitter cold outside. She guided him to her room, then pointed to the far corner beside a sturdy chest of drawers. The purebred moved there, laying out the blankets in a makeshift bed.

Olira watched him for a moment, her mind whirling with the awkwardness of seeing the strange man in her private space. She left the room briefly, returning with the heated rock from the hearth. She placed it carefully beside him, close enough to offer warmth but far enough not to disturb his rest. The purebred didn't acknowledge her gesture. He simply lay down on the floor, pulling the blankets over himself and turning to face the wall. Almost instantly, his breathing slowed, becoming deep and even, as he drifted off to sleep without a care.

Olira stood over him, uncertain, the silence of the room amplifying the quiet sounds of his breathing. She crawled into her bed without shedding her clothes off. She was doubtful that she would find any rest tonight. But as the minutes passed, the warmth of the room and the rhythmic sound of the man's breathing lulled her into a sense of calm.

27

LION

Lion groaned as consciousness seeped back in, every inch of his body throbbing with a fiery ache.

"He's up," someone said.

"Put him in decent clothes," a familiar voice grunted. "Hurry up!"

Rough hands grabbed Lion's arms and pulled him up to a sitting position. He screamed in pain. When he opened his eyes, he saw bandages covering his upper arm, the left side of his stomach and his back. Sand mixed with blood had dried hard on his skin. He was swimming in a sea of agony. His head felt heavy. Unconsciousness threatened to take him back, but a forceful slap brought him back to where he was.

Karhad. That was whom the familiar voice belonged to.

He was back in Castle Brinescar, in a room he didn't recognise. The walls were lined with shelves overflowing with jars of strange herbs, dried roots, and vials of liquids. The air smelled faintly of burnt sage and something bitter he couldn't place. This wasn't Vanalten's room, though it looked similar. The head physician's room, then? Lion's head throbbed with a dull ache. He felt too heavy to even think.

Karhad's earring jingled when he turned to the other man. "Give him something to sober him up. He looks like he'll faint at any moment."

He was right. Lion was on the verge of passing out and he was looking forward to it. Each breath was an agony. He wanted to close his eyes and never wake up.

"I could give him *pemitoin*, but the aftereffects will kill him, even with the antidote. He's too weak," the bearded man — the head physician — responded.

"Anything else?" insisted Karhad. "Anything to keep him awake for twenty minutes, at least?"

The head physician sighed. Nevertheless, he went to his workbench to mix up a drink for Lion. "You better not need him after half an hour," he said as he worked. "He'll be out for three days."

Three days break from pain and misery? Fantastic!

Lion closed his eyes for a moment and woke up with a slap on his face. The head physician brought a cup to his lips. Lion coughed and spurted. Rough hands pinched his nose and grabbed his mouth, forcing the drink down his throat. He passed out again briefly while they dressed him. When he opened his eyes again, his mind was somehow clearer, the pain dulled. He remembered his fight against Marzul, then he remembered the riot that broke out in the arena. His name was chanted throughout the Switchblade Arena.

Oh, he was fucked.

With Karhad's gesture, two guards appeared and dragged Lion out of the bed. He tried and failed to suppress a scream when one of them grabbed his left arm.

"Quiet," the guard snarled and punched his midsection, which elicited a louder cry.

"Stop it!" scolded Karhad. "They want him conscious, dimwit."

"I apologise, Master Karhad," the guard said sullenly. He moved his hands away from the arrow wound, but his fingers tightened like clamps.

They took Lion to the king's living quarters of the castle. Beyond the massive double doors that separated the king's living area from the rest of the castle was a vast room furnished with useless decorations: tapestries, statues, paintings and other junk. Lion ignored them all. His attention was focused on the two dozen Vogros soldiers and knights, all glaring at him with open hatred.

A familiar face amongst them caused Lion to look twice.

Sir Gennald!

The knight who used to be assigned to protect Lion during many public events and feasts stared back at him. He looked comfortable in his bear-engraved new armour. Sir Gennald frowned at Lion until he was forced to look away.

They made their way to the door at the far left of the room, where heated voices could be heard arguing on the other side. One of the four knights guarding the door stepped forward. He had short, black hair, a trimmed beard, and a missing ear. "We'll take it from here," he said, placing a firm hand on one of the guard's chest.

If the guard was annoyed or offended at this take over, he didn't show it. "Yes, Sir Gwodd," he said without a hint of resentment.

Sir Gwodd motioned two of his knights to take the guards' places. When he knocked on the door, the arguments behind it ceased as if cut by a knife.

"Master Karhad and the slave are here, Your Majesty," Sir Gwodd said, sticking his head inside.

"Send them in."

Sir Gwodd stepped back to let Karhad pass. Two knights followed him, with Lion between them.

This was the king's private library and study. The walls were lined from floor to ceiling with towering bookshelves, each crammed with leather-bound volumes. The smell of parchment and leather filled the room. A fire crackled in the heart, and dozens of candles lit the room. Several tables and chairs scattered the room, but no one was seated. Less than ten people crammed the room, all too tense and uneasy to sit. Lion recognised Kastian's family from the feast. His short-haired queen was standing in a corner. Two princes frowned at Lion from where they stood. The others were the advisors, high lords, and other important figures whose duties Lion neither knew nor cared for, all piercing him with unfriendly eyes.

The two knights dropped Lion in the middle of the room. He fell on his knees and bent over, his forehead on the cold surface and hands on both sides. Not that he hoped grovelling would lessen his punishment. He simply didn't have the strength to sit up. The silence continued, stripping him of any hope he had for a peaceful death.

"Well…" The older prince broke the silence by stating what Lion already knew: "He has to die, that's for sure."

"I agree with my brother," said the younger. "Your Majesty, say the word, and I will make arrangements for his public torture and execution."

Lion's stomach twisted.

"Your Highness, with all due respect," said an old man in silk clothes, "a public execution at this stage will only agitate the riots even further."

"Fine. Then we kill him in the dungeons."

"I advise against that as well, Prince Dienus. If the public finds out how we murdered the Lion of Zarall for no reason other than fighting and winning in the arena, this will anger them even more, not to mention making House Vogros look insecure."

"He has to go down in the arena," the queen spoke.

"Your Majesty is right."

"But we can't risk allowing thousands of people getting together in the arena again," said a large man in a velvet suit. "That would be begging for another riot."

"Lord Klaren is right," the older prince said. "People are already fuelled, looking for a single spark. If the slave doesn't go down exactly the way he should go down…" He didn't finish and nobody asked him to.

"Girl, fetch him some water, will you?" the queen mumbled to someone nearby, and Lion heard a hint of a foreign accent in those last two words.

There was a soft shuffle of feet across the floor, followed by water being poured into a cup.

"Then we'll *order* him to go down," Prince Dienus continued.

"And what do you suggest we do if he decides to disobey orders once he's out in the arena?"

A gentle hand touched Lion's shoulder and helped him to sit up. He recognised her scent before even seeing her face.

His heart stopped.

He remembered the tale of Elrimandel and Galeahil; how their first sight had stopped the time, filled their ears with sacred music, and their bodies with pleasure and devastation at the same time. Although those things hadn't happened to him the first time he had seen Saradra, they happened now.

The room disappeared with everyone in it. His physical pain went away. This moment was the only time that existed in all three Homes; there was no past, no future; just this moment and them in it.

She's alive, was the only thought he had. *She's alive!*

Saradra's red hair was tied in a tight bun. Her skin had a healthy flush and her clothes were neat and clean, but her expression was cold. No, not cold. Cautious. She didn't look at him, she didn't smile, she didn't show any indication that she knew him. There were eyes on them and any communication between them, verbal or nonverbal, would not go unnoticed.

Lion managed to keep his face still. He should have followed her example and stopped looking at her, but his eyes betrayed him by savouring her beautiful face just a couple of seconds longer.

"Disobey?" the younger brother retorted. "He won't disobey. He's a *pure-bred*!"

"We know he killed free men under suspicious circumstances. What if he disobeys? We can't take the risk!"

As the argument heated up, Saradra held an earthen cup to Lion's lips. He drank, not really tasting the water despite his thirst. He would give his right arm just to embrace her one last time. Breathe her in, kiss her lips, or even just to touch her.

As if sensing his longing, she shifted closer, until their knees almost touched. Lion moved his hand slightly forward and stroked her leg with the back of a finger.

"Lotheris is right," King Kastian spoke for the first time. "The slave has lied, killed, and I suspect he also attempted to escape before. I cannot rely on his obedience."

"We can drug him or injure him before the fight?" someone suggested. "It's not something that hasn't been done before."

"If the public sniffs a ploy, the repercussion will be even worse than before," the old man in silk clothes objected.

Saradra took the empty cup and withdrew to the back of the room. Although Lion's eyes yearned to follow her, he closed them shut and bent over again. He would welcome death with peace, now that he knew she was alive. That he hadn't killed her in his Rage.

"Then we'll wait out until people forget about him," Prince Lotheris suggested. "We can send him to the mines to rot."

"No, no, no, Your Highness," the old man objected again. "We can't risk anyone who has a remote claim to the throne getting their hands on him."

"What claim? There is no one left to claim the throne. Lord Thansor? He's married to a third degree Zarall, not even blood related. Lord Matthor is not rich enough to build an army, nor bribe allies. Anyone with the name Zarall is dead."

"Except *him*."

The prince scoffed. "Come now, Master Ulrian. What do you imply? Those idiots who call themselves public would prefer seeing a slave sitting on the throne rather than my father, just because he is called the Lion of *Zarall*? Is that it?"

"No, Your Highness. What I imply is, you have to understand, this slave has become a symbol in the public's eyes now. We kill him, we turn him into a martyr. We lose him, anyone who isn't even related to Zaralls might use him to rally people behind their cause. That genius who shot that arrow at him has made him a hero who defeated a full-grown bear, unarmed, injured, and naked. Now we have to deal with this mess carefully before..." He stopped when the door opened and a pair of timid feet walked in.

"Daddy?"

A small figure ran through the room.

Lion shifted his head, expecting to see a little girl, but found a mature woman of sixteen years snuggling in Kastian's arms.

The king's face softened instantly. He caressed the woman's dark hair gently. "Lareani," he said with a firm but tender voice. "What are you doing here? You should be in bed."

"I see triangles," the woman said in a flat voice. She buried her head in Kastian's shoulder, refusing to release her hands.

"Where is Min?"

"Triangles are pink."

A mixture of love and devastation etched on Kastian's face. "You shook her off again, huh?"

"Come on, sweetie." The queen stepped forward, untangling Lareani's hands off the king. "Your daddy is in a meeting now. You should go back to bed."

Lareani looked around at the room, blinking her eyes. Her lips trembled. She covered her ears and started singing a nursery rhyme quietly: "*It's raining, it's snowing, rainbow winds are blowing...*"

The queen curled a finger at Saradra. "Take her to her room and make sure she doesn't leave her bed."

"Yes, Owner." Saradra slid a hand through Lareani's elbow and led the little girl who was trapped in a young woman's body outside. The joyless nursery rhyme faded behind the doors.

No one in the room dared breaking the silence to pick up the argument where it was left off. Kastian walked over to the bar and poured himself a glass of wine.

"Until the name Zarall and anything *symbolising* them is completely destroyed, my family's claim on the throne will not be secure," the king declared after drinking half the cup in one gulp. He sat on one of the armchairs, leaning back and extending his feet. "Now, my advisers advise me. How do I destroy this *symbol* without causing any more damage?" He pointed in Lion's direction with his half-empty cup.

The old man — Master Ulrian — cleared his throat. "I believe Queen Inoeveth is right, Your Majesty. The slave has to go down in the arena. And it has to be a great event."

"The Serpent's Grip Tournament?" the older son suggested. "It's two months away."

"That was supposed to be his next tournament anyway, wasn't it?" the other man said, nodding slowly. "He fights there, he dies. It would quench the mob's thirst."

"But we have to make sure he makes a full recovery and gets a fair chance," the old man said sternly. "Then we have to make sure he loses indeed."

"And how do we do that? He won four grand tournaments. And he won the last one, Unraged and injured. How do we make sure he won't win the Serpent's Grip too?"

"I think I know how," Queen Inoeveth said. She crossed her arms, gazing at Lion with a slight curiosity. "We'll make sure he'll be begging to die by the time he walks out into the arena."

More torture. Great.

A sudden dizziness swept over Lion. His muscles lost all their strength, and he slumped to his side. A soft and fuzzy cloud pressed down on his mind, inviting him to sleep.

"We had to give him something to keep him awake," Master Karhad explained apologetically. "His injuries…"

The rest of his words were drowned under the fog of sleep. Lion escaped into the darkness, leaving them to argue and decide on his fate.

28

OLIRA

Olira lay in her bed, staring at the ceiling as she did on that bitter night three days ago. But tonight, it wasn't the cold keeping her awake. The farmhouse was warm, the fire in the hearth in the living area still crackling softly, but sleep kept its distance from her. It was the sound of the purebred, his voice low and troubled, that kept her from finding rest.

"No... please, don't..." he murmured, his voice trembling in the dark. It was barely more than a whisper, but in the silence of the room, it sounded like a shout. Olira stiffened, trying to block out the sound, but the desperation in his tone was impossible to ignore.

It had been three days since Frostbringer's Eve. Three nights since she had settled the man on the floor in the corner of her room. In that time, she and her four brothers had worked tirelessly, planting seeds for the last harvest before winter set in. She had put the man to work alongside them.

Andar and Kowas were obsessively fascinated with the purebred. Gilann and Torren kept their distance from the slave, wary and watchful. But the twins were drawn to him like moths to a flame. Olira had spent more time chasing them away than actually working, though as the days passed, she found herself less worried. The purebred seemed harmless enough, focused solely on his tasks, keeping his head down and interacting with no one. He completely ignored the twins' attempts at talking to him and didn't even look at them.

The slave hardly used his crutch anymore, though he still limped. The work seemed to be doing him good, helping him regain his strength. And it was helping Olira too. Although the slave was slow and unsure about farm work, his contribution was going to make a difference. She was even starting to get used to the man's quiet presence.

But now, in the quiet of the night, with nothing to distract her, Olira was once again confronted by doubt about the slave. His sleep was restless, his voice filled with fear as he begged and whimpered in his dreams.

"No... Please... Don't do this..."

Olira squeezed her eyes shut, trying to will herself to sleep, to ignore the pitiful sounds coming from the corner. It wasn't her problem. She had already done more for him than most would have. But despite her best efforts, the sound of his pleading voice gnawed at her.

She rolled over, pulling the blankets tighter around herself, her thoughts wandering to the idea that had been forming in her mind for days. Perhaps it was time to give him his own space in the house, somewhere other than the floor of her room. There was a small walk-in cupboard down the hall, barely large enough to stand in, but it could be converted into a tiny room. A place for him to sleep without disturbing anyone else.

"Please... run... please..."

Olira's eyes snapped open. She turned her head toward the man, her brow furrowed in confusion. Had she just heard him correctly? *Run?* The word hung in the air, making the hair on her skin prick up.

She propped herself on her elbow, her eyes locked on the man's large form, shrouded in blankets on the floor. He continued whimpering, "please, don't do this, please," stirring and flinching helplessly, but didn't repeat that word again.

Olira felt a chill that had nothing to do with the cold. Something about that word unsettled her and invited that doubt she had just defeated back in. The slave had passed all the tests Mistress Aeliana had suggested, but Olira had just thought of one more test.

One she deep down hoped he would fail.

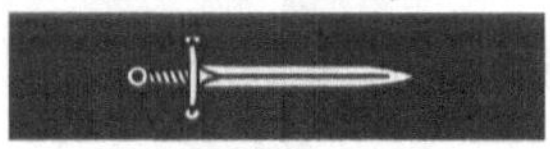

OLIRA STEPPED OUT OF the farmhouse with purpose. The morning sun was casting long shadows across the yard. Her boots crunched lightly on the dirt path as she moved quickly. Slung over her shoulder was a half-full sack.

She could smell the scent of damp earth on the soft breeze and see the rain clouds gathering on the horizon. They were still hours away. Her brothers were already in the fields, finishing the last tasks before the rain came. She could hear their voices in the distance, Andar and Kowas arguing over something insignificant, and Gilann barking at them to get to work.

She rounded the corner and caught sight of the purebred at the back, chopping wood, as he was asked to do every morning. His shirt was off, revealing crisscrossed, uneven scars, faded white against his tanned skin. He had countless other scars, and Olira had no intention of taking inventory of each mark that told a story of pain and survival. She couldn't even stomach imagining how he must have received those jagged lacerations that ran from his side across his ribs, or those clearly intentional burn marks on his chest.

What struck her the most was the way he always pulled his shirt back on when someone was nearby. She would have thought he was self-conscious about his scars if she hadn't known him any better. She attributed it to his discipline or a show of respect; something he was trained to do around his Owner. That was fine with her.

As she drew closer, his head snapped up. He set down the axe against the chopping block, reached for his shirt and pulled it over his head, covering the marks on his chest and back. The action was quick, almost without thought. He stood with his hands clasped in front of him, his head down.

Olira didn't comment. She simply said, "Follow me. Bring your crutch." Then she turned on her heel and headed towards the root cellar.

The slave limped after her without a word, his crutch tapping lightly against the ground with each step. He didn't even need it these days, but Olira made him carry it with him just in case, to avoid aggravating his leg.

The root cellar was dim and cool, a stark contrast to the mild morning outside. The scent of earth and stored provisions filled the air as Olira stepped inside. She motioned the slave to follow, then she handed him the sack she had brought.

"Keep it open," she instructed.

The slave set his crutch against the wall and held the sack open with both hands. His gaze flicked briefly inside, taking in the spare clothes, blankets, and waterskin neatly packed at the bottom. Olira began filling the rest of the sack with food: dried meats, hard bread, a small wheel of cheese, and a few apples. She filled the bag to the brim. Enough food to last a grown man for an entire week. Two, if he was careful. Then she tied the sack securely and handed it back to him.

"Come with me," she said, leading him back out of the cellar.

The purebred slung the bag over his shoulder, retrieved his crutch, and followed her.

Olira led him across the farmyard and towards the edge of the woods. The sun had risen higher in the sky, the rain clouds in the distance growing darker, but the weather remained mild for the moment. Still hours until that rain hit.

They reached the edge of the woods. The trees were dressed in shades of yellow, orange, and red, their leaves covering the ground like an autumn-coloured blanket. Sunlight peeked through the thinning branches, and the air carried the scent of fallen leaves and damp soil. Olira stopped, turning to face the man. She could feel the tension in her chest, the weight of the decision she was about to make pressing down on her.

"There's a small clearing in the woods," she said, her voice steady, but tinged with something she couldn't quite name. "You'll find it if you head straight in and keep going until you see a massive rock. It's impossible to miss. I want you to go there and sit for a bit."

The purebred glanced at her, his expression unreadable as ever. He waited, expecting more instructions.

"That's all," Olira said. "Off you go." She didn't tell him to return, nor did she tell him to leave for good. She was mindful to keep her instructions as vague as possible, open to any interpretation. Not a command, but an invitation. A choice for him to make.

The slave blinked. His eyebrows twitched as he looked ahead at the dense woods that stretched before him. Though his face was as expressionless as always, his body went rigid, as if alarmed. He glanced in her direction again.

"Go!" Olira said harshly, pointing at the woods.

The purebred looked at her a moment longer, then turned toward the woods. With the sack slung over his shoulder and his crutch in hand, he limped forward, his pace slow but steady. Olira watched him go, the figure of the man growing smaller as he made his way into the trees.

Olira stood there, rooted to the spot with goosebumps on her arms. She didn't know if he would return or if he would take the opportunity she had given him to escape. Her last test to prove that the man before her had no desire or will. No heart or mind or *rhoa* of his own.

She walked back home. Despite how much she needed him, and how her family's future depended on him, she deep down hoped the slave would just escape.

29

LION

IT WAS THE OLD slave with the weathered face who brought him his armour. Although he didn't look or say anything, his presence gave Lion comfort before the fight. And he was glad that the old man had survived. Things were nearly the same as they were before.

Almost.

It had been two months since Lion killed Marzul at the Switchblade Arena. King Kastian assigned his head physician to the responsibility of ensuring Lion's complete and speedy recovery. The wounds had healed but left scars. The torture and the beatings had long stopped. He was given a new room in the upper keep. The door was always locked and guarded by two Vogros knights.

He was fed regularly, and he was even allowed to train several times a day, under the instructions of the new Master of the Beasts. The man wasn't even as good as Doha, Badimar's least experienced assistant, but at least he set up some familiar drills. Lion pushed himself in each of them, utilizing his opportunity to improve his chances of surviving the Serpent's Grip. His efforts pleased the spectators, who showed up almost every training session. Badimar had never allowed spectators at training sessions, but King Kastian wanted to convince people that this was going to be a fair fight. So, some of the nobility, as well as Domestic Assets Trade Union representatives, Switchblade Arena administration, and some of the influential public figures had a standing invitation to come and watch Lion train whenever they wished.

Nothing so far betrayed the ploy Kastian was surely planning. Everything seemed fair. Lion had defeated his first three rivals over the first three days of the tournament. He was given armour, weapons and shields of his choice, helmet, and other appropriate equipment. He wasn't injured or drugged. They even Raged him before each fight, just to ensure he won. Kastian truly wanted him to advance to the final round.

And here he was, moments before the final, standing in the preparation room, getting ready. He listened to the eager roar of the crowd above, muffled by the walls and ceilings. More than a few times, he heard the name *Lion of Zarall* filling the entire arena. A sense of foreboding tugged at the back of his head.

Make sure he'll be begging to die... The queen's words rang in his head. Nothing they had done so far convinced him to do that.

Yet.

He had met his grand final rival the night before The Serpent's Grip started. Kastian had held a feast, as was the custom before a grand tournament. Lion was made to attend and watch as Kastian introduced his new champion: a purebred beast he named Laswen.

Lion and Laswen both stood on pedestals, facing each other across the room as the guests ate and mingled and were entertained. Laswen was a giant of a man, bigger and wider than Lion. His broad shoulders seemed to fill the room, and his thick arms hung with a quiet strength. He wore a bear's pelt on his back and a heavy armour that made Lion's look like a tin box. Based on the way they spent more time around him than Lion, the guests had seemed impressed by Laswen. Even Lion was apprehensive. And curious to see how he fought.

He hadn't watched Laswen's first three fights the previous days but heard the crowd's reaction as he sat in the preparation room. The fights didn't last long, which left the spectators craving for more. It told Lion that Laswen predominantly fought in Slayer's Pit or Red Gauntlet fights, which were very different from tournaments. Those fights between a Raged purebred beast against many freeborn beasts or civilians were designed for blood. They were less of a fight and more of a massacre; very different from what the spectators expected in a tournament. But Laswen's display of violence must have been so remarkable that it left the crowd cheering and clapping for a long time. They couldn't get enough.

And now the crowd was about to see Laswen fight Lion of Zarall.

Lion could see how this fight would end Kastian's troubles. He had impressed the crowd with his champion, evoked their thirst for blood, made them a fan of Laswen's bloody work. And now when Laswen killed Lion, they were going to be satisfied. Not angry, not even sad. No reason to continue the riots.

If Laswen killed Lion.

Lion wondered what would happen if he won instead. Would the mob take it as a sign Kastian didn't deserve to sit on the throne?

The old slave with the weathered face stepped back when he was done.

"This way," grunted the guard, who had been waiting by the door.

Lion wanted to say something to the old slave, something to acknowledge him. Or maybe he just wanted to say goodbye to someone, but he couldn't think of how to word it. So, he just stood and followed the guard without a glance back.

Sir Gwodd, the captain of the royal knights, was guarding the door leading into the launch room underneath the arena. His presence only meant one thing; Kastian was inside. Lion's stomach twisted. He wasn't expecting this to be a fair fight, not really. Kastian was here to ensure Laswen's victory.

Make sure he'll be begging to die...

Lion didn't need any intervention to lose this fight. He was at peace with his death. He had no intention of becoming the source of all the king's problems. He just had to convince Kastian of that. He had to...

The knight opened the door for him and Lion's heart skipped a beat.

No. Not this. Please.

Saradra stood in the middle of the room. Lion felt a stab at his heart when he saw her belly bulging under her dress. He stared at it for a long moment. His throat tightened, a lump forming as he struggled to keep his face blank. Saradra kept her head down, her hands together, her face neutral like a well-trained slave, but Lion could see that she was trembling.

Kastian leaned against the back wall of the room. A grin split his face as he took in Lion's reaction.

After closing the door behind him, Sir Gwodd took his stance next to the king.

Lion's mouth formed a grim line. Dispelling all traces of emotion from his face, he lowered his head down. He brought his hands together, but that didn't stop their shaking.

Why was she here? Why?

You know why, a small voice at the back of his head answered.

He swallowed.

Make sure he'll be begging to die...

"I already know you two have *feelings* for each other, so you can stop pretending like you don't know one another," Kastian spoke after watching them for several minutes. "Though I can't understand how a purebred slave *can* feel anything in the first place."

Lion didn't raise his head. If Saradra — and that little heartbeat growing inside her belly — had any chance at all to survive this, it depended on hiding *how much* Lion felt for her. Saradra must have been thinking the same thing, as she didn't raise her head either.

"I am giving you both permission to speak to each other, or hug, or do whatever you want for the next five minutes."

When the two slaves still didn't make any move, Kastian took a deep breath. He didn't smile, didn't even give any indication that he enjoyed this. "I already decided to kill you both. Pretending like you don't know each other won't change my mind. I wouldn't waste your last five minutes together if I were you."

Lion looked directly into Kastian's poison green eyes, and for the first time since his childhood, he begged: "Owner, please. Please, don't do this."

Kastian's face turned harder, but he didn't reply.

Hearing Lion's voice set something off in Saradra and she started shaking more violently. Lion couldn't bear seeing her like this, so he pulled her to himself and hugged her tightly. Her resolve crumbled as she sobbed in his arms.

"My older brother had a slave," Kastian started telling. "A purebred. Dinky, he used to call him. He was a beast, like you. A birthday present for Eltian's seventh birthday."

Saradra buried her face in the crook of Lion's shoulder. He caressed her hair. Their display of affection satisfied and disgusted Kastian at the same time. Sir Gwodd's blank expression didn't change. He watched Lion with vigilant eyes.

"Eltian was a little bit... how should I put this?" Kastian tapped a finger on his lower lip. "*Disturbed* should do fine. He was a disturbed child. He started hitting and kicking Dinky. He grew more violent as he grew up. He would torture him with his Pain Word. He would mutilate him. Raped him when he was old enough."

Lion kneeled, pulling Saradra with him. "Please, Owner," he begged on his knees. The lump in his throat reduced his voice to a whisper. "Spare her, please. Please..."

All his life, he had been taught begging would not change anything for a slave, if their Owner had set their mind on something. Begging was dangerously close to requesting. Nearly an Act of Defiance. Disrespectful at the least.

Yet, the words kept pouring out of his mouth. "Please, don't do this..."

"Eltian, may his *rhoa* rest in peace," Kastian tapped four fingers on his forehead at that, "did things to Dinky that you cannot even begin to imagine. Even our parents were disturbed by the things my brother was doing."

Helplessness was a powerful thing. Something shifted inside him. Desperation took over his thoughts. Begging was not going to work.

Sir Gwodd noticed the subtle change in the way Lion held himself. The knight took half a step forward. He neither made any move to reach for his sword, nor displayed any other intimidation. He simply pressed his lips together, ready to speak Lion's First Word if he so much as looked at the king the wrong way.

"But the slave did not break," Kastian continued, ignoring the tension in the air. "He never did. He would still walk when he could, and behaved and served like a perfect slave. A purebred."

"I'll lose the fight," Lion spoke like he was being strangled. "Please. I'll do whatever you ask—"

Kastian raised his voice to cut him off. "Everyone appreciates a well-trained purebred for being the perfect tools. A valuable property. However, I used to admire them for what they are." He smiled, but his green eyes lacked the joy of it. "I think a purebred is not a mere well-trained human. I think it is a different species; something more evolved than humans. They are easy to control, because they possess an inhuman amount of control over themselves. It's really surprising not everybody sees how remarkable they are."

Saradra's hand found Lion's and squeezed it. She sobbed and her tears fell on his armour. He pressed her against his chest, as if wanting to tuck her safely into his heart.

Kastian's smile faded. "If anyone had told me that a purebred could cause so much trouble for a king, I would have found it very amusing."

"I will obey," Lion whispered, his throat bobbing. "I'll do whatever you wish. I... I live to serve; I breathe to please. Please, Owner..."

"When I sent you into the arena with Marzul, I didn't think it was necessary to order you to die. I guess I underestimated what a purebred can do. And now I'm in a position where I can't trust your obedience."

Lion took Saradra's face between his hands and kissed her. He covered her face with kisses, every one of them hungrier than the last. His hand slid down to her belly, and he understood why she was so obsessed with her unborn child, even before it was conceived. He felt protective of the life growing inside. He wanted to hold it, guard it, care for it.

"Take her hostage," Lion said, his voice strained. "I'll die. I promise I'll die if you just spare her."

"No," Saradra whimpered as she held onto him tighter.

Kastian pursed his lips. "I could do that. I could promise you that I would spare her. But then you know why that would be a lie." Lion followed Kastian's gaze to Saradra's belly. The king didn't have to explain it further. He couldn't let Saradra live and give birth to the Lion of Zarall's child. He glanced at Sir Gwodd again, calculating the distance between them. There was no way he could get to the knight before he spoke his First Word.

"Please don't kill her," he whispered helplessly. He closed his eyes, his head down, his arms tight around Saradra.

"Oh, *I* won't kill her," Kastian said casually.

Lion's eyes snapped open. Colour drained from his face as the weight of the words sank in. He felt a crushing pain in his chest, as if the air had been sucked from his lungs. "No," he gasped. Tears ran down his cheeks. "No. Not this. Not this. Please."

"Your five minutes is up."

"Don't do this. Please." The room seemed to close in around him, the walls pressing in as a wave of nausea rolled over him.

Saradra wrapped her arms around Lion's neck. Tears still trailed down her cheeks, but that strong, fierce fighter returned to her voice. "Look at me," she ordered. "When you go out there, do whatever it takes to win. Do you hear me? *Whatever* it takes."

The blue of her eyes crushed Lion's heart. His mind raced in a chaotic storm of fear and helplessness, unable to accept what was about to happen. His heart pounded, every beat inflicting an ache.

"I love you," she whispered. She straightened her back and faced Sir Gwodd with those fiery eyes, brave and strong, promising a fight.

She didn't understand what Kastian meant! She thought the knight was going to do the king's bidding.

She was facing the wrong direction.

"Please run," Lion whispered. "Please run, please."

Utter confusion crossed Saradra's face. She still didn't understand. Lion sobbed, his lips trembling, choking on the lump in his throat. He opened his mouth to tell her he loved her back, but Kastian spoke before he could make another sound.

"*Dracistuecto.*"

A blackness pressed down, blurring his sight. Lion tried to shove Saradra away, but she clung to him.

"Run!" Lion pushed through clenched teeth. "Please run."

"No," Saradra refused. "You can fight it!"

He fought it. Twelve knew he fought it with everything he had. He focused on the colour of her eyes. A pressure started building inside his head. The blinding rage accumulated in his tense muscles.

"Fight it!" she yelled. "Fight it! Please!"

The purebred planted his fingers on the sandy ground, forcing himself to stay put. The Rage seeped into his mind, obscuring everything. Taking over his thoughts, his heart, his body. His breathing turned into a growl. A loud humming filled his ears, muffling all sound. Muffling her voice. Her words, her pleads. The pressure at the back of his head grew until it exploded in Rage.

30

OLIRA

OLIRA MOVED THROUGH THE woods, her boots not making any noise on the damp, soft earth. The rain from the previous night had left the forest soaked, the leaves glistening with water droplets, and the air thick with the scent of wet earth and pine. She had been dreading this moment all morning. She had done everything she could to delay going to the clearing and confronting what she might or not find.

The slave hadn't returned last night. There had been no sign of him in the morning either. She had checked everywhere, even the barn, half-expecting to find him sitting in the stall. But it was empty, the chain still attached to the wall. Her brothers had asked about him, their curiosity mixed with concern. Gilann, in particular, had thought she was insane for letting him go, but he understood why she had done it.

As she drew closer to the clearing, Olira's steps slowed. She didn't want to know. Part of her hoped she would find nothing, that he had taken the opportunity and run. It would put her in a difficult situation, with no other means to pay Master Tholthus, but she still hoped that he would run.

She pushed through the last line of trees and stepped into the clearing. At first, it seemed empty, the massive rock standing alone in the centre, a dark silhouette against the grey sky. Her heart sank, a mixture of relief and disappointment washing over her.

Then she saw a figure sitting against the rock.

The slave's knees were drawn up to his chest, his face buried in his arms. Despite his imposing size, he looked like a small, hunched figure that seemed to burrow into the damp stone behind him. His clothes were drenched, the fabric clinging to his skin as if trying to pull him down further into the earth. The bag she had given him lay untouched beside him. He hadn't used the coat inside, hadn't even tried to shelter himself from the rain, as if the cold and wet were things he no longer felt or cared about. He just sat there, motionless.

Olira's shoulders sagged. She was wrong. The slave was just an ordinary pure-bred, nothing more. A hollow shell. A mindless, broken thing with no will of his own. He couldn't think for himself, couldn't act in his own best interest, even something as simple as sheltering himself from the rain. As the realisation took hold, a flicker of something else stirred in the back of her mind: pity.

She crouched in front of him, her heart heavy with compassion. She sighed. "Why? Why didn't you run?"

For a long moment, he didn't move. Then, slowly, he stirred, lifting his head. He stared without focus at a vague spot past Olira's shoulder. His dirty blond hair clung to his forehead. His face was shadowed by dark blond stubble, and beneath his eyes were dark, puffy circles, like he hadn't slept all night. The glazed look in his grey eyes twisted Olira's gut in ways she couldn't fully understand. Despite his broad frame, the purebred beast looked utterly drained, bone-deep tired, as if he had been carrying the weight of the boulder behind him.

He opened and closed his mouth a few times until he could find his voice. "I live to serve," he said. He paused to swallow. "I breathe to please."

Olira hung her head. She nodded slowly. "Okay." The word was an admission of defeat, like she had lost an argument. "Okay," she repeated, taking a deep breath as she stood. "Let's just go home."

The man nodded slightly, pushing himself up from the ground with the slow, deliberate movements of someone who had long since given up on resisting the pull of gravity. They walked back to the farm in silence.

31

PUREBRED BEAST

"You can fight this!"

"Look at me! Please! Just look…"

"Fight it!"

Screams.

Soft skin against his knuckles.

Teeth biting into his hands.

Wet sound of bones cracking under his fists.

Blood. Only, blood.

32

LION

THE RAGE FADED, THE dark grip on his mind slowly receding.

His eyes were drawn to the wet pile of flesh at his feet.

He fell to his knees, tilted his head back, and howled.

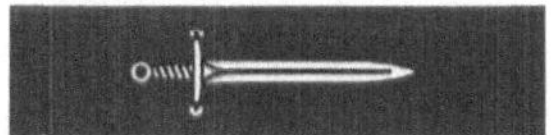

OUTSIDE THE ROOM, THE crowd demanded blood, their deafening cheers echoing through the Switchblade Arena.

Blood coated Lion's hands, arms, and the front of his armour.

He pulled Saradra's lifeless body to his chest. Her bones were broken in so many places that no matter how careful he held her, her limbs fell into queasy angles. The sight stole a senseless sob out of him. He buried his face in her scarlet hair. His tears mixed with her blood. A wild sound between a howl and a wail rose from the back of his throat.

He remembered.

He remembered more than he ever did.

He remembered how his hands felt when he hit and broke her face.

He remembered the sound of her skull when he bashed her head in.

He remembered how she begged and screamed and looked at him.

He cried. Howled. Rocked her shattered body back and forth in his arms.

In the arena, a cheerful music invited the Mid-Game actors on the stage to entertain the crowd. Their songs and the audience's claps hurt Lion's ears.

Kastian gave an order. There were other people in the room now. Lion neither heard nor cared what they were doing until hands grabbed him. They tried to pry his arms off her.

A primitive snarl escaped his lips. He yanked his arm free, buried his elbow in someone's face. He wrapped his fingers around someone else's neck. Crushed their windpipe before Sir Gwodd could yell out his First Word.

He collapsed next to Saradra's twisted body. Unable to turn his head away, he was forced to look at the slack angle of her broken jaw. One of her eyes was rolled back in her skull, the other was swollen and bloody. He couldn't look away. He couldn't turn his head. Tears ran down Lion's face. A deranged scream gathered in his chest, but his paralysed throat didn't let any sound out.

Hands dragged him away from her, pulled him to his knees. His head lolled loosely between his shoulders. Kastian grabbed his hair and tilted his head back to face him.

"I will say this only once," the king said quietly. A silent anger masked his face, looking more disturbed than pleased. Disturbed at watching what a purebred could do.

"Fight well, die well, give them a good show, and I give you my word; I will bury your bodies together in an unmarked grave. If those claims are false and purebreds do have *rhoas*, you might even find her in Farhome."

I will see you in Farhome.

Bury together. Find her in Farhome.

Together.

The words tore Lion's heart into shreds. He almost missed the surprising tone hidden under Kastian's words. The king was desperate. Afraid even. He was frightened of what Lion could do in the arena. What he could ignite.

The king of Chinderia was afraid of the slave.

He had no reason to be. Not anymore.

Make sure he'll be begging to die...

If Kastian had been more observant, he would know he didn't need to cast threats. But he cast them anyway.

"If you do *anything* other than fighting well and dying," Kastian snarled, pulling his lips back over his teeth. "I will defile her body in every way imaginable. I will have every single house guard fuck her corpse. Once they are done, I will rip your bastard out of her belly and feed it to my hounds. I will shred her body into pieces and dump them in every cesspit in Brinescar. And I will make you watch it all. So, you better not leave that arena breathing today."

Her belly...

His paralysis was fading. An inhuman whimper spilt from Lion's lips. He remembered how her arms were clutched over her belly, trying to protect it from Lion's blows.

"Clean him up," Kastian ordered before leaving the room.

Sir Gwodd stayed to supervise, as a pair of slaves stepped forward with a bucket of water and a washcloth. A different kind of pressure was starting to build up at the back of Lion's head. The slaves started washing the blood off his armour. Off his hands.

Her blood.

They were washing *her* away.

A clump of red hair, ripped from her scalp, was stuck at the base of his palm. When one of the slaves slapped the wet cloth in his palm, wiping it clean, Lion growled frantically.

"No! No!"

He punched the slave's throat. It was the old man with the weathered face.

"*Padlociatius!*" yelled Sir Gwodd promptly.

The other slave continued cleaning the blood off Lion, while the old man rolled on the floor, gasping and holding his throat. Sir Gwodd kicked him towards the door. "Get out!"

The old man scrambled out of the room, still coughing and wheezing. Others walked in; men wearing Vogros colours. As Lion lay helpless, they dragged Saradra's body out of the room. All he could do was watch. His eyes had spotted a bloody tooth in the midst of the blood-stained sand.

The pressure at the back of his head grew heavier.

The actors finished their show at the arena. The announcer started his final speech. The spectators stomped their feet in excitement.

Lion was aware of everything around him, but in a disconnected way. Almost as if watching himself from outside his body. He was slipping into *that place*, leaving his numb body behind. He wanted to stay in *that place* forever, never return. His thoughts were being crushed under a fierce headache. His paralysis faded, but no further sound came out of him. Sitting on his knees, he slumped in on himself.

Now that his hands were free of her blood, Lion noticed the scratches. Saradra had torn half the skin off his forearms. Her teeth had left deep marks in one of his hands.

She fought. She fought like the fighter she was. She drew his blood.

Lion took his head between his hands. The pressure inside his skull was unbearable. The headache throbbed violently. Hot tears burnt his face.

The announcer was introducing the competitors now, his voice booming through the arena. Switchblade buzzed with anticipation, the crowd stomping their feet in unison.

Everyone else had left the room. It was just Sir Gwodd and Lion now. The knight threw a shield, a lor'qas, and the lion mask in front of him. "Remember what the king said," Sir Gwodd hissed. "Fight well, die well, and give them a good show..."

Then, they could be buried together.

Together.

He let out a strangled breath.

The Gates of Life opened for the final time, inviting him to his death. Hungry shouts of the spectators filled the waiting room. The sunlight painted the blood-marked sand on fire.

Lion slipped the mask on. He picked up the shield and the lor'qas, pulled himself up on his feet, and stepped into the Switchblade Arena.

33

LION

Fight well. Die well. Give them a good show.

Laswen was Raged. He sprung out of his gate on a dead run, his face distorted in fury. He was stripped of any emotion, anything that made him human. A purebred beast.

Was this what freeborns saw when they fought Lion at this arena?

Was this what those Vogros men and Zarall traitors had seen when the mage unleashed Lion on them?

Was this what *she* had seen before she died?

Lion stepped aside to avoid Laswen's first attack. Although he'd rather greet the blow with his neck and end it, this wasn't what Kastian wanted to see.

Fight well.

His orders rang in his mind.

Get it done, Badimar had ordered before Lion took Saradra in his arms for the first time. The warmth of her body as they snuggled in his tiny bed was slipping out of his memories already, as if a lifetime had passed.

His head throbbed painfully.

Lion blocked the next attack with his shield and swung his lor'qas at Laswen's side. He jumped back and brought his sword down to meet his. Lion withdrew, raising his shield up.

Fight well.

Fighting well came natural to him. His body craved a good fight. It acted on its own, a primitive hatred boiling out of his muscles. He set himself free, and he fought.

Give them a good show.

Laswen was good. In his Raged state, he acted without thought. There was no hesitation, no fear, just pure instinct. But this was not a simple battle fever. Laswen's eyes saw everything; he saw how Lion shifted his foot before starting a counterattack. He saw how Lion slightly ducked his head between his shoulders before raising his shield up. He perceived everything, yet he didn't waste any time analysing any of this information in his mind. His body did that for him, while his mind stayed out of the fight.

Lion's did too, but it was different for him. His thoughts were a tangled mess. The memory of Saradra's dead body haunted him. He could still hear her screams and pleads. A weight pressed down on the crown of his head. The headache and the hollow pain in his chest became unbearable. He wanted to end this.

Die well.

It was time to pick the strike that would end his life. He decided the next blow would be as good as any.

He compelled himself to stand still and take it, but his body slid to the side. His sword went up just in time to meet Laswen's, throwing him off balance. Laswen recovered instantly and launched another attack.

Die well.

This one. This one was going to be the strike to kill him.

The headache became a blinding throb behind his eyes. He could feel the pressure mounting, pushing him to the edge of sanity. The crowd's roar intensified, but the sound was distant, as if underwater.

Stand still and die well.

He stood still, but his arm raised his shield up, deflecting the attack. Then his lor'qas lunged forward like a snake and gave Laswen a gaping slash on his side. An unstoppable chuckle rose from Lion's throat. The sight of first blood erupted into a roar from the spectators, which drove Lion's headache to a white-hot intensity.

Laswen, not even noticing his wound, lunged again, and something inside Lion snapped. The headache disappeared abruptly. Lion almost heard the sound of something *tearing* inside his mind.

He rolled to the side, narrowly avoiding the descending sword. A deranged laughter burst from his lips. His laughter was wild, unhinged, as tears rolled down his cheeks, concealed under the lion mask.

Give them a good show.

Lion laughed harder as he parried Laswen's next strike.

He will defile her body.

That was the threat Kastian had made. His head felt light and fuzzy now. No more headache.

She was dead.

She was gone.

He had killed her.

Laswen hurled a series of attacks and each one elicited another sob mixed with laughter from Lion. He met them all and followed up with his own sequence.

He killed her. And now, Kastian was going to...

Screaming something between a taunt and a laugh, Lion slashed inside Laswen's upper arm. Blood spurted at Laswen's breastplate. This wound had killed Laswen; he just didn't know it yet.

"Come on!" Lion yelled; his voice buried under the crowd's wild cheers. "Make me bleed!"

His rival's taunts didn't reach Laswen's ears, nor did his wound give him any concern. Any other fighter would have shown a flash of emotion after taking a deadly injury, but not a Raged beast. Laswen feigned a blow to Lion's left and sucker punched him with his shield. A sharp pain and the taste of blood inside his mouth told Lion he had gotten what he wanted.

He grinned. "That's it!" he said, deflecting a testing blow. "Make me bleed! Make me bleed! Come on!"

Laswen moved in and Lion swung his lor'qas to parry the next blow.

He had killed Saradra.

No, Kastian had killed Saradra.

They had killed Saradra?

He chuckled while tears streaked down his face. If there was one thing he was sure of, it was that Sir Gwodd *hadn't* killed Saradra.

He laughed so hard he almost got his head detached from his shoulders.

"He's gonna *defile* her body, you know that?" Lion asked. "That's what he said. He's gonna cut her... He's gonna..."

A wild laughter strangled the rest of his words. Tears blurred his sight. Laswen stepped in with a feign again. Lion raised his sword and Laswen dropped his, pivoting and attacking from the other side. He landed a clean slash on Lion's right thigh. Blood gushed down his knee.

"Attaboy!" Lion cheered, raising both arms up in celebration. The crowd shared his joy, screaming with excitement. Their screams reminded him of Saradra's. He still heard her voice in his head, begging, pleading for him to stop.

"Who's your *favourite* Owner, Laswen?" Lion babbled. He stumbled backwards while noticing Laswen's movements had slowed down, too. The wound on Laswen's upper arm had painted the side of his breastplate in red, and he was struggling to lift his shield up.

"They never found my map," Lion laughed. "Why did she have to look under my bed?"

His face still twisted in a mindless fury, Laswen stumbled forward, initiating another series of attacks. Lion greeted them clumsily.

"What's under your bed, Laswen?" Lion wondered. He stepped back and pointed a finger at him. "What secrets do you hide?"

He dropped on his haunches and chuckled as Laswen nearly took his head.

"Come on, beast!" Lion yelled, stretching his arms at his sides. "You gotta finish me off, friend. Or he's gonna defi—" Another giggle swallowed the word. "He's gonna def—" He didn't know what was so hilarious about that word, but he couldn't get it out.

Laswen, still completely indifferent to his wound, forced him to retreat against a series of quick moves. Lion's leg hindered him and he fell backwards.

That's it, he thought frantically, watching Laswen raise his sword over his head. *Die well.*

He didn't even have to do anything but lie still, and it would all end. Her screams would finally end. He would find peace.

Lion swung his shield from left to right and nudged Laswen's sword aside. He didn't deserve peace. He didn't deserve to be buried with Saradra. He reached for his lor'qas, but Laswen kicked it away.

Die well. Lie still.

Bury together.

I will see you in Farhome.

Do whatever it takes to win!

Lion flinched. Saradra's voice sounded so clear in his head.

Laswen threw his shield aside and grasped his sword with both hands. The next blow almost broke Lion's arm as he blocked it with his shield. He felt the violent tremors spreading from the shield all the way up to his teeth. His fingers curled around a handful of sand. When Laswen raised his sword again, Lion threw it at his face.

Do whatever it takes to win, do you hear me?

Lion lunged forward and jammed the edge of the shield against Laswen's kneecap. Without a single scream or a grunt, Laswen stumbled backwards, blinking the sand from his eyes. Lion didn't pause to see if he had broken his rival's knee or not. He rolled sideways and leapt to his feet.

Lion pulled his mask off and tossed it aside. He wiped the tears off his face, smearing blood all over. He didn't want to win. But he didn't deserve the peace of death, either.

Laswen stood — barely — between Lion and his lor'qas. He hopped on his good leg, trying to find his balance. He was almost done. Even the crowd knew this; they were demanding Lion to finish him off.

When he imagined how Kastian would be watching this right now, Lion couldn't contain another chuckle. He wondered if the king was secretly hoping Lion would lose at the last second, just to make it a bit more dramatic.

"You have to kill me," Lion begged. "Fight! Even she put up a better fight than you!" He lifted his free arm to show him the scratch and bite marks Saradra had left. Tears blurred his vision.

Laswen stumbled on one leg. A mindless fury was still etched on his face. He blinked at Lion's arm with unseeing eyes.

With a scream, Lion charged behind his shield. He knocked Laswen on his back, straddled him, and bashed his face with the shield.

The crowd had already started cheering for 'Lion'. That name Kastian had been trying to bury was being heard amongst the cheers as well.

Lion threw his shield and picked up his lor'qas. Then he grabbed Laswen by the scruff of his neck and dragged him towards the balcony where Kastian and his family were seated.

Demands of death filled the arena. Lion glanced at the armed men positioned on the outer walls of the arena. Some of them had their bows aimed at Lion, but he knew they weren't going to shoot. He didn't care if they did, anyway. But if they stripped the crowd off their champion, Kastian was going to have to deal with a lot more than the embarrassment of losing against Lion of Zarall for a second time.

He dropped Laswen underneath the balcony. Kastian watched him with a tight mouth. Even from a distance, Lion could see the king's knuckles were drained white as he grasped the arms of his chair. His queen displayed a forced smile on her face. Sitting next to his mother, Prince Dienus's face had turned an ugly tone of red. Prince Lotheris on the other side was better at hiding his anger. Their half-witted Princess's chair was empty, like it had been at every feast. They hadn't invited any guests or lords to sit with them today. Just the Vogros family, enjoying a pleasant day in the arena.

Laswen started blinking and moaning. His nose was broken. His face was completely covered in blood. He rolled to his side and coughed.

"You fought well, beast," Lion said, grinning at Kastian. "Stay down and I'll see you in Farhome."

Laswen looked around, disoriented. He started groaning from his injuries now as he noticed them. Lion kicked him on his back and stared at Kastian expectantly.

Grudgingly, Kastian raised his fist and turned his thumb upside down, signalling Lion to finish the fight.

The spectators roared their appreciation.

Lion's grin widened. He raised his lor'qas over his head. His blood rushed with the same unruly energy that possessed the crowd. He craved for blood. Death was what he had been bred for, raised for, trained for. Death was his sustenance. It was the only purpose of his miserable life.

Victory dissolved like ash in his mouth.

He threw his weapon aside.

Consumed by his injuries and on the brink of unconsciousness, Laswen didn't even realise Lion had spared his life. Although half of the audience sighed their disappointment, the majority of them found humour in Lion's disobedience. Kastian's face turned a glorious red.

Lion stepped closer to the balcony and without even thinking about what he was doing, he took his member out of his pants and started pissing.

Kastian was going to castrate him for this!

The thought hurled him into an uncontrolled laughter. The crowd howled with him. He laughed so hard, more tears flowed down his cheeks and his aim started to become an issue. With every burst of laughter, the dark patterns on the sand became more intricate.

Oh, Kastian was going to *defile* his member for this.

He doubled over, holding his stomach and wiping the tears off his face as he yanked his pants back up. His ribs hurt from laughing. His chest hurt even more. He wanted to cut his chest open and rip his heart out.

"Where's that mage when you need him?" he mused, though his voice was lost within the turmoil.

The audience was loving it! This was becoming their *favourite* moment in Switchblade Arena.

Oh, Saradra...

"How did I hurt you? How..." He sobbed uncontrollably and fell to his knees.

The audience's joy turned into angry protests, and Lion knew the guards were coming for him now. He jumped up just in time to dodge the first attacker: a young man, very eager to get to the unruly slave first that he had outrun his comrades, leaving them behind. Lion stepped out of the man's way with a clumsy half-turn, grabbed his cloak, and threw it over his head. The young man flapped his hands, trying to untangle himself from his cloak. This elicited more laughter from the audience.

Give them a good show.

The other guards spread around him cautiously. Instead of swords, they were wielding clubs. Lion taunted them, raising his arms to the side.

The crowd was cheering for him to fight. Moreover, some of them were attempting to climb into the arena. Sir Gwodd and a group of knights were escorting the royal family out of the balcony. The air in the whole arena was tense, only moments from exploding.

"Like a boiling pot," Lion explained to the nearest guard. "It's gonna explode!"

The guard scowled, glanced at his comrades, uncertainty paling his face.

Lion chuckled and sidestepped to dodge an attack from behind. He smacked his elbow just over the attacker's ear, sending him to the ground. The next club met with the back of his skull and stars flashed in his sight.

Lion went down under half a dozen clubs, landing on his head and legs.

People booed and hooted at the guards and at the name Vogros. Guards with spears entered into the arena. Covering his head against the clubs and kicks, Lion watched as someone from the crowd threw a rock the size of a fist at one of the guards. Someone else jumped into the arena, followed by others.

The riot erupted fast.

It almost looked like somebody had Raged all these people. An odd sense of satisfaction grasped Lion. This was exactly what Kastian had been trying to avoid.

Give them a good show.

He laughed like a mad man until they beat him unconscious.

34

OLIRA

Olira added the finishing touches to the Crimsonplum Harvest Tart and stepped back, examining the dark purple dessert with a critical scowl. It didn't look as crispy as her mum's baking, but it smelled right. The sweet, rich scent filled the kitchen, mingling with the warmth of the oven and the faint chatter from the other room. She wiped her hands on her apron and set the tart aside to cool.

Jygan was in the living area, his deep voice punctuated by the occasional giggle from Andar and Kowas. The boys worshipped him. Olira could hear them playing some sort of game, the sound of their laughter bringing a smile to her face.

She turned to the cupboard, pulling out six plates. "Take these to the table," she told Torren as she handed them. Her hand paused as she reached for a seventh plate. She had been contemplating inviting the slave to eat with them for weeks now, the idea lingering in the back of her mind. Why not, she kept thinking, but tonight didn't feel like the right time. Not with a guest in the house.

She set the plate aside and heaped it with food. "You can start dishing," she told Gilann, who had been helping her with the stew. "I'll be right back."

Olira carried the plate to the small cupboard that had become the slave's room. Three months had passed since Olira was first forced to take the dying man, and now, he had his own space in her house.

He had settled into the rhythm of farm life and had made a full recovery. An ugly white scar still remained on his thigh, but he didn't even limp anymore. His strength had returned, and his presence on the farm had proven to be more of a help than she had expected. The last harvest before winter was only a few days away, and Olira knew that having another pair of strong hands would make the work easier.

She didn't even feel the need to watch him around her brothers anymore. Andar and Kowas still tried to talk to him, but he continued to ignore them. Sooner or later, the twins would give up and stop trying. Like Olira did.

She knocked gently on the cupboard door, then pushed it open. The small space was dark, the single candle she had given him unlit. The room was sparse, with just a bedroll on the floor and a few belongings she had provided: a blanket, some clothes, a towel, a jug full of water, a wooden cup, and a candle.

The slave sat up, blinking and turning his face away from the light that flooded into the cupboard. Olira set the plate down and reminded him softly, "Just put a towel or something under the door, to stop the draft." She picked up the candle and ducked into the hallway to light it from another candle. "Or move the candle away from the door," she said, returning to the cupboard and handing it back to the slave. "You don't need to sit in the dark."

The slave nodded without looking. He had changed in the past few months, looking more decent, with his face clean-shaven and his hair trimmed. He looked healthier, though his demeanour was still vacant.

Olira had found herself entertaining the idea of keeping the purebred. She had already started looking into other ways to pay her debt. With the root cellar stacked for the winter, and a rich harvest to collect in a few days' time, she could make some extra money. She was even contemplating making another trip to Kiore before the winter rolled in, or to Kilrer, which was further and more dangerous to travel. But she could take the man with her. A purebred beast's presence would surely deter any bandits.

She could let him stay here and be content.

Leaving the slave to his meal, she returned to the kitchen. Gilann and Torren were busy setting the table. She joined them, her thoughts momentarily drifting back to the purebred in the cupboard. He needed a name. If he was going to stay here, she couldn't keep calling him 'Hey' or 'You' for the rest of their lives. She pushed the thought aside. Tonight wasn't the time to think about the awkwardness of naming a grown man.

Dinner went better than Olira could have hoped. She didn't remember the last time she had let herself relax and have this much fun. Twins chattered away nonstop, while Torren listened to Jygan's stories eagerly. The tanner sat directly across from Olira, their glances meeting over the table more than a few times. He was as charming as ever, his deep voice sending a pleasant jolt down Olira's stomach as she listened to him talk to Gilann about hunting.

When she brought the Crimsonplum tart over, Jygan's eyes lit with delight. His smile stole Olira's breath. He pretended to fight Andar and Kowas for the dessert, pinning one under his arm and the other with his leg, as they reached for the largest slice. When Olira kept that slice for herself, Jygan laughed.

After dinner, Jygan volunteered to help Olira with dishes. They worked side by side in the kitchen, the tension seeming to grow between them at every accidental touch.

And yet, at the end of the night, Jygan did his usual act and left Olira confused and fuming.

She had sent the boys to bed, and Gilann had retreated to his room. She walked Jygan out, lingering in the doorway. The air was heavy, a storm brewing in the distance. A soft rumble of thunder echoed in the night. Jygan hesitated, turning to Olira with a look that made her heart skip a beat. For a moment, she thought this was it. He would finally take the step, lean in, and kiss her.

Then, a sudden lightning split the sky, followed by a deafening thunder. Jygan glanced up, and when he looked back down, his expression had shifted. He pulled back, his gaze becoming avoidant. "I'd better hurry home," he said, his voice cold and distant.

Olira forced a nod, ignoring how her heart tightened. The sharp retort came out harsher than she intended. "Right, wouldn't want you to stay long enough to actually make up your mind."

Jygan grimaced, a flicker of embarrassment passing his face. "You guys be safe," he said. "That lightning sounded pretty close."

"Not close enough," she murmured, loud enough that he would hear, but not enough to demand a reply. "Ride safe, Jygan." She retreated inside and closed the door, barely keeping herself from slamming it shut. She heard the sound of his horse's hooves as he drove off into the night, the sound quickly drowned out by the rising wind.

She let out a long breath, trying to release the tension from her chest. She returned to her room. As she passed the cupboard where the slave slept, Olira noticed there was no light seeping from underneath the door. She frowned. The draft must have blown it out again. She considered lighting it again, but decided against it. The slave was probably already asleep, and she wasn't in the mood to deal with anyone else tonight.

She went to her room. The sound of rain drummed against the roof and filled the house with noise. As she changed her clothes and climbed into bed, the wind picked up and rattled the windows. Olira curled up tighter, ignoring the hurt in her chest, and fell asleep to the sound of the storm raging through her.

35

LION

LION'S FIRST FEW CONSCIOUS thoughts were sane: he wondered where he was, he cursed at the hundred different sources of pain piercing through his body, and he tried to remember what had happened.

When he finally did remember, the insanity flooded back.

His strained groans were interrupted by chuckles. Every sharp breath hurt.

He had fucked Kastian Vogros! He had *royally* fucked the king of Chinderia!

That brought his attention to between his legs. He groped his crotch and sighed when he found his manhood still intact. For now.

He laughed and regretted it immediately, wincing at the pain it brought. He gasped for air, but he couldn't keep it inside for long; the air found a way to slip out of his lips in the form of a moan or a giggle. Sometimes both.

He dove back into the peaceful pit of unconsciousness.

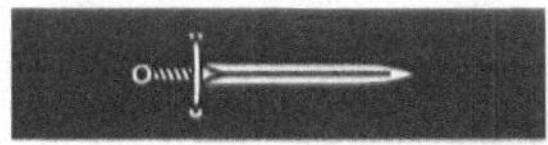

HE WOKE SEVERAL TIMES to find the world still inhabitable.

He was lucky to crawl back into the comfort of sleep the first few times. Nonetheless, there came a time when his mind was too stubborn to let the darkness back in. It invited the madness instead.

His cries and laughter attracted several figures to come and check on him. One of those figures was Karhad. The long, dangling earring on Karhad's right ear jingled annoyingly. He was arguing with someone about shutting the *stupid* slave up.

Lion snatched and pulled Karhad's *stupid* earring, ripping part of his ear with it.

Karhad jerked back. For a brief second, he didn't realise what Lion had just done. Then the pain hit him, and he started wailing, cupping the bleeding remains of his ear with both hands.

Lion laughed until his stomach cramped. He looked at the earring and at the piece of ear curiously. Why in Darkhome had he just done this? He had no idea, but it was hilarious!

"You stupid cunt!" growled Karhad. "*Prihjtivaviula! Prihjtivaviula! Prihjtivaviula!*"

Lion's back lifted off the bed in a painful arc. Was it possible to snap one's own back with the force of convulsions? He came too close to learning. His body was paralysed in an anguish like he'd never experienced before. The amount of pain was stacked when the Pain Word was repeated. His eyes rolled back inside his skull, teasing him with the prospect of unconsciousness, but one of the useful things about his Words was that they didn't allow fainting.

The torture went longer than usual until Lion heard a roaring blast. Something had ripped inside his mind. He had heard a sound like this, the distinct sound of tearing, back at the arena too. A dark presence creeped into his head. It didn't like the torment and the madness occupying there, so it retreated to the back, like a wounded animal. It stayed hidden in the shades of Lion's distorted thoughts. Waiting. Recovering.

When the pain finally faded, Lion's well-trained purebred body itched to roll facedown and assume submissive posture. His right leg was wet, bleeding out from an injury he forgot about. He raised one fist to his neck, requesting permission to speak. He slipped the other hand under the bandages on his leg.

"Speak," snarled Karhad.

Kiejain's balls! There were real tears in Karhad's eyes! What a wuss!

"Fuck you, Master," Lion chuckled and stabbed two fingers inside the wound.

The result was more blood, a sharp pain spreading from his leg, and a wonderful trip into unconsciousness before Karhad could speak his Pain Word again.

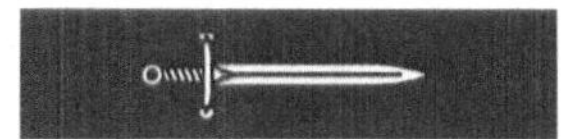

THEY THREW HIM FACE down on the floor.

He was comfortable lying there like a sack of happy potatoes, but somebody wanted him on his knees. They were kind enough to assist him by grabbing his hair and yanking him up. Nice blokes.

He saw the bookshelves spreading the length of the walls and smelled the dust they gathered. He was back in the library and not surprised to see Kastian's jolly bunch glaring daggers at him.

"Hi," Lion smiled, all teeth. His friendly attitude was rewarded with an immediate punch.

"He's broken," Karhad said. His right ear was wrapped in a bandage. "Gone mad. I've never seen a purebred lose his mind like this."

"There's something in my mind," Lion said and received another punch.

"Keep his hands off his leg," Karhad instructed. Two men did as they were bid and twisted Lion's arms behind him. Bummer. He was hoping to escape from this confrontation.

"Seriously," Lion snickered. "There's something *inside* my mind and it's bad."

"Don't speak without permission!" Karhad spat. "*Prihjtivaviula!*"

Their conversation became buried behind the haze of pain for several seconds. When Lion submerged from the pain, they were talking about the possible causes of his insanity.

"You should cut down with your use of Pain Word, Master Karhad," the old advisor said. "It doesn't seem to have a good impact on him."

"Pain Word does not cause insanity," Karhad said coldly. "I've never seen the Pain Word do this to a purebred."

"It's evil," Lion said. "It wants to get out, and it's very, *very* evil."

"Shut up!" grunted one of the men behind him, and slapped him with the back of his hand.

"Master Karhad is right," Kastian said. "Pain Word does not break their mind like this."

"How's Dinky doing?" Lion spat blood on the expensive carpet. Sitting on his large, throne-like chair, Kastian narrowed his eyes into slits. "It wasn't your brother. It was you, wasn't it?"

It wasn't really a question, and Lion didn't expect an answer from him. But one of the men answered on behalf of the king. "Don't you talk to your king, you piece of meat!" He backed his command with a slap.

"Stop damaging him," Queen Inoeveth said in a serene voice. "We've seen that does not work."

"As you wish, Your Highness."

Lion tilted his head back and laughed. Then he stared at the queen's grey eyes. *Look at me*, Saradra whispered in his head. *Fight it.*

"How did you know?" Lion asked, grinning a joyless grin. "How did you know? Huh?"

Inoeveth knew what he meant by that. Corners of her mouth curled into a tight smile.

"How did you know?" Lion yelled louder. Every time he repeated the question, his careless, lunatic humour diminished. "How did you know? How did you know?" He lunged forward with a deranged scream. He broke free of the surprised guards, yet the queen didn't even flinch.

Kastian reacted before anyone else did. "*Padlociatius!*"

Lion sprawled onto the floor. The guards, terrified of what their lack of attention could have caused, grabbed his arms and dragged him back to where he was. His head lolled back and forth, presenting him with a colourful view of the speechless faces.

Kastian stood up to give his queen comfort she didn't need. Queen Inoeveth allowed her husband to hold her hand, but she kept her cold stare on Lion, still smiling that goat's ass of a smile.

When the paralysis cleared, Lion broke the gasped silence with a laughter.

"He… He attacked the queen!" a lord in a fancy jacket breathed in a shrill voice. "How dare *anyone* do that, let alone a purebred! Master Karhad?"

They all turned to the Master of the Slaves, demanding an explanation. "I told you," Karhad said, touching his bandage self-consciously. "He's gone rabid! Your Majesty, he has to be sent to White Tower."

"No," Prince Dienus objected. "Father, we should execute him. Publicly. And if the people riot, we strike hard and crush them. Show them the power of House Vogros."

"This thing in my head," Lion said, still laughing. "If it gets out, bad things are gonna happen!"

"Shut up," growled one of the guards, but upon his queen's orders, he didn't do more than squeeze Lion's arm.

"What Prince Dienus suggests would be the best solution to clean up the mess that's caused in Switchblade," the old advisor said. "However, using our military forces to provoke and then stamp out a riot would leave us weak against an attempt by rival families. Even as we speak, they are gathering their courage to question the legitimacy of our king."

Kastian growled, rubbing his temples.

"I promise you, king," Lion said. "I won't let that thing out. It's locked deep inside."

Prince Dienus took his belt off and handed it to guards. "Shut him up."

The men stuffed the belt between Lion's teeth and tied it around his head. He let out a muffled protest.

"We have to do something to prove our strength," Prince Lotheris said. He had to raise his voice because Lion started to hum the tune of a made-up song. "We can stop the people from talking by hunting and arresting the loudest ones. But we still have to do something drastic to remind the Houses of our capabilities before any of them uses these riots as an opportunity."

What the older prince said didn't seem to relieve his father's headache. Kastian pressed the base of his palm against his forehead. "We all know that, but what? I have a room full of advisers who do nothing other than bewailing at our situation. Whichever of you is waiting to snatch the most desperate moment to come up with a solution, it is now."

"That would be me, my love." Queen Inoeveth put a gentle hand on her husband's cheek. "I know how to turn this around. We'll talk."

"Talk?"

The queen smiled and nodded. She stepped closer and wrapped her arms around Kastian's shoulders. Their eyes glistened with affection for each other. Watching their love hurt Lion more than any punch. Not long ago, Saradra was looking at him like that. Lion was watching her sleep with the same eyes as Kastian watched his queen. Now, a hole was ripped open inside Lion's chest, scorching everything.

Inoeveth glanced at him out of the corner of her eyes and flashed a cruel smile. A stiff growl rose from the back of Lion's throat.

"But who are we going to talk to, Your Highness?" asked the old advisor. "And about what?"

"You all have been getting worried about how other houses might use these riots for their benefit. Why don't *we* use them?"

Kastian, finally catching a brief glimpse of what his wife had in her mind, smiled. "Elaborate, dear."

"But first, we have to agree that the slave is going to White Tower. We need him to obey."

"I'm not releasing him into an arena again!"

"We won't. But we can still use him. After we get him... repaired."

Kastian ordered Master Karhad to take Lion to the dungeons and start packing up for a long trip. They dragged him out of the room before Queen Inoeveth revealed the rest of her heinous plan.

36

LION

THE DARKNESS WAS PEACEFUL. It had always been peaceful for him. He never dreaded being alone in the dark, and he doubted if he ever would. He could easily spend the rest of his life left alone in the peaceful, pitch black.

It had been nearly two weeks. He knew it because he counted the long stops they had made. Thirteen. Thirteen nights spent on the road to White Tower.

He was chained at the back of a wagon, covered by tarp on all sides. He sometimes heard the coachman talking to Master Karhad at the front of the wagon. There was not much conversation, mostly Karhad sneezing and complaining about the cold and rain. He was not a big fan of travelling. This was another reason for him to hate Lion.

Karhad hadn't acted on his hate, though. Both he and the other guardsmen Kastian had assigned left Lion alone most of the time. For the first few nights, Lion had laughed and howled so loud, they had no other option than to beat him unconscious so they could get a bit of sleep. Soon, Lion had become quieter. But not because of the threat of the beatings. Whatever had made him scream and cry and laugh until tears flew down his face was trickling away.

Darkness was healing his mind.

Lion rarely remembered having dreams before. Some slave breeders claimed that purebreds didn't dream, because they didn't have any *rhoas*. Lion didn't know where these dreams came from now, but he welcomed them.

He dreamed of his room at Castle Brinescar, making love to Saradra in the tiny bed they shared. She was warm, tender, and passionate. She didn't let him speak to say how sorry he was. She didn't let him beg for forgiveness, nor cry for her loss. She just took him by the hand and showed him how ready he was to trade everything for an eternity with her body.

Then, there was the dream that had felt like another life; a real life that was being lived by another Lion of Zarall in another Earthome.

The alternate Lion and Saradra had escaped on the night of the coup. All they did differently was pick another bedroom in the guests' quarter. They never encountered that mage and the fiend. They escaped the city, crossed the border, and reached the Chamber of Twelve Saradra had been talking about. They lived there. Pyres devoted to Goddess Alunwea showed them mercy and kept them safe. Saradra gave birth to a blond-haired boy with bright blue eyes. It had been terrifying at first. The Dream Lion had confided in Dream Saradra that he had received no training to become a father, which she had responded nobody ever had. It was the oddest feeling in Earthome, and nothing could have prepared him for it.

The whole dream was so realistic that Lion felt disoriented when he opened his eyes back in the wagon. He could almost hear his son's laughter.

Then, Karhad yelled him to shut up and Lion remained there, his eyes closed shut, trying to go back to that dream. No matter how hard he tried, it was gone.

Some other dreams involved blood and violence, and they felt just as good.

In them, he was back at the Switchblade Arena. He was wearing his usual armour with a lion engraved on his chest, complete with the mask. The arena was empty; there were no spectators, no announcer, no guards. It was just him and his rival.

Kastian.

In the dream, Lion fought and defeated Kastian, but he didn't kill him. Not quickly, anyway. He tortured him for days. He flayed him and buried him deep in the sands of Switchblade. He watched fire ants eat him alive, vultures rip his tongue and carve his eyes out. He stuffed him inside a steel bull and lit a fire under its belly, cooking him slowly. He lashed him until his back resembled nothing but a slab of meat. He killed Kastian with his bare hands, savouring every second.

Not just the king. Queen Inoeveth had become a guest in these dreams, too.

Lion erased that bitchy smile off her face in the castle torture room. He branded her with a hot iron, scalped her, stabbed her over and over again. He tortured her until she lost her mind, just like he did. Then he finished her off with his bare hands.

Surprisingly, these dreams had done more healing to his mind than the others. They gave him a sense of peace and satisfaction that had eased some of his suffering.

At the end of the first week, Lion had stopped laughing and screaming, and switched to staring at the darkness, yearning for the dreams. He started eating the stale food they served twice a day. He didn't know what had brought those dreams, but he didn't complain. They were almost constructed specifically to banish that madness out from his mind.

To open room for something else.

They had been exactly what he needed to see, and they threw him a rope to climb out of that pit called insanity.

And the dream that had done the most healing was the last one.

In that last dream, Saradra was there in the wagon with him. She cradled his head in her lap and he breathed in the smell of her hair. He moved his hand across the length of her leg, feeling the soft, warm skin. His heartbeat picked up, his breathing becoming quick and shallow, as the seconds piled up on top of each other. Realisation grew like a throbbing bump on his head.

"You're... you're here," Lion whispered hoarsely. "You're really here."

He clutched her hand, squeezing it tightly as if fearing she would disappear. Saradra winced and used her free hand to loosen his fingers, but didn't let go of his hand.

Lion attempted to sit up. His chains restricted his movements, and his body was still sore from the beatings, but he could straighten up enough to see the outline of her face in the semidarkness. "But... You... How are you here? How...?"

Saradra placed one of her delicate fingers — warm and alive and unbroken — against his lips as she hushed him into silence. "I can't stay," she whispered apologetically.

"No, no, no, no…" Lion struggled against his chains, shaking his head violently. "You're here! Don't… Don't go, don't go…"

She hushed him again, reaching out and taking him in her arms. Her hands gently cradled his head against her chest, muffling his protests. Lion sobbed and whimpered silently, uncontrollably. He breathed her in, soaked in her warmth, too afraid to move. He didn't want to break this moment.

Saradra held him until the wagon started slowing down for another camp on the road.

"I'm sorry," Lion whispered. "I'm so sorry. I… I tried to fight it. I did…"

"I know," Saradra whispered. "It's okay, I know…"

"But… But you're here now. You're okay! You…"

"I have to leave," Saradra interrupted reluctantly. "But you'll find me in Farhome. One day."

Lion started shaking his head. "I can't go to Farhome. Purebreds don't have…" He stilled. The hair at the back of his neck stood up, a shiver running down his spine. Slowly, he pulled himself back, searching her face in semidarkness. He let out a long, shuddering breath as he finished his sentence in a whisper: "*rhoa.*"

A weary smile played across Saradra's lips. Her silence encouraged Lion to arrive at the conclusion himself: This was Saradra's *rhoa*.

His chains didn't let him raise his hands to caress her face, so he stroked her knees with the back of his fingers. He swallowed the lump in his throat. "It's a lie," he whispered.

Saradra nodded. "We all have *rhoas*. Purebreds too."

The wagon came to a stop. Outside, men jumped down from their horses, moving around the wagon to set up camp. Saradra held his face between her hands.

"Don't go," Lion begged, his voice only a whisper. "Take me with you. Please."

Footsteps rounded the wagon, approaching the flaps that served as the entrance to the back.

"You have somewhere else to be," Saradra replied. Her eyes sparkled with passion and excitement. Her voice had an urgency as she whispered; "Twilight of Infinity."

Lion's eyes grew large and his heart plummeted. Saradra sealed her words with a kiss. Her lips were hungry. Warm. Real. "Do whatever it takes to win," she whispered into his lips. "Be free. Whatever it takes."

Lion leaned forward, his chained hands aching to take her between his arms, to angle her head back, to deepen the kiss. A desire like he'd never experienced before boiled out of him. His blood rushed, his muscles tensed, a growl humming in his chest. He wanted nothing more than to scorch the whole Earthome until there was nothing left but Saradra and him.

"Who were you talking to?"

Karhad pulled the flap back, filling the wagon with the cursed light of the setting sun.

Lion opened his eyes to find the space in front of him empty. He slumped like a brick, sinking into the muddy, filthy, airless bottom of a lake. Invisible hands cut his chest open, ripped his heart out. Ripped Saradra out of him. But this time, they replaced the empty space she had left behind with something else.

Twilight of Infinity.

Karhad climbed into the wagon. He asked another question, but Lion's heart was thumping in his ears. He didn't hear it. Saradra's last whisper echoed in his mind, louder and louder.

Be free. Whatever it takes.

Karhad muttered something about Lion's head losing it completely before he left, closing the flap behind him.

When Lion thought of his tattoo being removed from his neck, a new kind of desire set his blood on fire. No more chains. No more collars. No more pain.

Freedom.

For a brief, intangible moment, he wanted it more than he wanted death.

After that day, Lion didn't have that powerful compulsion to laugh or scream any more. Days flew past in a blur. He was so quiet that at one point, Karhad ordered the convoy to stop so he could check up on the slave. Lion's silence unnerved the Master of the Slaves more than his crazed laughter did.

Even when Lion had greeted him on his knees and responded to his questions with his head down, Karhad still had difficulty believing Lion was behaving again.

He thought this was a ploy and ordered the men to beat him. When they started moving again, Lion's silence was replaced by pained groans.

Now, when the convoy stopped for the thirteenth night, Lion was still bruised from the last beating. An hour later, the covers at the back of the wagon slid open and Karhad brought a bowl of goulash and a cup of medicine. Kastian's head physician had given Karhad a mixture to make Lion drink every night, in order to assist with the recovery of his leg. The wound throbbed and itched now and then.

Karhad had removed the bandage from his ear, which now resembled a half-eaten, dried prune. He was wrapped tightly in a woollen travel cloak. His nose was red and runny. He looked miserable.

Lion sat up on his knees and dropped his head down to greet him. Karhad scoffed at Lion's show of obedience. "You think this is a joke, huh?"

"No, Master."

Karhad sneezed and wiped his nose with the back of his hand. "You think just because you're behaving again, we'll turn back to Brinescar after traveling this far, huh?"

"No, Master," Lion repeated.

Karhad banged the bowl and the cup of medicine on the floor, splashing grey juice and meat everywhere. "Up," he said, fumbling for his keys. "Get up, you mongrel!"

Karhad's keys jingled as they slipped and turned in the lock. He released Lion's chain from the wagon and dragged him outside, jerking the chain roughly.

Although the sun was out of sight, remaining daylight still blinded Lion's eyes. He stumbled after Karhad, barely aware of the men setting up camp around the wagon.

"Master Karhad," a voice called behind them. "Where are you taking him?"

"Just up on that hill, Sir Quewlan."

"Is that a good idea?"

When Karhad ignored him, Sir Quewlan trailed behind them. The king had assigned two of his knights to oversee his escort, along with five soldiers.

The hill Karhad dragged him to was not exceptionally steep, but Lion still tripped and fell several times. His leg bothered him. When they reached the top, his knees were bleeding, and his eyes were still blurry.

"Look!" Karhad urged him with a slap. "Open your eyes, worm."

Lion blinked rapidly, shading them with chained hands. It still took a minute to get used to the light and more than a few seconds to understand what he was looking at. Karhad waited with a stunning amount of patience, staring at his face to catch the moment Lion would figure out what the shape on the horizon was.

This was the first time Lion saw the sea. The vastness of it was frightening and beautiful at the same time. The blue, glassy surface stretching from one end to the other, reflecting the last gleam of light left in the sky. If there had been more daylight, the colour would have been the same as Saradra's eyes.

The map of Chinderia flashed across Lion's mind. This must have been the Wasted Sea. Then, that piece of land right near the edge of the horizon was the Deep Island.

Lion's stomach heaved with nausea.

Karhad grinned as Lion shivered, suddenly feeling queasy. He couldn't take his eyes off the structure that stood in the middle of the island. Its grey-white walls were washed by a touch of orange light. It was an ugly, coarse, and tall building that presented nothing worth looking at. Yet, White Tower imprisoned Lion's eyes and started torturing him even before he had stepped a foot inside the building.

"Three days," Karhad said. "Three days and you'll be exploring all the different sounds you can produce from your throat."

Lion's heart sank deeper with every word. The promise of more torture didn't terrify him. Free men and women believed slaves feared White Tower because of torture. They were wrong.

Inside White Tower, the Hunters didn't simply torture a slave until he behaved again. They took away the only thing a slave was allowed to possess.

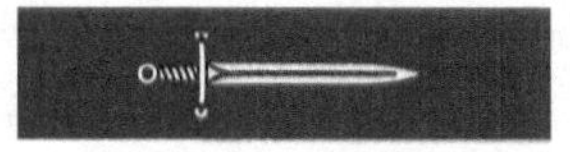

BREEDER ASTALDO DRAGGED HIS *hawkish gaze amongst the blank faces of his property.*

Their eyes were firmly fixed on the floor. Their stances were identical. Each one of them were now old enough to be allowed simple, identical clothing: coarse cotton tunics and dust coloured pants. Even their hair length was identical; shorter than one finger above the scalp.

"Sit," Astaldo said.

He hadn't even raised his voice, yet ten scrawny bottoms dropped to the floor promptly.

The young slaves had formed two rows; five at the front and five at the back. Astaldo started walking amongst them, the whip hanging on his belt making that dull thud every time it touched his thigh. It was a sound all the young purebreds were familiar with. Astaldo completed a circle around the slaves, dragging every step and filling the air with the threat of punishment for one reason or another, or none at all.

He stopped when he reached the front of the classroom. "Bring him in," he said, raising his voice for whoever was waiting outside.

The door squeaked open and two men walked inside. One was the weapons trainer they had all spent half their days with. He was carrying a wooden box the size of a pillow between his hands.

The other was a slave.

"Stand there," Astaldo pointed at the slave, who obeyed and stood at the front where all young purebreds could see him.

"All of you, look at him," Astaldo commanded.

For a split second, one of the nameless purebred boys feared the breeder would ask them to make eye contact with the new slave. To his relief, the new slave had kept his eyes on the floor.

The boy had noticed the slave's tattoo; a freeborn labourer. He looked well-trained for a freeborn, though. He must have been enslaved at a very young age, though the ink on his tattoo seemed fresh.

Astaldo stood with his feet apart, hands on his hips. "I want you to watch and see. Listen and hear. Whoever closes their eyes or looks away will spend the next week in the hole. Acknowledge."

"Yes, Owner!" said ten eager-to-please voices.

Astaldo turned his face to the freeborn, watching the purebreds out of the corner of his eyes. "Tell them who you are."

"I am the property of Astaldo Luuhun, Slave Breeder, Master of Faychill Ranch."

"And what are you called?"

"You have named me Ratsack."

As the purebred boy with blond hair and grey eyes listened to Ratsack speak, he felt all the hair on his arms and legs stand up. The freeborn's voice reminded him of the sound decaying bones made as they were dragged on dry land. His eyes never left the ground, which was not unusual for a well-trained slave. In fact, it was what would have been expected from any slave. However, this freeborn's eyes seemed different. They were nothing more than two empty, black holes carved on a corpse's face.

"Tell them what you did, Ratsack."

"I escaped."

Nobody gasped or looked at each other in fear. They were too disciplined for that. But an invisible shudder passed between them.

"And then what happened?"

"Hunters found me, Owner."

Astaldo raised his voice to indicate he was addressing the purebreds this time. "What do we say here, maggots?"

"Hunters always find you!" the boys yelled, loud and clear.

Slave Breeder nodded. "What happened when they found you, Ratsack?"

The boy who would become the king's champion beast one day already knew the answer, but hearing it still filled him with terror.

"They took me to White Tower," Ratsack said dully.

"Tell them about how time flows inside White Tower."

"For every hour outside, three days pass inside the tower."

"And how long did you spend there?"

"Six months had passed outside when I was returned to my Owner."

If every hour outside equalled three days inside, six months would have been...
The boy who would one day defeat a giant bear, naked and unarmed, held back a

gasp. He didn't have the knowledge to calculate how many days that would make, but he knew it was a lot!

"What do they do to escaped slaves in White Tower?"

"They Wash their flaws away."

"How?"

"They torture until death, then bring back intact, to torture more. Countless deaths wash off everything."

Everything, until all that was left, was an empty shell.

"Do you obey now, Ratsack?"

"Yes, Owner."

"Then take your clothes off."

As the slave undressed, Astaldo borrowed a knife from the weapons trainer. He handed the knife to Ratsack. "Cut yourself."

Ratsack dragged the knife over his naked chest, leaving a red trail behind.

The boy who would one day fall in love with a flame-haired girl, didn't find this impressive. Had Astaldo given him the knife and the order, he could have done this as well. He doubted if he could keep his face as impassive as Ratsack's, but he would still obey.

"Cut your ear off."

Ratsack took the knife to his ear without hesitation. He pulled it with one hand and cut with the other. His face didn't even twitch as the blade scraped against the bone and cartilage. He dropped the cut-off ear and stood there, blood seeping down his neck, ready for his next order.

"Cut your balls off."

The boy had to spend every drop of his willpower to stop himself from looking away. Astaldo's vigilant eyes studied their faces carefully. This was what he wanted the boys to watch and see, listen and hear.

To learn. This was another lesson to be learned.

Dark blood rushed down Ratsack's legs. He almost looked as if he'd peed himself, if not for the colour.

"Eat them," was Astaldo's next order.

The boy stabbed his fingernails at his knees. The pain drove the nausea away, and he forced himself to keep watching.

"Now, stab yourself in the stomach and leave the knife there."

Again, no hesitation, no sound, no twitch.

"Carve your eyes out with your fingers."

Astaldo's hand moved in a blur and his whip lashed at one of the other boys. The boy stifled a moan and turned his gaze back on the slave, just in time to witness fingers curling into hooks and pushing inside. Ratsack gouged his eyes out of their sockets, releasing a wet sound as he tore off the tendons.

"Rip your tongue out."

Ratsack obeyed. It took several attempts to grab his tongue, as it was soft and slippery, and his fingers were wet with blood. He bent his head down to let the gravity help him. He wrapped both his hands around and pulled it free with another wet sound that would haunt the young purebreds for months. Blood poured, followed by vomit. Ratsack straightened up, gawking at them with empty sockets and blood pouring down his chin.

Next, Astaldo made him bite all his fingers off. After three slushy crunches, Ratsack dropped to the floor, unconscious from the blood loss.

Astaldo's whip lashed five more times, bringing back each pair of eyes which had strayed off the demonstration. A fair number of purebreds were going to visit the hole tonight.

The Slave Breeder didn't grant Ratsack's mutilated body a second glance. He had brought the slave here for this demonstration — maybe even bought him solely for this purpose. Losing his property for the occasion didn't bother him in the slightest.

He stepped over the puddle of blood and scrutinised the effects of his latest lesson. However, the way he took a deep breath and tilted his head to the side indicated what he wanted to teach them today wasn't over yet.

"I hear that some of you," he started, lowering his voice and stretching the silence between each word, "have been dreaming of running away."

The boy who would one day kill free men and attempt an escape with the woman he loved shuddered. He turned his head down, cold sweat running down his spine. Who would even dream of something like that? Not him. Not ever!

I live to serve, I breathe to please, *he repeated in his head like a prayer. He had no wants, no desires, let alone dreams of running away. Even the thought petrified him.*

The silence was pregnant with punishment. "Remind me," *Astaldo said, blinking his eyes lazily.* "What happens if you escape?"

"Hunters always find you!" *This time, they didn't speak in perfect unison. Each one of them was rushing to finish the sentence before the others, to prove how well they knew the consequences.*

"They already did," *Astaldo said quietly.*

They heard the shuffle of his heavy robes before seeing him.

The boy almost flinched. There was someone behind them! But how? The door had never opened after the weapons trainer and Ratsack walked in and there was no one else in the classroom when the purebreds had first entered.

He moved his head an inch to the side to see a pair of boots dragging a long black robe behind them.

A Hunter! There was a real Hunter in the room!

"Stand up and form a single file," *Astaldo ordered.*

They stood. The back row took a step forward between the front row, forming a quick and orderly line. With Astaldo's gesture, the weapons trainer opened the wooden box he had brought with him and handed out a knife for everyone.

Sweat poured down the boy's back as he picked up his knife. Was Astaldo going to order them to cut their body parts off? The thought of doing what Ratsack had done drained all his breath out of his lungs.

"Cut your palms and hold your hands behind your back."

The boy sliced a shallow cut on his left palm. His blood flowed readily. He took both hands at the small of his back.

A rustle of rough cloth sounded as the Hunter approached. The boy at the start of the line flinched, and a yelp escaped his mouth before he could bite his lips shut. Astaldo narrowed his eyes at the purebred, but the whip didn't leave its resting place. The young slave bit his lips bloody. His body shook intensely, yearning to get away from the Hunter behind him, but he held his stance.

Whatever the Hunter did to him, it didn't last long. The next boy flinched only seconds after the first one. Then, the Hunter moved on to the next one, who managed to strangle a yelp, but cried silently.

The boy who would one day kill the woman he loved with his bare hands had the time to prepare for his turn. Yet, he still gasped when he felt the Hunter's touch.

The Hunter's hands were cold and clammy, but not like someone who spent a few hours in the snow. They were cold, as if made of ice. His fingers were thin, bony, and wrapped in a dry, creased tissue that the boy couldn't bring himself to call skin.

The boy's eyes popped wide open when he felt something cold, rough and wet rubbing inside his palm, licking his blood. Frozen lips closed around each one of the boy's fingers, sucking the blood off them. There was an unusual number of sharp teeth inside that mouth.

He's not human, the boy screamed in his mind. Hunters are not human!

The Hunter even licked the knife clean before moving on to the next purebred.

"Now you know," Astaldo spoke when the last one of the young slaves exhaled a relieved breath. "Hunters always find you, because they know your blood."

Because they were not human.

"No doors or gates are ever locked in Faychill Ranch," Astaldo continued. "They will be unlocked tonight as well. Those of you who have looked away, go and put yourselves in the hole. The rest of you, weapons training in fifteen. And feel free to take your chances to run away tonight if you dare. Now, drop the knives and get out."

They raced each other to be the first one out of the room.

The boy wiped his hands on his pants and risked a glance over his shoulder. The Hunter, who was nothing but a shadowy hood and a tall robe, had kneeled beside Ratsack's dead body and leaned over. The boy pried his eyes off them before seeing any more.

Spending years with Hunters in White Tower... Never. He would never disobey, never do anything that might bring that fate to him. He would serve, he would please, and never even dream of being free.

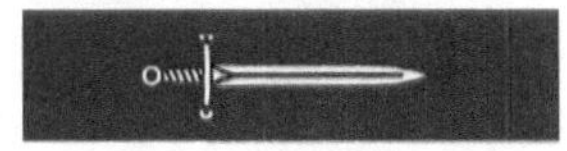

A SLAVE WASN'T PERMITTED to possess anything. Not a name, not emotions, not desires, not even a body. His body was their property. That was the phrase Astaldo had taught them.

But his mind was his.

He could behave like a perfect slave, hide all his thoughts, suppress every drop of emotion. Yet still cling to his own mind. It was the only thing the Owners and Masters could never own. It was all his. It was all him.

Now, they were going to take that away, too. He would still breathe, but he would be no more.

He sunk to his knees and shuddered.

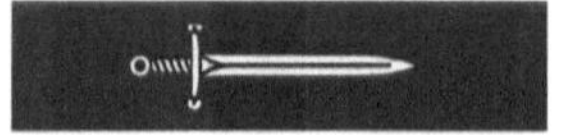

HE DIDN'T REMEMBER HOW he climbed back down from that hill. He had slipped a number of times and the knight walking behind him was the only reason he hadn't tumbled all the way down. Breaking his neck would have been a better fate than White Tower. After the second time he slipped, the knight, Sir Quewlan, hooked his fingers in Lion's collar and supported him all the way down.

What Lion did remember before hopping back inside the wagon was that none of the guards around the camp — including Sir Quewlan and the other knight — were wearing House Vogros uniforms.

They want to keep this a secret.

Kastian was afraid of what might happen if one of the opposing families got their hands on the Zarall symbol. Hence the secrecy and the black tarp around the wagon.

Lion didn't touch the food or the medicine that evening. It was too late to starve himself to death, but he just didn't have any appetite. He wanted to pray for a miracle to save him from this end, but he didn't know whom to pray to. The Twelve Riders had failed Saradra; the Goddess of Mercy was a deaf whore. He hated Alunwea. He hated every one of the Twelve Riders.

He played with the idea of praying to the sands and the steel, the only meaningful things in a beast's life, but they seemed to fail one in every two beasts, which didn't sound promising either.

So, he prayed to the darkness.

Darkness was peace. Darkness had always protected him from harm. Free men and women were afraid of it. Therefore, he prayed to the darkness to save him from the light of free men and women. Then, he leaned against the side of the wagon, and stayed up all night.

When the fighting begun, sleep still hadn't showed itself. Lion couldn't say the same thing for the guards, though. The darkness had lulled them to sleep, just like it wrapped the attackers like a blanket and hid them from the eyes of the sentries. Someone shouted and woke the others up, but not until the attackers had killed at least half of them.

The darkness served confusion to the Vogros men, and the attackers exploited it.

Lion sat there, in the darkness of the wagon, and listened to the sounds of the battle. A compulsion to laugh creeped in and he had to cover his mouth to suppress it. This was not the laughter of madness; this was pure joy.

He had prayed to the darkness to save him from White Tower, and the darkness had answered.

37

OLIRA

Olira stood in front of what was left of the root cellar.

Her breath caught in her throat as she took in the devastation. Last night's storm had turned violent in the blink of an eye. By the time she was startled awake by the hail pounding against the roof and the loud crack coming from the barn, the fury of the storm was already unleashed at the farm. Now, in the pale morning light, the extend of the damage brought tears to her eyes.

The fields were a sodden mess, her delicate, precious, exotic herbs and plants battered and broken, half buried in mud. The crops she had been counting on had been ripped from the earth, or flattened beyond recognition. The barn had taken a hit too. Part of the roof was gone, claimed by the storm. The torrents of rain and hail had drenched everything inside.

Olira had rushed to the barn in the early hours, while the storm still raged, to secure the animals. She'd found the two cows and Warrior huddled in a corner, shivering and their eyes wide with horror. The goat and half the chickens were missing, a few lay lifeless, their feathers ruffled. Gilann was right behind her. Surprisingly, the slave had rushed out of his cupboard and came after them, too. He helped them drag the cows through the storm and into the house, and he half carried Warrior, who fought so hard that he nearly hurt himself.

Now, the surviving animals were inside the house, drying and recovering from the horror. Olira surveyed the devastation that forced her to confront how insignificant humans were against the wrath of nature. The hopelessness built inside her like a rising tide until she had discovered the root cellar. There, she sank to her knees.

"It's okay," Torren said, his voice trembling. "We can rebuild it."

Olira could see the broken wooden beams through the collapsed rubble. She knew some of the beams were rotten, and she was arranging for them to be repaired before the winter set in. She should have acted quicker. The roof came down, burying their stores of food under the mud, most of the food already ruined.

"Andar, get the wheelbarrow," Gilann said as he approached the remains. His jaw was set as he started clearing away the debris. "Kowas, get a tarp. We'll see what we can salvage."

Torren kneeled beside Olira and squeezed her hand. Tears ran down Olira's cheeks and she swallowed hard against the lump in her throat. She wiped her face, smearing mud all over. She stood back up and followed Gilann's example. No point wailing. There was work to do.

The slave was already working without being asked to. He gave Gilann a hand as the two of them lifted a large piece of rubble. Underneath, they found sacks full of spoiled grains. The slave's eyes met Olira's for a brief moment and caught her frustration and despair. With all their stored food gone, the slave had just become a burden. Another mouth to feed. And he had also become their only chance at survival. She had no other choice. The decision was made.

The slave's expression didn't change, but a flicker of a dread passed his eyes. It made Olira's chest tighten. She spent the rest of the day avoiding the slave and working herself to exhaustion, so she could escape the guilt that burdened her *rhoa*.

38

THE SLAVE

THE SLAVE, WHOSE NAME wasn't Lion of Zarall anymore, turned and tossed in his sleep.

The nightmare came almost every night. He didn't have the words to describe the dream; there weren't clear, coherent images that played out like a story. It was a fragmented collection of impressions that assaulted his senses. He smelled and tasted blood, thick and metallic. He felt his skin tore under her teeth and nails. He heard the wet sound of bones and skull crushing under his fists. And the worst was the screams and the terrible silence that followed.

The nightmare clung to him, suffocating him, weighing on him. The makeshift bed beneath him felt like sand pulling him in, as if wanting to swallow him. His breathing quickened, hands clenching into fists, his body drenched in sweat. And then it was over. He jerked awake, his heart aching in his chest.

He was grateful for the confined space, small and dark. The walls felt like they were pressing in on him, like he was buried alive. He lay there, staring at the shadows, not even trying to pull himself back to reality. The dream still shrouded his mind, and the echoes of her screams filled the space. He was torn between wanting the screams to stop and clinging onto them, because they were all that remained of Saradra.

Despite his resistance, the last echoes of the nightmare faded. He rested his elbow over his eyes, breathing through his nose, his heart slowing. Then he heard it. The whispers. They were faint, almost too quiet to catch, like the murmur of voices from another room. When he strained to listen, they stopped abruptly. He only heard the whispers when he was expecting them the least, and the words could never quite reach him. It was like there was a thick mud or a fog in his mind, muffling the words.

He had been hearing them most nights now. A faint echo that never quite broke through the fog in his mind. Something — or someone — was calling to him, trying to get his attention. But no matter how hard he tried, he couldn't make out the words. It was maddening.

With a frustrated sigh, he sat up just as Olira knocked on the door. She didn't bother waiting for a reply and let herself in. He kept his head down, shielding his eyes from the light, and he stamped out the fear in his chest.

Olira stepped inside, a plate of food balanced in one hand. He kept his face carefully blank, though a knot of fear twisted in his gut. This woman... He didn't understand her fully, but he knew enough to be cautious of her anger. She was capable of things that she probably wasn't aware of herself.

She put the plate down and reached for the unlit candle. She lit it using another candle in the hallway and brought it back. The soft glow of the flickering flame illuminated the small space. When she didn't leave immediately, he glanced at her, cautious and alert.

She leaned against the wall, her expression unreadable. For a moment, she stood like the words weighed on her. Finally, she spoke with a low and steady voice. "I'm taking you to the town tomorrow."

He kept his expression vacant, while the fear twisted tighter inside him. He was expecting this, since that storm a week ago. The last of the debris was cleared, the barn fixed, and the spoiled crops removed from the field. She didn't need him anymore.

"Master Tholthus is a good man," she said. He didn't understand why her voice sounded strained. She hadn't asked a question or gave an order, so he wasn't obliged to respond. She lingered for another moment, as if expecting some kind of reaction. He offered no response, and she turned away, closing the door softly behind her.

He pulled the plate and forced himself to eat. As soon as the plate was cleared, he blew out the candle and lied on the bed, with his hands tucked under his head. Sleep didn't come easily this time. Tomorrow, he would wear a collar again. He would be sold to a stranger. His stomach churned, and he gritted his teeth. He didn't care how good this Master Tholthus was. All free men and women were selfish, and he was done letting them decide his fate.

Besides, as soon as he stepped out of this farm, he would be recognised. He was still surprised she didn't know what the brands on his chest meant. He was certain she had seen them before, though he still kept them hidden, just to avoid evoking her curiosity. But this Master Tholthus, or someone else in town, would eventually recognise the brands and identify him as the Lion of Zarall. Then, the word would get to Kastian.

Then, he would be on his way back to White Tower.

No, he couldn't let that happen.

His little respite in this forgotten corner of Chinderia was over. So, what now?

He heard Saradra's voice in his head again, as clear as it was before: *Twilight of Infinity*.

The thought of freedom was both thrilling and terrifying. If he could get to the city of Euroad, and fight at *Twilight of Inifinity*, he knew he could win it.

He touched the left side of his neck, imagining what it would be like to have his tattoo removed. His heart raced, and something deep stirred inside of him. He could live without a collar around his neck. Without the fear of free men and women. He could decide his own fate. The map of Chinderia flashed across his mind, and his heart pounded even faster. He could travel every corner of it. He could go to Ascain and find that little town called Bellmouth.

He could discover other maps. Earthome had more to offer than just Chinderia.

With that excitement came a ripple of fear. Letting himself desire something so badly was frightening. Because the idea of not getting it was devastating. The fear of failure and disappointment threatened to paralyse him.

He rolled to his side, willing himself to sleep, despite knowing rest was out of his reach tonight. The whispers returned, faint and distant, carrying with them a subtle hint of questioning. He stilled, staring at the darkness that surrounded him. He still couldn't make out the words, and couldn't quite hear the question. But he knew the answer.

His answer was *anything*.

He would do *anything* for his freedom.

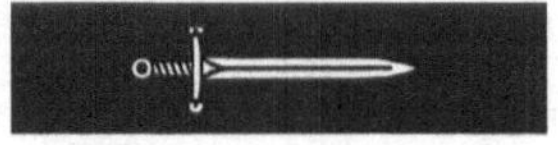

Twilight of Blood series continues in
Beast of Zarall

ACNOWLEDGEMENTS

I HONESTLY DON'T KNOW where to begin. There were so many people who helped me get this book to your hands.

To my husband, Jason, thank you for your honesty and for keeping me grounded when I push myself too hard. I love writing so much, it's so easy to lose myself in it and burn out. My husband was adamant at making sure I found a sustainable pace that wouldn't stress me. He also genuinely believed in my work and the way he encouraged me gave me confidence. So, thank you.

To my beta readers—Ash, Steph, MJ, Tamika, and those who didn't want to be named—thank you for the passion, support, and thoughtful feedback you poured into this book. I'm truly grateful for the time and energy you put into helping me shape this story.

To Bora, for being my beta reader and 'lore expert'. People think writing fantasy books is easy—just make things up and explain everything with magic—but fantasy needs logic and consistency like any other genre. When there is a steel pole in the middle of an arena, that has implications for the technological state in that world. When people pay tax in the cities, that has implications for the society structure, civilization, and economy. Bora, with his insight and experience with the fantasy genre, was extremely helpful in catching these things and ensuring I have internal consistency.

To my author friend Dr Joy Lim, for her insightful input on medical practices. I thoroughly enjoyed our conversation about the draining procedure, recovery, and septic shock, and her guidance was invaluable in ensuring Lion's recovery was realistic. Of course, any unrealistic moments are likely due to me taking a few creative liberties for the sake of the plot. Let's just say, I'm very thankful for modern medicine!

Writing this book was the fun bit – publishing it is a whole other challenge. Navigating that process can feel overwhelming, but the indie author community has been incredibly supportive. I'm especially grateful to Whit, Nicole, and all the other authors I pestered with my questions over the last few months. Your guidance and encouragement mean a lot to me!

To my editor, Gabby, thank you for your keen eye and thoughtful feedback, which helped shape this book into its final form. To Miblart, for the stunning cover design that perfectly captured the essence of my story.

To the reader, thank you for taking the time to immerse yourself in this story. Your support means everything, and I'm honoured that you've chosen to spend your time with these characters and their world. This book exists because of readers like you, and for that, I am deeply grateful.

STAY CONNECTED AND SHARE THE JOURNEY

THANK YOU FOR JOINING Lion and Olira's journey, I hope you enjoyed it. Please leave a review, it really helps the book find new readers. Your thoughts can make a huge difference in helping others discover the story.

I'd also like to invite you to stay connected. Join my newsletter for updates on future releases, behind-the-scenes insights, and special content.

Check out my website: **www.eddyrose.com**

Books have a way of bringing us closer, and if this one resonated with you, don't hesitate to recommend it to a friend or share your passion with others by leaving a review on Amazon, Goodreads, or any preferred platform.

ABOUT THE AUTHOR

Eddy B. Rose started her writing career when she was in third grade. Her first readers were a small but dedicated group of her classmates who stopped by at her desk at recess to read the next chapter of the story she wrote on a notebook in class, instead of listening to her teacher.

Eddy lives in queensland, Australia with her husband, toddler, and her two German Shepherds (the original babies) Kara and Kal-El. She enjoys getting up at 4.30am in the morning to write.

BEAST OF ZARALL

PROLOGUE

KALLIS

Kallis

The slave merchant hated the *Mad Lion*.

The tavern was located in Swuglus East, a lower-class section of the city of Coldpost. The street stank of vomit and piss. The single-story building was old, its stone walls weathered and cracked, with moss creeping through the mortar. And the regulars of the establishment — including the person whom he was going to meet — were the kinds of people he wouldn't see out in daylight.

But none of these were the reason he felt antsy as he approached the place. It was the name.

Soft light spilled onto the street from the *Mad Lion*'s front windows. Music and raucous voices carried farther than the light. There was a bard singing inside, but the lyrics were lost beneath the slurred attempts of drunken men trying to sing along.

A large man slouched on a stool just outside the doors. His head fell on his chest as if he was asleep, but the slave merchant doubted that. Swuglus East wasn't the sort of place you could nap with both eyes closed. The bouncer at the *Mad Lion* watched the street through narrowed eyes, fully awake and alert.

The slave merchant tugged at his heavy coat against the cold. Beyond the dark hills that overlooked the city, he could see dark clouds swallowing the stars. He was hoping to strike a good deal with the supplier and get home before the storm hit. He shivered at the idea of walking all the way to the other side of the city through rain and mud.

The bouncer didn't stir as the slave merchant climbed up the stairs to the porch and walked into the *Mad Lion*. The mixed smell of sweat, tobacco and oily food greeted him. He stood by the open doors, waiting for his eyes to adjust to the dim light.

Once again, he was reminded how much he didn't like this tavern.

The common room was filled with rows of tables, benches and stools, all occupied by eating, drinking, singing and gambling men. A stage the size of a bed was built on the corner where a bard played his lute and sang an obscene version of a popular folk song. The *Mad Lion* didn't look all that different from an ordinary, lowlife tavern, with the only exception being the ugly, rebellious decor.

Gold and black banners were hanging from every wall and column. Behind the bartender, there hung an elaborate tapestry that portrayed the Lion of Zarall's battle against the Bear of Vogros. A round, wooden shield with House Zarall's coat of arms was displayed proudly above it.

Sarte 'Lucky' Hamgard, owner of the *Mad Lion*, was a veteran house guard who had served late King Leonis Zarall and had the luck to retire several years before the coup. The man's blood ran golden and black and he was not shy about showing his colours, despite the fact that another king with different colours was now sitting on the throne of Chinderia.

The slave merchant could never understand the blind loyalty free men felt for each other. It was a good quality on a slave, but was not useful otherwise.

He wondered if Lucky would still feel lucky enough to openly show Zarall colours if it wasn't for the ongoing riots.

Kastian Vogros was sitting on the throne, and he even had the support of all the noble families, but Vogrosses did not have a solid grip on the country yet. At least not in the Northern Chinderia, where people had been louder and more reluctant to accept the change.

The slave merchant didn't think the instability would last for long. Zaralls were gone and there wasn't anyone else well-connected enough to have a claim on the throne against Kastian Vogros. People could whine all they wanted; Kastian Vogros was still the head of the strongest family in Chinderia. His line still went all the way back to Merduth the Axe, founder of the country. And he still controlled the largest army of slaves and free men.

Riots would go on until the common folk started to realise Leonis Zarall wasn't coming back from Farhome to feed their throats, so they would go back to worrying about themselves. People like Lucky would continue to rant about how Kastian Vogros couldn't even defeat Leonis's slave, but he would lose ears every day until one morning he'd wake to find those Zarall banners burnt down, along with his piss hole of an establishment.

It took the slave merchant a moment to spot the man he was going to meet. He started towards the table at the back of the room. It was a time of uncertainty for most businesses, but not for his. Times like these were when the slave business thrived most.

Public disorder meant people went unaccounted for, leading to a fresh wave of tattoos on the market. Kastian's soldiers were busy securing Brinsescar and the main roads leading to it, leaving the lesser-used routes dangerous. Travellers vanished, and the slave merchant was about to meet one of the men responsible.

Tonight's deal could potentially double or even triple his investment.

"Master Kallis," the man at the table said, gesturing for the slave merchant to join him. He was a large man with streaks of grey in his beard. The heavy leather armour he wore was faded and creased at the joints. It looked old, but bore no scars. Kallis wasn't sure if that meant the man was skilled enough to avoid being hit, or if he simply avoided fights altogether.

But you didn't become the bandit king of the Kilrer region by avoiding fights, so Kallis assumed it was the former.

"Master Vurkom," he greeted, offering the criminal a deep bow. He shrugged off his coat before lowering himself onto the bench. A massive fireplace burned fiercely in the centre of the room, and the windows had been blocked against the night breeze. Kallis would be sweating soon, and he didn't want the man getting the wrong impression.

Vurkom grabbed one of the serving girls by the arm and ordered two ales. Kallis didn't even like ale, but he didn't make any comment. He'd rather let the bandit think he was in control. For the same reason, he kept his silence until Vurkom decided to talk.

"I understand you're interested in my merchandise," Vurkom said. He was sitting sideways with one elbow at the table, the other hand on his knee, appearing to watch the bard across the room.

Kallis sipped his ale before speaking. "With all due respect, Master Vurkom, I wouldn't call them merchandise."

Vurkom glanced at Kallis, his lips curved with amusement. "And what would you call them?"

"Raw materials." Kallis imitated Vurkom's body language by facing towards the bard. He was vaguely aware the bard switched to a song about a fierce lion and a fluffy bear. Enough of the lyrics were caught in his ear to know this was another song about the mighty Lion of Zarall. He pushed his dislike aside and prepared himself to make the speech he'd done to others before.

"Go outside the city, Master Vurkom, and you'll see trees everywhere. Anyone with an axe can cut one down, but not everyone can turn it into good furniture. It takes time, skill, resources, and connections to craft merchandise from fallen logs."

Vurkom took a sip from his drink and stayed silent for a while. Kallis didn't break the quiet.

"Let me guess," the bandit said. "This is the part where you start haggling about how hard it is to find a good inker with steady hands."

"Finding a tattoo artist who can forge a genuine slave tattoo isn't the hardest part, Master Vurkom. At least not for me. Training is the most expensive and time-consuming part."

Vurkom's brows drew closer. "I can train them," he grunted. "Cut their tongues so they won't talk back, beat the shit out of them until they learn to do as they're told."

Kallis tried not to grimace. "Mutilated slaves lose at least a sixth of their value, Master Vurkom. Not everyone wants a mute. And training isn't just about beating the shit out of them. If you've believed the sky is blue your whole life, it takes more than pain to convince you the sky doesn't exist anymore — no matter the colour."

He paused, watching for a reaction. Vurkom's scowl faded into a vague grin. Kallis suspected the bandit already knew what came next, but he said it anyway.

"I have connections with breeders at slave ranches — people who can turn freeborn men and women into good slaves, regardless of their age. But time, Master Vurkom, time is my enemy. Every day they spend in those ranches costs me money. And they lose value as they age. It takes at least two years to break a man properly, if he's over twenty. Even then, some wills won't bend. It's hardly worth it."

Kallis stopped speaking. Vurkom's grin had spread into a smug smile. That wasn't the intended effect of his speech. He waited until the bandit spilt what he had.

"I've got kids," Vurkom said, leaning back in his chair.

Kallis took a long sip to cover his smile. He glanced around the room, hoping the bandit hadn't caught the anticipation in his eyes.

"How old?"

Vurkom pursed his lips. "A couple about this size." He held his hand at the height of the table. "Three more a bit older. That should reduce your costs, huh?"

"Indeed." Kallis licked his lips, finished the rest of his ale, and ordered some wine from one of the serving girls. He didn't expect them to have *Serpentblood*, and was pleasantly surprised to find they did. This business meeting had just proved worthy of a bottle of the most expensive wine.

Moreover, Kallis had noticed Vurkom was holding something back, and he had a good guess at what it was.

"Too bad they're not young enough for Wording."

Vurkom grinned. "One of the bitches is due next month. Could find more."

"Mother should have proper paperwork in place, of course."

"Which I'm sure you can handle, being a registered trader yourself."

"Finding a mage who's authorized to do the Wording is going to be expensive. Casters Board of Chinderia is extremely strict with their regulations."

"I bet you already know someone." Vurkom leaned forward at the table. His mouth was still smiling, but his eyes were sharp and cold as steel. "Let's cut the bullshit, shall we? I already know you have all the permits and the connections I need. I could swing my dick and hit another slave merchant in this city. Why do you think I'm meeting you? You wanna do business, or not?

"As they say, Master Vurkom," Kallis said. "Children are the future of this country."

They started negotiating before their wines were served. It wasn't the fastest service Kallis ever had, but they were lucky to be served at all. The serving girl stumbled, nearly dropping the *Serpentblood* as she approached their table. If it wasn't for the quick reflexes of a patron sitting nearby, Kallis's expensive liquid gold would have washed the mud and sawdust off the tavern's floors.

But even the clumsiness of the serving girl couldn't spoil Kallis's mood. He was going to leave this meeting already feeling like a richer man.

By the time the slave merchant poured their cups, they had already agreed on the rough terms. Details were to be discussed next morning at Kallis's office. Vurkom accompanied him for another cup of wine, then left. Five brutes, armed to the teeth, who had been blended in other tables, stood and left with the bandit leader.

The bard started another repetition of *The Lion and The Bear*. Kallis made an annoyed sound from the back of his throat, which turned into a cough. He rolled his eyes at the patrons joining in with the chorus. He didn't understand the passionate admiration these people felt for a non-compliant, broken slave.

It wasn't the slave himself that people cheered for; it was the idea of a worthless piece of property making fun of the strongest man in the country. They found it amusing. It *was* amusing. But also disturbing for a man who made his living from selling slaves.

Kallis picked up the bottle of *Serpentblood*. There was still enough left for two more cups. He decided to finish his bottle before heading back home.

He was just starting to notice the persistent itch on his throat when a stranger sat down at his table.

A frown creased the slave merchant's brow. He glared at the man, his displeasure at the invasion of his privacy quite evident.

The stranger wore an expensive shirt and vest, though both were creased and dusted with the grime of travel. A short sword hung from a plain belt at his hips. His blond hair was cropped short, his features sharp and youthful — early twenties, at most. Bright blue eyes scanned the room with confident, effortless charm. An arrogant grin curled at the corner of his mouth. Something in the way he carried himself — relaxed, assured — unsettled Kallis.

The song finished and the patrons cheered for another repetition. The bard, enjoying the ecstasy of a powerful crowd, climbed up on a table and started his tune again. Kallis straightened and stared at his uninvited guest.

"I don't remember —" the slave merchant started, but his throat spasmed and choked the rest of his words. He coughed on his hand, cleared his throat, and tried again. "I don't remember — inviting —" He coughed, glaring at the man. To quench the itch in his throat, he drank a large gulp of wine.

That's when he saw the little green vial between the stranger's gloved fingers.

The young man was looking at Kallis, his head tilted slightly, turning and twisting the vial in his hands. His arrogant grin widened when comprehension dawned on Kallis's face.

The slave merchant gawked at his cup of wine. He knocked it down, the red wine spreading on the table like blood. The sound was lost beneath the bard's tune and the voices of the patrons. Kallis moved to stand.

A hand clamped down on Kallis's shoulder, forcing him back into his seat. A second man slid onto the bench beside him, sitting with his back to the table, eyes scanning the tavern crowd. He was as young as the first — mid-twenties, maybe — with light brown hair, a ready smile, and the faint scatter of freckles across his nose. His features marked him as foreign. Kallis had dealt with enough foreign-born merchandise to recognise the long, narrow facial lines of a Kaldorian.

Unlike the first man, this one wore armour — a strange, overlapping kind that looked like layered plates — and carried more weapons: a short bow, a pair of daggers, throwing knives. Kallis made another attempt to rise, but the Kaldorian's hand stayed firm on his shoulder.

"You'd rather be sitting," the blond young man said, his voice calm and confident. "Take five steps and you'll drop dead." He shook the little vial at Kallis. "This is the only antidote within your reach."

Kallis's eyes grew large at the statement. "What do — Who are —?"

A surprised shout turned a few heads toward the back of the room. Kallis saw Lucky Hamgard rushing through the tables, shoving patrons aside. He knelt down, briefly vanishing among the curious crowd, then straightened with the serving girl in his arms. The patrons had already turned back to the bard as Hamgard carried her toward the back of the bar.

While Kallis watched the tavern workers gather around the girl, he noticed a third man. He knew at once this one was with the other two at his table. Larger and older than the others, the man's bulk was impressive — as big as a purebred beast. He had dark, short-cropped hair, a somewhat flat nose, and a serious expression that didn't waver. Kallis could make out the bulging outline of a heavy breastplate beneath the man's baggy tunic. A long sword and a short sword hung at either hip, and the hilt of a massive two-hander jutted over his shoulder. He stood several paces away, casually leaning against the wall. A beer mug in one hand, eyes on Kallis's table. He didn't look away when Kallis noticed him.

The blond young man took the bottle of *Serpentblood*, poured some into Vurkom's cup, and raised it to his lips. Kallis blinked, confused. He didn't understand — then he did. His eyes flicked to the bottle, to the man's gloved hands, to the unmoving body of the serving girl, and finally to his own fingers. The faint discolouration was already there.

"The bottle," he said and coughed again.

The blond man smiled and took another sip of wine. "There's no reason to spoil a good wine like this."

"What —?" Kallis gasped between his coughs.

The blond man put the cup aside, indicating he was ready for business now. "You are hard to track down, Master Kallis. Or would you prefer Master Gladwiel?"

Kallis blinked. "What do you —" he once again attempted to ask their intentions and failed.

"I'm looking for a slave," the man said, leaning forward on his elbows. "A purebred beast."

"Come to — come to my office. Take — take what you want."

The Kaldorian took his hand off Kallis's shoulder and crossed his arms over his chest. He still didn't look at the slave merchant and continued studying the crowd, but his mouth was twisted as if he'd tasted something nasty. The larger man with the heavy armour hadn't moved from where he stood. It was clear this conversation was going to be resolved between Kallis and the young blond man.

The blondie's smile had nothing to do with pleasure. "You misunderstood me, Master Gladwiel," he said smugly. "I'm not buying a slave. I'm searching for a specific one; a purebred beast with a certain fame."

Kallis's eyes widened with understanding for the third time since the blond man sat at his table. He shook his head. "I don't — know what —" Kallis coughed so hard, he couldn't breathe for a few long seconds. "Please..."

The blond man's smile disappeared from his face and he was silent for a while. "I know you had him," he said impatiently. "We've found the thugs who'd intercepted a convoy of disguised Vogros soldiers. I know they sold you a dying purebred beast for twenty Chinderian Blues."

Kallis was shaking his head violently. "I don't — I don't do business with —" He shook with another violent cough.

The blond man rolled his eyes, then rubbed his temples. "I don't care about the legitimacy of your business activities, Master Gladwiel. I'm not here to report you to the Domestic Assets Trade Union."

The Kaldorian scoffed softly, but the blond man continued without skipping a beat. "Give me a name, Master Gladwiel..." He pulled the cork off the vial with his teeth and set the antidote at the edge of the table. He placed his hand right behind it, ready to push it off the table and spill Kallis's life on the floor.

Kallis attempted to reach for the vial, but the Kaldorian grasped his wrist without looking and twisted it until Kallis buried his face into the crook of his elbow and whimpered.

The bard riled the crowd to join him on the last chorus of *The Lion and The Bear*. Several mugs rose to the air as the drunken patrons sang to the obnoxious things a lion with a long spear did to a soft, fluffy bear. Kallis's coughs were lost in the noise.

When the Kaldorian let his wrist go, Kallis cradled his arm in his lap.

The young blond man leaned forward on the table. He didn't bother raising his voice to be heard over the crowd. Kallis read his lips clear as day: "A name, Master Gladwiel."

Kallis closed his eyes. "Olira — Aryanna —" he coughed.

"And where can I find this Lady Olira?"

"Farm — West Kilrer."

The man's eyebrows twitched upwards. "You sold King Leonis's Lion of Zarall to a farmer girl in West Kilrer?"

"Please —" Kallis's face had turned purple from gasping and coughing. "Tell King Kastian — I didn't know."

The man's grin disappeared, and danger sparked in his eyes. "I'm afraid I can't do that, Master Gladwiel." He leaned further. "When I see Kastian Vogros, there won't be much talking."

With that, he stood. Kallis reached for the vial, but the Kaldorian snatched it off him.

The blond man walked out of the *Mad Lion* with not so much as a one last glance at the slave merchant. His heavy armoured companion followed him closely. The Kaldorian lingered long enough to walk over to the bar and leave the vial there, before following the other two outside.

Kallis looked at the vial with longing. He pressed his fist in his mouth, forcing himself to stop coughing and breathe. Five steps, he thought. According to the blond man who'd poisoned him, that was all he had left.

Lucky Hamgard, who was towering over his unconscious employee, his face creased with concern, straightened up and noticed the mysterious vial left at his bar. He narrowed his eyes.

No, Kallis thought with panic. *That's mine.*

Five steps.

He stood and took the first.

www.ingramcontent.com/pod-product-compliance
Lightning Source LLC
Chambersburg PA
CBHW051316190726
48290CB00001B/171